KU-725-935

Simon Kernick is forty, lives near London and has two young children. His novels, *The Business of Dying*, *The Murder Exchange*, *The Crime Trade*, *A Good Day to Die* and *Relentless* are published as Corgi paperbacks and his new novel, *Severed*, is available as a Bantam Press hardback.

The research for Simon Kernick's novels is what makes them so authentic. His extensive list of contacts in the police force has been built up over more than a decade. It includes long serving officers in Special Branch, the National Crime Squad (now SOCA), and The Anti-terrorist Branch, all of whom have plenty of tales to tell.

For more information on Simon Kernick and his books, see his website at www.simonkernick.com

www.**rbooks**.co.uk

# Acclaim for Simon Kernick

'A rising star of gritty London crime, in which morality and violence dance an awkward waltz against a familiar landscape of crooked cops, villains and lost souls'
Maxim Jakubowski, *Guardian*

'A terrific novel' *Independent on Sunday*

'More gritty urban crime from a writer with an increasingly keen following … Kernick is excellent at capturing the mean streets where crack deals go down and tourists don't linger' *Daily Mail*

'A taut gritty novel in which Kernick fine-tunes the narrative and uses every trick in the book to keep the narrative breakneck. This is British crime fiction in the hard-edged traditions of *The Sweeney*, David Peace and Derek Raymond' *Time Out*

'Taut, gripping, disturbing – a most assured and original début' Reginald Hill

'Not for the faint-hearted. Kernick, with all the freshness and fluency of a newcomer, revels in portraying the seedy, amoral, hidden world of Britain's capital city where conscience is a luxury, where humour is gallows black. *The Business of Dying* caught me with its gut-wrenching reality. A compelling début' Gerald Seymour

'The first person narrative compromises the reader into collaboration with Milne from the outset and sets up an exquisitely tortuous piece of characterisation that should challenge both author and readers in the books to come' Peter Millar, *The Times*

'The crime début of the year so far … Kernick tells it straight with no embellishments, which is exactly how I like my crime fiction. A prize winner if ever I saw one'
Mark Timlin, *Independent on Sunday*

'A most auspicious début which leaves me looking forward eagerly to Mr Kernick's next book'
Susanna Yager, *Sunday Telegraph*

'A gem of a book that will have the reader cheering ambiguously for the protagonist and narrator ... Gallows humour and a sardonic voice mark Kernick's remarkable début. Pathos, pace, twists and a savage sense of place make this a guilty pleasure' *Guardian*

'An uncommonly assured first novel, quite brilliantly plotted ... done with the kind of dash which inspires total reader confidence and involvement. Rancidly rendered King's Cross setting, credible cops and robbers (with an especially sympathetic Indian DC), sex seen resignedly as both the folly and the force which makes good and bad things happen. Formidable stuff. There is a pro at work here' Philip Oakes, *Literary Review*

'A gripping police thriller with original twists and moral depths ... A gritty portrait of a man struggling to regain some moral sense in a world bereft of it'
Jane Jakeman, *Scotland on Sunday*

'A crime début well worth the luggage space. Det. Dennis Milne is a professional hitman. You will either like or hate him, rather similar to Rankin's Rebus. I like him and am on his wavelength'
Jonathan Spencer-Paine, *Booksellers' Choice, The Bookseller*

'Tough, gritty and very exciting ... A really splendid start to what promises to be an outstanding new series – it's totally convincing' Tim Manderson, *Publishing News*

'Just the sort of fast-paced intelligent thriller that cries out for a TV adaptation ... Both gripping and thought provoking, Kernick weaves his web with the assurance of a seasoned professional' *Time Out*

'Laces urban noir with a touch of laconic humour, and doesn't overdo the tough stuff' *Sunday Telegraph*

'A good old-fashioned British gangster story'
*Birmingham Post*

'Simon Kernick is one of the hottest new names in crime'
*Crime Time*

'A finely honed thriller which unravels with admirable unpredictability, sweeps the reader along. Pure edge-of-the-seat crime thriller' *Sherlock*

'I love this book. It's fast, hard, and tight and it blasts through the London underworld like a cigarette boat on the Thames' Lee Child

'An accomplished and convincing narrative that flows naturally, is rich in detail and yet is crafted with gratifying economy. Twist and turns are in plentiful supply throughout, and the cast of characters are satisfyingly trashy and dysfunctional. The result is a highly plausible and self-assured thriller' *The Leeds Guide*

'Dark and complex . . . From hard-boiled cops to ruthless women on the make and sadistic north London crooks, Kernick generates a potent cocktail of thrills that makes contemporary London feel like Dodge City. A knucklehead ride' *Guardian*

'Relentlessly pacy, with rousing, recreational sex, grisly torture, credible macho bonding and truly wicked heavies, all edgily projected against the mean streets, pubs and clubs of non-tourist London' *Literary Review*

*Also by Simon Kernick*

THE BUSINESS OF DYING
THE MURDER EXCHANGE
THE CRIME TRADE

*and published by Corgi Books*

# A Good Day
# to Die

## SIMON KERNICK

**CORGI BOOKS**

**A GOOD DAY TO DIE**
**A CORGI BOOK : 9780552150705**

Originally published in Great Britain by Bantam Press,
a division of Transworld Publishers

PRINTING HISTORY
Bantam Press edition published 2005
Corgi edition published 2006

3 5 7 9 10 8 6 4

Copyright © Simon Kernick 2005
Foreword © Lee Child 2006

The right of Simon Kernick to be identified as the author of
this work has been asserted in accordance with sections 77
and 78 of the Copyright Designs and Patents Act 1988.

All the characters in this book are fictitious,
and any resemblance to actual persons, living or dead,
is purely coincidental.

*Condition of Sale*
This book is sold subject to the condition that it shall not,
by way of trade or otherwise, be lent, re-sold, hired out or
otherwise circulated in any form of binding or cover other
than that in which it is published and without a similar
condition including this condition being imposed on the
subsequent purchaser.

Set in 10½/12½pt Palatino by
Falcon Oast Graphic Art Ltd.

Corgi Books are published by Transworld Publishers,
61–63 Uxbridge Road, London W5 5SA,
a division of The Random House Group Ltd

Addresses for Random House Group Ltd companies outside the
UK can be found at: www.randomhouse.co.uk

Printed and bound in Great Britain by
Cox & Wyman Ltd, Reading, Berkshire.

The Random House Group Limited supports The Forest Stewardship
Council (FSC), the leading international forest certification organisation.
All our titles that are printed on Greenpeace approved FSC certified paper
carry the FSC logo. Our paper procurement policy can be found at:
www.rbooks.co.uk/environment.

**For my Mum and Dad**

# Foreword
## by Lee Child

What's up with English crime fiction?

It's a question that is asked often, and right now – early 2006 – it's a relevant question, because our genre's Third Age is drawing inexorably to a close. A century ago the First Age was all about Arthur Conan Doyle and Sherlock Holmes. Then the Second Age – in full flower seventy years ago – was dominated by Agatha Christie and Dorothy Sayers. Then, perhaps thirty years later, the Third Age took over, with Ruth Rendell and P.D. James hitting their magisterial strides. For a hundred years, very little was published in the genre that didn't owe practically everything to one of those five authors. Sleuths that were amateur, or brainy, or aristocratic, or 'more than' mere policemen, or eccentric, or unlikely, or who had arcane hobbies and enthusiasms . . . we've been there and done that. And what a fabulous ride it was. But after the *grandes dames*, what comes next?

Or, what's up with English crime fiction?

The same things that are up with England itself, really. Three factors are becoming increasingly important – the nation is more than ever metrocentric, more than ever multi-cultural, and less than ever dominated by class.

London is now a huge ethnic mosaic, in my experience easily rivaling New York City for diversity. It's another fact of life, so well accepted that it's no longer even worthy of notice or comment.

And London is an increasingly middle-class city, which in traditional English terms means no class at all. Birth and accent mean very little there anymore. When I opened my first bank account – too many years ago to happily contemplate – you could pretty much guarantee that a bank manager would be white, from sturdy English stock, and educated at one of a narrow band of schools. Now you could pretty much guarantee she won't be any of those things.

The Fourth Age English crime fiction writers grew up with these changes. They've internalized them. To their elders, class was always an issue. Stock, semi-comic stereotypes were plucked from the lower orders and paraded for our amusement. Lord Peter Wimsey could quell a street riot with his accent alone. And wasn't he wonderful to accept a middle-class Scotland Yard Inspector as his brother-in-law! Faint but clear echoes of the same attitudes are clearly audible in some Third Age fiction, too.

Fourth Age writers are past all that. That class is a dead issue is beyond being taken for granted by them.

Their elders put people of colour and non-English ethnicity into crime fiction from the start, but mostly as curiosities, often as villains, and never quite to be trusted. Their casts of characters are as instinctively multicultural as the London phone book.

And their elders usually glamorized London itself: Scotland Yard was presented as an effortless centre of excellence in comparison to dull provincial capabilities. 'They've called in Scotland Yard' was as great an accolade as a rural crime could ever earn. Addresses in London were chosen for their glitter: Piccadilly and Belgravia – or maybe Bloomsbury, if some sense of bohemian edge was required.

London is where life happens for Fourth Age writers; nothing more, nothing less: in the outer suburbs, near the M25, out at Heathrow, in grimy parts the world has never heard of, but should have.

Fourth Age writers have moved on. And we should move on with them. Perhaps with Simon Kernick in particular, because he might just be the best of them. I've read all his books, purely as a fan. They've got great plots, great characters, great dialogue, great action, and some spectacular violence. But what strikes me most is how they're rooted in a kind of effortless modern authenticity. They're real. They're what England is today. In fact all the above musing was generated by one simple question I asked myself: 'How does he *do* this?'

So, what's up with English crime fiction? Simon Kernick is, that's what.

# A Good Day to Die

# before

Richard Blacklip wanted to kill someone.

He'd been told before he left England that the man now sitting across the table from him could make the necessary arrangements. Mr Kane was, apparently, a fixer of such things, and in the sprawling, dirt-poor and life-cheap metropolis that was Manila, where almost anything could be bought and sold if the price was right, he had ready access to a constant supply of victims. It was now simply a matter of finding that price.

A call to Kane's mobile phone an hour earlier had set the meeting up, but now that his guest had arrived in the hotel room, Blacklip was beginning to have second thoughts about the whole thing. Not because he didn't want to go through with the act itself (after all, the truth was that it wasn't his first time), but because he was alone in a strange city thousands of miles from home, and was unsure of discussing his innermost thoughts and secrets with someone he'd only just met. Kane was supposed to be reliable, but what if he wasn't? What if he was a conman? Or worse still, working for the police, here to entrap him? Blacklip was aware that he was being paranoid, but that didn't mean his fears might not be justified.

'Is everything OK?' Kane's voice was calm and controlled, designed to reassure.

It worked, too. Blacklip smiled and used a handkerchief to wipe sweat from his forehead. 'It's fine,' he answered, sounding falsely jolly, even to himself. 'It's just this heat. I'm not used to it.'

The room was stifling. He'd changed into lighter clothes and turned the ceiling fan up to maximum, had even pulled down the blinds to keep out the fiery sun, but nothing seemed to be doing any good. He was conscious of the wetness under his armpits, and wished now that he'd rented a room with air conditioning. But then, of course, he was saving his money for bigger things.

Kane said something about Westerners getting used to the heat after they'd spent some time in the Philippines, but Blacklip wasn't really listening. He was too busy studying his guest while trying to act like he wasn't, a task he believed he performed much better than most people. He was used to discreet observation.

Kane was younger than he'd been expecting, probably no more than forty, and dressed casually in jeans and a light sports jacket over a cotton shirt.

He was a lot taller than Blacklip and of slimmer build, and his tan, coupled with his narrow, well-defined features, suggested that he was a fit man who spent plenty of time outdoors. His hair and neatly trimmed beard had been bleached by the sun and contained only the faintest hint of grey. Some people might have considered him good-looking, although his eyes were narrow and a little bit too close together.

A bead of sweat ran down from Kane's hairline, making swiftly for an eyebrow. He flicked it away casually. If the humidity in the room bothered him, he didn't show it. He stopped speaking about the Filipino weather and focused his eyes on Blacklip. He looked ready to do business.

It was now or never, the moment of truth.

Blacklip took a deep breath, aware that he was about to take a huge risk, but equally aware of the potential reward. The pleasure he'd get from it. The hunt. The act. The kill.

'You know what I want,' he said at last. 'Can you get it?'

'You want a girl?'

'That's right.'

Kane nodded agreeably. 'Sure, I can get you a girl.'

Blacklip cleared his throat, felt a joyous tingling sensation going up his spine. 'She has to be young,' he said, savouring that last word.

'Whatever you're after, I can get it for you. For a price.'

The tingling in Blacklip's spine grew stronger, spreading to his groin as he pictured what he was going to do. His mouth felt dry and he licked his lips.

Kane waited, his face registering nothing more than mild interest.

'Anything? You can get me anything?' Blacklip's voice had dropped to a whisper, his mind now entirely focused on the task ahead. His whole world had become reduced to the few square feet of this tiny, dimly lit room, its stifling heat temporarily forgotten.

'Anything.'

The word was delivered calmly, yet decisively. Blacklip knew the fixer did indeed mean anything. Even murder.

So, with a shy, almost childlike smile, he shared his bloody fantasy. Occasionally he stole brief glances at the man opposite him to check that what he was saying wasn't going too far, but each time Kane smiled back, reassuring him that everything was fine, that there was nothing wrong with what he wanted.

When he'd finished, Blacklip gave Kane the sort of look that a dog gives his master. Asking to be understood. Begging for his bone.

'I see,' said Kane, after a short pause.

'Can you do it?'

'It'll cost a lot. There's the logistics of it, for a start. And the risk.'

16

'I didn't think they'd be missed in a place like this. After all, there's plenty of them.'

'True, but the authorities are cracking down. That's not to say I can't do it, but it will cost.'

'How much?'

'Five thousand US.'

Blacklip felt a lurch of disappointment. 'That's an awful lot. I don't think I've got that sort of money. I was hoping for nearer two.'

Kane appeared to think about this for a moment, while Blacklip watched him, praying he'd take the bait.

'I'll see what I can do,' Kane answered eventually. 'But I'm going to need a deposit so that I can set things in motion. Obviously this sort of thing requires a lot of effort. Can you give me two hundred US now?'

'Please tell me you'll do it, Mr Kane,' Richard Blacklip said quietly.

'All right,' Kane sighed, appearing to come to a decision. 'I'll do it for two thousand.'

Blacklip got to his feet. 'Thank you very much,' he said with genuine appreciation. 'Now let's find this money, shall we?'

He stepped over to the bed, pulled open his suitcase and rummaged inside.

Then he turned round.

And looked straight at the black pistol pointed directly at his chest.

Fear stretched Blacklip's pudgy features into a grotesque parody of an astonished circus clown. His legs went weak and the wallet he was holding fell uselessly to the floor. The banknotes he'd already removed fluttered down after it.

His first thought was 'Police.'

But no-one else was coming into the room. There was no other noise. And jutting out from the pistol's barrel was a fat cigar-shaped silencer that couldn't have been police issue.

The man who'd introduced himself as Kane wasn't moving, or telling him he was under arrest. He said nothing and his expression remained impassive.

'No, please, please,' Blacklip begged, his voice high-pitched. 'Mr Kane, what are you doing? I've got money. Don't kill me. For God's sake.'

The gunman pointed the revolver purposefully in the direction of Blacklip's groin, his finger tensing on the trigger.

'Why are you doing this? There's been a misunderstanding. Please.' He felt a wetness travelling down his trouser legs. Ignored it. Desperation rose up in him like bile. He wanted to do something – anything. Scream, run, charge down his tormentor. But nothing moved. He was rooted firmly to the spot.

Pissing himself in fear.

The gunman looked him in the eye. In that moment, Blacklip knew there was no hope.

But he had to try. 'Whatever they're paying you,' he whispered, 'I'll double it.'

'I'm choosy who I work for,' said the gunman, and pulled the trigger.

Blacklip felt a sudden burning sensation like an electric shock. He gasped and fell back onto the bed, his hands grabbing at the wound.

He managed one last word, uttered with a final hiss of venom as rage overcame fear for just one second.

'Bastards.'

Then the gunman stepped forward and put two more bullets in Blacklip's head.

A splash of blood like aerosol hit the wall, and the gunman turned and walked from the room.

# Part One

## MINDORO ISLAND, PHILIPPINES

### One Year Later

# 1

I was sitting in Tina's Sunset Restaurant, watching the outriggers shuffle lazily through the clear waters of Sabang Bay, when Tomboy took a seat opposite me, ordered a San Miguel from Tina's daughter, and told me that someone else had to die. It was five o'clock in the afternoon, there wasn't a cloud in the sky, and up until that point I'd been in a good mood.

I told him that I didn't kill people any more, that it was a part of my past I didn't want to be reminded of, and he replied that he understood all that, but once again we needed the money. 'It's just the way the cookie crumbles,' he added, with the sort of bullshit 'I share your suffering' expression an undertaker might give to one of his customers' relatives. Tomboy Darke was my business partner and a man with a cliché for every occasion, including murder.

Tina's was empty, as was usually the case at that

time of day. It was right at the end of the collection of bars and guest-houses that pass for the small tourist town of Sabang's main drag, and tucked away enough that few of the tourists ever used it, so I'd known as soon as Tomboy had asked to meet me here that something was up. It was the sort of place you went to when you wanted to talk without anyone else listening. So I talked. 'Who's the target?'

He paused while the beer was put down in front of him, then waited until Tina's daughter was out of earshot. 'The bloke's name's Billy Warren,' he said quietly. 'He's on the Thursday flight out of Heathrow, arriving in Manila Friday morning.'

'Today's Wednesday, Tomboy.'

'I know that,' he answered, running his fingers through what was left of his hair. 'But you know what they say. Time waits for no man.'

'What's he done, this Warren?'

'No-one's saying anything at the moment, it's all very hush hush. But he's running away from some-thing – something serious. Just like you. Except this time, someone wants to kill him for it. He ain't going to be whiter than white, put it like that.'

'How much are they offering for the job?'

'Thirty thousand US. A lot of money.'

He was right, it was. Particularly here in the Philippines. The business we ran – a small hotel with dive operation attached – didn't take much more than that in a year, and thanks to Al Qaeda's continued efforts to mangle Western tourism in the Far East, things weren't likely to improve much in the year ahead. By the time we'd paid the staff, the local authorities and covered our running costs, we cleared maybe a third of that in profit. Paradise is nice, but it rarely makes you rich.

I took a sip from my beer. 'Someone must want him dead very badly.'

He nodded and pulled a soft-top pack of Marlboro Lights from his pocket, lighting one. 'They do. Not only that, they want him to disappear. No trace.'

'That's not going to be very easy in Manila.'

'It ain't going to be in Manila. As soon as he arrives, he's getting a cab down to Batangas, and a boat across to Puerta Galera.' Puerta Galera was the nearest main town to us and Mindoro Island's main port. 'He's got a room booked at the Hotel California on East Brucal Street. It's already been paid for. He's been told that you're going to meet him there to give him instructions and a briefcase full of money. What you need to do is get him out of the room and take him for a drive. One that he don't come back from.'

'If I accept the job.'

'Yeah,' he said with some reluctance, 'if you accept the job. But you know how things are at the moment. We need this cash. Badly. I wouldn't ask you if we didn't, you know that.'

'We've been in this place how long? A year? And

you want me to take someone out five kilometres down the road. Don't you think that's just a little bit risky?'

'No-one'll ever find the body. We're getting fifteen grand up front. All we need to do is provide photos proving it's been done and we'll get the balance of the cash. And that'll be the end of it.'

That'll be the end of it. I'd heard that one before. 'Last question. Who's the client?'

'Pope. Same as last time.'

'No doubt doing it on behalf of someone else?'

Tomboy nodded vaguely. 'No doubt.'

The mysterious Mr Pope. An old criminal contact of Tomboy's from London, he'd first got in touch a year ago with a business proposition, having tracked down Tomboy all the way to Sabang, which must have taken some doing. The business proposition had been the execution of Richard Blacklip, a British paedophile on the run from the law in the UK who was heading to Manila on a false passport. Someone Pope knew – apparently one of his victims, who was now an adult – wanted Blacklip dead, and Pope had asked Tomboy if he could organize someone reliable to carry out the task.

It might have seemed like a strange request for most people, but Tomboy Darke had been a career criminal all his life (albeit more of a ducker and diver than a man of violence) and had spent many years moving in the sort of circles where such things occasionally happened, and where people weren't so hesitant in asking the question.

And, of course, Tomboy had known just the man.

I sighed loudly, not wanting to get involved in a repeat performance.

He took a huge gulp from the neck of the beer, dragged on the cigarette and looked me right in the eye. 'I know you don't want to do it. I don't much want to do it, to be honest with you. But this is big money, and I'm telling you, this bloke's no angel. He's fleeing London for the back-end of nowhere, meeting someone to get a caseload of cash off them so he can start a new life a long way from prying eyes. Does that sound like someone with a clear conscience to you?'

He had a point there, but if there's one thing I've learned in life, it's never to take anything you're told at face value. I'd made that mistake before, and it had almost cost me my life. In the three years since I'd left England, I'd tried to put all that behind me, to start afresh. Just like this guy Warren was trying to do. But you can never escape the past for ever, as he was about to find out.

I continued looking at Tomboy and he continued looking at me. I was thinking that there might be a way round this. A way of getting the money, doctoring a few photos, and not having to kill anyone. I suspected that he was just thinking about the money. Even so, I told him what he wanted to hear.

'All right,' I said. 'I'll do it.'

# 2

Tomboy drank the rest of his beer and ordered another one from Tina's daughter. He then spent the next few minutes flirting with her while she leaned against the table opposite, a cloth in one hand and a smile on her face that was wide enough to be friendly but had little in the way of depth.

He said he bet that all the boys were chasing after her, and told her what a pretty young thing she was. She was a pretty young thing too but I doubted if she was a day over sixteen – while Tomboy was, if my memory served me correctly, the grand old age of forty-two, which made the whole thing look a little tasteless. He winked at me now and again, between jokes and compliments, just to demonstrate that it was nothing more than light-hearted banter, but I could see the hint of desperation in his act. He might have thought he was messing about, but, like a lot of men whose looks are fading as their waistlines expand, he needed to believe he still had that elusive 'something' the girls always go for. Unfortunately, he didn't. As well as being about three stone heavier than he had been back in the old days in London, the booze had reddened his nose and cheeks and scattered them with clusters of broken veins, while his precious blond locks – the pride and joy of his youth – had been reduced to a few desperate strands on top and a scraggy ponytail at the back.

But that didn't stop him. He asked Tina's daughter what she liked most in a man. 'Apart from the obvious,' he added, chortling.

She giggled. 'I don't know,' she said. 'Don't ask me that.'

'You should make it multiple choice, Tomboy,' I told him. 'You know, A: beer gut; B: loud London accent. That sort of thing. It'd give you more of a chance.'

'Sense of humour,' she said, looking pleased with herself. 'That's what I like.'

Tomboy turned my way with the makings of a glare. I think he wanted to say something – a similarly barbed comment aimed in my direction – but remembered that he'd just asked me to kill someone, so decided to let it go.

'You have a good sense of humour, Tomboy,' said Tina's daughter. She didn't say the same to me, but then I didn't know her as well.

Tomboy smiled. 'Thanks, love.' But he'd lost

interest in the banter now. Like an unwelcome heckler, I'd messed up his routine.

He quaffed the rest of his second bottle of beer and announced he had to go. He had things to do, he said. Phoning London, for one. Letting the man called Pope know the job was on.

I finished my own drink in silence, still watching the outriggers in the bay, but with nothing like the pleasure that I'd taken in the view earlier. I liked Tomboy, and hadn't meant to piss him off. He was a big man with a big personality, and he'd been good to me since I'd arrived at his Philippine hotel three years ago, on the run and without a friend left in the world. So I figured that I owed him. But killing someone on our very own doorstep? That felt like one payment too far.

Which was one reason why I still wasn't sure whether I was actually going to go through with it or not. The other reason was that I'm no cold-blooded murderer. I've done jobs before. Blacklip was one, and there were others before him in England. Jobs where I've had to end the lives of people who deserved it. Drug dealers; child molesters; the worst kind of criminals. They weren't many in number, and they never interfered with the work I did as a detective in London's Metropolitan Police, so I never thought that I was doing much wrong. However, all that changed three years ago, when I made a mistake and shot some men I was told were bad guys, but who were actually anything but. That's what I mean about not taking things at face value. People lie. They also double-cross, even the ones you're meant to trust. Anyway, the result of that particular mistake was that I ended up on the run, with the police, Interpol and God knows who else after my blood. None of them were successful, and after a long and indirect journey, I made it here to the Philippines, going into business with a man who used to be one of my best informants back in the old days, when I was still on the side of the forces of law and order and people had known me as Detective Sergeant Dennis Milne.

Originally, Tomboy had owned a hotel and beach bar on Siquijor, a tiny island way down in the south of the Philippine archipelago, and I worked for him there. When I'd arrived it had been doing quite well, but then the Islamic rebels of Abu Sayyaf began to extend their kidnapping and bombing operations closer and closer to where we were, and the visitor numbers had slowed to a trickle. Tomboy and his Filipina wife Angela had sold up at a significant loss just over a year earlier and we'd headed north to start again in the Puerta Galera region of Mindoro, a large island a few hours' boat and taxi ride from Manila. It was a lot busier here, and a lot safer too. Unless your name was Billy Warren, of course.

I paid my bill and left Tina's daughter a fifty-peso tip, then headed out onto the narrow concrete walkway that was Sabang's equivalent of a promenade, stepping over a couple of three-year-old kids playing on the ground with a mangy-looking puppy. I made my way along the beach, past a group of local men who were stood watching a cock-fight on the sand in front of the boats, then cut into the narrow, dirty backstreets of the town. The journey took me past the ramshackle stalls selling raw meat and fish, where the women gathered to barter in staccato tones; through gaggles of raucous schoolkids, heading home in their immaculate uniforms; past cheap tourist shops and girlie bars; across planks of wood that acted as bridges over the streams of effluent-laced water trailing beneath; under washing lines; through people's backyards; past noisy games of pool played under tin roofs. And all the way I nodded to people I knew, greeted a few of them by name, breathed in the hot, stinking air, and thought how much I loved this place. The vibrancy, the heat. The freedom.

When I emerged at the other end of town and stepped back onto the promenade, the sun was setting in a blaze of gold and pink above the headland in front of me.

It was beautiful. It should have made me happy.

But I was too busy thinking about the fugitive coming from across the sea, and wondering whether he was going to be the man who ruined it all for me.

# 3

Two days after the meeting at Tina's Sunset Restaurant, I drove the potholed road from Sabang to Puerta Galera, a gun in my pocket and a lot on my mind.

East Brucal Street's a quiet and surprisingly leafy little road about fifty yards long and dotted with mango trees, just off Puerta Galera's raucous main drag. The Hotel California, halfway down it, is a small, two-storey establishment with an open-air restaurant on its second floor that fits in nicely with the surroundings. It's owned by an ex-Vietnam War veteran who's not the sort of man you'd want to get in an argument with, but who was quite friendly with Tomboy and could be trusted not to take too much notice of who was passing through his establishment. At three hundred pesos a night for a double room with bathroom, it's a good-value place to stay. Particularly so for Billy Warren, as his one night there had already been paid for in cash by Tomboy.

It was two thirty on a hot, sunny Friday afternoon and the street was quiet. A couple of cars were parked up but there didn't seem to be anyone around. I pulled up ten yards past the front of the hotel, outside a collection of rusty corrugated-iron sheets that had somehow been fashioned into a shop selling house plants, and dialled the mobile number I'd been given.

Warren answered after five rings. 'Hello?' The tone was neutral, a little rough around the edges, and not betraying any nerves.

'My name's Mick Kane,' I told him without preamble. 'I've been told to deliver something to you, and to give you certain instructions. I'm outside, just up the street in a blue Land Rover. Can you come down?'

'I've never seen a blue Land Rover before,' he informed me helpfully.

'Well, now's your chance. You can even have a drive in it if you want. There's a bar at the Ponderosa golf club. It's fifteen minutes up the road. It'll be quiet up there this time of day, so we can talk.'

'So, you want to take me for a drive, do you?' His tone was suspicious, but there was something mocking in it too, as if he was letting me know he knew my motives. 'Here I am all on my lonesome in a fleapit of a country where, according to the

34

BBC, life is dirt fucking cheap, and I've just been invited to get in a car with a man I've never met before, but who's apparently got a load of money for me, and go for a country jaunt?'

'Listen, I don't mind how we do it,' I told him. 'My job's to give you the case I'm carrying and provide you with a few instructions to help you on your way. You can just come out and grab it if you want. It makes no difference. I just fancied a drink, that's all.'

'Has it got aircon, this place? I'm not going anywhere without aircon. Not in this heat.'

'Of course it has,' I lied. 'And it's got nice views, too. You'll like it.'

'We'll see,' he said enigmatically and hung up.

This guy fancied himself, no question; and he wanted me to know he was no fool. I've met plenty of men like him before. Men who are sure they know the score on everything; who are streetwise enough that they can smell trouble a mile off. But everyone's got a weakness. It's just a matter of knowing where to look.

Five minutes passed, and I was just about to phone the cheeky sod again to see what the hell he was playing at when he emerged from the hotel entrance, dressed in a white, short-sleeved cotton shirt and jeans. He made his way straight to the car without looking around, which meant that he'd been watching it from his hotel room. Fair enough. I'd have done the same in his position.

He was medium height, early forties, with short dark hair and a thick moustache that followed the curves of his mouth and didn't look right on him at all. He had a muscular build that suggested he worked out regularly, and his face was fairly non-descript in so far as nothing actually stood out, except perhaps that it belonged to a man who knew how to handle himself.

I couldn't help but smile as I watched him approach in the rear-view mirror. So the man I'd once known as Billy West had changed his name – or part of it, anyway. I hadn't seen him in maybe ten years, but he didn't look much different than he had done then. Except for the 'tache. This was a new edition, and presumably part of his disguise. Because there was no way Slippery Billy West wasn't on the run. The man had spent a lifetime struggling to extricate himself from the jaws of justice, and with more than a little success too, especially where his dealings with me were concerned.

I'd first come across him back in London around 1991, when my colleagues and I in CID had put him under surveillance on suspicion of gun-running. He was an ex-soldier who'd served in the Falklands conflict and Northern Ireland, and who'd ended up being court-martialled when he and a fellow squaddie had held up an army payroll truck at gun-point and relieved it of its contents. That was the only time, as far as I was aware, that he'd ever spent any time behind bars. Our surveillance of him for the gun-running lasted close to a month, and when we nicked him and raided the lock-up he was using for his business, we recovered three handguns and an AK-47 assault rifle. But in court, Slippery claimed to know nothing about the weapons, and used as his defence the fact that he wasn't the only keyholder to the premises, which was true. Two of his cousins, both of whom did work for him now and again, were indeed keyholders, and in the end it came down to the fact that it couldn't be proved beyond doubt that he was the one the guns belonged to, particularly as there were no prints on any of them. So he'd been acquitted.

I had the same trouble with him again a couple of years later when, acting on intelligence, I'd led a raid on his flat in King's Cross in the hunt for a significant quantity of cocaine. Unfortunately, the bastard had reinforced not only the front door but the bathroom door too, for a reason that quickly became apparent. We'd managed to batter down the front door after much effort, but by the time we'd got inside he'd already made it to the bathroom, along with his stash. I'll always remember the frustration I felt as we tried to force open the second reinforced door before he flushed the whole stash down the toilet. What was worse, we could hear him doing it. And he was whistling a jaunty tune at the same time, as if the sound of us trying to break into his place was the most natural thing in the world. After about five good heaves with the Enforcer, we'd finally got the door open, only to find old Slippery sitting comfortably on the throne with his trousers round his ankles, a recent copy of the *Sun* in his hands. He even managed a loud fart to add to the authenticity of his situation, before greeting me with a cheery 'Morning, DS Milne, I wondered what that noise was.' Which was him all over. As cocky as they come.

All that was left of the suspected half-kilo of cocaine he'd been in possession of were five plastic bags each containing trace amounts of the drug, which turned out to be enough to warrant only a two-hundred-pound fine.

Three weeks later, the guy who'd supplied us with the information that led to the raid, a former business associate of Slippery's named Karl Nash, was found dead in his Islington townhouse. At first his death was thought to have been due to a heroin overdose, but further investigation revealed that he'd been asphyxiated. There was, of course, an obvious suspect. Nash and Slippery had fallen out very publicly, but although Slippery was arrested and questioned in connection with the murder, there was insufficient evidence to proceed.

I think even he realized at this point that he was living on borrowed time, and shortly after that he'd quietly disappeared from the scene, and I hadn't clapped eyes on him since. Until now, that was. I wondered whether he'd recognize me or not. After all, we'd spent plenty of less than quality time in each other's company.

As he came by the side of the car I saw him glance casually at the back seat, just to check there wasn't anyone sat waiting there to garrotte him, before opening the door and getting inside.

'Mick Kane,' I said, putting out a hand.

He shook it with a softer grip than I'd been expecting and looked me in the eye. 'Billy Warren.'

For a couple of seconds there was nothing, and he even started to turn away, but then he looked at me again.

'What is it?' I asked him.

A slow and deliberate grin spread across his face. 'Fuck me, it can't be. Dennis Milne. Christ, you've changed a bit. Have you been having a bit of a nip and tuck, you vain bugger?'

So much for my disguise. 'I could hardly have announced my real name, could I?' I said, not bothering to deny his claim.

'Too right. I'd never have come down here. I wouldn't know whether you were going to nick me or shoot me.' He shook his head, still grinning. 'Blimey, it's a small world, innit? And full of sur-prises, too. Who'd have thought the copper who spent so much time trying to put me behind bars because he said I was a – what were your exact words, Dennis? – a lowlife bastard who's going to get what's coming to him, I think it was . . . Who'd have thought the copper who called me that would

39

turn out to be a mass murderer?' His expression was full of mockery, but then it turned serious and his grey eyes hardened. 'You ain't gonna try and shoot me now, are you, Dennis? You have actually come with the money?'

'Unlike you, Slippery, I've got morals. I've only ever killed people who deserved it, and when I've had good reason.'

'What about them customs officers?'

'They were a mistake, and not one I'm ever going to repeat. I'm happy here. I don't need to complicate things by going back to that old game.' I turned the key in the ignition, put the Land Rover in gear, and pulled out into the road.

He was still watching me and I sensed a tension in him. He obviously wasn't entirely convinced. 'I bet you've always thought I deserved it,' he said.

'I did,' I told him. 'And I still do. But then again, when I came here this afternoon I didn't expect to be running into you. It's what you might call an interesting surprise.'

'Fair do's,' he said, and pulled a pack of Marlboro Reds from his pocket. He flashed it in my direction. 'Want one?'

'No, I quit. A while back now.'

'So, where's the case?'

'In the boot. You don't drive round the Philippines with cases full of money on your passenger seat. Not unless you want to lose them.'

He nodded, accepting the explanation, and we

pulled out of East Brucal and turned right into the chaos of Concepcion Street, the noisy, fume-filled and dusty thoroughfare that was the heart of Puerta Galera. The traffic was heavy as usual, and the pot-holed road filled with all manner of exotic vehicles: hulking, multicoloured buses known as jeepneys that had people hanging precariously from every square inch of space; tiny mopeds with covered sidecars that often contained three generations of one family; battered old American Buicks and Fords; brand-new 500 and 1,000cc motorbikes ridden by bare-chested, helmetless and most definitely uninsured Europeans with their Filipina girlfriends on the back. The whole lot of them blast-ing on their horns as if their masculinity depended on it, and none of them going any faster than the choking pedestrians walking along the sides of the road.

Slippery lit one of the Marlboros with a match and opened the window, letting in a fiery waft of pollution. He chucked the match out and immedi-ately shut the window again. 'Christ,' he said, taking a long drag. 'Is it always like this?'

'Always like what?'

He waved his arm expansively. 'Like this. You know, hot, smelly and noisy.'

'You get used to it,' I told him, wondering at the same time if he actually would, or whether I'd deny him the opportunity. He'd been right when he'd suggested I thought he deserved to die. I think he probably did. He was almost certainly a killer himself, with few redeeming features and not even the first semblance of a conscience. But if there was a way of avoiding a murder and still getting our money, I was keen to take it. And no-one, apart from Slippery and me, would ever know the truth.

'So how long have you been out here for now, Dennis?' he asked, puffing on the smoke again. 'The whole time since you disappeared?'

'Pretty much.'

'You know, I couldn't believe it when I read about what you'd done. I really couldn't. You always struck me as one of the good guys. You were obviously a very decent liar.'

I knew the bastard was baiting me, but I ignored it. 'I couldn't even begin to compete with you in the bullshitter stakes, Slippery. I reckon the only time you ever told me the truth was when you spoke to confirm your name, and you've even managed to change that now. Or half of it, at least. What happened? Didn't you think you'd be able to remember it if you changed the first part as well?'

'I always keep it simple, Dennis. There's no point trying to confuse things.' His voice was even, but there was an underlying irritation in it. I'd obviously annoyed him a little, which suited me fine. 'And what's this fucking Slippery business?'

'Don't you remember? It was the name we used to have for you in CID. Slippery Billy West. On account of your ability to wriggle out of every situation we put you in.'

He snorted loudly and derisively. 'What? And you ain't a wriggler? How many people did you kill? Six? Seven? And here you are with a nice suntan, living the life of Reilly. You've wriggled just as well as I ever did, mate, and don't pretend otherwise.'

The car fell silent as we crawled through the traffic past the turn-off to the harbour, before finally speeding up as we came out the other side of Puerta Galera. The road here was relatively new, the best in the north of the island, and I'd soon passed all the crawling jeepneys and built up a half-decent head of speed. The sea appeared to our right through a coconut-palm grove – a brilliant, cerulean blue – but almost immediately the view was obscured by a ragged huddle of tin and wood squatters' shacks that had sprung up by the side of the road. In the Philippines, you're only ever one step away from abject poverty.

'So,' I said eventually. 'You know why I had to come here. What about you? What are you running from this time?'

He opened the window and chucked out his cigarette butt. The air outside was clearer and fresher now that the traffic had thinned. He didn't answer for a while and I thought that maybe I'd upset him, but then he sighed loudly. 'Something I should never have got involved in,' he said at last and he sounded like he meant it.

'Isn't that always the way?'

'I'm normally a good judge of these things,' he said, which is something I would probably have agreed with, 'but I fucked up this time.'

'What happened?'

He turned and looked at me carefully. I think he was trying to work out whether it was something he wanted to tell the man who, for a short time at least, had been his nemesis. I got the feeling that his instincts were erring on the side of caution, but that he also wanted to talk about it to someone he knew. Criminals love to tell people about their crimes but in general it's not very practical for them to do so, so when they're in the presence of other criminals (and I suppose to Slippery I was one), they tend to let rip.

'I did a job for a bloke. Your sort of job. A hit.'

'Oh yeah?'

'Yeah. I got approached by someone I knew to take out a bloke in London. The pay being offered was ten grand and I needed the money. It was a rush job, though. That's why I should have turned it down. I didn't have time to put him under surveillance, find out about him, or anything like that. I was told I had twenty-four hours to put him in the ground. That was it. So I told them I needed fifteen grand for a job like that, we did a bit of negotiation and I settled for twelve.'

He sat back in his seat and drummed his middle and index fingers against the side of his face in a rapid and irritatingly noisy tattoo. I suddenly remembered it as a habit of his from the past. He used to do it during interrogations, usually when he was mulling something over.

'The problem was,' he continued, 'I didn't have a clue how I was going to do it, and I didn't have time to come up with any sort of proper plan. I reckoned I was going to have to knock on his door, hope it was him who opened it, and let him have it there and then. The client said he wouldn't be armed, so it should have been no problem. Anyway, I drove down to the victim's place the next night and I was waiting outside in my car, just checking everything out and psyching myself up to make my move, when I got a call on my mobile. It was the client again. He told me that our man was at home, but was about to go out to an all-night café in Clerkenwell to meet someone. If he got there and met the other bloke, then I had to take out both of them.'

He sighed. 'And that was my second mistake. Rather than just say I was outside the target's house and ready to pop him there and then, I sniffed the chance to make some more cash. The client sounded really worried, like he was getting desperate, so I told him it would cost more to do two. Twenty grand in all. He was pissed off, but, like I explained to him, it meant a bigger risk for me, and so he went for it. He hung up, and then a couple of seconds later the target came walking out of his place, and I just watched him go when I could have taken him out.'

I couldn't believe Slippery's stupidity, especially after telling me the importance of keeping things simple. He was no master criminal, but he'd always been pretty good at covering his tracks, so to make a sloppy and extremely risky decision in order to pocket a few more quid showed what I'd long suspected: that his successes against the forces of law and order had finally made him think he was untouchable.

'And it fucked up?'

'Well, that's the thing. Not at the time, no. I got the directions to the café and went straight down there. Then I just walked in with a crash helmet on, spotted the target chatting to the geezer he was meeting, and went straight over. They were the only customers in the place and they were so deep in conversation that they didn't see me until it was too late. I pulled my shooter, and that was that. Two bullets in each of them, then head shots just to make sure. Only one witness, the bloke behind the counter, and he did the right thing and kept his mouth shut and his hands in the air. I reckon the whole thing took about ten seconds.'

'So what went wrong?'

He shrugged and started the old finger tattoo again. 'This is it, I don't know. The whole thing happened a few weeks back, and there was a bit of a hoo-hah in the papers because one of them was a copper. I didn't know that, of course. I'd never have touched him if I'd known he was Old Bill.'

'That's nice to know.'

'Not 'cause I respect them, but because it's too much hassle. Anyway, I got paid the full amount and I didn't hear nothing more about it until a couple of days ago, when I got a phone call out of the blue from the client saying I had to get out of the country, and fast. I asked him why, and he said he had information that the coppers investigating the murders were on to me. He didn't say how they'd got so close, but he was pretty convincing. Course I wasn't keen on upping sticks, but when he told me that he had a false passport and a ticket to the Philippines, and that someone would meet me there with ten grand to get me settled, I decided he had to be serious and that it was probably an idea to take him up on his offer. And that's it. The rest you know.'

'And who was your client?'

He gave me a look that bordered on the suspicious. 'Don't you know?'

'I'm here on behalf of someone called Pope. He supplied us with the money to give to you.'

'He's the one I did the job for. The client. Les Pope.'

Les Pope, I had to admit, was a man with access to supremely good intelligence. A year ago, he'd been so many steps ahead of Richard Blacklip that he'd been able to lead me right to his hotel room.

Now, he was far enough inside a major police investigation to tip off the prime suspect and get him out of the country.

It was then that I made my decision. 'I'm going to be honest with you now, Slippery.'

'Call me Billy, please.'

'All right, Billy. The fact is, you're in a lot of trouble.'

'What do you mean?'

'Pope wants you dead, and he's hired me through a mutual acquaintance to make sure you get that way.' He started to shift in his seat and I had a feeling that he might try and go for me, so I kept talking, still staring at the road ahead. 'Now listen, I've got no intention of hurting you. Like I told you before, I'm out of that game now, and if we play this right, you can walk away in one piece and completely off the hook, and I can still get my money.'

'How are you going to manage that?' he demanded, his eyes boring into the side of my face.

'Because Pope doesn't just want you dead, he wants you to disappear off the face of the earth as well, which means we've got scope for faking your demise.'

'He's going to want evidence that you've done the job, though.'

'Of course he is. He's a criminal, so he's not going to trust me, but there's an easy way round that. He wants photographic evidence that you've been killed. If you look in the glove compartment, you'll see a Coke bottle filled with fresh rooster blood, which looks exactly like its human equivalent.'

'Lovely.'

'It pays to make the effort, Billy, as well you know. There's also a small jar of black paint that we'll use to mark the entry wounds of the bullets. All you have to do is lie on the ground, act dead while I pour the contents of these two bottles over your abdomen and do a bit of a paint job so it looks realistic, and then I'll stand back and take a couple of snapshots. They'll get sent back to Pope, he'll be happy with a job well done, I'll get paid, and that'll be that. You head down south and live quietly and anonymously, because with the British police and presumably Interpol after your blood for two murders, it's in your interests to lie as low as possible, and I'll never mention your name again.'

'How do I know you ain't gonna kill me anyway?'

I slowed down as a jeepney in front of me stopped to pick up passengers by the side of the road. 'If you're a shooter then you should know better than anybody that your best weapon is the art of surprise. I've just told you exactly what I've been hired to do. Now why would I bother saying anything if I still intended to kill you?'

He thought about that one for a few seconds, then opened the glove compartment. Seeing the blood-filled Coke bottle and the paint, he shut it again and lit another cigarette. At the same time, I overtook the stationary jeepney. 'That bastard,' he said, taking a drag. 'I knew I should never have trusted him. And the ten grand in the boot?'

'Behave. It doesn't exist. Be thankful that you've still got your life. So, are you in agreement with my plan? It's a lot better thought out than the one you used for your little job.'

'You want me to lie in the dirt and have chicken blood splashed all over me while you do a David Bailey?'

'That's about the size of it.'

'It doesn't seem like I've got much choice, does it?'

'No,' I said. 'I don't think it does.'

He emitted a loud sound of consent that sounded like someone impersonating a fart.

'I'll take that as a yes, shall I?'

'All right,' he grunted. 'Let's do it.'

# 4

A mile short of the resort of White Beach, there's a left turning that leads up to the Ponderosa, Mindoro's only golf course, a truly terrible collection of nine holes built high up on the side of a steep, forested mountain, where the wind whipping across the greens makes hitting a decent shot next to impossible, but where plenty of the expats try on the basis that there's nowhere else for them. I've never liked golf so I've not given it a go myself, although they do have some spectacular views over Puerta Galera and the islands beyond. Some say that on a clear day you can even see Manila eighty miles to the north, although I never have and wouldn't particularly want to either.

The road starts smoothly enough, which is useful as it's so steep, but quickly degenerates into a dusty, potholed and winding track, like so many of northern Mindoro's roads. The money's been made available more than once to pay for resurfacing them, but it always seems to disappear into someone's pocket before a square foot of tarmac's been put down.

On the way up, while Slippery was complaining about the road's state after banging his head on the roof for the second or third time, I asked him how he knew Pope.

He responded by asking how I knew him, which I recalled as another irritating habit of his from old. Answering a question with a question.

'I don't,' I said. 'A friend of mine here does.'

'He's a solicitor – a bent one. I was up on some charges and he represented me.'

'And got you off, no doubt.'

He nodded evenly. 'He did, yeah, and we kept in contact after that.'

I thought about this for a moment. I hadn't figured Pope as a solicitor. I had him down more as some sort of gangland Mr Big, since he obviously had such influential friends. It surprised me that they might include someone from within the team investigating the two murders that Slippery had committed. Defence lawyers and coppers rarely mix well, not when you consider that the former are always trying to fuck things up for the latter, and making far more money in the process.

'And when Pope, your brief, asked you to commit murder for him, you weren't a bit shocked?' I asked.

'No,' he said simply, reaching into his shirt pocket for the cigarettes. 'I wasn't.'

'Don't light up now,' I told him. 'We're almost there. You can have a celebratory smoke afterwards. To usher in your new life.'

He grunted irritably, but put the pack back in his pocket. 'Don't try anything, Dennis. And I mean that. I'm no fucking pushover.'

'I have no doubt about it, Billy. You were always the hardest, and dare I say it, the slipperiest target I ever chased. I'm not going to try anything.'

I slowed down as the road flattened out just before it came to a blind bend, still a good mile from the golf club. There was a slight grassy incline on the right where I could pull up without blocking anyone else coming either way, not that there was much chance of that. On the way up we hadn't run into anybody and the Ponderosa's not the busiest of places, especially on a weekday.

I managed to get right up onto the verge and cut the engine. 'We'll do it down there,' I said, pointing to a path that led into bushes.

'Why there?'

'Because it needs to be a place where no-one's going to disturb us, so they don't wonder what on earth we're doing. Believe it or not, there's hardly any places on this island where you can go without running into someone.'

'I'm watching you,' he said, all semblance of his earlier good humour now gone.

'You're getting paranoid,' I told him and slowly took the snub-nosed .38 revolver from the waistband of my jeans, showing it to him as I did so. I then placed it in the side pocket of the driver's door so that it was out of sight. 'See? I'm now unarmed.' I gave myself a quick pat down and leaned forward in my seat so he could see I wasn't bullshitting.

His expression relaxed a little. 'All right, all right. Let's get this over with, then.'

'Bring the bottles with you, can you?'

He retrieved them from the glove compartment while I pulled a small digital camera out of the storage space between the two front seats, and then we both got out of the car. I clicked on the central locking and waited for him to join me. There was a gentle breeze in the air and it was cooler now that we were over a thousand feet above sea level. The only sound was the incessant chatter of the cicadas in the undergrowth.

We started walking down the path in single file, with me leading. The route ahead opened up into grassland and a hundred yards to our left a huge ravine appeared, beyond which another forest-covered mountain rose up. In the distance, beyond the mountain, I could see the sea and the red-and-white telephone mast that stood on the hill overlooking White Beach – the only sign of man visible in the whole spectacular vista. Take that away and we might as well have been standing there a thousand years ago.

The path forked and I took the left-hand route,

which followed a gentle gradient through a grove of palm and mango trees in the direction of the ravine.

'Where the fuck are we going?' I heard Slippery demand behind me.

'I told you, somewhere quiet.'

'I don't like this.'

'Look,' I said, turning round so I was facing him, 'you can see I'm unarmed. What am I going to do? Kung fu you to death? And if you're that worried, look behind you.' I pointed up to a collection of neat two-storey wooden huts with pointed roofs that stood on a hill behind the road we'd been driving up. 'See, we're not that far from civilization.'

He looked in the direction I was pointing. 'Who lives there, then?'

'People called Mangyan. They're farmers. They tend to keep themselves to themselves, but I still don't want any of them seeing us.'

I resumed walking and he followed, his complaints temporarily silenced.

'I've just thought,' he said after a few seconds. 'Have you brought another shirt with you? 'Cause my one's going to be ruined.'

'Shockingly enough, no,' I answered. 'But you must have packed a spare. When we're finished I'll drop you back at the hotel, you can have a nice warm shower, and then you'll be as right as rain.' I stopped by a palm tree and turned around. The

Mangyan huts were almost out of sight. 'Here'll do,' I said.

He stopped a yard or so behind me and I pointed to a clump of long grass a few feet away. 'Lie down there on your back, legs together, arms outstretched and head to one side, like dead people do on the telly. And put the bottles down next to you.'

'Are you sure there are no snakes in there?' he asked, giving the grass a useless kick.

At the same time, I leaned down and felt round the back of the palm tree, locating the Browning with silencer that I'd taped to the bark the previous day. I pulled it away and peeled off the tape, pleased that I'd planned ahead enough to keep my options open. Then released the safety.

'Hold on,' he said, turning round, 'we ain't brought anything to put the paint on with . . .' The words died in his throat as he saw the gun, the shock rapidly giving way to resignation as I pointed it at his chest.

'I can't fucking believe I fell for that. I should have known a bastard like you would have tried something. And you've got the nerve to call me slippery.'

I had to admire his guts. He knew what was going to happen, that this was the end of the line for him, but he didn't beg and plead. I felt an unwelcome twinge of doubt that I had the strength to pull the trigger. Then I remembered why I was going to.

'You know that copper you killed?' I asked him.

'Don't tell me . . .'

'He was my friend.'

'Ah, fuck it, Dennis. It was just business. Like it always is. Nothing personal.'

'Well, this is personal. Now tell me everything you know about Les Pope and the people behind that shooting, and don't leave a single thing out, or the first bullet'll be in your kneecap.'

He sighed loudly and nodded his assent. Then he turned away slightly, dropped the bottles, and quick as a flash he was pulling a throwing knife from beneath the ankle of his jeans. With astonishing speed he swung round to take aim, and I cursed. It had never occurred to me that he'd be armed, but then he wasn't called Slippery Billy for nothing. This bastard didn't know the meaning of the word defeat, and I felt a sudden heartfelt admiration for him, coupled with the unwelcome knowledge that in many ways there really wasn't that much difference between us.

Then I started firing. The first bullet caught him in the shoulder, knocking him sideways before he could release the knife. The second missed, I think, while the third and fourth struck him in the upper back as he continued to spin round. He fell to his knees and tried to face me again, still holding on to the knife, and once again I got that tiny twinge of doubt that I'd be able to finish him off. But perhaps I was just deluding myself, because a moment later

I aimed the gun at his head and pulled the trigger twice more.

His body bucked sharply as the bullets struck him just below his left eye, but somehow he managed to retain his kneeling position, holding it for what seemed like an awfully long time before slowly, almost casually, he toppled onto his side.

I waited a few moments just to make sure that his luck had finally run out, then looked behind me to check that no-one had heard anything (there was no-one there, so I assumed they hadn't), before finally approaching the body. Blood ran in thin, uneven lines down the side of his face and onto his neck, but his eyes were closed and he looked peaceful, as the newly dead do. Standing there watching him, I reasoned that he had killed at least twice for no other reason than money (one of his victims being a police officer and my friend), and wouldn't have lost a second's sleep if the boot was on the other foot and he'd been the one shooting me. So I really had nothing to feel guilty about. But I wasn't entirely convinced. It didn't make me feel any better that I then used the camera to take half a dozen photos of his corpse, as per our contract, before searching his clothes until I found his mobile, the key to his room and the false passport he was carrying, all of which I pocketed in my jeans. I finally concluded matters by putting on a pair of surgical gloves, wiping the Browning's handle and picking up all the loose cartridges. I then grabbed Slippery by the shoulders and hauled him deeper into the undergrowth. Thankfully, he was lighter than I'd been expecting, because there was still some way for him to go before we hit his final resting place.

I dragged his body fifty yards in all, the path quickly giving way to a thick wall of bushes and trees, and I was hot and panting when we finally came to the edge of the ravine. The drop here was almost sheer and ran some five hundred feet into the tree-carpeted valley below.

I'd chosen this spot because the valley was pretty much inaccessible to people. There was always the chance that a resourceful Mangyan tribesman had somehow found a way in and was nurturing a vegetable plot there, but that was a risk anywhere on the island. The chances were that the body would lie undiscovered for months or even years, and if the remains were one day found, it was unlikely the police would be able to identify them as what was left of Billy West, and I don't suppose they'd be too worried about it either, even with the bullet holes in his skull. They'd probably conclude that it was a local who'd fallen foul of the NPA, the Marxist rebels cum anti-drugs vigilantes who operated in the mountains behind Puerta Galera, and who still made the occasional foray down to the coast, using their guns against those who didn't see eye to eye with them.

I didn't like the idea of depriving Slippery Billy

of a burial. I didn't know his family situation but I supposed he had loved ones somewhere, and that they'd be left wondering for the rest of their lives what had happened to him. But I had no choice. He'd made his bed and, uncomfortable as it was, he was going to have to lie in it.

As I toppled him over the edge and turned away, wiping sweat from my brow, I thought about the mysterious Les Pope, the man who'd commissioned this and Blacklip's murder, as well as at least two others. Would he be losing any sleep over his crimes? I doubted it. Like Billy West, I expected he'd just see it as business.

I pondered that particular matter as I returned to the Land Rover and continued my journey up to the Ponderosa golf club for a much-needed drink and a chance to think about the man whose murder I'd just avenged.

# 5

Asif Malik. He'd been a colleague of mine in Islington CID for more than a year during my last days in London. Originally I was his boss, and then, just before my ignominious departure, he'd got promoted to the same level as me, which hadn't been much of a surprise. He'd always struck me as a man who was going places. He was hard-working, bright and, most importantly of all, decent. Most coppers are decent people underneath it all, but some – myself included – get more cynical as the years go by and the crime rate keeps rising. I'd once believed in what I was doing, in my ability, as a police officer working within the strict frameworks the law sets, to change things and deliver justice to the people who needed it. But time, and the growing realization that what I was delivering was nothing more than a sticking plaster for a gaping wound, had corrupted me to the point where both my reputation and my conscience were now well beyond repair.

It was possible that Malik had changed too. After all, I hadn't seen him in three years. But somehow I doubted it. He'd always been unflinching in his view that what he was doing was right, and what the people he was trying to catch were doing was wrong. To Malik, life had been relatively simple. There was good and there was evil, and it was the duty of all right-thinking people to try to promote the former and stamp out the latter. That was why it had upset me more than I would have expected when I'd read about his death on the Net three weeks earlier. Because he was one of the good guys, and God knows there aren't very many of them left these days.

Since leaving home, I'd followed his career on its upward trajectory, in the expat papers and on the Net, from detective sergeant in Islington CID to detective inspector in Scotland Yard's SO7 Organized Crime Unit, and then to his final, brief role as a DCI in the National Crime Squad. It had pleased me to see him doing well. First and foremost, because I'd always liked him. I think he reminded me a little of what I'd been like when I'd started out, before the rot had set in. But there was more to it than that. For some reason, the evidence of his progress helped to ease the guilt I felt periodically over the fate of the only three innocent men I've ever killed – the two customs officers and the accountant whose deaths had led to the disintegration of my old life, and my subsequent exile. I guess I saw Malik as an extension of me: my good side. The young copper I'd mentored, and sent on to greater things. If I was capable of helping him, then I couldn't have been that bad a man. That's how I'd rationalized it on those occasions when the guilt had begun to get a grip. And it helped, because like a lot of things, there was a degree of truth in it. He had learned a lot from me, and before the secret of my other life had come out, most of it had been good.

Billy West hadn't even known who Malik was when he'd snuffed out his life along with that of the man who'd been sitting next to him in the Clerkenwell café that night. The job had just been an easy way to make some decent money. Nothing more, nothing less. And now there was a wife who was a widow, and two young kids who were going to grow up without a dad. I don't suppose Slippery had given them a second thought. He'd now paid the price, but Les Pope? At the moment, Les Pope slept soundly in his bed six thousand miles away, unaware and unworried that he'd made a new enemy. Someone like him probably had plenty anyway.

I had lunch in the open-fronted clubhouse at the Ponderosa, overlooking the sea and the islands beyond, but didn't see anyone I knew. Puerta Galera's a small place and the expats tend to stick together. When you're on the run for murder it's a lot safer to keep yourself to yourself, but isolation was next to impossible in a community this size. It wasn't a problem, though. They knew me as Mick here and, as far as I was aware, they accepted my cover story that I'd lived and worked in the Philippines tourist trade for years. Most of them had been out here a long time themselves and wouldn't have known who I was anyway; and those who had come in the last three years wouldn't have been able to pick me out unless they knew who they were looking for or, like Slippery, were already acquainted with me. My appearance had changed considerably since the days when my photo had been plastered all over Britain's newspapers. I'd had two very professional bouts of plastic surgery – one in Davao City when I'd first arrived, one in Manila a year later – that had changed the shape of my nose and chin and removed the dark lines beneath my eyes. My skin was a much darker hue thanks to its prolonged contact with the sun, and my hair, thinner now that I'd hit forty and tinged for the first time with grey, had lightened for the same reason. I also wore a small, neatly trimmed beard that fitted my long thin face comfortably, and which had never been there during my time as a copper. Despite all that, however, I was still a little disconcerted by the speed with which a man I hadn't set eyes on in ten years had known who I was. Maybe it was time to think about going under the knife again.

I'd taken the day off and was in no mood to hurry back to our place, so when I'd paid the bill and driven back into Puerta Galera, I turned south instead of taking the road north to Sabang, and drove along the winding and potholed cliff-top coast road in the direction of Calapan.

And all the time I was thinking.

# 6

It was early evening and already dark by the time I returned to the Big La Laguna Dive Lodge, the place I now called home. It was only a small hotel, with sixteen whitewashed guest rooms arranged round three sides of a tiny courtyard, containing an even tinier pool. In front of the courtyard, facing directly onto the beach, was our open-air bar and restaurant, and next door to that was the dive shop we ran. We'd given the whole place a complete refit and paint job when we'd bought it, and had even gone so far as installing expensive rattan furniture in the rooms and the drinking and eating areas, and although I say so myself, the place looked good.

My room was right at the back of the hotel and faced straight into a Filipino family's apartment, but since I didn't spend much time in it, the view didn't really bother me. I went straight up to it now, saying hello to a couple of our guests on the way, and showered and changed, before going back out to locate Tomboy.

I found him in the back room of the dive shop, sitting at the table with a load of paperwork spread out in front of him. He had a half-full bottle of San Miguel and a crumpled pack of Marlboros within easy reach. On seeing me come in, he smiled expectantly. 'How's it going, mate? I was beginning to get worried about you. It all went all right, didn't it?'

I stepped into the room and shut the door behind me, a signal that we could talk. 'It's all done.'

He nodded appreciatively. 'Good. Now we can get back to running this place. Did you get rid of everything?'

I told him I had and he asked me whether it had been in the place we'd discussed.

I nodded.

'You did a good job, Mick,' he said, calling me by my nickname, and sounding not unlike a man I used to do work for back in London. 'And it's going to tide us over for a long time. We won't have to do it again.'

I felt like taking him up on the 'we' bit, seeing as he hadn't done a lot, but I didn't bother. I was too tired for an argument. 'When are we going to get the balance of the cash?'

'As soon as he's seen the photos. You took 'em all right, yeah?'

I nodded and he reached over and picked up the

cigarettes, watching me with an expression that might have been sympathy. 'It's all over now. You can forget about it.'

I shook my head. 'It's not over, Tomboy. Billy Warren wasn't who he said he was. He was Billy West, a villain I had dealings with back in the old days. You must have known him. You knew every villain round our way.'

He scrunched up his face into an expression of acute concentration. 'The name rings a bell,' he said after a pause, 'but I can't picture him. It must have been after my time.'

'It wasn't. I hadn't seen him in at least ten years before today.'

He shook his head. 'Nah. Like I said, the name rings a bell, but that's it. I honestly don't remember him.'

I wondered why he was lying. Tomboy had known every villain on our patch, most of whom he'd put behind bars with his information, but if he had known Slippery Billy he wasn't saying, and I decided to let it go for now. 'Anyway, Billy West was also a shooter on the side. He'd moved into that line of business recently, and the last job he did, the one that brought him over here, was Asif Malik.'

'The two-man hit in the café?'

'That's the one.'

'Shit, how's that for a coincidence?' He shook his head, looking suitably taken aback. I decided he couldn't have known about Slippery's involvement in Malik's murder, otherwise he'd never have let me near him. Tomboy had never known Malik, but he knew he'd been my partner and was a man I'd liked and respected. 'I'm sorry about that, Mick. Or maybe I'm not. At least it gave you a reason to sort him out.'

'Who's Les Pope?'

Tomboy sighed and lit one of his Marlboros. 'I was afraid you'd ask that. Why do you want to know?'

'I'm interested,' I told him. 'Apparently, he was also the man who set up the Malik job.'

I thought he'd resist telling me too much, but I think he saw in my expression that I wasn't going to be fobbed off. 'He's a lawyer.'

I managed an empty laugh. 'Well, there's a surprise.' So at least Slippery Billy hadn't been lying about that. 'Go on.'

'He does defence work as a solicitor, and he knows a few bad types, but he's always kept his nose clean, so he's never really received much attention from the law. He's also well-spoken and well-educated, which helps.'

'How do you know him?'

'The usual. He defended me on a couple of cases years ago, before I knew you. We kept in touch, and I did a little bit of work for him now and again.'

Just like Slippery had. 'What sort of work?'

'The illegal sort. Providing other clients of his

with alibis, helping them out of binds. Nothing too serious, but put it this way: he's not the sort of geezer I'd like to mess with. He knows people who could make life very difficult for you if they wanted.'

'The sort who'd pay to have people killed?'

'I suppose so, although I've got to admit it was a bit of a surprise when he rang me out of the blue last year about our man in Manila.'

'He'd never asked you to get involved with anything like that before?'

'No, course not.'

I wasn't sure I believed him. The more I thought about it, the more it seemed odd that Les Pope would have asked Tomboy to help commit murder on two occasions in the space of a year, unless he knew something about his former client that made him confident he'd go along with it. I think I'd deluded myself that Tomboy's involvement in crime while he'd been an informant of mine back in London had always been on the periphery. I still didn't want to believe that it had been anything more. After all, I liked the guy. He'd helped me out when he could have earned himself a lot of money by turning me in to the Philippine authorities when I first arrived here, and we'd lived cheek by jowl for the three years since. He was a friend. Even so, the doubts that had prickled away all day remained.

'Why do you want to know all this, Mick?' he asked, picking up his beer bottle. 'What good's it going to do? We're thousands of miles away from Pope and London, and you know what they say. Let sleeping dogs lie.'

'Because,' I said, choosing my words carefully, 'he was responsible for killing someone I liked and respected. If it had been you he'd killed, I'd be asking the same questions.'

'Keep it down, can you?' he hissed, dragging on his cigarette.

'It's all right, I locked the front door. We can talk.'

'Look, I appreciate why you're asking the questions, but what's done is done. You know what I'm saying? It's spilt milk and all that. I'm sorry about Malik – I am – but nothing's going to bring him back, and the man who pulled the trigger ain't no more, so let's just forget about it, eh?'

'That's easier said than done.'

He took a swig of beer, banged the bottle down on the table and stood up, craning forward in my direction. When he spoke, his voice was a forced whisper. 'What the fuck are you going to do, Mick? Go back to London and pop Pope? Then get on a plane like nothing's happened and fly back here?' He raised his hands, palms outwards, in a gesture of 'What more can I say?' 'It don't work like that. You're a wanted man in London; chances are you'll be picked up before you even locate him, let alone pull the trigger. And if that happens you ain't ever going to see the outside of a nick again, are you? Not with your record. They'll throw away the key.

71

Are you willing to risk all that just to kill the bloke who had something to do with organizing the hit on someone who you worked with once, but ain't seen in over three years? Because I'm telling you, mate, if that's the case, it ain't worth it. Honestly.'

He was right, I knew that. And for exactly those reasons. In the end, it was far too risky. I'd built up my life here. I was happy, and even on those days when I got tired of the heat and the sight of palm trees, it was still a vastly preferable alternative to the inside of a cold English prison. Plus, I told myself for maybe the thousandth time in my life, injustices are perpetrated every day by people who will never be brought to book for their crimes. Take most politicians, for a start. I couldn't kill them all. Why tear apart my whole life just to get at one person, when there'd be a dozen more waiting to take his place?

Because Malik was my friend.

Because he was a good man.

Because I was not.

'Ah, forget it,' I sighed. 'I'm just talking.'

'I know it's pissed you off. I can't believe it myself, as it happens. Small fucking world.' He stubbed out his cigarette and got back down to business. 'You got the key to Warren's room? I'm sending Joubert over later to clear it out.'

I fished it out of my pocket and handed it to him, disappointed that his mind was already on other things. It struck me then that I didn't really know

Tomboy Darke at all, even after all these years, and it was a thought that depressed me, because it exposed my failings as much as his.

'Come on,' he said, taking the key and finishing his beer. 'Let's go get you a drink.'

I followed him back through the dive shop and next door to the bar, where, not for the first time in my life, the booze beckoned invitingly. For the moment, at least, I'd try and forget the ignominious fate of Slippery Billy West and those he'd murdered back in the old country.

# 7

But sometimes it's not so easy to forget.

The days passed and life carried on as usual. It was late November, the beginning of the drier, cooler season in Mindoro, and the lodge was about three-quarters booked, so there was more than enough to keep me busy. We had staff who did the cooking and cleaning, but now and again I helped run the bar, and most days I'd take groups of divers out on our outrigger to the many dive sites that littered the craggy Sabang peninsula, and which most of our guests were here to see. Diving had become something of a passion for me since coming to the Philippines. I'd learned while we'd been in Siquijor and was now a qualified instructor, unlike Tomboy, who couldn't even swim and had to make do with running the shop and doing the books.

In the week after Slippery's death, I took divers out every day, enjoying the opportunity to immerse myself in the island's warm, clear waters and forget the torments that were beginning to wear me down. It's easy when you're underwater. It's quiet, for a start. There's no-one to hassle to you, and there are enough breathtaking sights amongst the fish-covered reefs and canyons to take your mind off even the largest of troubles. The only problem is there's only so much time you can spend down there before your air runs out and it's time to come back to reality. And reality for me meant remembering Malik as a living, breathing, talking person, and remembering what had happened to him, and my own very indirect part in it.

I couldn't get it out of my head, no matter how hard I tried. One night in the week after Slippery's death, I had a dream. It was an almost exact replica of an incident that had occurred not long after Malik and I had started working together, about four years back. At the time, I hadn't been too sure about my new recruit. A five-foot-eight, slightly built Asian university graduate, who was already shooting up the ranks even though he was barely in his mid-twenties, I'd already come to the conclusion that he was only there to make up the ethnic numbers. So when we did our first op together, a raid on the home of a habitual burglar named Titus Bower, I decided to test my new partner's mettle and see if he was more than just a prime example of affirmative action and Met Police political correctness.

Bower lived in a small, terraced house with a

shoebox-sized rear garden that backed onto an alley. I was leading the team sent out to arrest him, which sounds a bit more glamorous than it actually was, as there was only Malik, me, and two of the station's uniforms. Since I knew that Bower might well make a run for it, I decided to post an officer at the rear of the property to intercept him. Ordinarily, I'd have used one of the bigger guys for this, but instead I chose Malik, much to his surprise and the surprise of the other two on the op. He didn't complain, though, I remember that. Just did what I'd asked, and when the rest of us had knocked on the front door and Bower had opened it a few inches, realized who we were and made a dash out the back, Malik had been there to greet him.

It had been a one-sided contest. Running through Bower's cluttered hallway in hot pursuit, I watched as our suspect tore open the rear door and charged straight into Malik, knocking him down onto his back and literally running right over him like something out of a cartoon, his Nike trainer trampling Malik's face as the poor sod tried without success to tell him he was under arrest. Bower was a big guy, and he'd run from us before, so I knew I'd been unfair on my new partner, but the thing that I remember about the incident was that Malik hadn't given up. Although shocked and probably in a lot of pain, he'd grabbed hold of Bower's ankle as he'd come past, and had refused to let go. Bower had staggered along the garden, struggling to shake Malik off, and had even tried to kick him in the head (an act that had caused him to lose his balance and fall over, much to our mirth). But Malik had grimly held on to that ankle right up until the moment we'd had Bower in cuffs, and I thought that there probably weren't that many coppers out there with that level of determination. He'd had to go to hospital for treatment to the injuries he'd suffered, which included a fractured cheekbone, and though I never apologized for putting him in the firing line (and he never held it against me, either), I always treated him with respect after that.

In my dream that night, the whole event played out exactly like it had happened that cold winter morning four years ago, except for one thing. As I'd come out the back door and seen Malik holding on to Bower's ankle, I'd produced a gun from my pocket and had started shooting. I'd hit Bower four, five, six times (I can't honestly remember the exact number), killing him instantly, but somehow one of the bullets had gone astray and hit Malik in the head, killing him too. He hadn't even screamed. Like Slippery Billy West, he'd simply fallen on his side and lain still. Then everything had stopped and I'd stared at what I'd done for an extremely long moment while the two uniforms stood silently on either side of me, one with his gloved hand on my upper arm as if effecting an arrest, before finally and mercifully I'd woken up.

I don't know how an expert would have interpreted that dream, but I knew exactly what it told me. That I was going to be tormented for God knows how long if I didn't do something about what had happened to him. For all Tomboy's arguments – and there were many – I simply couldn't let it go.

It was still there at the back of my mind a week after that. Every day I checked the Internet for news of a breakthrough in the case. Whenever I could, I checked the papers. But there was nothing, and I had little doubt that by shooting Billy West I'd severed the last thread of an investigation six thousand miles away. Here I was, living it up in paradise, staring at the same gorgeous scenery day in, day out while Malik rotted in the ground, Les Pope counted his money, and whoever had wanted my former colleague exterminated in the first place walked round scot-free.

I also wanted to know why he'd had to die. What did he know, or had he done, that had put him on a collision course with Pope's clients, the same people who'd wanted Slippery Billy out of the way? Plainly, they were people with power and influence, as well as access to intelligence; people who thought they could do whatever they pleased.

I wanted to find them.

I wanted to find them, and I wanted to kill them.

I knew it would be dangerous to go back home –

there was no getting around that – but not impossible. Three years had passed. A lot of water had flowed under the bridge; a lot more killers had emerged into the public consciousness; September the Eleventh had left the watchful amongst us looking in different places for our villains. Three years was a lifetime in the multimedia click-on-a-button world that I'd left behind, and Dennis Milne, copper turned hitman, was part of a dim and distant past that no-one was keen to resurrect.

So I made my decision.

Late on a Wednesday evening twelve days after the death of Billy West, and with the balance of the money for that contract now paid, I found Tomboy sitting in near darkness at a table facing the sea in the lodge's empty open-air restaurant, the remains of a San Miguel in front of him. He'd been working the bar that night so I knew he wasn't drunk. Joubert, one of the kitchen staff, was cleaning some glasses out of earshot. I could have got a drink if I'd wanted one, but I didn't. Instead, I sat down next to Tomboy and said I was going home.

Tomboy shook his head wearily and gave me a look of deep disappointment that seemed to accentuate every line on his face. It made him look five years older. The same conversation we'd had on the day of the Billy West killing then began to play out, but it didn't last anything like as long because this time he could see that I'd made up my mind. He called me a fucking idiot. 'Look what you've got here,' he declared, waving his arms expansively.

The night was calm and peaceful and the fronds of the coconut palms above our heads flickered and drifted in the gentle breeze. Stars swarmed and swept in a majestic canvas across the clear black sky, with only the faintest hint of man-made light to the north in Manila. The sea lapped gently against the shore; the joints on the older outriggers in the bay creaked in time with it; and from somewhere in the village behind came the bark of a dog and the faint but enthusiastic shouts of locals involved in a pool or card game. It was paradise, there was no question of that, but at that moment it was nowhere near enough. It struck me then that I was sick of nice weather. And healthy food. I wanted the next fish I ate to be in batter and sitting next to a pile of greasy chips.

'I know exactly what I've got here, Tomboy,' I told him, 'but you know my situation and why I've got to do something about it. I'm going to be taking my half of the cash from the contract. When I've finished in London—'

'*If* you finish – that's what you've got to think about, mate. You might never come back. I told you about Pope. He knows some dodgy people. Don't mess with him. Honestly. No good'll come of it.'

'When I've finished in London, I'll bring back what remains of my share and pump it straight

80

back into the business. But I don't know how much I'm going to need.'

'You ain't listening to me.'

'I am, but I've already thought everything through. And you know me. I'm stubborn.'

'Too fucking stubborn.'

'That's as maybe, but it's the way it is. I'm booked on the Friday flight out of Manila. I'll be back as soon as I can. It may be days, it could be weeks. I'll keep you posted.'

Tomboy sighed loudly, then shook his head again. 'Be very careful. I know you like to think you're a tough guy, and in a lot of ways you are, but there are tougher ones out there, and I'd hate you to run into them.'

I nodded. 'Thanks for the advice. It's appreciated.'

He started to say something else, but stopped himself. Eventually, he just wished me good luck.

I told him I hoped I didn't need it.

But of course I knew that I would.

# Part Two

**INTO THE VIOLENT CITY**

# 8

The wind hit me with an icy slap as I stepped out of the Terminal Three building at Heathrow, hopelessly underdressed in a light jacket and shirt. It was seven o'clock on a bitter Friday night in early December, and a few yards away, beyond the panels sheltering the entrance from the worst of what nature had to offer, a driving rain fell through the darkness amidst the crawling traffic.

England in winter. What the hell had I been thinking of, coming back here? On the plane over, I'd found it difficult to keep a lid on my excitement at the prospect of returning home after such a long time away, even though my business here was hardly pleasure. Now, however, the enthusiasm was dropping as fast as my body heat as I stood outside in temperatures hovering only just above freezing, looking every inch the ill-prepared foreign tourist. I needed to get into the warmth, and fast. An announcement in the terminal had informed everyone that the Heathrow Express to London was currently out of service due to an incident at Hounslow, which probably meant some selfish bastard had jumped under a train, so I joined the queue of shivering, bedraggled travellers at the taxi rank, feeling vaguely paranoid that I might run into someone who knew me from the past, but confident that my disguise was working. No-one had questioned me at immigration. I'd given the guy my passport, held in the name of Mr Marcus Kane; he'd taken one brief look at it and me, and that had been that. Not even a second glance. I was back.

It took ten minutes before my turn came, and I was fading fast as I got into the back of the black cab and asked the driver to take me to Paddington. He pulled away without saying anything and headed for the M4, jostling for position on the overcrowded Heathrow sliproad.

The traffic was as horrific as the weather. All three lanes heading into London were moving at no more than ten miles per hour, with plenty of stopping and starting, with the occasional angry honk of frustration drifting through the wind and rain. It was the same going the other way, maybe even worse, since the bulk of the vehicles were escaping the city, not entering it. I'd forgotten how overcrowded the south-east of England was. In the Philippines, outside the maelstrom of Manila and southern Luzon, the pace is slow, and what roads there are are generally empty. Here, it's as if the whole population's on the move, fighting each other for that most precious of commodities: space. We hadn't gone two miles before I decided that, whatever happened here, I'd be heading back to the Philippines afterwards. I'd needed to come back, if only to see what I was missing; but having seen it, I was quickly realizing that it wasn't a lot.

The cab driver was like a lot of cab drivers. Having broken the ice by asking me where I'd come from and got an answer (I told him Singapore, hoping it sounded boring enough that he wouldn't want to ask anything more about it), he took my answer as an invitation to talk, and quickly regaled me with his views on immigration (too much), taxes (too high) and crime (rampant). This last bit interested me a little, because I hadn't heard much recently about crime levels in the UK. I got the big stories, but not the overall picture. The driver told me it had gone through the roof since Labour had been returned to power, especially crimes of violence. 'I'll tell you, mate, you're twice as likely to get mugged in London than New York these days. Probably more. If you ain't been here for a while, you want to watch yourself, I'm telling you.'

I told him I would, and allowed myself a little smile. It wasn't that I didn't believe him, but where crime was concerned I remember the cab drivers saying exactly the same thing in the Seventies, the Eighties and the Nineties. They said it in Manila too. Maybe crime *was* rampant, but who could honestly remember a time when it wasn't?

Eventually our crawling, rain-splattered progress sapped even the cabbie's strength, and he lapsed into a bored silence while I stared out of the window and into the dark, wondering how I was going to get my investigation started. It wasn't as if I was a police officer any more, so I had no resources I could call upon for help. But I did have several key advantages. I knew who I was looking for, and I wasn't working within the constraints of the law. One thing that had always bugged me when I'd been a copper was knowing that the bad guys consistently had the upper hand. We not only had to find them, but we also had to gather huge amounts of evidence to bolster our case, even when we knew damn well that they were guilty. As often as not – particularly when a criminal knew what he was doing – those huge amounts of evidence simply weren't available, and our suspect walked free. Slippery Billy West was a case in point.

I had no doubt that Les Pope would also be a very difficult individual to pin down, from a copper's point of view, because as a lawyer he'd know how to work the system. With me, though, things would be different. I wasn't afraid to hurt him if he didn't help me. I might well hurt him, even if he did. But I had to be careful. Locating him wouldn't be hard, but it was important I played things just right. I wanted to find out who else was involved in Malik's murder without alerting anyone to what I was doing, and without getting Tomboy in trouble. It wouldn't be easy. But then I'd known that when I decided to come back.

The journey to Paddington took the best part of an hour and cost me almost sixty quid. Sixty quid would have got me from Manila to Malaysia and back again with a Filipino cab driver. It made me wonder what had happened to the low inflation they've been banging on about for so long.

I got the driver to drop me at the station, just in case my face ever appeared on TV and he remembered me, and paid him using three twenties. I then stood by his window waiting for the one pound twenty change, thinking there was no way I was going to tip him for a service that had cost so much, even though the bastard was giving me a look that said one pound twenty was the least he expected for so kindly transporting me from A to B. He continued to give me the look until I told him that I'd start charging for my own wasted time unless he hurried up. Reluctantly, he fished the coins out of his pocket and slapped them into my open hand. 'Tight ass,' I heard the cheeky bastard mutter.

I felt like saying something in return – after all, too many people get away with too much in this life – but decided that not drawing any attention to myself was probably the best option. I turned away, heading in the direction of Lancaster Gate.

I'd had a girlfriend round here once, back in the

late Eighties, not long after I'd come out of uniform. Liz, her name had been, and she'd been a part-time model; a real beauty who ordinarily would have been way out of my league, but a sweet person with it. We'd met after she got mugged and sexually assaulted while going to visit a friend on my home patch of Islington, and I was assigned the case. The relationship then hadn't exactly started in the best of circumstances, but something between us had evidently clicked, and after I'd been to her flat on a couple of occasions to update her on the case's progress, we'd begun an affair. Or sort of affair, anyway, since one side-effect of the assault was that she felt unable to have sex with a man. Instead, she just wanted to be held and kissed, and for a while that suited me fine. I could think of a lot worse ways of spending my time than cuddling up to a beautiful woman in a nice apartment with a good bottle of wine, but eventually – inevitably, I suppose – I got frustrated. She was seeing a psychiatrist and told me that she was on the mend – we even tried it one night, but at the crucial moment she broke down in tears and pushed me away – and a few days after that, I said that maybe it would be best if we went our separate ways. She begged me to give it a little more time, but I was young and I was selfish and in the end that's a fatal combination. I met up with her once after that, to tell her that we were winding down on the case in the absence of any leads. She took the news stoically enough and told me that she was leaving London. I never saw her again, and it was only now, for the first time in years, that I thought about her. I wondered briefly as I crossed Praed Street what had happened to her, and whether she'd put the past behind her and got the kids she'd always said she wanted, or whether her life was still crippled by the after-effects of that one night. My heart hoped it was the former, but my head was convinced otherwise. She'd been that sort of girl, and I've always been that sort of pessimist.

I found accommodation in Norfolk Square, a quiet area of fading Georgian townhouses, the majority of which had been transformed into hotels of varying quality, situated a short walk from the station. I chose one of the cheaper-looking ones and went inside.

The man behind the desk, who was either Turkish or Arabic and who showed a comforting lack of interest in me, wanted twenty-five pounds per night up front. I said I wanted a room for a week and asked what discount that entitled me to. Eventually, after carrying out some silent calculations on a slip of paper in front of him, he grunted that it would cost me a hundred and twenty if I paid him straight away. I didn't bother going to take a look at the room first. I had no doubt that it would be none too pretty, but then I wasn't planning to spend much time in it, so I counted out the money and placed it in his outstretched hand.

He pulled a key from one of the hooks behind him and handed it to me. And that was that. It made me think that most people tend to talk too much, and that there was something to be said for brusqueness.

I hauled my case up two flights of very steep, narrow stairs to my room, and wasn't surprised to discover that it was small, bare, and not very warm either. The paintwork, done in a long-ago off-white, was dirty, nicotine-stained, and full of bumps where the roller had gone straight over the original wallpaper, and there were ancient cobwebs fluttering in each corner of the ceiling. From outside came the rhythmic clatter of a train entering Paddington station; the wooden window-frame rattling in unison. It might have worked out at less than twenty quid a night, but I didn't feel like I was getting good value for money, especially when I reminded myself of the fact that our place on the beach in the Philippines worked out at nearer ten. And you got breakfast and use of the pool there as well.

But by this point I was too tired and jetlagged to care. My journey, which had begun that morning in Manila, had taken me across eight time zones, and although it was now eight thirty in the evening in London, it was actually four thirty the following morning for me and I badly needed to sleep.

I chucked the case on the bed, switched on the radiator and slowly unpacked while I waited for the room to heat up. As I did so, I tried to shut out the distinct feeling of anticlimax that had been slowly enveloping me ever since I'd been stuck in the taxi on the M4. For years this city had been my home. I'd worked, played and lived in it; had killed and made love here; seen much of the good but more of the bad. But always I'd felt that I belonged; that the city was a part of me. But tonight it was different. Tonight I felt like a stranger visiting for the first time. There was none of the familiarity I'd been expecting, no explosion of memories as the taxi crossed the boundaries and the familiar buildings sprang up like monoliths on either side of the road. Only the odd, unsettling sensation that my time here was something from another, barely remembered life.

I decided to have a shower and clean up a bit, then hit the sack and start everything tomorrow when I was more refreshed and less depressed. The city, I knew, would look a lot better in the morning.

I was halfway out of my clothes and waiting for the dilapidated shower unit to hit a temperature that neither burned strips off my back nor froze my balls off, when my mobile phone rang.

I strode into the bedroom, and pulled it out of the pocket of my jacket. I'd bought it the previous day in Manila, and only one person was aware of the number: Tomboy Darke. But as soon as I looked at the screen and saw that there was no incoming number showing, I knew it wasn't going to be him.

I pressed the Call Receive button and put the phone to my ear.

'Mr Kane, good evening.' The words were delivered slowly and with authority in an accent that was unmistakably middle-class London, and north of the river if memory served me right.

'Sorry, I think you've got the wrong number. I don't know a Mr Kane.'

'Really?' he said. 'Somehow I believe you do. My name's Pope. I think we should meet up. I've got a feeling we've got a lot to talk about. Don't you?'

'Let's make it tomorrow morning,' I said, pissed off that the element of surprise was gone, and way too tired to see him now. Tomboy must have talked, but why? Surely he'd have known he was putting me in potential danger.

'I'd prefer tonight. I don't want you to have to hurry tomorrow for the plane you've got to catch.'

'Which one's that?'

'The one taking you back to where you belong.'

I didn't bother rising to the bait. 'Well, tomorrow it's going to have to be. Take it or leave it.'

'In that case, I'll take it. There's a café in Islington, off the Pentonville Road. It's called the Lantern. Meet me there at ten o'clock tomorrow morning. I'll be sitting at the corner table on your left as you go in, next to the window.'

'What do you look like?'

'You'll know who I am,' he said, and rang off.

I stood there for a moment, still holding the

phone while I thought things through. It seemed that Tomboy hadn't given Pope my real name, but what if he'd described me? I couldn't believe that the bastard – someone I'd known for years, someone I had to admit that I trusted – had blown my cover. Maybe he was frightened I'd hurt Pope and cut off what was obviously turning into quite a lucrative little sideline. Or maybe I was being cynical, and he was just looking out for me. By telling Pope what I intended, he might just be trying to get things straightened out before they went too far, and get me back on the plane to Manila without anyone coming to any harm.

Either way, though, he'd betrayed me, and I couldn't forget that. It's funny how people you think you know can react when the going gets a little tough. I tried his number, but it was early in the morning and he wasn't answering. I didn't leave a message, but instead tried the lodge in the hope that someone on night duty might pick up. But no-one did, and eventually I hung up, hoping that the start I was having wasn't the shape of things to come.

**9**

First thing the next morning, I walked over to the Edgware Road and bought myself a thick waterproof coat with too many pockets. I then wandered round until I found a stationer's shop that printed personalized business cards. I ordered a hundred (the minimum number) in the name of Marcus Kane, private detective, from the old guy behind the counter. He said that he'd never met a private detective before and asked me what kind of work I did.

I told him missing persons. 'I've just come back from a case in the Bahamas,' I said, and when he asked for more details, spun him a cock-and-bull story about a runaway wife and her young lover fleecing the husband of all he owned before escaping to the Caribbean. I explained that I'd got them both arrested by the local authorities and they were now awaiting extradition. He said that it served them right, and that the cards would be ready by Monday.

By the time I walked out of the shop it was quarter past nine and I needed to get moving if I was to make the rendezvous. I'd thought about not turning up at all, since it wasn't immediately obvious what I was going to get out of it, but I guess curiosity got the better of me. I wanted to see what Les Pope looked like in the flesh and hear what he had to say.

I caught the Circle Line from Paddington station to King's Cross, the journey being less crowded than I remembered, probably because it was a Saturday, then walked the length of the Pentonville Road from west to east, through my old stamping ground, marvelling at how much things had changed in the past three years. The porn shops at the start of Pentonville Road were all boarded up now, and scaffolding covered the grime-stained buildings. Huge cranes towered across the skyline above the station and beyond. I'd heard somewhere that they were going to make King's Cross station the main terminal for the Eurostar rail service linking London to Continental Europe, and it looked like the powers that be were doing their utmost to clean up the area, so that those stepping off the trains from Paris and Brussels for the first time would get a good initial impression of Britain's capital. There was still a long way to go, and the place definitely had a mid-construction feel about it, but on the surface at least it looked better than it had done when I'd been a copper here.

All the way to my destination, I kept my eye out for anyone suspicious, but the pavements were quiet, as they always were in this part of town. Nothing much happens on the Pentonville Road, the only activity tending to be the steady flow of traffic heading between the West End and the City, and that's because there's really nothing on it, bar a handful of shops, the odd pub in need of refurbishment, and the occasional luxury apartment complex. It had a real windswept feel – you half expected to see a pile of tumbleweed dodging between the traffic. It suited me fine, because if anyone was following me, I'd have known about it.

The Lantern was a shabby little place in need of a serious paint job on a quiet backstreet no more than a hundred yards from the junction of Pentonville Road and Islington's Upper Street, and also not far from where I used to live. I got there at just before ten and walked past on the other side of the road, seeing immediately that the corner table Pope had mentioned was empty. I kept walking until I got to Chapel Market, fifty yards further on.

The market was in full flow and crowded, another familiar sight that was vaguely comforting. It was a dry day and chilly, with a blanket of unbroken white cloud overhead, and there was also the first sniff of Christmas in the stall decorations and the excited faces of the many young kids milling around with their weary-looking parents. It was December 6th, and Asif Malik had been dead, and his wife and kids grieving, for just over five weeks.

I turned and headed back in the direction of the café, watching the street like a hawk. Two Italian men in white tops were unloading vegetables from a van and taking them into a restaurant. Other than that, there was little to attract my attention.

As I passed the café, however, I saw that the corner table was now taken. I didn't get a good look at the occupant but continued on casually until I came to the door, then stepped inside. The interior was cramped, with no more than seven or eight tables. Two workmen in white hard hats and fluorescent jackets sat at one of the tables, piling into plates of sandwiches, while at the corner table sat a good-looking guy in his early forties and wearing it well, with a lean face, a full head of dyed blond hair and a very nicely tailored Italian suit. He was smiling at me with the sort of confidence that left neither of us in any doubt that he knew exactly who I was. It wasn't an unpleasant smile either. Tomboy's description had been basic in the extreme, and I think I'd been expecting some middle-aged, greasy individual with a lot of jewellery and bad hair. The name Les never seems to conjure up much in the way of sophistication. However, this guy was a cross between a stockbroker and a good timeshare salesman. A definite Tom or Greg.

He stood up as I walked over. 'Mr Kane, thanks

for coming. Take a seat, please.' The same authoritative voice I'd heard on the phone the previous night.

We shook and his grip was tighter than it needed to be. He kept his hand there for several seconds and I think he wanted me to flinch, although he continued to give me that welcoming smile. I didn't, and he let go.

I sat down opposite him, noticing that he had an orange juice and a black coffee.

'I've ordered a sandwich,' he told me, sitting down as well. 'Do you want something? It's on me. They do a good ham and salad ciabatta, I'm told.'

'No thanks. If the waitress comes over, I'll have a coffee. Otherwise, forget it.'

'Thanks for coming to see me. I'd just like to say, before we start, that I'm very happy with the services I've received from you and Mr Darke. It would be a pity to spoil it all now by getting involved in things that, frankly, don't concern you.' The same expression remained on his face as he spoke but the tone had changed subtly. He was telling me, not asking me.

The waitress walked towards us. She was young and thin, with a skimpy black halter-neck top that rode up past her cute, pierced belly button. With the temperature outside struggling to stay above zero, it gave me the chills just looking at it. I ordered a large filter coffee and a mineral water, since Pope was paying.

'Fine,' I said to him when she'd turned away. 'I understand what you're saying. The only thing is, they do concern me.'

'Why?'

So Tomboy hadn't told him about my relationship with Malik, which was good. I didn't want him to make any problematic connections. 'That's my business, I'm afraid.'

Pope stroked his chin thoughtfully with his thumb and forefinger, and eyed me with interest. 'I expected a stubborn man. I suppose you've got to be pretty strong-willed in your line of business. Now, I could sit here and threaten you, but I don't like that way of operating. It's too basic. And with a stubborn man, I'm not sure it works. So I'm going to appeal to your intelligence. By the look of you, you've obviously been away a long time and I'm sure the climate over there suits you, but things are very different here. You're poking your nose into affairs that are none of your business, and if you continue to do so certain people are going to get very upset.'

'Like who?'

'Like people who you're never going to get to, who are so far away from the coalface that even if they order your death, the order'll pass through at least half a dozen people before it gets to the triggerman. Do you understand what I'm saying, Mr Kane? People who are untouchable. Who you're not even an irritant to, even now. So by coming here asking questions, you're not only risking your neck, you're also wasting your time. Which is a pretty shitty combination, don't you think?'

I didn't say anything since at least part of what he said was right. Possibly all of it.

'Now, I know you've come a long way,' he continued, his manner polite and unhurried, 'and I appreciate that I'm asking a lot to get you to go back to where you've come from less than a day after you've arrived, so I'm going to make things easier for you.' He reached inside his jacket and removed an airline ticket, which he put down on the table between us. 'It's a business-class ticket to Manila via Singapore on Singapore Airlines. You're confirmed on the flight at eleven o'clock tomorrow morning. As soon as you've checked in, you'll receive a phone call and you'll be met by someone at the departure gates. That someone will have two thousand dollars US in cash for you to compensate you for your journey. I'm asking you to be on that flight when it takes off, Mr Kane. Because if you're not, we'll know about it.'

Again, I didn't say anything. My coffee arrived and I thanked the waitress with a smile that she didn't return. I'd forgotten what an impolite city London could be. It concerned me that since coming off the plane yesterday, the friendliest person I'd run into was Les Pope. It wasn't something you'd want to put in the guidebooks.

'I'd also like it if you returned to your hotel and

stayed there minding your own business for the next twenty-four hours. If you behave yourself, I'll even arrange you a car to the airport.'

'There's no need to take the piss, Leslie.'

'Just be on that fucking plane, Mr Kane.' The friendly act was faltering as Mr Pope began to show me his true colours which, unlike his face, were none too pretty. This was an arrogant man who thought he was holding all the cards. In a movie, I would have told him to take his plane ticket and stick it where the sun don't shine because I'd do whatever the hell I wanted, even if it meant stepping on the toes of him and his friends. But this wasn't a movie, and if there's one thing I've learned in life, it's never to let an adversary know what you're thinking.

I picked up the ticket, turned it over in my hands, then put it in my pocket. After a long pause, during which he stared at me intently, I finally spoke. 'All right, Mr Pope, you win. I'll be on that plane. But I don't want you to try anything in between times. If one of your buddies has a pop at me before I get to the airport, then I'll be back, and I'll be none too happy either.'

I think I caught him out there, because I'm sure he'd been expecting me to start playing up. He gave me a hard stare that revealed deep frown-marks on his forehead, before the expression eased and he smiled again. 'I'm glad you're doing the right thing, Mr Kane. And nothing will happen to you if you do me this favour. Just make sure you don't get any second thoughts between here and Heathrow. Otherwise, things for you might suddenly take a turn for the worse.'

'I'm presuming the coffee's your treat,' I said as I stood up. At the same time, I gave the table a bit of a nudge and half my cup's contents slopped out, much of it missing the saucer and landing on the table. A thin line of liquid made a rapid charge for Pope's end of the table and started dripping over the edge and onto his lap.

He jerked back in his seat, not quite avoiding the first drops, and his eyes met mine again. They were very blue, and they burned with a hatred that I'd seen only a handful of times before, and which I knew spelt trouble.

'Sorry about that,' I said, turning towards the door while he dabbed angrily at the offending stain with a tissue.

The waitress walked over looking pissed off. She had a cloth in her hand. 'You can clean that up,' she snapped, thrusting it in my direction.

I smiled and started to tell her that I was sure my colleague could manage when she lunged at me and I saw that she had a syringe in the other hand. She was aiming it at my upper leg, one of the few places on my body that wasn't well covered by the new coat, and I stepped instinctively to one side, grabbing her by the shoulder.

I felt the sting of the needle hitting my thigh just

as I shoved her bodily into the table. More coffee spilled out of the cup, but by this time Pope was already out of his chair.

The waitress went to jab me again but I caught the side of her face with a hasty but accurate right hook and, not being the biggest of girls, she went down on her behind, looking dazed. I would have felt guilty but there was no time for that. Pope was going for something in the back of his suit trousers and I didn't want to wait around to find out what it was.

As I went for the door, the nearest workman jumped to his feet and charged me, swinging a piece of piping in his hand. I grabbed the handle with one hand and used the other to pick up an empty chair that I flung at him. He knocked it aside and kept coming. I turned away and yanked at the door. It was halfway open and I was wriggling through what gap there was when I was sent reeling by a ferocious blow to the side of the head. My vision blurred and I struggled to keep my balance, knowing that if I fell down here, then I was finished. I had to get outside. In front of witnesses. Across the street, I could see a young couple walking past with a pram. I kept pushing myself through the gap in the door, but the workman, or whoever the hell he was, wasn't going to let me go that easily. A brawny hand slammed against the door's glass, trapping me halfway through. At the same time, he went to smack me again with the piping.

But he didn't get the chance. I gave an almighty push and the next second I was stumbling out into the cold air, and freedom.

A silver car pulled up just outside the café, blocking my view of the couple and their pram. Through the fuzz of my vision, I saw a man jumping out, although there was no way I could have described him.

I opened my mouth, started to say something.

And then I felt a second blow, this time to the back of my head. My legs buckled, and I remember hoping as I hit the ground that my brain was OK because it felt like it had been uprooted and sent flying round my skull like a pinball. I was vaguely aware of being lifted back to my feet, but before there was any time to wonder how the hell this was going to end, I blacked out.

## 10

I awoke in noisy blackness. When I opened my eyes, I couldn't work out whether this was because I was still unable to see properly, or because I was in a dark space. The cramped feeling in my legs and back soon confirmed it was the latter. I was hunched up in the boot of a car, travelling over very bumpy ground. My head thumped ferociously from the blow I'd received and there was a terrible pain behind my eyes.

I willed myself to remain calm and assess the situation – no easy feat when you've been kidnapped, locked up, and suffer from claustrophobia, but I figured I didn't have a lot of choice. I could hear voices – very faint – in the front. I listened for a moment, and concluded that there were probably two men. Next, I moved my hands and feet. They weren't tied. This meant they almost certainly hadn't managed to get me back into the café. They must have simply picked me up and chucked me straight in the boot. They probably hadn't searched me, either. And it was that which gave me a chance.

My fingers touched the top of my head. There was a lot of semi-coagulated blood, and the skin felt extremely tender. I probed round and located a large, angry lump. The guy with the piping had certainly given me a couple of decent whacks, but not quite decent enough. I could move every part of my body, including the extremities, and my eyes were now becoming accustomed to the gloom. I was pretty sure I wasn't concussed, which was the good news. The bad news was that I was going to have to improve my survival skills substantially if I was going to get out of this situation intact.

I moved my hand down to the inside pocket of my jacket. The airline ticket was still there, but I wasn't interested in that. Instead, I reached in further and located a small aerosol can. CS gel. It's freely available in Manila as a legitimate defence against the street robbers who plague the poorer districts, and the gel's better than the gas because it's more accurate and only affects the person being sprayed, not the sprayer or anyone else close by. The cans can easily be smuggled in the cargo holds of planes, where they show up on the X-ray machines as innocuous spray-action toiletries. That's why I'd brought three of them with me, and why I was carrying two now.

The car went into a very large Puerta Galera-style pothole, jarring my whole body and giving me an even bigger headache. But we were slowing down rapidly and I got the feeling that we were nearing our destination. Wherever that was. I wondered whether I was going to get a beating – a warning perhaps that my adversaries and erstwhile employers weren't messing around – or whether it was going to be more than this: a loose end being tied up.

Pope's trap had been a sweet one, I had to give him that. He'd lured me into the open, to a supposedly neutral venue, pretending to make a reasoned approach, so that I would let my guard down, before striking just as I was pondering over what he'd said. Apart from her incompetence at the end, that waitress had been an inspired choice of attacker. There was no way I'd have ever suspected her. Even when plan A had gone wrong, Pope still had a B and a C. I was clearly dealing with someone who was well organized as well as ruthless.

I pulled the can of CS gel loose from my pocket, and placed my thumb over the release button as the car hit another pothole before slowing to a halt. A couple of seconds later the boot flew open, and daylight came rushing in. A hand grabbed me roughly by the collar and pulled me upwards. My headache intensified and my vision blurred again as I moved properly for the first time since the blow.

I made out a white hard hat, and vaguely recognized its wearer as the man who'd attacked me with the piping. I could see through the fuzz that he was grinning and that there was a crooked, glassing scar round his lip. He pulled me closer and started to say something. His breath smelt of eggs and bad coffee, and I wrinkled my nose while simultaneously raising my arm and pushing down on the can's release button, the action automatically breaking the security seal. A line of white gel shot out and got him right in the eyes.

The effect was immediate and incredibly satisfying. He staggered backwards, screaming and slapping at his eyes, and while he was otherwise occupied I hauled myself out of the boot, looking round for any further assailants.

Unfortunately, I'd been wrong about the numbers. There were three men altogether, and the other two were coming towards me from either side of the car. The one to my left was the other workman from the café, a stocky guy with a long head and a small moustache. Those were the only details I got, because I was too busy concentrating on the black baseball bat swinging casually from one hand. From the other side of the car and out of vision, I heard number three shout that I had gas.

Time's of the essence in these sort of situations. I sprayed the gel again, aiming at Moustache, but he turned his head to one side and I only managed an indirect hit. He rubbed at one eye and cursed. I'd stopped him, but he wasn't going to be out of the equation for long.

I swung round, the effort making my vision blur again, and tried to aim at number three through the fuzz. I sprayed wildly as he came towards me but I think I missed, and then I was pressing the button and nothing was happening. The gel had run out. I'd been told you didn't get much for your money. One or two sprays and that was that.

I turned to run as assailant number three's baseball bat came into view. He was holding it two-handed, and seemed to know what he was doing. He lashed out, striking me hard on the back of my legs before I could get out of range, the force of the blow sending me stumbling to the ground. I fell forwards into mud, fumbled momentarily in my pockets, then rolled round so I could see what my chances were.

They weren't looking too good. I was in woodland. A wall of pine trees rose up on either side of the muddy track that the car – a silver four-wheel drive, the same one from outside the café – had come down. I could make out the sound of an aircraft flying unseen through the unbroken white cloud, miles overhead, but there was no hum of nearby traffic. Moustache continued to rub his right eye, but still held on to the baseball bat. Assailant number three, shorter and thinner than his friend, with more hair, was smiling and swinging his bat jauntily. Number one, Scarface, was on his knees a few feet to my right, head in his hands. 'Fucking bastard,' I heard him hiss. I guessed he'd be out of

111

the equation for another five minutes or so, by which time I'd have either escaped or been battered back into oblivion. At the moment, it looked like the latter.

I shut my eyes, then opened them again, focusing on the two men coming towards me. My vision began to clear at what some might argue was exactly the wrong time.

'How's yer head?' asked number three in a thick Glaswegian accent. 'Must be hurting.'

'It's going to be hurting a fuck of a lot more in a minute,' said Moustache, gripping his bat as if he was getting ready to hit an almighty home run. His accent was East London, and he was still blinking aggressively against the effects of the gel.

They stopped on either side of me, looking down. 'You're harder than we give ye credit for,' said number three. 'But nae hard enough, ah'm afraid. Now shut yer eyes and we'll make it quick.' He lifted his bat, as did his colleague. 'That'll do you nae good, son,' he added, motioning to what he thought was the empty CS gel canister in my hand as I raised it slowly.

From somewhere off to the left, I heard a noise in the trees. Something running, getting closer. Then a man's voice, calling out, 'Tex, get back here!' The voice was still some distance away but the dog was a lot nearer. Perhaps he'd heard the commotion and was coming to investigate. If he had, I was grateful. I'd always liked dogs.

'Whattae fuck?' cursed the Scotsman, looking towards the trees.

Still lying on my back, I squeezed the button on the second canister and the gel shot upwards and straight into the face of Moustache, who I'd identified as the most immediate threat. He jumped back, but his muffled curses suggested I'd got him this time. I swung my arm round, still depressing the button, and more gel hit the Scotsman.

But he'd had that one second to react while I took out his colleague, and he used it to jump back out of the way. As the spray sputtered and died all too quickly, he came back fast, striking out with the baseball bat. The blow caught me on the arm as I tried to protect myself, then connected with the fleshy area between my neck and my chin, some of the force at least taken out of it. It hurt – it hurt a lot – but nothing was broken.

He stepped back, his face determined rather than angry, making me think that he in fact was the most dangerous of the three, and raised the weapon above his head for a better shot. But at that moment Tex, who was a young Alsatian, came bounding out of the trees, wagging his tail, and jumped up at my attacker. I don't think he was performing a Rin-Tin-Tin-style rescue; more that he thought what was happening was a game, and wanted to join in.

The effect was the same, though. The Scotsman panicked, kicked out at the dog, knocking him backwards, then went for him with the baseball bat, managing a glancing blow to Tex's side as the dog dodged out of the way. This only served to make Tex angry, and he began barking wildly and trying to find an opening in which he could extract a bit of canine payback. The Scotsman tried to keep an eye on me and deal with the dog at the same time, but by attempting to do both he was managing neither. I grabbed Moustache's baseball bat, and although the Scotsman saw me do it, he had to fend off Tex, who'd managed to get his teeth round the end of his bat and was now involved in a tug of war over it.

I'm a lot fitter than I used to be, but I'd taken something of a beating that morning and my head was still banging away, so when I came at my opponent and hit him across the shoulderblades with the bat I'd liberated, I don't think I did anything like the same damage I'd done to his friends with the CS gel, even though I had a clean shot.

The Scotsman lost his footing, but righted himself quickly and proceeded to kick the dog very hard in the throat. This time, the connection was far better and Tex went over on his back. Ignoring me, he made the most of his advantage and landed a sickening blow with the bat on the animal's head and I knew that this was the end of Tex's resistance.

'My dog! What the hell are you doing to my dog?'

Tex's owner stood by the track, ten yards away, his hair and clothes wet from walking through the undergrowth, the shock on his face as all-consuming as that of any crime victim I'd seen. He was a big man, a couple of stone overweight, and on the wrong side of middle age. He had the look of the long-term office worker about him, and I knew he wasn't going to be able to offer much in the way of assistance, bar calling for help, which was the last thing I needed. He also looked like he was about to break down and cry. His eyes were watery behind the thick-rimmed glasses.

'Get ta fuck, old man!' snapped the Scotsman, already turning back to me with the air of someone keen to complete unfinished business.

Which was when I summoned the last of what strength I had, leaned back with the bat as if ready to hit my own home run, and smacked him round the side of the head.

It still wasn't the best of blows, but at least I managed to daze him. He fell to one knee, clutching his head with one hand, but still holding on to his weapon with the other.

I went to whack him again, but out of the corner of my eye I saw the first guy I'd sprayed getting to his feet, his eyes now uncovered. He was pretty stocky as well, with the scar giving him the sort of face that you could imagine appearing on the cover of a book about pub brawls. He didn't look very happy either.

He turned in my direction and took a step forward, starting to say something less than complimentary, so I threw the bat straight at him and scored a direct hit right between the eyes.

'You fucker!' he yelped, stumbling backwards into a pothole on the track and losing his footing.

At that moment, Tex's owner howled an obscenity of his own and charged down the Scotsman like an ageing buffalo, grabbing him in an all-enveloping bear-hug that appeared highly effective. 'You're not getting away with this!' I heard him shout as he wrestled with the other man, using his ample weight in an attempt to smother him. He was crying too – loud, violent sobs – and I suddenly felt very sorry for him.

But this wasn't the moment for expressing sympathy. It was time for me to make a move, since this was a battle I was never going to win. Shouting to the owner to get out of here himself before the others recovered, and adding the immortal lines, 'It's too late for the dog! Save yourself!' I ran over to the four-wheel drive, slamming the boot shut. I hoped that the assault I'd launched from it a few minutes earlier had surprised the driver enough that he'd left the keys in the ignition.

He had.

I jumped inside and started the engine, slamming it into first and accelerating away. In the rear-view mirror, I saw that Tex's owner still had the upper hand, but that Scarface had now recovered and was going over to assist his mate. He also had the bat I'd chucked at him in his hand. Tex meanwhile lay motionless in the middle of the track, in the same position he'd fallen in.

I cursed. It wasn't my problem. The owner should have run while he'd had the chance. Why take on men like that, however upset you are? In the end, you've got to be pragmatic. Retreat when the odds are against you. But the guy was still an innocent who'd done nothing wrong, and if I left him there God knows what would happen. I was a copper for a long time – getting close to twenty years – and even if for a lot of that time I hadn't been a particularly nice one, I still didn't like to see an obvious injustice being committed when there was something I could do about it. I felt sick and I felt exhausted, but it didn't stop me from looking for a space to turn round.

I'd driven about a hundred yards when there was a break in the trees to my left. I changed down to second, swung the wheel and mounted the bank before reversing straight back into a tree on the other side of the track. Turning the wheel as far as it would go, I just managed to manoeuvre the vehicle round, and then I was heading back in the direction of the fight. I'd been gone no more than twenty seconds.

I was in third gear and coming fast when I rounded the corner and saw Scarface standing in the middle of the track, bat above his head, ready to strike. Beneath him, the Scotsman was now sitting astride the dog-owner, pummelling him with his

117

fists. The dog-owner's arms were in front of his face as he tried to protect himself, and his feet were only inches from the prone dog's head.

Scarface looked up when he heard the engine and he blinked rapidly as his reddened eyes tried to focus. He shouldn't have bothered. If he'd had any sense he'd have used the time to get out of the way. Instead, for me it was third time lucky. First the CS gel; then the bat; now the car, which put bluntly was more like a tank.

I hit him head-on and he flew over the bonnet and banged against the windscreen with a satisfying thud. He seemed to hold that position for a second, and then I slammed on the brakes and he rolled off the front, leaving a dirty stain of blood on the glass. I didn't bother flicking on the wipers. Instead, I flung open the driver's side door so that it was fully extended, and shoved the car into reverse.

The Scotsman was just getting off his victim to make a break for it. However, he'd also taken a bit of a beating so wasn't as quick as he should have been, and was only three quarters upright when the edge of the door struck him full in the face. The momentum sent him crashing over backwards with a pained yelp not unlike the one Tex had made when he'd been hit. I turned the wheel slightly, only just managing to avoid hitting the dog-owner's feet, before coming to a halt again.

It was a pretty grim scene. Scarface lay slumped

on his side, about ten yards up the track from Tex. Moustache was still writhing on the floor with his hands over his eyes. The Scotsman was on his back, arms outstretched, a huge gash running vertically down his face. He was conscious, but no danger to anyone. And the dog-owner, his face bloodied too, was sitting upright, his glasses broken, looking across in shock at his dog's body.

Still, I thought, putting the car back into first, it could have been worse. He might be traumatized now, but one day he'd tell this story to his grandchildren. And embellish it too, no doubt.

Without warning, my vision blurred again as I experienced a sudden wave of nausea, and I had to swallow hard to stop myself from vomiting. It took some seconds for the nausea to pass and the blurring to clear. Then, keeping my head low so he wouldn't get a decent description of me, I touched the accelerator and moved away, trying not to hit Tex but not bothering to avoid Scarface, who I drove straight over. His mug would fit even better on the cover of a book about pub brawls now.

Harsh, perhaps, but when you make your living breaking the heads of people you don't know, you shouldn't expect a rash of Get Well Soon cards.

# 11

The place where they'd taken me was an isolated wood just off the M25 near Hemel Hempstead, and the more I thought about it, the more I was convinced that this was where they'd planned to kill me and dump my corpse. My opinion was bolstered by the discovery of a brand-new loaded .45 revolver in the 4x4's glove compartment, which presumably was intended to finish me off, once they'd beaten the shit out of me. I'd been lucky that Tex and his owner had shown up, but the fact remained that Les Pope evidently wanted me out of the way very badly indeed, and was prepared to go to some extreme lengths to make sure he succeeded.

It took me well over an hour to get back into central London, and the whole way I was paranoid that someone would spot the streaks of blood on the bonnet and call the cops. But maybe blood-stained cars are more common in England these days, because no-one did. I parked up on a back-street in Bayswater, put the gun in my pocket (there were no spare bullets), and used a handkerchief to wipe the steering wheel, door handles and car keys clean of prints. I left the keys in the ignition and made a note of the number plate and the vehicle's make and model, before walking slowly and wearily back to the hotel, my head still thrumming away.

It was one-fifteen p.m. when I reached my room and locked the door behind me. Knowing I was going to have to do it sooner or later, I stumbled into the bathroom and stared at myself in the grimy round mirror above the sink. I looked a mess. A yellowish bruise had formed on my jawline where I'd been struck by the Scotsman's baseball bat, and there was a second bruise like a particularly enthusiastic lovebite on my neck, while several cuts and unidentified marks dotted my face. My eyes had taken on the dull, watery look you often get in the mugshots of the more unhealthy and badly nourished criminals, and even my hair looked dishevelled, sticking up in clumps on top and at the back where the blood from the initial blows with the lead piping had dried. I hadn't been expecting a pretty sight, and I wasn't disappointed.

Having little difficulty pulling myself away from the mirror, I took a long shower and felt the back of my head as I washed my hair. The lump was big, not quite golf-ball sized but enough to make me wonder whether I might have been optimistic concluding I wasn't concussed. My eyesight was back to normal, but the headache was showing little sign of abating.

When I'd finished in the shower, I knew I had to sleep. The thought unnerved me. If I was concussed, then there was always the possibility that I might not wake up again. There were also a lot of questions that needed answering. So far, I hadn't even got started on my investigation and already I'd come very close to getting killed. It would be a lot easier simply to give up and catch the plane back the following morning. To be honest, at that point I was tempted. I'm no masochist – I don't enjoy having the shit kicked out of me by people I've never met before – and I'm not suicidal either. I'd got my payback on the men who'd attacked me, and when they thought about me in the future, it would be with trepidation. I owed Pope, true, but sometimes you've simply got to let go. Tex's owner had made the mistake of charging headlong into danger because he'd got emotional, and if I hadn't been there, things would have ended up a lot worse for him. Who'd be there to help me if things went wrong?

But I'm stubborn. When I make up my mind to do something, I do it. Sometimes I have doubts about things – I wouldn't be human if I didn't – but I never let them stand in the way of a course of action. I'm not sure if that's a good trait to have or not, but it's irrelevant really. Like I'd told Tomboy, I've got it, and that's that. And it was the reason why there was no way I was taking the easy option now. Not until I'd brought down Pope, and whoever it was who was hiding behind him. I was just going to have to be a lot more careful, that was all.

The mobile rang. It was on the bedside table and I picked it up, guessing it would be Tomboy finding out how I was getting on. But the screen was once again showing no number.

Which meant it was Mr Pope.

'Hello, Mr Kane,' he said as I picked up. 'I'm sorry about what happened earlier, but I wanted to make sure you got the message fully. London's a very dangerous place. It's best you leave it.' There was nothing threatening in his words. Rather, his tone was sympathetic, that of a trusted friend dispensing advice.

'I am planning on leaving,' I said, my headache suddenly getting worse. My stomach was grumbling too. All in all, I was a very unhappy man.

'I wanted to make sure you knew how serious we were about you getting on the plane.'

'Well, you certainly got your message across, but somehow I don't think I was meant to be getting on it at all.' I didn't mention that I had the gun.

'It was a warning, Kane. If we'd wanted you dead, you'd have been taken out the moment you stepped inside the café. But next time I'll use someone better than those idiots this morning. I underestimated you there. And overestimated them. I won't make either mistake again.'

'Glad to hear it. I won't be making any mistakes again, either.'

'I hope that means you're going to be on tomorrow's flight. This time I guarantee that nothing'll happen to you en route.'

'That's very reassuring, but I'm beginning to get the sneaking suspicion that you might not be a man of your word. I'll make my own plans, Mr Pope, and the first you'll hear of them is when I tap you on the shoulder one dark night. Then perhaps we'll talk again.'

The laughter down the other end of the phone was frighteningly genuine.

'Pope?' he said, still laughing. 'Who the fuck is Pope?'

And he hung up, leaving me staring at the bedroom wall, thinking that I had one hell of a lot of catching up to do.

# 12

I slept for three hours that afternoon and when I woke up I felt like shit and my stomach's growling had reached dangerous proportions. Rising thick-headed but still alive, I grabbed myself a large drink of water from the tap, got dressed and headed out to look for something to eat. Darkness had fallen and the streets were cold.

There was a Burger King fifty yards down the road, and since I hadn't had one in a good long while, I went in and ordered a large Whopper meal with Diet Coke from a man who looked remarkably like a Filipino, although I didn't bother asking him if he was or not.

I ate in the upstairs area, the only person in there, and finished the food in about two minutes flat. It wasn't that it was especially good, just that I was very very hungry. While I sat at the table slurping away at my Diet Coke, I pulled a crumpled news-paper article from my pocket.

The article was written by someone called Emma Neilson, billed as the Investigating Crime Reporter for the *North London Echo*. It was dated 3 November, just over a month earlier, and concerned the fact that one week after the double murder of former Islington police officer DCI Asif Malik, thirty-one, and Islington resident and convicted street robber Jason Khan, twenty-two, in a Clerkenwell café, the police seemed no nearer to solving the case. The article went on to suggest that DCI Malik, one of the National Crime Squad's newest and most talented ethnic-minority officers, had been tipped for rapid promotion within the ranks, and could possibly have become the Met's Chief Constable one day, which might have been taking journalistic licence a little too far. Malik had been an extremely good copper, there was no doubt about it, but even so he'd been a long way from the top of the pile.

Still, journalists aren't interested in presenting the bare facts. They're interested in stories, and it seemed from my trawling of the Internet over the past few weeks that Ms Neilson had been very interested in this particular one. She'd written a further three articles for the paper concerning the murders. One was simply an account of Malik's life and career, but the other two examined possible motives for his killing. In the main, these centred round Malik's work for the National Crime Squad, which had seen him involved in investigations into

126

a heroin-importation gang and an organized paedophile ring, although he'd also made enemies in the North London criminal underworld during the two years he'd spent in Scotland Yard's SO7 unit, prior to joining the NCS. Not surprisingly, then, there was no shortage of suspects, but in the most recent article, published the previous week, Ms Neilson had concentrated on one criminal gang in particular, who, she said, had some questions to answer. She described the gang's leader as a shadowy thug who'd been responsible for a number of murders, but didn't name him. Instead, she implied in a none-too-subtle manner that he might be getting some inside help from within the team investigating the murders. 'Just what were Malik and Khan meeting about?' she'd demanded in the last paragraph. 'And why are more than a hundred full-time detectives still asking that question? Perhaps there are those amongst them who don't wish to find out.'

The ugly head of police corruption. I didn't suppose the feisty Ms Neilson had endeared herself to the investigating officers with articles like that, but then it wasn't her job to cosy up to them, and in a time when police officers could be unmasked as hitmen, it wasn't such an outlandish accusation either. And unlike anyone else, bar the ones who'd organized it, I knew there *was* an inside man. Someone who'd passed on the message that Slippery Billy was under suspicion.

There'd been plenty of articles in the nationals about what had happened to Malik and Khan (although none had contained quite the same polemic as Ms Neilson's), but as time passed and other news stories jostled for position, interest had begun to fade, particularly in the absence of any significant new leads. The articles had got shorter; the editorials praising the sacrifices of individual police officers in the face of lawlessness had disappeared; life had moved on.

The police wouldn't give up, of course, but five weeks with no arrests is a long time. And now that the man they'd been on to had disappeared into thin air before they could even question him (there'd been no mention of Billy West anywhere in the media), morale would be dropping fast and resources thinning out as officers were moved to newer and easier cases.

But Emma Neilson was still interested and that was good enough for me. It also helped that she didn't work for one of the bigger papers. It meant she'd be easier to track down and hopefully less suspicious of my motives. I might have had the advantage of knowing who'd organized the murders as well as whose finger had been on the trigger, but I needed to find out some background on the story, and she was the ideal person to start with.

Once upon a time, I could have phoned the *North London Echo* and spoken to my old mate Roy

Shelley, but now he'd gone, and as far as he was concerned, so had I. There was no way we'd ever be renewing our acquaintance, which was a pity, and one of the oft-forgotten disadvantages of running from the law and into exile. All your relationships are killed instantly. Both my parents were dead, but I still had a brother down in Wiltshire who I hadn't spoken to in the whole time I'd been away, and would probably never speak to again either. We'd never been that close, but it still seemed a waste.

I phoned the *Echo* and asked to speak to Ms Neilson, saying my name was DI Mick Kane of the NCS. The bloke on the other end sounded suitably impressed but told me that she wasn't there. Apparently she wasn't expected in until Monday.

'Lucky her,' I said. 'How come you drew the short straw, having to man the phones on a Saturday afternoon?'

'The management seem to like her,' he answered, with just a hint in his tone that he didn't share their admiration. 'And she's better looking than me.'

'I wouldn't worry about that,' I told him. 'They're all better looking than me.'

We both had a bit of a laugh, and with small talk over and trust established, I asked him if there was a mobile number I could reach Emma on. 'It's important we get hold of her. It's to do with the murder inquiry she's been covering in her articles. I'm part of the investigating team.'

'Er, sure, I suppose so. Hold on a moment.'

I waited while he put me on hold, and a few seconds later he was back on. He reeled out her number, then asked if she was in any trouble. He sounded like he'd be quite pleased if she was, and I wondered what he had against her, and whether it genuinely did have something to do with her looks. If so, she'd definitely be worth meeting. More likely, though, it was down to the fact that she was better than him at her job.

I told him she wasn't in any trouble, thanked him for his help and hung up, immediately dialling the number he'd given me.

Three rings later and a female voice answered. 'Emma,' she announced chirpily against a background of street noise. Her accent was upper middle class and educated, with a faint north-easterly brogue. I guessed she hailed from one of the wealthier areas of Yorkshire or Humberside.

'Hello, Emma. You don't know me but my name's Mick Kane. I'm a private detective.'

'Sorry, I can't hear you. Can you speak up?'

I repeated myself loudly. At the same time, the street noise faded somewhat.

'God, that's better. Sorry, I'm on Regent Street doing a bit of shopping. What can I do for you, then?'

'I've been retained by DCI Asif Malik's uncle to look into the circumstances surrounding his murder, and the murder of Jason Khan. I know that the police are still investigating, but my client's

130

getting concerned about the lack of progress. I understand you've taken an interest in the case yourself, so I was hoping that we could meet up, perhaps on neutral ground, to discuss your take on things.'

'How did you get my number, Mr Kane?' Her tone was firm but not hostile.

'I'm a private detective; it's my job to find out these things.'

'Why don't you talk to the police?'

'You know what it's like talking to them. There's a lot of professional rivalry. They won't tell me anything. Listen, I'm happy to pay for your time.'

She paused for a moment and I could almost hear her thinking down the other end of the phone. 'I'm meeting friends in the West End tonight, but not until nine o'clock. I can meet you round here at eight?'

'Sure. Whatever's convenient for you.'

'There's a pub on Wells Street called the Ben Crouch Tavern. Just off Oxford Street, at the Tottenham Court Road end. I'll meet you there.'

'Sounds good.'

'How will I recognize you?' she asked.

'I'm forty, I've got a suntan, and I look as if I've just been beaten up.'

'Oh. And have you?'

'I have. I'll tell you about it later.'

'Now I'm intrigued. I've got long, curly hair, by the way. Light red. And I'm thirty-one.'

'I'm sure we'll find each other. Thanks for your help, I'll see you later.'

We said our goodbyes and rang off. I looked at my watch. Ten to five. Plenty of time.

# 13

I walked down to the Marble Arch end of Oxford Street via Edgware Road and went into the first decent-looking menswear shop I saw. Inside, I bought myself a whole new winter wardrobe to add to the coat I'd got earlier, including a leather jacket, a couple of sweaters and a pair of black CAT boots, all from an enthusiastic teenage assistant who took absolutely no notice of my weather- and fist-beaten features and kept telling me that every item I put on suited me perfectly. I wasn't complaining. It's never a chore receiving compliments, even if they are commission-based, and it meant I was only in there about twenty minutes. They also sold Swiss Army knives, and I took one of them too, figuring it would probably come in useful at some point.

Having got rid of the best part of five hundred quid on gear that I was unlikely to use again once I returned to the sun, I made my way back in the direction of the hotel. The streets were busy with late-night shoppers, and there was a festive mood in the chill air which helped to improve my mood and made me yearn a little for a return to life in the big city. Even the beating I'd received earlier felt like a nostalgic throwback to a long-ago past when I'd worn the uniform of the forces of law and order and had spent my working days fending off abuse from the public I was paid to protect. In the end, though, I knew it was all bollocks. The reality was that London was a dark, overcrowded and increasingly foreboding place – at least for those without the wealth, the penthouses and the fashionable parties – a place of street robbers, and drugs, and seething sink estates; of police officers who no longer had the resources or the motivation to police; of politicians who talked up the statistics but ignored the fact that the problems were multiplying like bacteria; and where those who did stand up and place themselves in the firing line – men like Malik – ended up getting shot down.

Tonight, though, it was possible to forget all this. Tonight, families ruled the streets and Christmas carols blared out of open shopfronts. Smiling dads carried their babies in those kangaroo-style pouches you sometimes see; mothers, some of them laden down with shopping, shepherded their over-excited offspring and tried to keep them off the road and out of the path of the seemingly endless stream of red buses rumbling by in both directions. It was what Christmas was all about: rampant consumerism, and spending some quality time with the family. I began to feel a bit jealous, remembering my Christmas Day the previous year, just after we'd bought the lodge. The cook, Teo, had been off sick (with food poisoning, rather worryingly) and I'd had to sweat away in the kitchen preparing the food for our guests, while they'd got drunk out the front and Tomboy entertained them with his wit and bonhomie. Until, that was, he'd been forced to retire, incoherent, to his house up in the hills. It hadn't exactly been memorable.

As I turned the corner onto Edgware Road, I saw three kids of about sixteen across the street who'd surrounded a smaller kid. They had him in the entrance to an alleyway between a restaurant and a shop, and were making him empty his pockets. I watched as he handed over a mobile phone and some money, his face a picture of humiliation as he tried to catch the eye of the many shoppers walking past. But the shoppers kept going, either oblivious to the scene being played out only feet away from them, or choosing to ignore it; hoping that by shutting their eyes to what was going on, it would somehow stop it happening to them. It wouldn't. Let a criminal commit a small crime unchecked, and he'll commit a second, larger one the next day, and be a lot bolder when he does it. These shoppers reminded me of the peace-loving people in H. G.

Wells's *The Time Machine* – the Eloi, I think they were called – who accepted that some of their number would always be killed and eaten by the stronger, more aggressive Morlocks, and simply let it happen. And like the Eloi, these shoppers would one day find that steering clear of trouble was no defence when trouble came calling.

I stopped and went to cross the road, but muggers tend to be swift workers and, having got hold of his mobile and money, they'd disappeared up the alley by the time there was a break in the traffic. The kid gazed about him in some distress, probably wondering why the adults who told him how to behave were such hypocrites, and then disappeared up the road, running fast, before I could catch his eye. Poor bastard.

I watched him go, wondering what I would have done if I'd caught up with him. Comforted him? Given him forty quid for a new phone? Told him to buy a knife? Probably all of those things. He'd learn a lesson from this, anyway. When you head onto the streets, you're on your own, so you've got to be prepared and ready to protect yourself. I'd made a similar mistake that morning, and it had almost cost me a lot more than humiliation and lost innocence. I wouldn't make the same one again. I hoped the kid wouldn't either.

I'd just turned into London Street and was only about a hundred yards from the hotel when my mobile rang. I put down my bags and checked the screen, immediately recognizing the number on display.

It was Tomboy.

'Sorry I didn't phone you earlier,' he said with the same sort of forced breathlessness that I used to put on when returning calls later than I should have done. 'I've been up to my eyeballs, working like a dog. Everything all right?' The placating tone in his voice told me he knew it wasn't. I wondered whether he'd spoken to anyone here since the incident that morning.

'How long have I known you, Tomboy?'

'You've heard from Pope, then?'

'That's a good question, I'm not sure. I met a bloke who was roughly the same age, eye colour and build as the Les Pope you described. But I'm beginning to get the impression they weren't one and the same. Describe him again.'

'Fuck, mate, it's been a long time.'

'Is Pope good-looking?'

'Was this geezer?'

'That's not what I'm asking,' I snapped, stepping into an alleyway away from the traffic noise, and thinking that I'd really been slipshod not getting this sort of information earlier. It could have saved me a lot of trouble.

'Well, I don't think anyone's ever called him good-looking, as such. He used to dress well, mind. Savile Row suits and all that.'

'Did he have a thin face or a fat one?'

'Well, fattish really.' The face of the Pope I'd met had been more on the slim side. 'He weren't a fat bloke, particularly, but he weren't thin either.'

'Well, in that case I haven't heard from him,' I said, convinced now that it hadn't been the same man. 'But I've heard from some of his friends and they weren't too interested in talking. Why did you let on that I was coming over? You must have known it would land me in a lot of shit.'

I heard him sigh at the other end of the phone. The line was remarkably clear. It didn't sound much like he was in the Philippines. Or maybe I was just getting paranoid.

'I'm sorry, mate, I really am,' he said, ladling on the contriteness. 'What's happened, then?'

'Suffice to say that your friends wanted me out of the picture, and they went about it in a very direct manner. If they'd had their way, I wouldn't be talking to you now. In fact, it's unlikely I'd have been talking ever again.'

'Listen, I had nothing to do with any of that. Believe me on that one, please, for Christ's sake.'

'So, what did you do?'

He coughed, and I heard him take a lug of a cigarette. The line was that clear. 'I phoned Pope. That's all I did. I phoned him 'cause I wanted him to have a word with you, tell you what he could about everything, and, y'know ... smooth things over a bit. Then persuade you to get back on the plane so we can all get back to normal again. Which is what I want to happen.'

'It's a bit late for that now. Your talking to him almost got me killed. You must have had some idea that would happen.'

'I didn't, I promise you. I thought he'd just have a word.'

'Where can I find Pope?'

'I don't know. He used to live up somewhere in Mill Hill, but that was years ago. He's probably moved now.'

I exhaled loudly, concluding that he was telling the truth. 'Why did you do it, Tomboy? Did you think I'd thank you for grassing me up? I thought you'd retired from that game. Obviously I was wrong.'

'Fuck you, Mick, I was just trying to protect both of us. Pope's involved with some heavy-duty people; I told you that before you decided to go off on this fucking adventure. If I'd let you go straight after him, you'd definitely have got killed, and then they probably would have started looking for me.'

'Ah, that's the real reason, isn't it? You're watching your own back, never mind mine.'

'Listen here, I've built myself a decent business over here, and when you came over, on the run from just about everyone, did I turn you in? Did I? Did I fuck. But I could have done, you know, and I'd have made a few quid doing it, too, but I didn't, and the reason I didn't was because you was a mate of mine, and you treated me all right back in the old days. So don't give me all that about being a grass. I was trying to help you out again.'

'It didn't work.'

'And I'm sorry about that, but I did it for your own good. All right? And I'm going to tell you this for your own good, too: get the fuck out of there. Get on a plane and get back here. While you still can. Because otherwise you're gonna get into stuff you really don't want to.'

'Like what?'

'Just do it, Mick. Not for me. For you.'

And he hung up before I had a chance to say anything else.

I shivered. The cold was beginning to bite. For some reason, I felt guilty for being angry with him. He'd played the injured-innocent card like he played most situations in his life: with just the right amount of acting skill to sound genuine. He was right, too. I was getting myself into a dangerous situation. But there was no way I was changing course now.

Not before I'd even started.

# 14

The Ben Crouch Tavern was a big pub with a black wooden frontage about fifty yards east of Oxford Street. A chalkboard sign outside the door said that they served Monster Burgers, and a plaque pinned to the wall above it said 'Prepare to sample the eerie atmosphere of Ben Crouch', whoever he was. Scary.

Inside, it was dimly lit, and all the furnishings, including the wooden floor, the array of beams and pillars and the steps leading up to the open-plan balcony above my head were painted the same black as the frontage. A bar on the opposite wall ran the whole length of the pub, and there were a few stone gargoyles up amongst the bottles of spirits, but this was about as eerie as the atmosphere got. The place was crowded, but rather than the legions of the dead, the clientele consisted mainly of large groups of very loud students, and only the occasional refugee from the Rocky Horror Show.

The area in front of the bar was packed, which is always a bad sign for the ageing drinker, and the buzz of conversation and clinking of glasses was so noisy that it almost drowned out the music – a song from the Eighties which was either the Mission or the Jesus and Mary Chain.

I stood near the entrance for a few moments, wondering how the hell I'd find a red-haired girl of thirty-one I'd never seen before, when I felt a tap on the shoulder.

I turned round and looked into the smiling face of a very attractive young woman with soft, elfin features and a fine head of curly reddish-blond hair that fell down over her shoulders with the casual finesse of a fashion ad. She was quite a lot shorter than me, probably no more than five three, and dressed in an expensive-looking nubuck jacket and jeans, with a dinky red handbag hanging jauntily from one shoulder. She had a cigarette in one hand but no drink that I could see, and I would have put her at twenty-two or twenty-three if it wasn't for the eyes, a striking mixture of hazel and green, which betrayed a definite maturity. This was a girl who probably wanted you to take her lightly but knew you'd be making a mistake if you did so. Like a lot of journalists, really, and more than one or two coppers.

'Mr Kane?' she enquired above the noise.

I put out a hand and she took it. 'How did you know? Do I really look that out of place?'

She smiled broadly, showing deep dimples. 'You want me to answer that?'

'Probably not.' I gave her one of my old rueful smiles that years ago used to really get to the ladies.

'It's not that. It's just you do actually look like you've been beaten up. But you didn't tell me you'd be wearing glasses,' she added.

I hadn't known myself until an hour or so back, but had decided to put them on just to add a little to my disguise. It pays to be careful when you're in the vicinity of journalists.

'I've only started wearing them recently,' I answered, 'so I tend to forget. Anyway, I'm pleased to meet you. I thought your articles were very interesting.'

'Do you want to go somewhere else?' she asked, moving close enough so that I could smell a subtle dab of perfume. 'There's no way I can make myself heard in here.' Which wasn't strictly true. Her voice, though not loud, was strong and clear, the northern burr less obvious now than the fact that she'd obviously been educated at a school considerably higher up the educational scale than the one I'd spent my youth in.

To our left, a table full of drunken students were doing an atrocious version of some rugby song, banging away on the wood with open palms in an effort to find a rhythm. It was fair to say they weren't succeeding.

I nodded. 'Sure, lead the way.'

We stepped outside into the relative quiet of the night and walked across the road to a smaller, less crowded pub on the corner. Emma found a space at the bar, and I asked her what she wanted.

'A bottle of Beck's'll be fine, thanks.'

I got the barman's attention and ordered her Beck's plus a pint of Pride for myself, not knowing quite what to expect. It had been three years since I'd drunk English bitter and I wasn't sure whether it was going to taste like nectar or warm piss.

'So, how come we met in that other pub?' I asked as we found a spare table in the corner, a good few feet away from the nearest customers. 'Were you checking me out to see if I was worth talking to?'

'I didn't know you from Adam,' she said with a smile. 'What did you expect?'

I took a sip from my drink. First impressions were veering towards warm piss. 'You still don't know me from Adam.'

'That's true, but I watched you when you walked in and you seemed genuine enough. I can usually tell, I meet plenty of people who aren't. If you'd looked too shifty, I'd have just slipped out of there and you'd never have realized.'

'Fair enough,' I said, thinking if only she knew the truth.

'How did you manage to get beaten up?' she asked, changing the subject as she slipped a notebook and pen out of her handbag. 'What did you find out?'

'Well, first off, let me say this. I want you to help me, and I want to help you, but can you do me a favour and keep what we find out of your articles until we've got somewhere?'

'Why?'

'I've got a feeling that the last article you wrote was right – that there's more to this case than meets the eye. I just want us both to be careful, that's all.'

She nodded. 'OK, but if I turn up something that's a real scoop, I might have to change my mind. I don't want to be at the *North London Echo* all my life.'

'I understand, but please tell me if that's what you're going to do, all right? At least so I know.'

'Sure.' She took a pack of Marlboro Lights and a cheap lighter out of the handbag. 'Do you smoke?' she asked, pointing the nearly full pack in my direction. One of the cigarettes had been placed upside-down, with the tobacco end sticking out.

I told her that I didn't any more, but didn't mind if she did. Then I asked if she'd put the cigarette upside-down in the pack intentionally.

'Apparently it brings you luck,' she said, lighting up. 'I've always done it.'

I nodded. 'My first girlfriend always used to do it too. She wouldn't even accept a cigarette from someone whose pack didn't have an upside-down fag in it. A lot of people used to do it in those days.'

'And did it bring her luck, your girlfriend?'

'She ended up falling in love with a

representative from the Seventh Day Adventist Church who knocked on her door one day when she was a student. She became a born-again Christian, and ran off with him to America. My brother told me that she's had five kids. I don't know if you'd class that as luck or not.'

'Not five kids. Not for me, anyway. But I suppose it depends which way you look at it, doesn't it?'

'Exactly.'

She puffed lightly on her cigarette, taking care to blow the smoke away from me, and I took the opportunity to look at her more closely. She wasn't wearing any make-up, and didn't need it. Her skin was soft and pale and there was a cute smattering of freckles the same colour as her hair running across the top of her nose. But it was the eyes that held my attention. They stood out, not only because of their perfect round shape and unusual colouring, but because they seemed so full of life. Emma Neilson was the sort of girl who could turn heads. I don't think she was classically beautiful – some of her features, like her nose and cheekbones, weren't delicate enough for the rest of her face – but she had a real spark about her, and I'd have bet money she could wrap all but the hardiest of men round her little finger.

'You still haven't told me how you got beaten up,' she said, taking a sip of her beer.

'I know, and I will, but before I go into details of what's happened to me, and what I've managed to find out, I'd like to get some background on the case from you.'

'How long exactly is it you've been working on it?'

'Not very long at all. Since yesterday.'

'And you've already managed to get yourself on somebody's wrong side. That's quite impressive.'

It was obvious she was sceptical of my story. I'd have been, in her position. It made me wonder whether I should have thought things through a bit more before meeting her.

'I'll level with you, Miss Neilson—'

'Emma, please. No-one calls me Miss Neilson.'

'OK, Emma. Well, I've got a lead, something that'll require some help on your part to develop, but it's good, I can promise that.'

'What sort of lead?'

'A name.' She raised her eyebrows, but didn't say anything. 'Someone involved, and not necessarily one you know. But first, I want to hear what you've got. I want to know if there's anything I've missed out.'

'Where do you want me to start?'

'The background. My understanding is that the police think that Malik's death is connected to his work, either at the NCS or at SO7. That seems to be your take on it as well, if my reading of your articles is right. You also appear to have a particular individual in mind, one who has a motive but who might also have friends protecting him. Would that be right?'

147

She stared at me for a moment, weighing me up with those brown-green eyes, then appeared to make a decision.

'Asif Malik made some enemies in the past among organized-crime figures,' she said carefully, 'but the consensus of opinion is that those figures are now finished. However, there was one individual in North London that my sources tell me he was involved in investigating when he was murdered.'

'The one you mentioned in the most recent article but didn't name?'

'That's right. But I'm not going to name him now to someone who I've only just met. I hope you understand.'

'I do, but what makes you suspect him so strongly?'

'Jason Khan, the man who died in the café with Malik, was a member of this individual's organization.'

I raised my eyebrows. This was getting interesting. None of the information I'd gathered on the Internet had mentioned this connection. 'I heard Khan was a convicted street robber, but not exactly a big player. Not someone with the inside gen to bring down a major criminal enterprise.'

'I can't say for sure, but he knew something, and it must have been important.' She paused for a moment. I could tell she had some further information to bolster her case but wasn't sure she should share it. I didn't hurry her, but watched as she put out her cigarette and took a sip from her drink.

Finally, she took a quick look round, then leaned forward over the table. Once again I could smell her perfume. 'The reason why Khan must have known something important is that four days after he and Malik were murdered, his girlfriend died in very suspicious circumstances.'

'What sort of circumstances?'

'On the face of it, a heroin overdose.'

'Did she have a history of drug abuse?'

'She was a runaway who'd spent most of her teenage years in care, and yes, she did have a history of drug abuse . . .' She paused again. 'I know what you're thinking, Mr Kane.'

'Mick, please.'

'I know it's possible that she could have over-dosed when she heard about Jason, but it doesn't fit. I never knew her, but she was a very strong-willed girl, by all accounts. She'd been through a lot in her life, but she'd recently undergone a course of psychotherapy and, from what I can gather, she seemed to be getting her life back together. According to her friends, she and Jason were no longer using drugs, and Jason had never been involved in heroin anyway.'

'Why didn't you print your concerns about the girlfriend's death in the article?'

'It's coming out in the next edition. Tomorrow's.'

I raised my eyebrows for a second time. 'That ought to stir things up.'

'If it gets the police moving, that's good enough for me. At the moment, they don't seem to be doing much about it.'

'You're going to need to be careful. I'm sure you know how to look after yourself, but we're dealing with dangerous people here.' I pulled out my own notebook. 'What was the girlfriend's name, by the way?'

'Ann Taylor.'

I had to work hard to keep my expression impassive. Ann Taylor. A young girl with a spindly child's body and a big attitude. Once upon a time, I'd rescued her from an abduction while she'd been working the King's Cross backstreets as a teenage prostitute. It had been during my last days in London, when I'd been investigating the murder of one of her friends and fellow runaways, Miriam Fox. I'd hoped that maybe Ann had turned out all right in the period since. She'd always struck me as someone with a degree of intelligence as well as the street smarts you associate with runaways, but neither of these attributes were any substitute for luck, and in the end it was that which Ann had been lacking.

But in the short time I'd known her, my impression was that she wasn't the sort to take her own life. As Emma suggested, Ann had been a tough kid who was used to residing at the shitty end of most people's quality-of-life index. People like that are statistically far less likely to end their own lives than those from wealthier backgrounds. But then again, there was nothing to suggest that it hadn't been an accident either. Smack's an easy drug to OD on without actually wanting to.

I decided to let it go for now, and asked Emma what Malik's movements were on the night of the shootings.

'He and his wife, Kaz, were watching the television all evening. The phone rang just after ten p.m. Malik took the call, spoke for several minutes, and then announced that he had to go out. It's been confirmed that the call came from Jason Khan's mobile. Malik threw on some clothes, left the house, and the timings suggest that he went directly to the café where he was killed. And that was it. Kaz went to bed, and the next thing she knew she was being woken up by the police knocking on the door, telling her the bad news.'

'Did she say whether he'd told her what the meeting was about? My client, Mr Malik senior, wasn't sure.'

She shook her head. 'Nothing, but apparently that wasn't unusual for him. He does – did – a lot of very secretive work. From what I remember, she did ask him whether it was really necessary to go out at that time of night, and he said it was. She also mentioned that he looked very agitated. He was generally considered quite a calm man, but she made a point of saying he wasn't himself after taking the phone call. Whatever made him go to that meeting must have been important.'

We were both silent for a while. I wondered whether Jason Khan had been used as bait to lure Malik to a meeting so that Billy West could finish him off. If so, the man behind it had evidently had Khan killed at the same time to make sure his mouth stayed shut. Perhaps Khan had said something to his girlfriend about the meeting and they'd found out about it, effectively signing her death warrant.

At the moment, however, it was all conjecture.

'Now for the quid pro quo,' said Emma. 'Your turn to tell me what you know. Who's this man you've been having trouble with?'

'I want your word that it won't appear in any article until you've cleared it with me. We need evidence against him, for a start.'

'I've already said I'll do everything in my power to abide by your wishes.'

'Not good enough. I want your word.'

'It's nice to meet someone who still believes in that. OK, done.'

I paused for a moment, then spoke. 'The guy I'm talking about is called Les Pope.'

Her eyes widened and she sat back in her seat. 'You're joking!'

That caught me. 'What do you mean?'

'You don't know?'

'Obviously not.'

She shook her head, clearly concerned about my lack of detective skills.

'Les Pope is – or more accurately, was – Jason Khan's solicitor.'

# 15

'Tell me about Pope,' Emma demanded, taking a sip from her beer. 'How did you get onto him in the first place if you didn't know he was Khan's brief?'

I wondered then if I'd overplayed my hand. It's always risky trying to deceive someone whose job it is to sniff out untruths. It's even less of a good idea when you're still a wanted man in the country you're sitting in, and with a telltale suntan as well. Already she was looking at me over the rim of her beer glass with a healthy and fully justified scepticism, although thankfully without any worrying flicker of recognition. Her eyes reminded me of those of a cat – there was something hypnotic about them – and I got the idea that it would be difficult to hide your secrets from her for too long.

'Let's just say that over the years I've built up contacts with a lot of people who'd never voluntarily talk to the police, but who might be tempted to open their mouths with the promise of money. I heard about Mr Pope from one of those people.'

'How good was his information?'

'Good enough to get me a beating.' I gave her the cock-and-bull story I'd concocted in my room earlier, about how I'd been asking around about Pope when two of his thugs had accosted me outside my North London office and kicked me around, warning me to stay out of their boss's business. It was a bit clichéd, I suppose, but not a million miles from the truth.

Emma seemed to buy it as well. 'And there's you telling me to be careful,' she said drily.

'I speak from bitter experience,' I told her. 'That means you should listen doubly hard.'

She smiled, showing the dimples again, and pulled another cigarette from the pack. I saw her glance at her watch at the same time, and felt a vague twinge of disappointment. I think I'd been overestimating the excitement of my company.

She asked me where we went from here and I told her I needed an address for Pope.

'And when I get that, I'm going to pay him a visit.' My tone suggested that when I got hold of him, I wasn't going to ask my questions with a high degree of politeness and patience. It was in keeping with the image I wanted to project to her: that of a man who was essentially on the side of the good guys, but who wasn't afraid of trying on the tough stuff. I thought she'd like that because it would mean I was more likely to come up with some answers, which would help with her story.

'And,' I continued, taking a gulp of my beer, 'I want you to look into Mr Pope's background. Find out anything you can about him. Clients he's had, associates he's got, any controversy he's been involved in. Same with Khan.'

She looked at me in the way an old girlfriend of mine used to do when she thought I was taking the piss. Put-out, but in a playful sort of way. 'You don't want much, do you?'

'It'll help with your own investigation.' I pulled a piece of paper from the pocket of my new jacket and put it on the table in front of her. There were five phone numbers on it, taken from the records section of Slippery Billy's mobile. I didn't know if they'd elicit any information, but it was worth a try. 'Do you know anyone who could trace these numbers, and find out whose names they're registered in?'

She asked me whose phone I'd got them from and I told her that it belonged to Les Pope. 'And they're calls that he recently made and received.'

'How did you get hold of his phone?' she asked, taking the piece of paper.

I flashed her my most businesslike expression. 'One of his phones. I believe he's got several. Let's just say, by stealth.'

'Does he know it's gone?'

'It's back with him now.'

'I'll see what I can do. I can't promise anything.'

'If you use any of your police contacts, be very careful. Don't, whatever you do, mention Pope, and don't use the same source for all the numbers.'

She gave me a puzzled look, followed by a suspicious one. 'You've got a very unorthodox way of operating.'

'In a land of conformity, it's always best to be a little different. It boosts business.'

'I bet it does.' She looked at her watch again. 'I'm sorry, I've got to make a dash. But I'll see what I can do with this. I also need a number for you.'

She keyed my number into her mobile, then put everything in her handbag and stood up, stubbing out her cigarette. She put out a hand, but she was no longer smiling. She was more wary of me now. 'It was nice to meet you,' she said as we shook, 'and thanks for the drink. Let me know how you get on with Pope.'

I told her I would, said it was nice to meet her too, and watched as she walked out of the pub. It was, I thought, one of the terrible injustices of life that as a man grows older he still experiences the same sort of desire for attractive young women that he's always had, and yet, at the same time, age makes him become steadily less attractive to them. I'm not a bad-looking bloke, but I look my age, and in ten years' time, if I'm still here, I'm going to look fifty. Eventually, I'm going to get to the point where no-one wants me. Already I was too old for Miss

Emma Neilson. I could see it in the way she looked at her watch. She was interested in me because I might have some information relevant to her story, but that was all. When she'd heard what I had to say, she'd wanted to get away to see her friends. Even her boyfriend, maybe.

I thought about getting another drink, but decided that this place wasn't for me. It was beginning to fill up now as the evening's revellers arrived in force – mainly a twenties crowd, with a few thirty-somethings sprinkled in – their faces rosy from the cold outside, their laughter echoing through the bar. If I had to drink alone, then at least I was going to do it somewhere where I felt comfortable.

I drained my pint and left.

# 16

Out on Oxford Street, row upon row of Christmas lights were strung across the road in a riot of festive colour. Shops were still open and the pavements remained dense with the last of the hardened shoppers and the now far more numerous gaggles of boisterous and drunk youths, the girls among them looking worryingly underdressed for the weather conditions. No-one caught my eye as they passed, no-one took the least bit of notice of me. Given my situation, this should have been something that pleased me, but tonight it didn't. It made me feel even more like an outsider. Someone who'd long ago ceased to belong.

I was at the wrong end of Oxford Street for my hotel, so I started walking in the direction of Oxford Circus, and managed to grab a cab with a driver who thankfully wasn't interested in talking, and who took me back to Paddington without saying a word.

I got him to drop me off in Praed Street, and wandered along it for a few minutes, enjoying the relative quiet, until I found a pub that looked about right. A song by Oasis – I couldn't remember which one – drifted out of a gap in one of the stained-glass windows, accompanied by the buzz of conversation and clinking of glasses that I'll always associate with a proper London boozer, and which up until that moment was a sound I'd forgotten how much I missed.

I stopped at the door and stepped inside, immediately breathing in a lungful of warm, smoky air.

It was a nice place, recently decorated, with the emphasis on wood-panelling. The room itself was long and narrow with a bar running three-quarters of its length. Several irregular rows of round tables took up the rest of the available space, and tonight they were filled with a loose collection of drinkers, exclusively white and almost exclusively male, and varying in age from twenties to seventies. Most of them seemed to be facing roughly in the direction of a raised platform in the far corner of the room, which I took to be some sort of stage. At the moment it stood empty. About half the stools lining the bar were in use, but there was a cluster of three spare at the end furthest from the stage, and I took the middle one of these. A couple of punters looked round as I passed, but their expressions registered no interest as I ordered my second pint of Pride of the evening from a barman with a sagging head and a prehensile lower jaw who bore more than just a passing resemblance to a well-built Barbary ape. Not someone you'd want to pick trouble with.

No longer having to worry about impressing attractive female company, I took a huge gulp from the pint this time and sunk about a quarter of it down in one. Now, finally, it was tasting like nectar, but as I drank again, I realized that a vital ingredient was still missing, and I knew immediately what it was.

Two seats down, an old geezer in a grey raincoat and cloth cap, who must have been knocking on the door of his eightieth year, puffed thoughtfully on a Lambert & Butler while staring at his reflection in the mirror on the other side of the bar. I watched him for a few moments, following the cigarette out of the corner of my eye as he dipped the tip in his mouth and noisily sucked in smoke, then slowly withdrew it and, with bony soft-veined fingers, tapped the end against the side of the Heineken ashtray, before repeating the process all over again.

It had been three years since I'd last had a cigarette, and for most of that time I hadn't missed having one, but then for most of that time I hadn't been in a smoky London pub drinking Pride. It was, I had to admit, difficult to do one without the other.

I drank some more of the beer, trying to supplant the urge by wondering what Emma Neilson was up to now and whether her efforts would turn up anything of use. But it was no good. The seeds of doubt had been planted. Three years might have gone by, but that was irrelevant. I needed a smoke, and, worse still, I'd already subconsciously made the decision to have one. I could see that, unlike a lot of pubs, the landlord here sold them behind the bar. They were stacked in four separate rows on a shelf beneath the spirit optics – Marlboro, Marlboro Light, Bensons and Silk Cut – like whores beckoning a happily married man. I couldn't take my eyes off them.

I finished my pint, motioned Apeman over and ordered another one, along with a pack of Bensons and a box of matches. It felt like a momentous, life-changing decision, and I hesitated before I removed the cellophane wrapping. People who start smoking again usually justify their decision by saying they're only going to have the one, or that they're only going to do it when they're out socially, or whatever, but this was different. I knew straight away that if I had this one then that was it, I was back on thirty a day. Which represented supremely bad timing, since they cost twenty-five times more per pack here than they did back in the Philippines.

Still, the line had been crossed, and it was a testimony to smoking's long-standing hold on me that as soon as I'd taken the first sip of the new pint, I was ripping off the wrapping and pulling one out. I lit it without further thought and took a short, hesitant drag. There was no lightheadedness, no feeling of sickness from the poison pouring down my throat and into my veins. Instead, there was just an easy feeling of coming home. I took a longer drag and finally found myself relaxing properly for the first time since I'd got back.

A tuneless, half-hearted cheer went up from the tables and I turned to see what it was in aid of. A tall young lady with very long legs had entered the room from a door beyond the end of the bar and was strutting towards the platform. She was wearing about an inch of make-up and not much else – just a glittering gold bra and thong, and high-heeled court shoes of the same colour – and her overall demeanour suggested she thought she was one hell of a lot better looking than she actually was. Not that you could call her unattractive. It was difficult to tell through all the foundation, but I suspected that she would always look better in a pub at night than in bed the following morning.

A song I didn't recognize by a female singer I also didn't recognize started playing loudly as the girl reached the stage, stopping to smile and blow a seductive kiss at a group of half a dozen young drunks at the nearest table, who whooped appreciatively. I had to give her her dues: she was doing a good job of acting like she was enjoying herself, which couldn't have been easy in a place like this. It reminded me of the beautiful young girls in the Philippines you often saw on the arms of older, badly dressed Western men. Always smiling, regardless of how ugly the guy they were with was – and they were usually pretty damned ugly. All part of a woman's natural ability to pull the wool over a man's eyes, I suppose.

She got up on the stage and started doing a slow, supposedly sexy dance routine which involved a lot of swaying and wiggling and not even a negligible attempt to stay in time with the music. Not that the audience seemed to mind. As the bra came off to reveal a pair of small but perky breasts, a louder cheer went up from the audience, and someone at the drunks' table yelled at her to get the rest of it off. I noticed Apeman screw up his face into a scowl when he heard this, as if he sensed that that particular table might give him trouble. Overall the atmosphere in the pub was jovial, but I'd spent enough of my life in this town to know that things could change in an instant, especially when drink was involved.

And they did.

It was after the stripper had removed her thong and was gyrating naked with her back to the audience that it happened. Slowly, ever so slowly, she bent down to touch her toes, her naked arse rising higher and higher in the air as she did so, giving the whole room an eyeful of her nether regions, which were so cleanly shaved they could have featured them on an advert for Gillette. As her fingers touched the floor in an impressive show of physical flexibility and her arse reached its zenith, one of the drunks with impeccable timing blew a loud, dry and very realistic raspberry.

Which was the moment all hell broke loose.

Several older members of the audience jumped to their feet and began remonstrating angrily with the drunks, who were all out of their chairs in an instant. There was the usual pushing and shoving, accompanied by loud threats, and one of the drunks threw a punch that sent the recipient stumbling backwards. Scuffles erupted and a table went over in a cacophony of breaking glass.

But the drunks had made a mistake. They'd turned their backs on the stripper, who, not surprisingly, was none too happy with the way her routine had been hijacked. With a deft movement, she pulled off one of her shoes and turned it round in her hand so that the heel was jutting out like a weapon. Then, snarling and cursing (all pretence of sultry seductiveness now gone), she launched a ferocious surprise attack that I'm not afraid to admit had me wincing.

The nearest drunk got the heel right in the top of his head, the blow landing with such force that I swear it actually penetrated bone. In fact, she had to work hard to get it out again, but it finally came free, and as he shrieked in pain, she let him have it again, although this time her technique for retrieving her weapon had improved, and it was out almost as soon as it went in. The victim went down to his knees, clutching his head, and one of the older regulars took advantage of his state to catch him with a sly kick to the ribs.

'You fucking bastards!' the stripper yowled in a voice so high that one more octave and only dogs would have heard it. The rest of the drunks turned round in unison, and she let the nearest one have it with a scything swipe of the heel that opened up a vicious gash on his cheek. He was hurt but he ignored that fact and lunged forward, trying to grab her by the legs. With a deft movement, she hopped backwards on her bare foot like a naked gymnast, and launched a karate kick with the other foot, the one with the remaining shoe on, the heel catching him right between the eyes. Which was him out for the count.

'Christ, she's good,' I said to the old geezer who, like me, had turned in his seat to watch events unfold. 'She should be in a martial arts film.'

'Does judo,' he rasped, turning my way with an amused expression. 'Don't ever want to mess with Judo Julie. Got a wicked fucking temper on her.'

'Do you think she'll be all right?' I asked, taking a sip from my drink and watching as a bottle of beer sailed through the air in her direction. It narrowly missed her head before smashing against the wall behind the stage. The whole group of drunks – at least those still standing – started to fight their way towards her en masse.

'Don't you worry,' he cackled. 'Ernie'll sort it out.'

'Him?' I said, motioning towards Apeman, who was coming round from behind the bar, huge fists bunched somewhere down near his knees. He didn't look very happy.

The old geezer continued his cackling. 'Yeah, that's Ernie.'

The drunks caught sight of Ernie only after he announced himself by bellowing incoherently – a sound that was not unlike a cross between a bull and a donkey – and when they did, the fight drained out of them with an impressive rapidity. Unfortunately for them, it was too late. For a big man Ernie was surprisingly swift of foot, and within a few bounds he was on them, the other battling punters parting like the Red Sea to give him easier access.

'All right, mate, leave it!' yelled one of the drunks desperately, but his words were unceremoniously cut short when his chin came into contact with Ernie's left fist, the force of the blow lifting him bodily off his feet. He came crashing down on the floor somewhere out of sight, leaving the rest of his mates in the firing line. I'm sure I heard one of them let out a high-pitched scream.

Ernie charged into them with a couple of swinging roundhouse rights that had those who were still on their feet scrambling madly for the door, not even bothering to pick up what was left of their mates. Ernie then allowed himself to be restrained by a couple of the locals while Judo Julie the stripper, a stiletto in each hand, stalked the pub floor naked, like something out of a pornographic version of *Lord of the Flies*, swearing and cursing, and occasionally administering punishment to any of the injured drunks who weren't quick enough in following their mates out the door.

Like all good pub brawls, the whole thing was over very quickly. The initial offending fart noise to the final denouement had taken less than a minute and the girl singer I didn't recognize was still pining away on the CD. Something about her baby cheating on her. It made me think that I wouldn't want to cheat on Judo Julie.

But by this time even Julie's anger had dissipated and she stepped back onto the stage to bring her act to a final, anatomically educational conclusion while the area around her was cleared up and a couple of the wounded locals bought themselves fresh drinks from the bar to ease their pain. No-one seemed to be too bothered by what had happened, not even Ernie, who was having to do most of the clearing up, and I guessed that most of those present saw it as an event that was incidental to their evening. Something for them to chat and have a laugh about in those moments when their conversation hit an unwelcome pause.

Welcome to London. Home of Big Ben, the Houses of Parliament and the traditional pub brawl.

I finished my pint and looked at my watch. The

stage was empty now and the place back to normal, with the buzz of conversation drifting through the smoky air. I pulled two cigarettes from the pack, and lit one while I pondered a third pint.

'Another drink?' asked Ernie, lumbering over and lifting my glass, his expression the most friendly I'd seen it that evening. There was even the hint of a smile there. Obviously, inflicting a bit of pain lifted his spirits. I'd met a few people like him down the years.

'Sure,' I answered, replacing the second cigarette in the pack upside down, figuring that in this town I was going to need all the luck I could get. 'Why not?'

# 17

I woke up the next morning with a sore head. It was difficult to tell whether it was courtesy of the whacks on it I'd received the previous morning, or the six pints of Pride I'd consumed on what was pretty much an empty stomach the previous night. Either way, I knew I needed some sustenance. I lay where I was for a while, my feet sticking out the end of the bed, mulling over whether it was worth going back to sleep for a few minutes or not, but the sound of kids running about and shouting in the corridor and the banging of doors coming from the floor below convinced me that it wasn't. I leaned over and picked up my watch from the floor. Five to nine. Late, for me.

I rose from my pit and showered and dressed, before heading into the big wide world. The weather outside was cold, grey and wet, and not unexpected for the time of year, but I didn't fancy spending very long in it, not now my blood had thinned from my time in the tropics. I found a newsagent's, bought the *Sunday Times*, *Independent* and *News of the World*, then ducked into an Italian café a couple of doors down and ordered a chicken-salad ciabatta with orange juice and coffee.

I ate in a booth next to the window while I read the papers. There wasn't a lot of interest: more violence in the Middle East; further warnings of the threat of Al Qaeda suicide bombers in London; a big article in the *Sunday Times* about pensions, the gist of which was that anyone retiring in twenty years wasn't going to have one. Which might have been true, but who wants to read about it over their cornflakes on their day of rest?

Only in the *News of the World* did I find any mention of my kidnapping and subsequent escape the previous day, and even that was very indirect. Under the headline DOG SLAIN DEFENDING MASTER on page five, there was a short piece describing how 'brave Alsatian' Tex and his owner, Ralph Hatcher, fifty-four, had stumbled across a sus-pected drug deal gone wrong while walking in woodland in Hertfordshire. The two of them had then been savagely attacked by several of the thugs involved, and Tex had died defending his master. Mr Hatcher had received facial injuries but had been discharged from hospital after treatment. And that was it, really. There was a photograph of a dog who may or may not have been Tex (it was hard to tell) staring at the camera with his tongue lolling out, but no photo of Hatcher. Obviously he wasn't interesting enough.

When I'd finished the ciabatta, I lit my first cigarette of the morning and smoked it all the way down to the butt. Did it taste good? Sure it did. Good enough for me not to feel guilty about it, anyway. I thought about phoning Emma, but it was still pretty early and I knew she wouldn't have anything for me yet. She'd probably still be in bed, and good luck to her. If you couldn't rest on a Sunday, when could you?

Instead, I ordered myself another coffee, lit cigarette number two and thought about my position. Emma Neilson had an inside link to the investigation of Malik's murder, and her information about the unnamed gangster was probably accurate. This guy clearly had a lot of resources at his disposal, including at least one copper working on the case, as well as the ability and ruthlessness to have a number of people killed. Obviously, I was going to have to find out who he was, but what then? He was a big player, which meant he was going to have serious protection. I remember once visiting the home of a major North London crime lord, Stefan Holtz, to question him in connection with the shooting of a business rival, and having to go through two sets of wrought-iron gates topped with barbed wire and a metal detector at the front door, and past at least ten moody-looking blokes in suits and half a dozen CCTV cameras before we finally got face to face with him in his office at the back of the house. Even then he sat ten feet away from us and four of his men remained in the room. People like that had enemies, and they weren't stupid. They took precautions. I was up against someone similar, someone I didn't even know, and all I had was a .45 revolver and six bullets. It didn't have the makings of a fair fight.

But that, of course, was the challenge.

# 18

The phone call finally came at half two in the afternoon while I was eating a lunch of fish soup with aioli mayonnaise in a small French place down in the West End on Goodge Street. I hadn't felt like heading back to the hotel after breakfast, and since there was a pause in the rain I'd started walking in the direction of the Thames, taking the opportunity to reacquaint myself with the sights and sounds of the city I'd left behind.

I put down my wine glass and pulled the phone from my pocket, wondering whether it was going to be Blondie, the man who'd claimed to be Les Pope, re-establishing contact. I hadn't heard from him in close to twenty-four hours, so was expecting to receive another of his threats at some point, now that it was obvious I'd missed my plane.

But this time a number was scrolling across the screen, so given his penchant for secrecy, I figured it wasn't him. I was right, too. It was Emma, and I felt a twinge of excitement at the sound of her voice. I think I was getting sad in my old age.

'How was last night?' I asked her.

She made a dismissive noise. 'It was all right. Nothing special. I spent a lot of money and I've got a hangover. Like a lot of Sunday mornings, really.'

'Well, take it easy for the rest of the day. That's what Sundays are for.'

'Do you think I've just been lying in bed, then?'

'No, of course not.'

'Because I haven't. I've been doing work. Work that you requested. You wanted Les Pope's home address.'

Suitably chastened, I asked if she'd got it.

She reeled off the address and phone number of a place in Hampstead, while I scribbled them down.

'He's been there two years,' she added, 'and he lives alone. I can't get hold of his mobile, though. I don't think there's one registered in his name. But you must have his number if you had his phone.'

'I've got it somewhere, don't worry about it. Did your article come out this morning?'

'Front page.'

I could hear the pride in her voice, and resisted the urge to remind her yet again to be careful. 'Well done. And thanks again for your help.'

'I haven't had a chance to look into Pope's background yet, but I will do. How are you planning to get him to talk, by the way?'

'I have my methods,' I answered cryptically, wondering about that myself.

'Don't do anything that's going to get you into trouble.'

'It's very nice of you to be concerned.'

She laughed. 'I don't want anything happening that's going to mess up the story.'

'I'll pretend I didn't hear that,' I said, thinking that that was the first time I'd actually heard her laugh. Maybe it was a good sign.

We said our goodbyes and I hung up and went back to my fish soup, which was tasty enough but curiously devoid of fish. I finished it off, though, then ordered a coffee and a slice of apple tart.

There was no point making my visit to the elusive Mr Pope on an empty stomach.

# 19

Grantley Court was a pleasant T-shaped cul-de-sac made up of large semi-detached mock-Georgian houses, built on a gentle incline a little way west of North End Road. It was a new development, five years old at most, and open plan in its design, so there were no hedges or walls blocking the view of the buildings or the uniformly turfed front gardens. No trees had been planted on the pavements, either, giving the road something of an exposed look, which didn't bode too well for any long-term observation of Pope's place.

I hadn't hurried there, preferring to arrive in darkness, which at that time of the year in southern England was usually with us by four o'clock. I got there just after four, following a lengthy journey by bus and foot. Pope's place, number twenty-two, was in the middle of the cul-de-sac, directly oppo-site the entrance and close to where the two strokes of the T joined. A newish silver Lexus was parked on the one-car driveway and a light was on on the ground floor, but I couldn't tell whether or not he was at home. A burglar alarm, complete with flashing blue light, was attached to the second-floor exterior brickwork.

Tomboy had lived round here once when he'd been a snout of mine, but in considerably less opulent circumstances. I didn't have much recent experience of London house prices, but I couldn't see that you'd get much change out of a million for one of these houses, given the central yet quiet location. That meant Pope was making some tidy money from somewhere, a lot more than he'd be paid for defending small-time crims like Jason Khan.

I slipped onto the driveway of a house with no lights on across the road, and stood behind a parked people-carrier. From here I couldn't be seen very easily from the road but still had a decent view of number twenty-two. I pulled out my mobile and called Les Pope's landline.

It rang for more than a minute, but no-one picked up.

So he wasn't there.

No matter. Time for plan B. It seemed logical to me that one of the last people Slippery Billy West would have spoken to before his death was Les Pope, since, as far as Billy was aware, Pope was the only man in the world aware of his plight. He was bound to have called him, if for no other reason than to let him know that he'd arrived at his destination. So I rang the last number dialled from Slippery's mobile.

Once again, the phone at the other end rang for a good long while before it was finally picked up. The voice that greeted me was male. An ordinary middle-class London accent, no obvious signs of stress. And also, definitely not the same man with the blond hair I'd met yesterday.

'Ah, the elusive Mr Pope,' I said, hoping it was him. 'You sound different.' There was an audible intake of breath at the other end and I knew that I had the right man. I continued before he had the chance to speak. 'We need to meet again, and this time I want to make sure that it is you. I've seen a photo now so I know who to expect. Don't bother contacting your friends. They didn't get rid of me last time, did they? If you want to stay in one piece and get yourself out of this situation alive, then you're going to need to give me some information, and quickly. We're going to meet in one hour's time. Five fifteen. At a pub called the Cambridge Arms on Charing Cross Road, just down from the Palace Theatre. Come there alone.'

'I'm not in London,' he said hurriedly. 'I'm miles away.'

'Then you'd better find some very rapid means of transport back. One hour's time, and it's non-negotiable.' He tried to protest, but I ignored him. 'And don't try anything to get me off your back either. If you're not there, I'll come looking for you, and since I know that you live at twenty-two

Grantley Court – it's a lovely place, by the way – I don't think you'll prove that difficult to find. This is your last chance. I'd take it, if I were you. Understood?'

There was a long pause. 'How do I know you're not going to try and kill me?'

'The Cambridge Arms is slap bang in the heart of the West End. The whole area'll be swarming with people. I won't get the opportunity to do you any harm, and no-one'll be able to harm me either. Which is the way I like it. So make sure you're there. Otherwise I'll burn the house down, and that'll just be for starters.'

Having given as good a tough-guy act as I could, I ended the call while he was still talking and continued to watch the house, just in case he was actually in there, lying low.

I stayed where I was for the next fifteen minutes, staring at Pope's front door twenty yards away, knowing that if he was there he was going to have to make a move soon if he wanted to get to the pub in time. But he didn't. Nothing happened. During the whole fifteen minutes, only one car came past, driving slowly by before dislodging its contents – a family with two young kids and a baby – at a house a few doors down. Otherwise, the street was quiet. The wind had picked up and high, jagged clouds streaked across the night sky. The temperature had dropped, too, and I felt myself shivering. Then it began to rain.

I came out from behind the people-carrier and crossed the road, moving quickly. An eight-foot-high wooden fence at the side of the house joined Pope's place with his neighbours', blocking access to the rear of both properties. Presumably a deterrent to casual burglars, it was never going to stop the more determined intruder, and it didn't stop me. I jumped up, grabbed the top and hauled myself over with only the minimum of fuss.

Pope's back garden was small and square, with half of it paved. A large, near-impenetrable leylandii hedge at the end obscured whatever it was that the garden backed onto.

I crept round to the back of the house and found myself staring through half-pulled blinds into a substantial and surprisingly tidy kitchen-diner, with plenty of gleaming pots and pans hanging from hooks above gleaming work surfaces. It looked like something out of a cookery show. For a man under pressure, Pope wasn't letting things go. A single ceiling light was on, but the room was empty and the door at the far end was shut.

Now for the hard part: getting in. Once upon a time, people were a little bit slack about their home security, making breaking-and-entering an altogether simpler affair, but in the last two decades burglary had become endemic in England, so now everyone was a lot more careful. Doors and windows were far more secure. Alarms were commonplace. People made sure they double-locked everything.

Life for your casual burglar, just like your casual car thief, had become far more difficult, which was why successive governments were always harping on about the fact that under their careful steward-ship, overall crime was on the way down (they never mentioned the fact that violent crime was on the way up, as frustrated thieves started targeting people rather than their property). But you always got one idiot, someone who didn't listen to the advice of the crime-prevention officers, and it looked like I'd found him.

The back door of Pope's place was locked, but I could see a key poking out of the lock itself. I took my notebook out of my pocket and ripped out a blank page, then knelt down and pushed it through the gap at the bottom of the door until only an inch or so of it was showing. Getting back up, I dug out the Swiss Army knife I'd bought the previous day in Oxford Street and located the smallest screw-driver. It was then simply a matter of fiddling in the lock with the screwdriver until the key was dis-lodged on the other side, a process that took about ten seconds, but only because I was a bit rusty. When the key hit the paper, I bent down and pulled it back through. And that was it, I was in.

I shut the door gently behind me and crossed the kitchen. The house was silent and it was obvious that, unless he was hiding under his bed hoping all his problems would go away, Les Pope wasn't here.

I stopped at the kitchen door and listened again,

but the silence remained. At least, that is, until I opened the door. As I did this, one of the alarm's motion sensors picked up the movement, and the silence was shattered with a high-pitched, metallic shriek. Ignoring the noise, I strode into the hallway, found the light switch, then went through the ground floor opening doors, knowing what I was looking for.

The telephone rang. This would be the firm managing the alarm system responding to the message sent to their control room that the alarm had been tripped. Their next call would be the police, but I wasn't too concerned about this. Burglar alarms going off are not a top priority for the Met, because they're usually tripped by accident. Unless I was very unlucky, it would be twenty minutes at least before someone arrived. More of a concern were the neighbours. I checked my watch and decided to give myself two minutes.

I found the study at the front of the house, and went straight over and closed the curtains before switching on the lights. There was a large and immaculately tidy antique desk facing one of the walls, with well-stacked bookshelves directly above it. One of the other walls was also lined with bookshelves, while the third contained a number of photos hanging in frames.

I tried the desk drawers but they were all locked, then had a quick shuffle through the thick piles of paperwork stacked in boxes marked IN-TRAY and OUT-TRAY. But in the few seconds I had, I didn't see anything of interest. Turning round, I scanned the photos on the opposite wall. One man appeared in most of them, and it made me think that either Tomboy hadn't seen him in a long time, or, more likely, he was trying to hide something from me, because Les Pope – and I was sure it was him – was a supremely ugly individual. A twelve-by-eight colour photo of him standing next to an ex-footballer I recognized, but couldn't put a name to, had pride of place on the wall. Pope was grinning from ear to ear, while the footballer just looked vaguely embarrassed, his eyes drifting towards one of Pope's pudgy hands which had appeared round his shoulder. I could sympathize with the footballer's plight. Pope might have been in his early forties but he looked nearer fifty. He was balding fast, even though wedges of oily black-grey hair were combed across his pate in a desperate bid to stave off the inevitable, and his features all seemed misshapen and oversized, as if they'd been very badly moulded. His face sagged; his lips were like chipolatas; and his crooked, snub nose was the largest of its kind I'd ever seen. Only the eyes – big, blue and smiling – acted as redeeming features.

Either way, he was now going to be extremely easy to recognize.

I started to turn away, knowing that time was running short. Then I stopped and did a double-take.

A photo higher up the wall had caught my eye. It was black and white, in a dark wood frame. Quite how I noticed it I still don't know, since it hardly stood out. A group of men on a golf course, posing in front of the clubhouse. Seven or eight of them standing in a row, smiling as they faced the camera. I looked again, closer this time, but there was no mistake. You don't forget the faces of men you've killed, and you don't forget the face of a man who's asked if you can supply him with a young girl to murder. When Les Pope had been setting up the execution of Richard Blacklip in a Manila hotel room a year ago, he'd claimed that he'd been acting on behalf of someone the target had abused as a child. That was what Tomboy had told me, anyway.

But here were Blacklip and Pope in a photo together, only one person between them.

I pulled it down from the wall, roughly removed the frame and folded the picture in half before shoving it into the back pocket of my jeans.

There was movement outside the window. Torchlight. Then a knock at the front door. It was time to go.

I retreated swiftly through the house and out the back door, not bothering to shut it behind me, then made straight for the leylandii at the back of the garden. I couldn't hear any movement behind me and I didn't look back.

Three minutes later I was through the hedge, across someone else's back garden and out onto a different street.

No-one followed.

'I'm changing the time,' I told Les Pope when he picked up his phone. 'It's now six thirty. Same place.'

'Listen, I've got a better idea,' he said quickly.

'I bet you have. The problem is I'm not interested in hearing it. It's six thirty at the Cambridge Arms. And if you get a call from the people who manage your home alarm, don't worry. Nothing's been stolen and the place is as tidy as I found it. Your desk's very neatly kept, by the way.'

'What the hell do you think you're doing?' he demanded, full of righteous indignation.

'You know exactly what I'm doing.'

'I'm not going to be blackmailed,' he blustered.

'What you're going to do is provide me with the information I want. Then I'm out of your hair. Six thirty. And don't try anything, or next time I visit your place I'll make sure you *are* in residence and then there really will be a mess.'

He started to answer but I wasn't interested in a debate so I flicked the phone off. It had been a productive call. Now I knew he was in town. Otherwise he'd have tried to put me off again.

I looked at my watch. Quarter to five. I was back on the North End Road and heading south. Plenty of time.

# 20

An hour and a half later, I was standing outside the entrance to a Spanish restaurant in the bright orange glow of the Charing Cross Road, a black 'I love London' cap pulled low over my face. It was raining steadily and the streets were quieter than usual. Across the road, the Cambridge Arms was busy with theatre-goers taking shelter from the inclement conditions. Pope had yet to arrive.

I stepped back under the restaurant's canopy and lit a cigarette to pass the time. It was my seventh of the day; I was counting. A couple in evening dress, sharing an umbrella that was too small for them both, hurried across the road and in the direction of Soho, dodging between the traffic. A bus appeared, slowing down and obscuring my view of them. When it sped up again, they were gone.

All the way here, I'd been thinking about one thing. What did Richard Blacklip, a small-time paedophile, have to do with Malik's death? Maybe nothing of course, but something about it didn't seem right. Blacklip had been arrested for abusing his daughter – I'd seen that from a newspaper clipping that Pope had sent Tomboy, as well as from trawling the Net. But he'd also known Pope, and had presumably trusted him enough to reveal that he was going to Manila. Whereas Pope, for whatever reason, had wanted him dead.

I dragged slowly on the smoke, conscious that water was dripping from the canopy above my head onto the cap and running slowly down my neck. Shifting my position so that I was no longer in the firing line, I looked back at the street and suddenly saw Les Pope no more than five feet away, hurrying past with another man. Neither of them noticed me. Instead, they turned and crossed the road, and as they reached the door of the pub, the man with Pope turned to say something to him and I saw the long cut running like a tribal marking down the middle of his face. It was the Scotsman from the previous morning's little incident. I figured that I still owed him. And owed Pope too, since he'd disobeyed all instructions by turning up accompanied.

I retreated into the shadows and watched as they disappeared inside, ten minutes early.

There was no desperate hurry so I finished my cigarette, then meandered across the road and took up position a few yards down from the front door. I knew Pope's number by heart now, so I pulled the mobile from my pocket and called it.

He answered to the sound of pub noise. 'Yes?'

'Change of venue, Mr Pope.'

'Look, what is this? I'm—'

'There's a pub called the Three Greyhounds just up the road from the Cambridge Arms, in Moor Street. It's safer there.'

'What do you mean, safer?'

'The Cambridge is under police surveillance. I assume you're there. Go out, turn right, then right again. Walk for thirty yards and you'll see it. Meet me in five minutes.'

I rang off immediately, counted to twenty, and moved over to the Cambridge's front door. Further down the street, I could see a group of students approaching, but they were still some way off and larking about in a manner that suggested they weren't likely to notice anything untoward.

The door opened and the Scotsman appeared, looking across the street to where I'd been standing until two minutes ago. He was probably on the hunt for the non-existent surveillance. I stepped forward and lifted the .45, smacking him on the bridge of the nose with the handle. It was a perfect shot, his nose breaking with an angry crunch. There was a second's delay and then twin waterfalls of blood came pouring out of his nostrils. I smacked him again on the top of the head before yanking him out of the way. He fell awkwardly on the pavement, moaning in pain and clutching what was left of his nose.

Pope appeared in the doorway. 'Oh dear,' he said with admirable understatement, and turned back to go inside.

But he was neither the speediest nor the most dexterous of individuals, and I'd grabbed him by the collar and pulled him backwards before he'd even made it round ninety degrees. I turned the gun in my hand and shoved the barrel into his ample midriff.

'Make a fuss and I'll put a bullet in your gut right here, right now. Understand?'

He mumbled something unintelligible and I could tell from his tone and body language that he understood all right. With a face like his, he definitely wasn't a lover but it didn't look like he was much of a fighter either. A typical defence lawyer, really. Good at making money. Good for nothing else.

I brought him away from the door and pulled him nice and close. Then took a brief look down at Scotsman. He was sitting up, but his hands and face were a bloody mess and his eyes didn't appear to be focusing properly, courtesy of the blow to the head. Now he'd have some idea what it felt like to get a whack when you weren't expecting it.

'Hey, what's going on?'

The accent was American.

A young couple in their late teens were

approaching, the girl with far more confidence than the man. She looked a feisty sort, not afraid to intervene in disputes that weren't her own, which would have been an admirable trait on any other day but this.

The expression I fixed her with was one of utter mortification. 'Oh Jesus, I can't believe this. I'm sorry but please can you get out of the way? We're filming here.' I motioned towards an undefined spot across the road and she stepped back instinctively, out of the way of the imaginary camera. At the same time, I pushed the gun harder against Pope's belly just in case he got any ideas of escape.

'Man, that's realistic,' she said, gazing round in an effort to see the hidden camera.

'That guy's good, too,' said her friend, looking down at Scotsman.

'He's great,' I said, giving Pope a push and starting up the street. I kept my head down as we passed the group of students, who were all staring at the bloodied Scotsman sitting in the middle of the pavement.

I heard the American girl asking her companion if he could see the camera crew, before the Scotsman interrupted by shouting out angrily that there were 'nae fucking cameras!' Then I'd turned the corner and that was the end of that.

'Where are we going?' demanded Pope, trying to put some authority into his voice.

'Somewhere nice and quiet where we can talk.

Just keep walking. I'll tell you when to stop. I'm going to let go of you now, but if you try and make a break for it, you'll be telling me what I want to know with your dying breaths.'

I released my grip on his arm and put the gun back in my pocket, as we walked side by side into the narrow streets of Soho, the West End's sleazy heart. It was busier here, thanks to the profusion of bars and restaurants, but we were heading further in towards the peep shows and sex shops. Away from the bright lights.

'I don't know what it is you're after,' he said, looking my way.

I had to step aside to avoid a group of wet but giggling Japanese tourists, so I didn't answer him immediately. I half thought he might make a dash for it, since for a couple of seconds we were separated by two or three yards and several people, but it seemed my threats had scared him enough because he didn't try anything, even going so far as to slow down so I could keep up.

'I think you might have made a mistake,' he continued. 'I'm not really involved in all this.'

I smiled at him. 'I don't think I have. Now, who did you organize Billy West's murder on behalf of?'

'I didn't have anything to do with it, I promise. All I did was make some calls to Thomas Darke on behalf of another client of mine.'

'Who?'

'You know I can't tell you that.'

'All right, have it your own way.' I took him by the arm again and steered him across the road.

He continued to protest his innocence and I told him to save his breath.

Up ahead there was a narrow pedestrian walkway that led through to Rupert Street. We turned into it and I felt Pope stiffen. It was darker here and there were fewer people about. We walked past the entrance to one of Soho's infamous clip joints, where unsuspecting male punters were lured in on the pretext of having some sort of relationship with a pretty, semi-naked girl, only to find that this relationship was very much of the platonic kind and the obligatory drink was going to cost him the best part of a week's salary. The girl at the door of this one had the body of an East German shotputter and a face to match, and would have had difficulty enticing a sex-mad adolescent OD-ing on Viagra into her establishment, but she gamely tried anyway, and even winked at Pope.

Just past the clip joint was a small porn cinema offering 'XXX' films, a rarity in these parts now with the proliferation of DVDs and the Internet. 'In here,' I told Pope, bringing him to a halt and opening the door. 'After you.'

He stepped reluctantly into a shoebox-sized foyer that smelt of damp. I squeezed in after him, managing to find enough space to stand in. A small, weaselly-looking bloke in a threadbare cardigan who'd probably been here since the place opened in the Sixties sat behind a chipped wooden counter a couple of feet away. He stared at us blankly from behind glasses that were far too big for his face.

'Go on then, Leslie,' I said, 'pay the man.'

Pope sighed, then asked how much he wanted.

The bloke told him it was twenty-four quid for two and Pope sighed again, more loudly this time. 'That seems an awful lot,' he complained.

'It seems very reasonable to me,' I said. 'Give him the money.'

Reluctantly, he pulled a bulging black wallet from the pocket of his Savile Row suit and removed two crisp, clean twenties from the end of the half-inch-thick wad. He had to force himself to give them over, and he kept his hand there while the change was counted out and handed back with an equal lack of enthusiasm. It was like watching a bad comedy sketch about two ageing tightwads.

Pope was really beginning to annoy me now, and before he could return the change to his wallet, I gave him a push and manoeuvred him through the door that led into the cinema.

We were greeted by the sight of a naked woman on the screen as she serviced three men at the same time amidst a lot of grunting, groaning and muffled wails. The theatre itself was small, with no more than a couple of hundred seats. There were only three other people in there, all middle-aged men by the look of the backs of their heads, and they were spaced well apart. No-one turned round as the door clunked shut behind us.

Ignoring the stale smell in the air and the telltale arm movements of the men in front, I guided Pope along a row near the back and shoved him all the way into the far corner, pushing him down in the last seat. I took the seat next to him, returned the .45 to its earlier position against his midriff, and used my other hand to locate the Swiss Army knife. Flicking open the main blade, I jabbed it gently against his crotch.

He looked down and took a sharp intake of breath. I jabbed him again, a little harder this time.

'My God,' he hissed, his voice cracking. 'Be careful. Please.'

I leaned close to him, my mouth inches from his ear. He had a musty, unwashed smell that was only partly disguised by the expensive cologne he was wearing. When I spoke, it was in a whisper. 'Now that I've got your undivided attention, I want you to listen to me very carefully. I'm going to ask you a series of questions and you're going to give me nothing but honest answers, and without any hesitation. If you lie, or pause for more than one second, I'm going to start cutting you with the knife.'

'Please, you're—'

'Do you understand?'

He tried to protest again but I pushed the knife hard against his balls, not enough to break the skin, but not far off it either. He let out a little squeak which was all but drowned out by the ecstatic noises on the screen, and nodded frantically. 'Yes, yes, I understand.'

'Who's the client? The one you hired Billy West for, and the one who got you to organize the hit on him?'

'His name's Nicholas Tyndall. For God's sake, don't tell him it was me who told you. He'd have me skinned.'

'Who is Nicholas Tyndall?'

'He's a gangster, a real thug. I've done work for him before. I—'

'Why did he use you to set up the hit on Malik and Khan?'

'I don't know anything about that . . .'

I brought the knife up to his face with a rapid movement and jabbed him in the cheek with it, creating a shallow wound half an inch across. He flinched and this time cried out properly, but once again the sound was all but drowned out. A thin line of blood appeared, getting thicker as I watched. I didn't like having to do this, but I couldn't afford to listen to bullshit. I also couldn't afford to keep making threats without being seen to carry them out. I returned the knife to his crotch while he wiped the blood from his cheek and stared at it on his fingers. He looked pale.

'Why did he use you to set up the hit on Malik and Khan?' I repeated, leaning close to his ear again.

'Because he didn't want it carried out by any of

196

his own people, and he wanted it kept as quiet as possible.'

'What's Nicholas Tyndall got to do with Richard Blacklip?'

He tried looking at me blankly, one hand still on his face where I'd cut him, but it didn't work. 'Who?'

'Don't fuck me about,' I snarled, bringing the knife back up to his cheek again and slicing it across three of his fingers.

He shrieked in pain and quickly shoved the fingers into his mouth. I pulled the knife away and out of sight, just as one of the other punters turned round and gave us both a dirty look.

I gave him one back and mine must have been dirtier because he quickly turned away.

'Him,' I said, dropping the knife into my lap and producing the photo of the men at the golf course. I stuck it right in front of his eyes so that he had no choice but to look, using my index finger to point out Blacklip somewhere in the middle.

What colour there was drained from his face.

'No hesitation, Pope.'

'He was different,' he answered between pursed lips. 'He owed me money.'

'Then how did you know where to find him in Manila?'

Again he hesitated, and I was just about to give him another warning when a strange thing happened.

His face broke into a sly, confident smile, a sight made all the more odd by the blood dribbling down the side of his face. 'I don't think I'm going to tell you that,' he said, still smiling, and then there was a popping sound not unlike a champagne cork being dislodged and Pope's head snapped back against the wall, a black mark appearing in the centre of his forehead. Dark liquid splashed against the paintwork. Two more popping sounds followed in rapid succession and he slumped sidewards in his seat, blood pouring down his face. His body immediately went into wild spasms, the legs kicking out against the seat in front.

For a second I was too shocked to move as I watched him die in front of my eyes, then instinct took over and I tumbled out of my seat, rolling over so that I was crouching with my back to his corpse.

I caught sight of the assassins immediately. There were two of them, both dressed from head to toe in black, with flat caps on their heads and scarves pulled over their faces. They were standing purposefully in the aisle, no more than fifteen feet away, each armed with a silencer-equipped pistol that was pointed in my direction.

I scrambled backwards in the narrow space between the rows of seats, trying to make myself as small and as difficult a target as possible, but Pope's legs blocked my retreat. At the same time, I desperately worked to manoeuvre my .45 up into a firing position. One of the gunmen fired, a flash of light shooting out of the silencer, but the bullet ricocheted up off a seat and pinged into the ceiling.

A second bullet hissed above my head and there was a dull thwack as it hit Pope. Then the two gunmen were making for the door.

Sitting up as fast as I could, I pulled the trigger on the .45 before realizing that I was only holding it one-handed. There was a deafening explosion as the bullet roared out and the gun bucked dramatically in my hand, the kick from the shot surging right up to my shoulder with a pain that made my arm feel like it was on fire. A huge white hole appeared in the far wall of the theatre as the bullet struck it, way above the heads of the fleeing assassins, sending bits of plaster flying off in all directions. One of the punters cried out in panic.

Ignoring the pain in my arm, I pulled myself to my feet, which was the moment I saw the shock of blond hair sticking out from under the cap of the assassin nearest the door, just before he disappeared from view.

The man who'd claimed to be Pope. Blondie. Like a bad penny, he kept coming back.

But how the hell had he known we were here?

No time to think about that. I took aim, two-handed this time, and pulled the trigger as the second gunman reached the doorway.

There was another deafening blast of noise and the gun kicked wildly, but now I was better prepared and I held it steady. I heard the second gunman yell and stumble, his hand going up to his left shoulder. I'd hit him but not with a direct shot because he kept on moving and was gone from sight before I could fire again. But even a graze from a .45 calibre bullet would be enough to slow him down.

On the screen, the action was building to a noisy finale, but unfortunately it was being played out without the participation of the audience, who'd all sensibly hit the decks, not wanting to get involved.

Pulling the cap down over my face, I hurried along the seats to the aisle and ran in the direction they'd taken.

You have to take snap decisions in a situation like this. There's no time for thinking things through. The shooters might be waiting to ambush me in the foyer, but if I went through slowly, listening out for them, I'd risk giving them time to get away, and I couldn't have that – not now my main lead was missing most of his brains. So I yanked open the door and charged through. To my right, the proprietor with the cardie and the big glasses was sprawled back in his seat, spindly arms hanging limply by his sides, a bullet hole slap bang in the middle of his head. Aside from him, the foyer was empty.

I hit the street at a run, almost slipping on the pavement's slick surface, and spotted them straight away, running out of the passageway and into Rupert Street. They rounded the corner and disappeared from view before I could fire and I ran after them, knowing that if they got away then that was it, I was back to square one.

As I came out the end of the passageway, I saw that the trailing gunman – the one I'd hit – was clutching his shoulder, although he still had hold of his weapon. He must have heard my pursuit because he swung round, the scarf still covering his face, and saw me stride out into the road, the .45 raised to fire.

He pulled the trigger first and I heard a loud female scream from somewhere behind me, but he was running and he was injured, and that put him at a serious disadvantage. He missed. He fired again and missed with the second bullet too, though not by so much this time.

It's strange to recount, but I had no time to feel fear as I stopped, took aim and pulled the trigger for the third time in less than a minute. In that sort of confrontation, when everything begins and ends at such speed, you've got no time for anything bar the physical actions needed to stay alive. And mine, it turned out, were more effective than his.

He was maybe two yards from the junction with Brewer Street when the bullet hit him somewhere in the upper chest, lifting him off his feet and sending him spinning out of control.

Blondie, now right at the corner, swung round and fired off four rounds in quick succession, moving his arm in a careful, controlled arc.

A window shattered behind me; someone screamed again and I threw myself to the pavement, managing to get off another shot from my hip as I did so. It was inaccurate, hopelessly so, and I could tell this because it hit a garish blue-and-pink neon sign saying 'JOE'S ADULT VIDEOS' at least ten feet above Blondie's head. The sign exploded in a shower of sparks and the lights went out. Blondie took this as a cue to make good his escape, disappearing onto Brewer Street, where, as far as I could see, all the pedestrians were huddled in the doorways of the various establishments, taking shelter from the battle in their midst.

From somewhere in the distance came the inevitable sound of police sirens. Knowing that time was short, I got up and ran over to where the first assassin lay motionless, rifling through the pockets of his leather jacket with one hand while clutching the .45 with the other, trying to ignore the sound of my heart hammering in my chest.

Nothing. Not a thing. I stopped to look around me and saw the woman from the clip joint had come out from her kiosk and was now at the bottom of the passageway, staring over at me, eyes wide. There was a big bloke in a suit with her who looked like he might be going to do something, so keeping my face as obscured as possible beneath my cap, I pointed the .45 straight at him and the two of them jumped for cover into separate doorways.

The assassin's scarf had come loose and hung limply round his neck. His mouth was open and a thin trail of blood was leaking out the side of it. He was young – no more than late twenties, at a guess – and wearing a plain black sweater and trousers of the same colour. I patted the trouser pockets hurriedly. Keys in the left, nothing else.

Something in the right, though. It felt like a wallet. I pulled it out. It was.

Thrusting it into my pocket along with the gun, I got to my feet and began to run down Rupert Street as fast as I could, in the opposite direction to Blondie, heading for Shaftesbury Avenue and the crowded safety of Piccadilly Circus.

But if I thought that was the end of the evening's drama, I was sorely mistaken.

# 21

Twenty-five minutes later, I called Emma Neilson from a backstreet off the King's Road. I was exhausted. I'd run and walked a long way across the West End and by my estimations I was well over a mile from the scene of the gunfight. I wasn't taking any chances. It wasn't so much that I was worried about being caught in the net that the police would be throwing across the whole area; I was far more concerned about the prospect of CCTV cameras getting a decent shot of me and being able to pinpoint my route of escape. London's teeming with CCTV cameras and I knew the police would spend dozens of man-days going through the available film in an ever-increasing circle in order to find out where I'd gone and whether I'd used a getaway car.

Only when I was confident that I'd covered enough ground to make checking every camera a logistical impossibility for my former colleagues in the Met did I finally stop and catch my breath. It was raining hard and I was pretty sure that the street I was on – a run-down residential area in the shadow of a Sixties council block – wasn't going to be covered by Big Brother. There wasn't a lot worth covering and there was so little street lighting that they wouldn't have been able to pick up anything of use anyway.

Emma answered on the fifth ring and I could hear the TV in the background. It sounded like the *Antiques Roadshow*.

'Hello.'

'Emma, it's Mick. Mick Kane, the private detective from last night.'

'Are you all right? You sound a bit stressed.'

'I'm fine, but I've had some trouble.'

'What kind of trouble?'

'The kind that involves our Mr Pope. I need to see you urgently. Look, I wouldn't ordinarily ask, but can I come over to your place? I've got information. Stuff I think you'll want to hear.'

She was silent for what felt like a long time, although anything feels like a long time when you're standing out on a cold night street with the rain tumbling down on your head and half of central London's cops after your blood.

'I don't know you at all,' she said eventually, her tone uncertain. 'You could be anyone. This could be a trap. You said yourself that people weren't going to take kindly to the articles I've been writing. What if you're one of them? Or you're working on their behalf?'

I could see her point. I'd have had the same suspicions in her position. Unfortunately, this wasn't much help to me now. 'I'm not, I promise you.'

'But I don't know that.'

'No, you don't, so all I'm going to say is this: Pope's dead, and someone's just tried to kill me.'

'Oh, God.'

'I think the people who killed him work for the man you suspect is involved in the murders of Malik and Khan. Is his name Tyndall?'

'I'm sorry, but this is all getting too heavy for me. I may be a journalist but I don't want to get involved in murder. I think you're going to have to call the police.'

'I can't.'

'Why not?'

'Just take my word for it, I can't. I'm sorry to have bothered you. I've got to go.'

'Wait a minute. Where are you?'

I told her the name of the street and the approximate location.

'That's only about five minutes from me.'

'By foot or by car?' I asked, hoping that didn't mean she lived round Soho.

'Car. I'm in South Kensington, near Gloucester Road Tube.' She sighed, and I knew that she was trying to come to a decision as to what to do. It didn't take her long. 'Stay where you are and I'll be there in a few minutes. I'll be driving a navy blue Volkswagen Golf.'

'Thanks,' I said, but she'd already rung off.

I stepped back into the doorway of a dilapidated-looking stonemasons' offices, reached into my pocket and found the wallet I'd taken from the dead gunman. I didn't much want to open it, since I didn't think I'd find anything of any use. The two men who'd come into that cinema to kill Pope were professionals and weren't likely to be carrying anything that identified themselves, which would leave me at something of a dead end, as well as being wanted on suspicion of a new murder. But you've always got to try to look at the positive side of things, so I offered up a silent prayer and opened it up.

Whoever was paying him was paying him well, that was for sure. There was at least five hundred in cash, probably more; but as I suspected, not a lot else. A cheap-looking, dog-eared business card was sticking out of one of the credit-card slots and I tugged it free. Something else – another card – came out from behind it. It was impossible to read either in the dim light, so I put them in the back pocket of my jeans and kept on searching, finding nothing else bar a used dry-cleaning ticket, which I pocketed as well, along with the cash (the latter on the basis that he was no longer going to need it, and I might).

A car – a Toyota, by the look of it – turned into the street and I sank back into the shadows as it passed, the tyres slicking over the wet surface of the road. When it was gone I stepped out again and walked over to a three-quarters-full skip about twenty yards down the street, parked outside a house that looked like it was in the early stages of renovation. The skip was full of all kinds of junk, from pieces of interior wall to a rusting pushchair, and I buried the empty wallet and the black 'I love London' cap under a pile of cement chippings. These days, if you're a criminal, you really can't be too careful. I'd bought the cap earlier that day near the Embankment, paying cash to an Eastern European stall-holder who didn't even bother to catch my eye, so I didn't think it would provide any of the officers examining the CCTV footage of the shooting with much in the way of clues. But I didn't want it to still be in my possession if they released any details into the public domain, particularly if I was going to be spending any time round Emma.

Three minutes later, a blue Golf pulled into the street and slowed down.

When it was no more than ten yards away I stepped out into the road and waved at her. The Golf came to a halt and I strode round to the passenger door and jumped inside. Something by Coldplay was playing on the CD.

'Thanks,' I said with a weak smile, immediately pushing myself right down in the seat so that my head was level with the top of the dashboard.

'Oh, God,' repeated Emma Neilson, staring at me wide-eyed. 'I can't believe I'm doing this. What is it you've done? Oh shit, forget that. Don't tell me.'

Even from my cramped position and after the drama that had unfolded over the last couple of hours, I couldn't help noticing how nice she looked. She was wearing the same suede jacket she'd had on the previous night, but underneath it was a pink or lilac halter-neck top that showed just enough pale midriff to be tasteful. Her hair was tied back in a ponytail, accentuating her girlish appearance, and the nervous expression on her face made me want to put a reassuring arm around her and tell her not to worry, everything would be all right. Not that it was looking too promising at the moment.

'I'll explain everything when we get back to your place,' I told her.

'I'm not sure I want you to. I think I'd rather not know.'

'It's not as bad as it looks,' I continued, which was one of the bigger lies I've told in my adult life.

She fixed me with a suspicious expression, then turned away to concentrate on the road ahead while I continued to push myself even further down the seat and counted the seconds to our destination.

# 22

Five minutes later, Emma pulled into a parking space. 'It's just round the corner from here,' she explained, 'but I'm afraid you're going to have to walk.'

I managed to squeeze myself out of the seat and onto the road, putting on my glasses at the same time. Having also lost the cap, I was now looking significantly different than I'd been during the shootout. It always amazes me what a couple of props can do.

We were on a typical Kensington street. Wide, grand and very well lit, with immaculately kept, five-storey whitewashed Georgian townhouses on either side. London for the millionaires and the tourists.

'You don't live in one of these, do you?' I asked, following her through the rain.

'Not quite,' she answered, without turning round.

I pulled out the business cards I'd retrieved from the wallet and examined them in the light of the street lamps. I raised my eyebrows. A clue. It wasn't a lot, but it might be something.

I put the cards back in my pocket.

After a minute or so, Emma turned into a narrow, cobbled cul-de-sac of pretty, painted mews houses. She walked up to the second one on the left (it was painted a deep red colour) and unlocked the front door. Feeling sheepish and more than a little unwelcome, I followed her in.

The front door opened straight into the living room. It was a striking place, like something out of an MTV video. The walls were a soothing pale orange; the furniture (the sofa, two chairs and a footrest) a brighter orange; and the carpet, along with the dining table and chairs on the far side of the room, were a matt black. It sounds awful, particularly when the fact that it was a mess was taken into account (there were books, CDs and two fullish ashtrays hanging about, none of which were orange or black), but somehow it worked. I liked it, in spite of my better judgement. Maybe it was because it demanded attention. A flight of well-polished wooden stairs at the far end of the room led up to the top floor.

'Nice house,' I commented, but she ignored me as she pulled off her jacket and picked up a half-glass of red wine that was on the floor by one of the chairs.

'Do you want a drink?' she asked without looking at me.

'Please,' I said, realizing suddenly that I was very thirsty.

'There's beer in the fridge.' She nodded towards an open door that led off from the right of the living room. 'Or there's wine on the top. The glasses are in the cupboard above the sink.'

I walked through without bothering to remove my coat or gloves. Somehow I didn't think she'd be too pleased if I made myself at home. I heard her phone ring in the living room.

The kitchen was small and modern, with appliances that looked brand new. Evidently they'd upped reporters' wages since the last time I'd been round these parts. I poured myself a glass of water and drank it in one, repeated the process, then finally filled the glass from the bottle of red wine sitting on the worktop. An Australian Shiraz from the Barossa Valley. I took a sip, felt myself relax, then walked back into the living room, where Emma was still standing.

Only this time she was pointing a gun at me – the second one in less than two hours. London, it seemed, was getting more dangerous than Manila.

The gun was a small-calibre revolver, a .22 or a .32, and she was holding it as if she knew what she was doing. Not the most lethal weapon in the world, but more than enough to bring down a fully grown man at close range, particularly one who'd been through what I had in the past couple of days.

'Who the hell are you?' she demanded, looking and sounding significantly less girlish and vulnerable than she had done a few minutes ago. Her soft elfin features were suddenly taut and focused, the big round eyes narrowed to slits.

I told her that I was exactly who I said I was. Mick Kane. The expression I adopted was one of righteous indignation, but I was pretty sure I wasn't convincing her.

'What's the name of Asif Malik's uncle?' she continued, without relaxing her grip on the gun. 'The one who's supposed to have employed you to find his killer?'

'Mohammed,' I said reflexively, 'and he's not his actual uncle. He's his second cousin or something. They just call him uncle.'

She shook her head dismissively. 'You're lying. I just took a call from one of my sources. There's no private investigator in the whole of South-east England called Mick Kane. I think you'd better try again.'

I suddenly had a huge and terrible desire to unburden myself, to tell her exactly who I was and why I was here. And I almost did it. Almost.

But not quite.

'My name's Mick Kane and your source is wrong.' I nodded towards the gun. 'And aren't those things illegal round here?'

'Very much so. And it's illegal to shoot people,

too, but if you try a bloody thing on me, I'll be breaking two laws rather than just the one. And I'm not bluffing, either.'

'I can see that.'

'And in case you're in any doubt, this is real. It's a Colt Diamondback LR. A limited edition. It was a gift from my father for my eighteenth birthday.'

'Shit, and I only got a pair of jeans and a V-neck jumper.'

'Don't try to be funny. I know how to use this thing. I grew up on a farm and I could fire a gun before I could count to twenty. I shot competitively right up to the day they made it illegal. I even go to France sometimes for a bit of target practice. That means I won't miss. Understand?'

'I think we're getting off on the wrong foot here. I came to you because I needed your help. I still need it. And I've got no intention of hurting you.'

'Who are you working for?'

'I'm not working for anyone.'

'I don't believe you.' She was about to add something else, but at that moment the lights went out. All of them.

Everything fell silent. The curtains were drawn and only the faintest glow filtered in. We were only ten feet apart, but I could barely see her in the gloom.

'Don't move,' she said, 'I'm still pointing this thing at you.'

'I know. I can see.' The gun hadn't moved but

214

she'd subtly changed position so her face was pointed towards the door. 'Do you often get power cuts?' I asked.

'No,' she said, and for the first time since she'd pulled the gun, there was uncertainty in her voice. 'I can't remember the last one, and I've been here two years.'

'Then it seems like a very unfortunate coincidence, if you believe in such things.'

She took a tentative step towards the door, turning her head so that I was back in her field of vision. 'This had better be nothing to do with you.'

'How could it be? I'm in here with you.'

'Why are you whispering?' she demanded.

'I'm listening.'

'Do you think—'

The front window exploded, the sudden crackle of breaking glass shattering the room's eerie quiet.

Instinctively, we both dropped to our haunches, and I reached for my .45, dragging it free with an angry tug and pointing it at the window.

The curtain hadn't moved. I waited for the second shot, wondering why they hadn't tried to take us out earlier when we'd been coming from the car.

Five seconds passed and still the second shot didn't come. I could hear Emma's breathing. It had accelerated with the surge of adrenalin but was still under control. I admired her for that. She didn't speak, and I could see in the gloom that her gun was also pointed at the window. You had to give her ten out of ten for guts. Most people would have been curled up in the corner, shaking with fear.

I let another five seconds pass, and asked her in a whisper whether she was all right.

'I've been better,' was the answer, but the uncertainty remained in her voice.

I moved towards the front door, keeping low, and only raised myself to my full height when I got there.

'Where are you going?' she whispered.

'I don't think it was a bullet,' I answered. 'It didn't sound right. I'm going to go and take a look.'

'They might still be out there.'

'They won't. Not now. The window made too much noise. And if they wanted to kill us, they'd have done it when we were on our way in.' But I wasn't as confident as I sounded. I listened at the door, but couldn't hear anything. I told Emma to move to one side so that I could open it up without exposing her to danger, and she did as she was told.

Stepping to one side and keeping close to the wall, I turned the handle and let the door swing slowly open. The only noise came from the traffic out on the main road.

I peered round inch by inch, keeping the gun pressed against my hip.

The narrow cobbled street was empty, with no sign of the assailant, or anyone else reacting to the commotion. But what caught my attention were the lights that were on in the windows opposite. Coming out further, I saw that the houses to either side also had power. I was trying to work out exactly what that told me when I spotted the brick lying on the ground amongst shards of glass a few feet away. A hole several inches across and surrounded by spider's-web cracks had appeared in the window where the brick had made contact, but the safety glass had been strong enough to deflect it.

There was a note attached to the brick by two elastic bands. I leaned down and removed it, then retreated inside and shut the door behind me.

'Is everything all right?' Emma asked from somewhere in the darkness.

'It was a brick,' I answered, slipping the .45 back into my waistband. 'Whoever chucked it's gone.'

'Not exactly sophisticated.'

'No,' I said, 'I suppose it's not.' As I spoke, I unfolded the note and tucked it under my armpit, before producing the box of matches I'd bought in the pub the previous night and lighting one. I retrieved the note and read it in the match's small light.

Two words, typed in bold, large font.

## Look upstairs

The breath stopped somewhere in my throat and I could feel my stomach constrict.

'What are you looking at?' she asked, coming up behind me. 'Don't tell me that was attached to the brick?'

I blew out the match and refolded the note, pushing it into my jacket pocket, then turned to face her. She was standing a few feet away, the pale contours of her face just visible in the darkness. I couldn't see the gun but assumed it was down by her side.

'Stay down here,' I told her. 'I need to go upstairs.'

She started to protest but I moved past her, fumbling my way over to the staircase and banging into the sofa on the way. I didn't want her to follow in case of what was up there, but it was clear from the sound of her footsteps that she wasn't planning on hanging back. As I reached the staircase and found the banister, she asked me again about the contents of the note.

This time I told her.

She cursed under her breath, but stayed behind me as I reached the staircase. 'I should go up first,' she whispered. 'I know where I'm going.'

'No way,' I said, and made my way up the stairs, thankful that they weren't creaking. As surreptitiously as possible, I brought the .45 back out, hoping that Emma wouldn't see it.

And then when I was close to the top of the staircase, the power came back on. I had to blink rapidly to reaccustom my eyes to the light and immediately thrust the gun out in front of me in case this was some sort of trap.

But it wasn't. No-one suddenly appeared. No shots rang out. The whole upper floor was quiet. It also looked remarkably ordinary, in so far as anything in Emma's house looked ordinary. It was a lot tidier than downstairs, and there was no obvious sign of intrusion. The walls were painted the same orange as the sitting room, and several abstract paintings – little more than symmetrical patterns created in black and white – hung from the available spaces, along with an expensive-looking metallic silver clock shaped like a very thin oblong. Three doors, all painted white, were positioned round the small square landing.

'Which one's your bedroom?' I asked her.

'The one to your right. Why?'

'Just an educated guess,' I said, and pushed the door open rapidly. I flicked on the light switch and ran inside, keeping low, and moved the gun round one hundred and eighty degrees in a covering arc, taking in from left to right the desk with PC, the neatly made queen-sized bed with stuffed animals reclining impassively on the pillows, the huge wardrobe that took up most of one wall.

At first, I missed it. But as I swept the gun back round from right to left, my eyes stopped and focused on something in the middle of the bed.

It was a small African woodcarving of a narrow tapering face, about six inches long, that blended in

219

well with the midnight blue of the duvet, but definitely didn't belong in the room. Thick, straw-like hair sprouted up wildly from the face, through which two large chicken feathers had been passed in opposing directions. Each feather had what appeared to be dried blood on the tip, and there were further flecks of blood in the hair as well.

As I lowered the gun, Emma came into the room and saw what I was looking at. I heard her take a sharp intake of breath and out of the corner of my eye saw her put a hand to her mouth. Despite the fact that her other hand was still attached to the Colt Diamondback, she looked very vulnerable again. 'Oh God, they've been in here. In my house.'

She took a step towards the bed but I put out an arm to stop her. 'Don't touch anything. You might contaminate evidence.'

And then a thought struck me, something that I should have cottoned onto as soon as I'd seen the lights showing in the other houses in the street.

Unless whoever had cut the power had some supremely good contacts within the local electricity company, the only way they could have shut it off was if they'd done so manually.

From inside the house.

'Where's your fusebox?' I demanded.

'Downstairs. In the utility room. It's off the kitchen.'

I didn't hesitate. I went out of the room and hit the stairs at a run, almost stumbling in my haste to cut off any escape, the gun waving wildly in front of me, although, God knows, I really didn't want to have to use it in here after what had happened in the cinema.

But, of course, I was too late anyway.

The front door was wide open. The intruder had gone. He'd even had the nerve to turn the power back on while we were otherwise occupied, before calmly emerging from his hiding place and walking straight out the front door.

I went over and closed it, not even bothering to attempt a pursuit, then pulled the bolt across. Next I pulled back the curtain and inspected the window in more detail. It was going to be expensive to repair because the whole pane would have to be replaced, but overall the damage was limited, and even another couple of heaves of the brick wouldn't have shattered it. It definitely wasn't an emergency job.

When I was satisfied that everything was in order, I found a plastic bag in one of the kitchen drawers and went back upstairs.

Emma was sitting in the swivel chair by the desk and staring into space. She was no longer holding the gun, and the exhaustion in her face suddenly made her seem very much her age. Even her hair seemed to have lost its lustre. The woodcarving remained on the bed.

I stepped across and carefully picked it up, turning it round in my hands. It was an ugly-looking thing, the pitted eyes staring out malevolently from amidst the straw, but not much different from any of the other traditional African face-carvings on sale in hundreds of shops across London and the South-East. I put it in the bag, tied the handles and placed it on the floor by my feet.

'The man you're investigating,' I said, turning round in her direction, 'is his name Nicholas Tyndall?'

Which was when she said something that truly shocked me.

'I know who you are now.'

There was no fear in her words, simply a weary resignation. Our eyes met, and I knew there was no point lying about it. She knew. I said nothing.

'When I first saw you, I thought you looked familiar,' she went on, breaking eye contact and looking at a point above my left shoulder, 'but I couldn't place where it was I'd seen you before. Then, when you lied to me about who you were, that started to get me suspicious. But it was only when you pulled that bloody great revolver that I remembered where I'd seen your photo. Three years ago in the papers. Dennis Milne, police officer and killer.' She emphasized that last word and I flinched involuntarily. 'They mentioned your name when they were writing about Malik's murder. They said he used to work with you a long time ago. Is that why you're here?'

I nodded slowly. 'He was a good friend of mine

once. I don't like to think of his killers running free.'

'But you're wanted for murder. You're risking everything by getting involved.'

I shrugged. 'Sometimes we do things we don't understand.'

She ran a freckled hand slowly down her face, and I could see the tension in her features. When she looked at me, I saw an attractive, vivacious girl who'd suddenly found herself in terrible trouble. I wanted to reach down and hold her. Press her head against my chest and tell her that it was all right, it wasn't as bad as it looked, and breathe some of the vibrancy that had been there the previous evening back into her.

Then, in a soft voice, she asked a question that ripped me apart. 'You've come here for my help, but what's to stop you killing me when I'm no longer any use to you?'

For a moment I didn't say anything as I absorbed the blow. It still hurt to know that this was how the world viewed me – as a murderous pariah – because somewhere, somehow, they were wrong to do so.

'I haven't got a heart of stone,' I told her. 'I've done things I'm not proud of, things I've regretted, but I honestly never meant to hurt anyone who didn't have it coming to him, and I'm not going to do anything to you either. I promise you that.' She didn't say anything so I continued. 'You can call the police if you want, report you've seen me, but I'd ask that you don't. I'm here to find out who was behind Malik's murder, which is something I know you want too.'

'I don't know if I want it any more,' she said, rubbing her face again. 'Not after this. I'm a small-time bloody journalist on a small-time bloody newspaper. Why are they targeting me?'

'That's the problem: you're not small-time. You're doing too well on this, because you're unearthing information that's making life very difficult for Nicholas Tyndall and his people. That's why they're doing this.'

She didn't try to deny that Tyndall was the man she'd refused to name the previous night, which only confirmed what I already knew. Instead, she looked round the room as if it was suddenly unfamiliar. 'I can't believe it. Last night everything in my life was going fine, now it's just ... I don't know ... it doesn't seem real. I can't believe I'm sitting in my bedroom with a man who's wanted for mass murder.'

'I told you, Emma, you're safe with me.' But perhaps what I should have been asking was: was I safe with her, an investigative journalist who'd send her profile skywards if she decided to turn me in? No-one would dare to call her small-time after that. The problem was, at the moment, I didn't have much choice but to throw in my lot with her.

'What happened tonight with Pope?' she asked.

I gave her a brief rundown of the events in the

cinema and the shooting in the street outside, but I left out any mention of Richard Blacklip. There was no point in letting her know that I'd been carrying out hits during my time abroad, or where I'd been residing.

'You killed someone, before I picked you up?' Her tone was understandably shocked.

I looked away. 'It was self-defence. I had no choice.'

'But the police are going to be after you, aren't they? And they're bound to have CCTV footage.'

'I was well disguised, and when I was outside I was keeping my head down. I was also wearing gloves. I don't think they've got a lot to go on.'

'A true professional,' she said with educated sarcasm.

'Maybe.'

She sighed. 'I can't believe all this. I need a cigarette.'

'Here, have one of mine.' I reached into my pocket and produced a pack of Benson & Hedges.

'I thought you didn't smoke.'

'I didn't yesterday. Today I figured I'd live dangerously.'

She managed the beginnings of a smile, removing some of the tension in the room. It made me feel sorry that I was causing her all this anguish, although you could say – depending on how uncharitable you wanted to be – that she'd brought at least some of it on herself.

I stepped forward, proffered the pack in her direction and waited while she took one.

'The upside-down cigarette,' she said, spotting the one I'd switched round in the pub the night before. 'It doesn't seem to have brought you much luck.'

'I don't know whether it has or not,' I answered, lighting us both up. She gave me a puzzled look as I fished for the two business cards I'd taken from the wallet of Blondie's dead colleague earlier. One was for a restaurant somewhere in the City, but the other was more interesting. It was this one I handed to Emma.

She turned it over. 'What is this?'

'It's the card of a guy named Theo Morris, from a company called Thadeus Holdings.'

'I can see that, but what's it got to do with anything?'

When I told her where it had come from, she looked at me as if I was some sort of grave robber, which I suppose wasn't that far from the truth.

'And the photo on here. It's not the man you . . . ?' Her words trailed off.

I shook my head. 'No, it's not him. It was behind another card that I took out of the wallet, so I guess it was left there by accident. A shooter would never be carrying ID. There's a mobile number written in pen on the back which is going to need to be followed up.'

She started to say something, but I kept on talking. 'Now I understand your position, and after what's happened here tonight I'd advise you very strongly not to write any more articles about Malik's murder, at least until it's safe to do so, but you can still help me without putting yourself in any danger – providing me with bits and pieces of information. Nicholas Tyndall doesn't want to hurt you; I can promise you that. He just wants you to leave him alone. And if you stop sending the spotlight his way and instead leave me to do the legwork, then you'll be safe. The police aren't getting very far in solving this murder, and the more time passes, the less the likelihood is that they will. But I think I'll be able to, and without blowing your cover. I'm a good detective – it's not something you ever lose – and I've come a long way to make sure I get justice, so I've got the motivation. And I'm not easily scared, either. On the other hand, if you turn me in, we might lose a real opportunity to bring some very bad people to justice.'

I was using my best persuasive tone, and even though parts of what I said might have been exaggeration, I believed the crux of it to be the truth.

She continued to stare at the card in front of her. Finally, she turned her gaze in my direction. 'What bits and pieces of information do you want from me?'

'First off,' I said, pointing towards the mystery business card, 'I want to find out who the hell Theo Morris and Thadeus Holdings are.'

# 23

Emma booted up the PC and connected to AOL while I fetched a stool from near the door, brought it over and sat down beside her. Directly above the desk was a large skylight, on which the rain outside beat a steady, comforting tattoo.

When we were online she typed Thadeus Holdings into the search engine. A list of the first twenty matches appeared, with the company's own website at the top. Emma clicked on it and a bland site map appeared with the company's logo, the letters TH in bold Gothic lettering, in the top right-hand corner of the screen. There was a drab yellow circle in the centre of the screen connected to a number of smaller yellow circles by spoke-like blue lines, and in it was a summary of what Thadeus was supposedly all about: *Helping clients develop a cost-effective and holistic corporate security policy. With offices and associates in twenty-nine countries world-wide.* In other words, the usual corporate bullshit. It made me wonder whether whoever penned such inanities actually thought they were saying something useful, or whether, more likely, they knew perfectly well it was a load of crap.

The smaller circles represented Thadeus Holdings' various subsidiaries. They included a data-processing company; a software house specializing in the construction of anti-virus firewalls; and a total of four outfits with the word 'Security' in the title: *Thadeus Security Solutions*; *Winners Security*; *Timeline Security (Europe) Ltd*; and *Thadeus Security Products Ltd*.

Emma clicked on the subsidiary companies in turn and got a brief rundown of what each one did. The work of those involved in software and data processing was pretty much self-explanatory, but it was the security companies that caught my attention. As well as providing bodyguards and general security for companies operating in countries considered dangerous, much of Thadeus Holdings' business revolved round manufacturing and selling hi-tech electronic surveillance equipment to a wide variety of businesses, governments and individuals around the world, and the consultancy required for their effective implementation.

'This is interesting,' I said, leaning over Emma's shoulder and pointing at a picture of one of the company's products. It was a microchip-sized personal tracking device, barely a centimetre long, which allowed a third party to keep track of where the wearer was. It was, the blurb said, an innovative device specifically designed for parents wanting to keep tabs on the whereabouts of young children.

'What's interesting about it?' she asked.

'I've been wondering how the two shooters who took out Pope found us in the cinema. I was keeping a very close eye on everyone and everything when we were walking through Soho, and if they'd been following us, I'd have spotted them. But I didn't.'

'But if Pope had been wearing one, surely that means he must have been expecting them.'

I nodded. 'He was.'

'How do you know?'

'I was asking him a question – we were inside the cinema and I had my back to the door – when this big smile spread across his face. He must have seen them coming in, because until then he'd been as nervous as hell.'

'So he thought they were going to kill you?'

I nodded, noticing that much of the tension had left her and a spark of excitement had appeared in her eyes. It reminded me of how I used to feel when I was working on a particularly interesting case. The thrill of the pursuit. It doesn't come along very often, but when it does, you know about it.

'But what do these people have to do with Malik or Khan?' she continued. 'Or Tyndall, for that matter?'

'God knows,' I said, re-examining the business card. 'Can you look up the name Theo Morris? It doesn't give a job title here and I want to see what he does for them.'

She tapped his name into the website's internal search engine and came up with a match. As soon as she hit that, an unsmiling photograph appeared of a middle-aged man with a mop of curly black hair and a thick moustache. It was the same man as the one on the card. Next to the photo his name appeared in black print, along with the fact that he was Head of Operations for Thadeus Holdings. A short biography beneath stated that he'd joined the company in 1983, was married with two children, and was responsible for the management of all Thadeus Holdings' UK offices.

We both looked at each other, wondering what this told us. It didn't seem much. I thought about phoning the number on the back of the card, but decided against it. It was almost certainly Morris's mobile, and I didn't want to speak to him just yet.

'Let's have a look at the company history,' I suggested. 'See what that throws up.'

Emma went back to the home page and pressed the Company History icon on the far left of the screen. A couple of seconds later a beaming photo of a jowly, fifty-something businessman with a big smile and thinning, straw-coloured hair appeared. This, according to the byline, was Eric Thadeus: the founder, chairman and chief executive of Thadeus

Holdings. A potted history of the company followed.

It had been founded in 1978 by Thadeus, an electronics engineer who'd started out developing commercial bug-sweeping devices, and had grown rapidly, thanks to the sophistication of the products and Thadeus's supposed management skills. It was now a market leader in the provision of the whole package of security services.

Emma worked her way through the rest of the site while I got up and stood watching and smoking my tenth cigarette of the day, but there was nothing else of interest. According to the company blurb, Thadeus Holdings was a highly reputable, environmentally aware, dynamic organization who treated their employees with dignity and care, and who only used recycled paper in their head office. Very nice, and very above board. Except that their Head of Operations' business card and private phone number were in the wallet of a man who'd tried to kill me less than two hours previously.

Emma finally pulled out of the site, and clicked on some of the other Thadeus hits that her search had initially brought up, but there was nothing of any interest, and after another twenty minutes she gave up and went offline. 'If Morris is involved, then we're not going to find it out from here,' she said with a sigh, the excitement in her eyes having faded as it became clear that, as with most things in life, there were going to be no easy answers.

I knew how she felt. I was beginning to feel the same way myself. The leads were drying up, just as they had done for everyone else working this case.

'Did you find anything else useful on Pope or Jason Khan?' I asked hopefully.

She shook her head, lighting a cigarette. 'Nothing that I didn't already know. I haven't managed to get anything on those numbers you gave me from Pope's phone yet, but I expect I'll hear something in the next couple of days, although I'm not going to chase them up. Not after this. I spoke to a couple of contacts about Jason Khan, but they didn't have anything new. It seems he was on the lower rungs of Tyndall's organization.'

'Yet he was able, with one phone call, to lure an experienced police officer out of his house late at night and on his own, to a place where he was unprotected and vulnerable.' I sat back down on the stool, facing her. 'We're missing something here. We've got to be.'

'He knew Malik from the past,' she said, retreating a little in her seat, as if she was trying to put some distance between us. 'Malik arrested him a couple of times when he was with Islington CID.'

'Really? The name Jason Khan doesn't ring any bells with me.'

'Perhaps that's because it wasn't his real one. He changed his last name when he converted to Islam. My source said he made the conversion to get out of a prison sentence for mugging an old lady.

233

Apparently the judge felt that his finding religion demonstrated an urge to reform. Not that it seems to have worked.'

'It usually doesn't. What was his real name?'

'Jason Delly.'

I made a surprised noise that was halfway between a laugh and a snort.

'You remember him, then?'

'Oh yeah, I remember him all right. The whole family were thugs. His mum once whacked me with a frozen leg of lamb when I tried to arrest her for shoplifting. It almost broke my arm.'

Emma smiled. 'Really?'

I nodded ruefully. 'Really. Jason Delly was a real piece of work as well, probably the worst of them all. I nicked him when he was about fifteen for attacking one of his schoolteachers. She was six months pregnant at the time. He broke her jaw and two of her fingers, and then kept kicking her while she was on the ground. The little bastard grinned the whole way through the interview. He still kept grinning when we told him she might lose her baby. I can't imagine any decent person wanting to even be in the same room as a piece of dirt like him. Whatever he said on the phone that night to Malik must have been dynamite to have got him down there.'

'God, what a bastard. Did she lose the baby?'

'No, but she never went back to teaching.'

'You know, the more I see of this case, the more I

regret ever getting involved in it.' She stood up and stretched, moving away from the desk with her back to me. 'It's introduced me to a part of life I wish I'd never seen, and to people I wish I'd never come across.'

The sadness in her voice betrayed her privileged background. This was a girl who'd obviously been shielded for much of her life from the realities the rest of us have to face, and was finding those realities difficult to take. It made me wonder what on earth she was doing working as a reporter on what was effectively little more than a provincial newspaper. And why on earth such an educated, well-brought-up girl felt the need to keep a handgun in the house.

'What are you going to do now?' she asked, noticing me watching her.

It was a good question. 'I think I'm going to pay a visit to Jamie Delly, Jason's youngest brother. I want to see if he can throw any light on what Jason was up to in the last few weeks of his life.'

'Isn't that a bit dangerous?'

'Jamie won't recognize me. The last time I saw him was years back and he was just a kid then. I know this is a bit of a liberty, but do you think you might be able to get me an address for him? I'll let you know anything I find out.'

She gave me an oddly intense look then, as if she was examining some interesting new insect under a microscope. 'I don't know how you can be so confident. You've shot someone, you've seen two men die right in front of your eyes, and you've almost been shot yourself. And yet you're already thinking about the next step. And for some reason I still want to help you, even though my inner voice tells me to run a mile.'

'That's because we both want the same thing – to solve a double murder that looks like it's been covered up, and to get back at the people who've been trying to bully and threaten us both. I haven't done you any harm. They have.'

She flicked at a loose strand of hair. 'I'll see if I can help, and I'll keep your secret. But remember, I'm not going to risk my career or my life to help you. If someone comes asking, I'm not going to lie. You understand that, don't you?'

I nodded.

She didn't say anything else, but remained standing where she was, which I took to be a hint that it was time for me to go.

I stood up. Above me the rain continued to batter the skylight, harder now. 'Thanks for all your help,' I said.

She surprised me then by offering me a lift to wherever it was I was staying.

'Forget it,' I answered. 'You've done enough for me today.'

'You can't walk back in this. How far are you from here?'

'Not that far. Up near Paddington.'

'It's still too far to walk. Come on, I'll drive you

236

there.' She didn't sound thrilled at the prospect, but acted as if she was performing some necessary duty. It must have been her breeding.

'You're not worried about them coming back?' I asked.

She shook her head. 'As you said, they wanted to scare me. They've succeeded there, so I'm probably safe for a bit now. Come on, let's go.'

There's no point looking a gift-horse in the mouth, as my mother would have said, so I followed her out of the room, thinking it was a pity she hadn't asked me to stay.

We talked a little more about the case on the short drive to the hotel, and Emma seemed a lot calmer as she tried to put the evening's events behind her. She might have been closeted from some of the harsher things that life had to offer, but she was a tough girl underneath. For some reason I couldn't explain, I genuinely did trust her to keep her word and not reveal my true identity. I'm a cynic – made, not born – and throughout my adult life I've tended to see the worst in everyone. It's almost certainly why I've never married or had kids, and it's probably why I ended up circumventing the very law I was meant to have upheld in the first place, and why I graduated to putting bullets into villains in return for financial reward. But even taking all that into account, I still felt safe knowing that Emma knew who I was. In truth, I'd developed a real soft spot for her. Which was why I should have thought of her rather than myself, and not put her straight into the path of danger. But things always look simple with hindsight, don't they?

I got her to drop me off opposite Hyde Park on the Bayswater Road. She'd wanted to take me right to my door, but soft spot or not, I didn't want to give too much away.

'I'll be fine here, honestly,' I said. I got out of the car, thanked her, and said I'd speak to her the next day.

I watched as she pulled away from the kerb and drove off in the direction of Marble Arch, then turned and walked back to my hotel through the rain. And as I walked, something bugged me. Something I'd missed. I racked my brains all the way back, hardly noticing that I was getting soaked to the skin.

It was only when I was halfway up the stairs to my room that I realized what it was.

When I'd been in the cinema questioning Pope with my back to the door, and his face had broken into that irritating and ultimately futile smile just before he'd been shot, both Blondie and his friend had had ample opportunity to shoot me. It wasn't as if they weren't good at finding their target. Not one of their bullets had missed Pope. They could have taken me out if they'd wanted to. And yet they hadn't. They'd let me live, and had only tried to deal with me when I'd chased after them and they'd had no choice.

In the aftermath, that fact had slipped my mind. Now it was back there with a vengeance.

But what did it mean?

What did any of it mean?

I yawned, let myself into my room, and locked the door behind me. Whatever it was it could wait until tomorrow.

# 24

Jason Khan's brother, Jamie Delly, had never
known his dad. I don't suppose his mum had,
either. He was eight years old when he'd first been
nicked, after making a valiant effort to burn down
his primary school. Since the age of criminal
responsibility in the UK is ten, he'd been let off with
a warning, which when you're a kid like Delly is
the same as a letter of encouragement, and over the
next six years he'd been arrested on numerous
occasions for offences which ranged from the
minor, like shoplifting and possession of dope, to
the potentially far more serious, like knife point
muggings and aggravated burglary. He'd been four-
teen when I'd left the force, and even then I hadn't
seen him in close to a year. He'd be seventeen now,
and doubtless making a mess of his life. Like his three
brothers, he was a nasty little bastard, but I felt that
he'd also be the easiest to talk to. He was the
youngest and the smallest of the Delly boys, and he

hadn't been the brightest of sparks either, with nothing like the animal cunning of, say, Jason. Or indeed Bryan or Kyle, the other two. If he knew something, I'd get it out of him. I also thought he'd be the least likely to recognize me. But I put my glasses back on, just in case.

On that Monday morning the rain had stopped and the sun was shining. My head still ached, but a lot less than it had done the previous day, and the lump from Saturday's blow in the café had shrunk considerably. I rose at eight o'clock, dressed in fresh clothes and got something to eat from the Italian place round the corner. I took the paper with me and was surprised to see that the shootings in Soho weren't the top story. In fact, they only got a small initial mention in the bottom left-hand corner of the front page, supplanted by another Palestinian suicide bombing in Jerusalem, plus something about GM crops, and I had to turn to page three to get the full report. There was a photo of the street in which I'd gunned down the assassin. It had been sealed off with scene-of-crime tape and a uniformed copper was standing in the background. Aside from that there were a few sentences describing how three men had been shot dead in a gunfight, part of which had taken place in an adult cinema. None of them had so far been formally identified by the police.

And that, pretty much, was it. Twenty years ago, an incident like that would have been front-page news. Now it was just one more shooting. For a country with some of the strictest gun-control laws in the world, Britain has a remarkably high incidence of gun crime, and it always amazes me that by and large the police remain unarmed.

I'd finished breakfast and was on my way to collect my new business cards when Emma phoned. Our conversation was short and formal, but at least not awkward. Clearly, she was still prepared to work with me in the cold light of day. She gave me Jamie's last known address in Islington, on an estate east of the Essex Road, in the direction of Hoxton. I recognized it as a place I'd visited before on police business, and I told Emma I'd let her know how things went.

'Careful, Dennis,' she told me, and I felt mildly touched at the way she used my first name. No-one had called me that for a long time.

'Don't worry about me,' I told her. 'I have a knack for surviving. How about you? You haven't had any more unwanted deliveries?'

'No, everything's fine. They're replacing the window this afternoon.'

'Well, you be careful too. We'll talk later.'

I hung up and looked at my watch. Nine thirty-five a.m. I didn't suppose a lazy no-hoper like Jamie would be out of bed yet, which made it the perfect time to visit.

The estate he lived on consisted of a series of

L-shaped grey-brick buildings five storeys high, arranged in a loose square, with each one connected to the other by a covered passageway built at the level of the third storey, giving the whole thing the appearance of a giant puzzle. As with most London council estates, there was a map at the entrance to give the visitor some idea how to find his way around. Jamie lived in Block D, which according to the map was on the left-hand side.

A twenty-yard-long tunnel carved out of the block in front of me led into the interior of the estate, and as I walked through it, I wondered what the designers of these places were thinking about when they made their plans. They were a criminal's paradise. Built like fortresses, they could be defended with ease by the local youths against the encroachments of the police during street disturbances, and the profusion of passageways offered all kinds of ambush sites and escape routes for even the slowest and noisiest of muggers.

One night in October 1985, when I was still a probationer in uniform, I'd been sent to a similar estate in Tottenham, along with hundreds of other Metropolitan Police officers, to deal with a bloody riot, during the course of which we were petrol-bombed, shot at, and bombarded with paving slabs by a mob who were able to defend their territory with terrifying effectiveness, thanks to its design. The estate was Broadwater Farm, a byword for infamy in the Met, and by the end of that night more than two hundred of my colleagues were injured, and one, PC Keith Blakelock, was dead, having suffered multiple stab wounds at the hands of machete-wielding rioters. I swear that if the site had been more open-plan we would have brought the riot under control a lot quicker than we did, and with far fewer casualties.

At this time in the morning, the place was quiet: a couple of young mothers were pushing prams; a frail pensioner still in his dressing-gown was standing about on one of the balconies that ran round each block. Not much else.

I found Block D, and climbed the steps that led up the side of it until I came to the fourth floor. Delly lived at number 42 and the balcony that ran its entire length was empty. When I got to his door, I could hear the radio playing from inside and I knocked hard. There was no answer. The curtains were pulled and I couldn't hear anything above the radio. I knocked again, harder this time.

I'd come a long way this morning and was loath to go back to the hotel without seeing Jamie, so since there didn't appear to be anyone else around, I decided to resort to more radical measures than I would usually have considered. Taking a step backwards, I kicked the door as hard as I could just below the handle. It wobbled but held, so I kicked it again, and this time it flew inwards with a loud crack.

I stepped inside and shut the door behind me. The place smelled terrible. Fat; unwashed sweat;

domestic rubbish; smoke. The only way I could have spent a night in there was if I'd been wearing a gas mask.

'Who the fuck are you?'

The voice belonged to a well-built, square-jawed white guy of about thirty, dressed in a black leather jacket and holding a foot-long cosh in his right hand. He was standing in a doorway on the other side of the room, and without waiting for an answer, he raised the cosh menacingly and advanced across the mess-strewn living room.

'I'm the man with the gun,' I answered, pulling the .45 out of the waistband of my jeans and pointing it directly at his chest. 'Drop that fucking thing. Now.'

He stopped dead, held his ground for a couple of seconds while he assessed the situation, then reluctantly dropped the cosh as I walked towards him, cocked the gun and pushed it against his chest.

'I don't think you know who you're dealing with here, mate,' he snarled.

'Well, why don't you enlighten me? Because you sure as hell aren't Jamie Delly, and that's who I'm here to see.'

He looked down at the gun, then at me, and could see that I wasn't messing about. When he spoke again, it was with another menacing growl. 'I'd advise you very strongly to turn round and walk away. Because I am here on behalf of someone who has a lot of clout round this neck of the woods, and who does not like people doing things that fuck up the smooth running of his business. You know what I mean?'

I took a step back, and raised the gun so it was a millimetre from the bridge of his nose. 'Where's Delly?'

Through the doorway came another voice, above the music. 'What's going on, Jer? Who you talking to out there?'

'Don't answer him,' I said, keeping the gun where it was. 'Go back in there.'

He started to tell me again that I was making a mistake, so I let him know that I'd count to three and if he hadn't moved by then, he wouldn't be moving anywhere again. He glared at me through slit-thin eyes until I made it to two, then slowly did as he'd been instructed.

I gave him a nudge and followed him through the door and into the flat's small interior hallway. The voice called out again, asking what Jer thought he was doing. It was coming from the first room on our right. The door was half open and I shoved Jer inside. At the same time, I used my foot to push it as far open as it would go, and was immediately confronted with a sight that I could have done without at that time in the morning.

A skinny, unkempt teenager who I recognized as Jamie Delly was hanging by one arm from the shower hook above the bathtub. He was wearing nothing but a pair of threadbare boxer shorts that had probably been white once but were now a murky grey, and he was staring at me, his eyes wide with fear and pain. Blood ran in rivulets from his nostrils down to his chest, but it wasn't this that caught my eye. It was the fact that the top third of his left ear was missing where it had been freshly sliced away. The bottom two-thirds and the area of the neck beneath it were just a red mess. In front of Jamie, and slightly to one side, stood another white man with a shiny bald head, a dark goatee beard and a smile like a gash. He was holding a pair of bloodied secateurs, the blades of which were now pressed against the little finger of Jamie's free hand, ready, by the looks of things, to lop it off.

When the guy with the secateurs saw me, the smile disappeared, to be replaced with a glare of annoyance much like the one Jer had just given me.

'Hello,' I said, pointing the gun in his general direction. 'Am I interrupting something?'

'Who the fuck are you?' he demanded.

'What is it with you two? Didn't anyone ever teach you manners? I'm this boy's guardian angel and I'm here to tell you both to get going while you're still in a position to do so.'

'I think he means it, Tom,' said Jer, staring at the gun.

'The fuck he does,' snarled Tom. He turned to me. 'You ain't gonna do nothing in here. Not with that fucking thing.'

I laughed. 'I think you could be in for a shock, but

don't worry, I'm not going to kill you. Just make a mess of your kneecap.' I changed the angle of my gun arm to make my point. 'Now, I'm going to count to three. After that, if you're still standing here they're going to be calling you Pegleg until the day you die.'

'You don't know who you're messing with.'

'That's what Jer said. I wasn't interested then, I'm not interested now. One . . .'

They exchanged glances, then Tom slowly eased the secateurs away from Jamie's finger, cutting the skin as he did so. Jamie gasped, but said nothing.

I stood out of the way as they exited the bathroom and turned in the direction of the door, Tom leading.

'You'll regret this,' Tom told me as I followed them into the living room.

'Life's too short for regrets.'

'Yours is gonna be. You're a dead man, mate.'

'Can the threats and keep moving, baldie,' I said, realizing that I was beginning to enjoy myself. Detective work was infinitely more rewarding when you didn't have to play by any rules.

He glared at me, but opened the door and did as he was told. Jer also managed a glare, but his lacked conviction. I watched them as they walked along the balcony towards the steps, Tom already talking on his mobile phone, doubtless calling up reinforcements with guns.

I didn't have much time.

# 25

I shut the door again and put the chain across, then replaced the gun, before returning to the bathroom, where Delly was trying without much success to free his hand from the rope that bound it to the shower hook. The blood from his ear was running down onto his left shoulder. It was a messy injury.

He swivelled round as I came in, no sign of recognition in his eyes. 'Can you get me down from here?' he whined in a high-pitched voice that hadn't changed a great deal since he was thirteen years old. 'Please.'

'I need to ask you some questions. You answer me quickly and truthfully, I'll cut you down.'

'Come on, man, you can't—'

'What did those two want?'

He gave me a pleading look, but it didn't work. I stared him down and repeated the question.

'I dunno,' he answered. He pronounced it Adanoo, using the same harsh, ghetto-style pronunciations that seemed to be all the rage amongst the kids round here these days. 'There was this knock on the door. I opened it and one of them smacks me with an 'ammer. Doosh! Just like that. Then the bastards dragged me in here and strung me up like this. I tried asking them what the fuck they wanted, but they didn't say nothing. Not a word. And then the one with the goatee pulled out that chopper thing and sliced me ear with it. You seen it anywhere? The bit he took off?' He began scanning the filthy linoleum floor for his missing body part.

'We'll find it in a minute,' I snapped, keen not to waste time. 'And what did they do after that? Did they ask you anything, or were they just cutting you up for the fun of it?'

'They wanted to know about me brother.'

At last, we were getting somewhere. 'Your brother Jason? The one who was murdered.'

He nodded rapidly. 'That's right. They wanted to know why he was meeting with that copper on the night he got killed.'

'And what did you say?'

'I didn't know,' he shouted, beginning to lose patience. 'I hadn't seen me bro for weeks before he got wasted. That's what I told 'em, but the bastards never believed me. They was gonna start on my fingers. Then you turned up.'

I was confused. 'You don't know who these men were? They told me when I came in here that they worked for someone big, someone not to be fucked around with. Who do you think that might be? Who do you think those two were working for?'

He rubbed his free hand – the one I'd saved – against the wounded ear, watching me at the same time through screwed-up features. It made him look like a rat. It struck me then that he'd always looked like a rat. Cunning and vicious. I had no doubt that he deserved to lose a few fingers.

'Look, man, just cut me down from here, OK?'

'No. Answer the question.'

'Why the fuck should I?' he demanded, not in the least bit appreciative that my intervention had saved him from further injury.

I pointed the gun at his groin. 'Because if you don't, I'll blow your fucking balls off. That's why.'

He exhaled theatrically, and I think he knew that I had no desire to shoot him. I noticed that a rivulet of blood from his ear had now reached his ribcage. 'You heard of Nicholas Tyndall?' he asked, swivelling round slightly on the hook.

I told him I kept hearing of Nicholas Tyndall.

'Me brother used to do some work for him, dealing gear. A while back. I saw him with one of them geezers before, so I reckon Tyndall's the one who sent them here.'

Which meant that Tyndall hadn't known what Malik's meeting with Jason Khan had been about. So he couldn't have set it up. Not for the first time in the last few days, I felt myself being pushed towards a dead end.

I looked at my watch. I'd been in here about three minutes, and didn't want to hang around much longer. It was no way to conduct an interview. Jamie started trying to free himself again, turning his back on me.

'Who do you think wanted your brother dead?'

'I don't know, man. Like I say, I never saw him much, y'know. He lived with his woman over near Caledonian Road.'

'And now she's dead too.'

'Cut me down, man. Please. Me ear's doing me in.'

'Give me a name.'

'Wassat?'

'A name. Someone who knew your brother and his girlfriend. Someone I can talk to. Then I'll cut you down.'

'I told you, man. I didn't see him much. I dunno who his mates was.'

'A name.'

He jerked his right arm back hard, trying either to break free of his bonds or pull the shower rail from the wall, whichever came first. Except neither did. He cursed with frustration while I waited and watched, counting the seconds, knowing Tyndall's men would be back soon. And knowing too that if he couldn't provide me with at least something, I would have wasted my time here.

'I used to sell a bit of weed to one of Annie's mates. Y'know, Annie who was Jason's woman.

The mate's name was Andrea or something. Last name began with B.'

'I need to know how to find her.'

'How the fuck am I meant to know how to find her? I ain't seen her in months.'

Four minutes, and I was losing patience. I came forward fast, grabbed him by the hair and shoved his head back against the mildew-stained wall, pushing the barrel of the gun into his bloodied cheek. 'If I were you, I'd start racking your brains,' I hissed. 'Real fucking quickly. Else a misshapen ear'll be the least of your problems. Understand?'

He finally got the message. 'All right, all right, cool it, man,' he begged, the words spilling out fast. 'I got an old address book in a drawer in the lounge. Beneath the telly. It'll be in there. That's where I keep all me contacts.'

I released the pressure on the gun and left him hanging there while I strode back through to the lounge, conscious of the ticking clock. I pulled open the drawer beneath the TV and rummaged round until I found a crumpled pocket-sized address book under a pile of DVDs and a huge bag of grass. I flicked through the pages until I got to 'B' and was pleased to find that Islington's schools had at least taught Delly something. There was an Andrea Bloom in there, along with an address in Hackney and a mobile phone number, scrawled in barely legible childlike handwriting. Since she was the only Andrea in the 'B' section, I felt it safe to assume it was her. I pocketed the address book and went back into the bathroom.

Jamie had given up struggling. He hung there limply, his head bowed, looking a terrible mess. I almost felt sorry for him.

He looked up as I came back in, and I thought I saw a flicker of recognition in the cunning rat eyes. It was time to go.

Trying to avoid his gaze, I used the Swiss Army knife to cut through his bonds, wrinkling my nose at the sour smell coming off him. While I was slicing away at the ropes they'd used, I asked him how well his brother had known Asif Malik.

Not surprisingly, he hadn't known. 'But when Jason was gonna become a Muslim an' that, I know he talked to Malik about it,' he said. 'He wanted some advice.' The last strand of the rope came free, and Jamie collapsed in a heap in the filthy bathtub. He touched his ruined ear tenderly, then looked up at me. 'Who the fuck are you, man?' he asked, and I knew then that he still had no idea of my true identity.

'The person who made sure you stayed in possession of all your fingers and toes,' I told him. 'Remember that.'

I switched on the shower, thinking he needed one, and walked away, ignoring the yelp of shock he let out as the cold water soaked him.

When I was back on the balcony, I looked at my

watch. Six minutes since I'd kicked out Tom and Jer, the irony of their names only now sinking in. I didn't think it'd be long before they were back with numbers, and I didn't want to be here when they were.

I was confident they wouldn't do any more harm to Jamie. It should have been obvious to them that he didn't know much about his brother's death and was therefore going to be of no great use. Most serious criminals only inflict injuries when they need to and I suspected that Tyndall would be no different. However, I was fairly sure that Jamie would tell them what he'd told me and that they too might want to track down Andrea Bloom. It was important that I got to her first. She might only have represented a very slim lead, but there wasn't a lot else vying for my attention right at that moment.

As I turned to go, I spotted a man and a woman, both smartly dressed, emerging from the tunnel into the estate proper. Even from this distance, I could tell that the woman was young and pretty, late twenties tops, with brown hair cut into a neat bob; while the guy was about my age and height but carrying more than a few extra pounds, mainly round the belly. Straightaway I knew they were cops and, as if I needed confirmation, they both looked up towards Block D. It didn't take a genius to know they were coming here.

I started along the balcony towards the far end of

the block, walking fast, then breaking into a run as I hit the stairwell. I didn't look back.

I was still running when I came out of the back of the estate, onto a litter-strewn pathway that ran alongside a particularly unattractive stretch of Regent's Canal. Decrepit, long-deserted warehouses with rows of broken windows loomed up on each side of the coal-black water, reminders of a time when there was still some real industry round here. I kept going until I found a bench that hadn't been uprooted and chucked into the canal, and sat down, giving myself two minutes to recover. When my breathing was back to normal, I pulled out the address book and found Andrea Bloom's entry. But when I called the mobile number, it was out of order.

I recognized the road she lived on. It was about a mile from where I was sitting. And once again time didn't feel like it was on my side.

So I got to my feet and started walking.

## 26

According to the address book, Andrea Bloom lived just off the Kingsland Road in Hackney. It might have only been a few hundred yards as the crow flies from the bistros and restaurants of south Islington, but the Kingsland Road was a world away from them. It's the sort of place you end up in when you've taken a wrong turn – a long, straight, desolate road lined with council estates and heavily fortified shops selling cheap goods – where gangs of kids in hooded tops hang round on their mountain bikes waiting for something to happen, or someone to mug. It hadn't changed much since I'd been away and still didn't feel that safe, even at eleven o'clock in the morning, but I walked most of its length south to north, unchallenged and unscathed, which either meant I looked too hard to take on or, more likely, it was still too early for the local street robbers.

Andrea's street was quieter and a bit more

upmarket, being made up mainly of three-storey townhouses, most of which could have done with a decent exterior paint job. Hers was about thirty yards down on the right-hand side, and was one of the more ramshackle residences.

I had to ring the bell several times before an early-twenties white guy with a dreadlocked mane of naturally blond curly hair answered. He must have been getting on for six foot six, but was as lean as a rake. He had a large ring through his nose, and a smaller one through his right eyebrow. The expression on his face was suspicious, but it didn't sit that easily there. I guessed he was quite a friendly sort to the people he knew, but maybe a little earnest. He was dressed in a light green T-shirt with a photo of Che Guevara on it, and combat trousers of the same colour, while his feet were bare. I'd have put money on the fact that he was a vegetarian, and that he was better educated and from a family higher up the social ladder than either his garb or current location would suggest.

'Yes?'

'I'm here to see Andrea Bloom.'

He looked me up and down carefully, like a man examining a fake designer shirt on a cheap market stall. Even after all this time, I must still have had the demeanour of a copper, and I doubted that any members of the law-enforcement fraternity were very popular round here.

'I don't know any Andrea Bloom.'

I could tell he was lying. It wasn't difficult to spot. 'Yes, you do,' I told him. 'Is she in?'

'Who are you?'

I was beginning to get tired of this question. 'It's personal. Is she in?'

'She's at work.'

'And where's her work?'

'I'm not telling you,' he snapped.

'Fair enough. I'll come in and wait for her, then.'

I pushed past him and stepped into the hallway. The carpet was threadbare, but the general décor a considerable improvement on Delly's place. I turned left and walked into a small sitting room with a cheap-looking TV in the corner and a profusion of different coloured beanbags on the floor. I found a chair and plonked myself down.

He came stomping in after me. 'I don't know who the fuck you think you are, but you can't just come walking in like this.'

'Tell me where I can find Andrea and I'll walk right back out again,' I said, making myself comfortable.

'I want to know why you want to see her. She's my girlfriend.'

He added this last with a hint of pride in his voice and I felt a bit sorry for him. 'I want to talk to her about her relationship with Jason Khan and Ann Taylor.'

Something happened then. His body tensed, and

a perceptible flicker of fear crossed his face like a storm front. He knew something.

'Andrea hardly knew them,' he said, talking far too fast. 'I don't think there's much she can tell you. Now if you give me your card, I can—'

'I promise you I don't mean her any harm. I'm a private detective. So, please, why don't you just make it easier by telling me where I can find her?'

'Hold on a moment,' he said, then left the room.

I stood up to follow him, taking my time, keen not to spook him any more than he was already. But very interested, nevertheless, in his reaction to the mention of Jason Khan and Ann Taylor.

I hadn't taken more than two steps when he suddenly reappeared. Only this time he was carrying a gleaming kitchen knife with an eight-inch blade. He waved it at me as menacingly as he could manage, the tension in his features telling me that he liked this situation even less than I did, which, given that I was standing only three feet from the end of the blade, took some doing.

'Put that thing down,' I said, taking a step back, reluctant to go for the gun and ruin any chance of a meaningful discussion with either him or his girl-friend. 'You use it and you'll be going to prison for a long, long time.'

He stepped forward, gaining in confidence. 'I want you out of here now. Andrea's got nothing to say and she doesn't want to see you.'

'I think you should let her decide that.'

He took another step forward, waving the knife for effect. 'Out.'

I shrugged. 'All right, have it your way.' I went to go past him and he moved to the side. As we came level, I lunged forward and grabbed the wrist of his knife arm, twisting it away from him. He didn't immediately let go so I balled my other hand into a fist and slammed it down on the upturned forearm. He cried out in pain and the knife clattered to the floor. I kicked it out into the hallway, then forced the arm behind his back and pushed him down to his knees.

He tried to struggle so I pulled the arm higher up his back, and he quickly stopped. I put my mouth to his ear. 'I repeat: I am a private detective. I mean your girlfriend no harm, but it's important I speak to her. Two people have been murdered and she may have information that could help one of the dead men's families. Please. I need to know where to find her.'

'How do I know you're not going to hurt her?' he demanded.

'Why should I?' I asked, genuinely interested in his answer.

But he didn't tell me why. Instead, he asked me to let him go.

'Are you going to tell me where I can find her?'

'I'll come down with you. If you want to talk to her, you'll have to do it with me present as well.'

'Fair enough.' I released my grip and let him stand up.

'I'll need to phone her,' he said, starting to walk into the hallway, but I pulled him back by the neck of his Che Guevara T-shirt.

'Use mine,' I told him, handing over my mobile and picking up the knife. 'And please don't try and get her to disappear for a bit. I'll just come back.'

He nodded, looking shaken, but didn't take my phone. Instead, he produced his own and dialled the number. When she answered, the two of them conducted a hushed conversation, with him standing in the corner of the living room next to the TV, his back to me. I couldn't hear everything that was said, but the gist of it was that he'd heeded my warning and was trying to persuade her to meet me.

When he'd finished, he shoved the phone into the pocket of his combat trousers and told me that she'd join us in a café they both knew in twenty minutes. 'But you're wasting your time. She doesn't know anything.'

'We'll see,' I said, ignoring his hostile stare.

Twenty years in the Met had left me immune to that sort of look.

The café was called the Forest, and it was a ten-minute walk further north in the direction of Stoke Newington, which we made in near silence. I did introduce myself, however, giving him one of my flashy new business cards, and also got his name, which was Grant. He didn't really look much like a Grant. More a Nigel or a Tim. Not that I told him that.

When we stepped inside the door, it was eleven thirty-five by my watch, and there were about a dozen people in the place – mostly young, studenty types similar to Grant. A basic but colourful mural of a woodland scene took up most of the available wall-space, and sounds-of-the-rainforest type music was being piped from the speakers at each corner of the ceiling. A menu behind the fat woman at the counter offered 'Healthy Vegetarian Fare', but I got the feeling she preferred to eat at Burger King.

'I'm not stopping in this place,' I told Grant. 'Let's wait for Andrea outside.'

'What's wrong with it?' he asked, but I'd already walked out the door.

'It's horrible. And too busy. Let's go to a pub.'

He mumbled something under his breath but didn't argue, and we stood in the cold for a few minutes until I saw a look of recognition cross his face as an attractive black girl of about eighteen, with her hair in braids, approached. She was dressed in a three-quarter-length purple leather coat and embroidered flared jeans, and her manner was cautious, as if she expected to get arrested at any moment.

Grant stepped between us and explained who I was and why we were outside.

'I'd rather talk somewhere a little more intimate,' I told her, putting out a hand. 'My name's Mick Kane, and I appreciate you coming.'

'I don't know if Grant's told you,' she said, reluctantly shaking my hand and watching me with very large and very beautiful brown eyes, 'but I honestly don't see how I can be of help.'

'I did tell him,' put in Grant.

'Well, if I could buy you both a drink and just ask a few questions, then at least I'll feel like I'm doing my job.'

'OK,' she agreed, with the same reluctance she'd put into the handshake, 'but I haven't got a lot of time.'

I told her that this didn't matter and suggested we try the pub opposite.

Nobody argued so I crossed the road, and after a couple of seconds they followed.

# 27

Five minutes later, we were sitting at a corner table in the lounge bar of the pub across the road, the only customers in the place. I was on one side with a double orange juice. They were on the other: Grant with a pint of Stella, Andrea with a mineral water.

'How did you find me?' she asked.

'A friend of Jason's said you knew his girlfriend Ann.'

She nodded, before asking in a voice that was more mature than her years suggested what it was I wanted to know.

'Anything that could point to why Jason Khan was murdered.'

'I can't really help you. I knew Jason, but not that well. I knew Ann better. But why are you involved? There are plenty of police on the case, aren't there?'

'There are, but my client's concerned that things aren't progressing.'

'And your client is . . . ?'

I smiled. This one was no fool. I told her it was Asif Malik's uncle, and she seemed to accept the answer. She then told me that she couldn't think of any reason why Jason would have been murdered. 'I can't see how he would have got himself involved with anyone big enough or nasty enough to have bothered killing him. He was just a small-time dope dealer and thief. He thought he was one of the big boys, but from what I could see, he was just a loser.' She shrugged, as if there wasn't anything else she could add of any relevance.

I decided to change tack, and asked how she'd known Ann.

She relaxed visibly. Grant too.

'I first met her a couple of years back,' she said, fiddling with her glass. 'I'd been in foster care for ages before that, but then my foster mum got cancer and she couldn't look after me and my brother any more. We got split up and I got put into a care home in Camden while they tried to find another family for me. Ann already lived there, and she showed me the ropes and looked out for me. We just became mates. I liked her because she didn't take shit off people, but she was nice underneath as well, you know what I mean?'

I did. That had been my take on Ann as well, although I couldn't admit that to Andrea. I motioned for her to continue, keen to let her talk at her own pace.

'I was at Coleman House – the place in Camden – about six months and when I left and went back into foster care, me and Ann kept in touch. My foster family were living up in Barnet so it wasn't that difficult to get down and see her. We used to go out drinking, smoking a bit, having a giggle. But to be honest, I got sort of tired of all that. I didn't want to piss my life away. I wanted to do something a bit different. You know, get a job, get a life, go back to college. I met Grant . . .' At this point, she put her hand in his, and he pulled one of those yearning expressions you sometimes see in crap romance films. Somehow it endeared him to me. It's nice to see a bit of young love. 'Me and Ann drifted apart for a while,' she continued, 'but recently we'd started seeing more of each other again. She was beginning to grow up herself, and thinking of changing the way she lived her life.' She sighed. 'But it was all too late, wasn't it? Always is, for girls like Ann. You know, a lot of people wrote her off, and I bet quite a few of them think she got what was coming to her, because she did have a real temper. And she didn't like doing what she was told, either. But I tell you this: she was a good sort, she really was. She meant a lot to me.'

The mention of Coleman House brought back memories for me too. Memories of my last days in London, and how they'd ended in violence and murder. How a brief affair – a potential relationship – had ended before it had even begun. The woman had been Carla Graham and at one time she'd managed Coleman House. I think I might have even been in love with her. The image of her in my mind was unwelcome. It reminded me of events I'd rather not have remembered, both for my own part in them and for other people's.

I had my notebook out and made a point of writing down the details of Andrea's testimony. When I'd finished, I looked her in the eye and asked if Ann had committed suicide.

'That's what the police said, isn't it?' she answered, trying to sound casual. Avoiding my gaze.

'Yeah,' added Grant. 'And they ought to know, right?'

'Perhaps,' I said. 'But what do you think?'

'I think she did,' said Grant, with far too much in the way of conviction. 'She'd had things hard in recent months. And then with Jason dying, I think it all just proved too much, you know?'

Andrea sighed. 'I think Grant's probably right. It seems the most likely way it happened.'

'Did you both make statements to the police?'

Neither of them said anything for a moment. Grant looked furtive. Then Andrea spoke. 'They never asked, and because they didn't seem that interested in what had happened, I never approached them. My experiences of the police haven't been that great over the years. I tend to avoid them when I can.'

'From what I've gathered during my investigations,' I continued, 'Ann Taylor was a tough girl who'd been in care for many years. Statistically, people with that type of upbringing, or lack of it, tend to be the least likely to commit suicide. It's because they're tougher than most of us, more used to the hard knocks that life has to offer, so they don't get brought down so often. They're already there. Would you agree with that assessment of Ann, Andrea?'

'She was tough, but she had a vulnerable side, too. She hurt the same as anyone else, you know.'

And she had done, I remembered that. She'd cried in front of me once, three years earlier, when she thought that a friend of hers from Coleman House, who'd gone missing, was dead.

'When was the last time you saw Ann alive?' I asked.

Andrea hesitated, and I saw Grant glance at her, trying to catch her eye.

'About a week before she died, I think. Something like that.'

'Before Jason was murdered?'

She nodded.

'You didn't go round to offer your condolences after his death?'

She shook her head. 'No.'

I didn't believe her. She was lying. So was he. The question was why. 'But she was your friend,' I said. 'Someone who'd shown you the ropes when you

269

first went into Coleman House. Who'd helped you when you needed her help.'

This was the cue for Grant to butt in angrily. 'I don't like the tone of your questioning,' he snapped. 'We're only here out of the kindness of our hearts. We don't have to talk to you, and I don't think we're going to any more. Come on, Andrea.' He started to get to his feet, and she moved in her seat as if to follow.

'If you leave, I'll go straight to the police and give them your names. I'll also hand over the evidence as to why I don't think Ann committed suicide. Then they'll come looking for you, only next time you'll have to talk. And if there's anything you're hiding, they'll find it.'

They both stopped moving.

'If you talk to me I'll do everything in my power to protect you as sources. No-one'll ever know I spoke to you and you won't be bothered again.'

Grant sat back down. Andrea shuffled in her seat. For a few seconds there was an awkward silence.

I was going to ask them again whether they thought Ann had committed suicide, but then I remembered something from my first meeting with Emma. 'I understand that Ann had recently been receiving treatment for psychiatric problems. Can you tell me about that?'

They looked at each other again. Nervously.

'How much do you know about it?' asked Grant, after a pause.

'Very little,' I said, 'but I can find out more, easily enough. Why don't you make it easier and tell me?'

It was Andrea who spoke. 'She got referred to a psychiatrist about a year ago, after she'd got arrested for GBH. It was part of her bail conditions.'

'GBH? That's pretty serious. What did she do?'

'It was when she was working the streets. She used to do that before she got nicked. She had a bedsit in Holloway she took the punters back to. One night one of them gave her a load of trouble. He tried to get her to do stuff she didn't want to do, so she pulled a knife and let him have it across the face. Then she chased him out of the bedsit and cut him a couple of times round the back of the head. He needed about eighty stitches.' There was an unmistakable pride in her voice as she recounted this story. It was clear that, eighty stitches or not, the punter had got what was coming to him. It surprised me hearing her talk in a manner that so readily condoned violence. She was an attractive, well-dressed girl, and clearly intelligent. It was easy to forget that she'd probably had a few hard knocks herself over the years.

'So what did this psychiatrist have to say?'

'She reckoned she was suffering from some sort of schizophrenia. Ann told me she even wanted her sectioned, but that didn't happen. What they did was put her on a psychotherapy course.'

'And did that help?'

Again she paused. 'Yeah,' she said after a few seconds. 'It did. The jury found her not guilty because of diminished responsibility.'

'And that was that? She was released?'

'Yeah, that was that.' She looked down at the table.

'The schizophrenia Ann was suffering from. Did the psychiatrist say what had caused it?' This time the pause was longer. 'I can find out, you know, but I'd rather hear it from you.'

Grant leaned forward suddenly. 'The doctor who diagnosed her said that she thought it stemmed from her past. Apparently she'd been abused by her father when she was very young, and it was something to do with that.'

He took a generous swig from his beer, before pulling a metal tobacco tin from his pocket. I watched his hands as he took out a roll-up and lit it with a cheap plastic lighter. They were shaking slightly. He took a drag and blew a mouthful of smoke towards the empty chair beside me. I took out my own cigarettes, watching Andrea now, and offered her one. She shook her head and told me she'd quit.

'Why are you so interested in talking about Ann's psychiatric problems?' she demanded.

I could have said that it was because she and Grant were so interested in not talking about them, but I didn't. Instead I asked another question. 'Ann's allegations about her father. Did anyone ever follow them up? Presumably, if the judge believed the psychiatrist about her schizophrenia and what had initially caused it, then the police must have launched some sort of investigation into her father's alleged abuse.'

'Yeah, they did,' said Grant. 'And they nicked him as well. But they never got him to trial. He got released on bail and absconded.'

I felt my skin crawl.

*A stifling hotel room in Manila a year ago. A man who wanted to kill a little girl.*

'And now he's got what he deserved,' added Andrea, her voice full of barely suppressed rage.

I turned to her and was surprised at the intensity of her expression. She was staring right at me, the earlier furtiveness now completely gone.

'What do you mean?' I asked her, even though I was suddenly very sure of exactly what she meant.

'After he absconded, he left the country,' she said, 'and the next thing anyone heard he'd turned up dead in a hotel room somewhere in Asia. Someone had shot him, and good riddance to the bastard too.'

'I read something about that,' I said. 'But I don't remember it involving someone called Ann Taylor.'

'No,' said Andrea. 'That's because Ann changed her name after she ran away from home. Her real name was Sonya Blacklip.'

# 28

Andrea clammed up again after that, as if she sensed she'd said too much. And I guess she had, because by now I was beginning to get an angle on things. Grant clammed up as well, and although I kept them there for another ten minutes, I didn't find out anything else of interest.

Before they went, Andrea told me that they just wanted to be left alone, and implored me to respect their wishes. I said I would, feeling sorry for them as I watched them leave with their heads down and shoulders hunched, fearful of the consequences of my unwelcome entry into their lives. But I wasn't sure it was a promise I could keep. They knew a lot more than they were telling me, and I could only assume that Ann Taylor had told Andrea something, which Andrea had then told Grant; something that with Ann's death they'd sworn to keep quiet.

Ann's father, Richard Blacklip, had appeared in a

photograph with Les Pope. Pope had ordered the deaths of Malik and Jason Khan. Khan was Blacklip's daughter's boyfriend. Connections. Plenty of connections. But where, and to whom, did they all lead?

Fifteen minutes later I was walking down the Essex Road, not really thinking where I was going as I talked on the phone to Emma. She hadn't found out anything of great interest about Thadeus, or any links they might have had with either Malik, Pope or Nicholas Tyndall, and was still waiting for her contact to come back with the phone numbers listed on Slippery Billy's mobile. When I told her I needed details of Ann Taylor's illness, and who had treated her, she was none too pleased.

'I've got a lot on, Dennis. We've got an editorial meeting at three o'clock and I've got to be home at five thirty for the window guy. I've already spent hours on this.'

'Please. It's important.'

'Why? What's it got to do with the case?'

'Just trust me on this, OK? This once. Honestly, Emma, I wouldn't ask if I didn't think it could lead to something.'

She sighed loudly, but said she'd do what she could and I said I'd call her later.

I hung up and realized that I was standing outside the Half Moon pub. I'd drunk in here a few times back in the old days and it was less than half a mile from the police station where I'd spent so much of my working life, and only a few hundred yards from Islington Green and the bright lights of Upper Street. I stopped and peered in the window. Two old guys were sat at the bar laughing and smoking, while a barman I didn't recognize polished a glass behind them. I'd known the landlord here once upon a time. I'd pop in on the occasional afternoon after I'd worked an early shift, and we'd have a few pints together and a chinwag in the welcoming half-light of the lounge bar. I wondered if he was still here and even thought about going in. Thought about it seriously for a couple of seconds. It looked warm and inviting.

It was also too close to the old stomping ground. Too risky. Even letting it cross my mind was a stupid idea. I could never go back in here. Not now. Not in a month. Not ever. It was the past and the past for me was a closed book.

But the past never truly lets you go, even the parts you wish to forget. In the three days since I'd returned to this city, the yawning chasm that had been the days, the months, the years away, had shrunk to nothing. Every step, every smell, every familiar street had dragged me backwards through time, and now, with Andrea's mention of Coleman House, the ghosts of my last bitter days here were rising to haunt me again: the innocent dead; the guilty dead; and, of course, the mysterious and beautiful Carla Graham, the woman who for a few

276

fleeting moments I'd felt closer to than any other.

I stood there in the pale winter sunlight for longer than I should have done, until the cold began to seep beneath my skin. Finally, I turned and retraced my steps, pleased to be escaping from reminders of the old days. But as I walked, the ghosts of the dead shifted and swirled around me, reluctant, as always, to release me from their grip.

# 29

'Sonya Blacklip,' said Emma, telling me something I already knew.

She was sitting cross-legged on her orange sofa, dressed in a plain, loose-fitting white T-shirt and blue jeans. Her freshly washed hair fell loosely over her shoulders, and she was drinking one of the four-pack of Fosters I'd brought with me when I'd turned up at her place a few minutes earlier. She looked remarkably fragrant and relaxed, given the twenty-four hours she'd had. I was drinking from one of the other cans too and smoking a cigarette while I sat on the chair opposite, listening to what she had to say. It had just turned seven p.m., and I was feeling pretty relaxed myself.

'. . . Was the real name of Ann Taylor,' I added.

'That's right.' She then gave me a thorough run-down of what she had learnt about Ann, corroborating everything that Andrea and Grant had told me earlier.

'The course of psychotherapy that Ann was put on began in October of last year, and the doctor in charge of it was a woman called . . .' She paused while she consulted her notebook. '. . . Madeline Cheney, and from what I can gather she's an expert in her field. She's spent years studying the retrieval and reconstruction of memory. And after a number of one-to-one sessions with Ann, she managed to coax from her aspects of her past that Ann hadn't talked about to anyone else. What Dr Cheney found out made grim reading. I haven't been able to get all the details – most of it's not in the public domain – but she made a written submission to the court in which she testified that, in her opinion, Ann had suffered extensive sexual abuse as a child at the hands of her father, starting when she was as young as four, shortly after her mother died, and continuing until the age of eleven, at which point she finally ran away from home, and ended up here in London.' Emma paused for a moment and looked at me. 'The claims were pretty horrific. According to the testimony, it wasn't just her father who abused her, but his friends too, and there were other children who also suffered at the hands of the same group. However, when the police investigated, they never identified any of them, and the only person who faced any charges relating to the abuse was Ann's father, Richard. But he skipped bail, and ended up murdered in a hotel in Manila before the case ever came to trial.'

'I need to speak to Dr Cheney,' I said. 'Where does she practise? Do you know?'

'You don't ask for much, do you? I've got her number and address here.' She waved her notebook in my direction. 'But I'd like to know what this has got to do with the murders of Malik and Khan.'

I sipped my beer, thinking once again that I had a real soft spot for this girl. I told her about my question-and-answer session with Jamie Delly, including the situation I'd found him in, and the second session I'd had with Andrea and Grant.

Emma seemed more concerned about why Tyndall's men were torturing Delly than the actual torture itself. 'That suggests that Tyndall didn't actually have anything to do with the shooting of Malik and Khan, doesn't it? Because if he had, surely he'd have known what the two of them were meeting about?'

'I don't know,' I said.

'And if that's the case, then who sent me that doll with the blood on?'

'I don't know that either.'

'But there's something you're not telling me,' she stated firmly. 'Because nothing you've said so far points to Ann Taylor's mental state having anything to do with any of this. So what is it?'

'I think Andrea and Grant know more than they were letting on. They were very keen to avoid talking about Ann Taylor – particularly her psychotherapy.'

Emma shook her head. 'No, there's more to it than that. And I want to know what it is.'

There was no way I could avoid the question now. We'd reached a crux in our brief relationship. It's always been a habit of mine to absorb as much information as possible from the people I talk to, while giving out the absolute minimum. There's nothing to be gained from telling people your innermost secrets; doing that just makes you vulnerable. But this time I knew I was going to have to come clean. If I gave her any more grounds for suspicion, our partnership was finished.

'I got the names of the people whose numbers you gave me on Saturday,' she continued. 'The ones that supposedly came from Les Pope's mobile. One of the numbers on there also belongs to Les Pope. So what was he doing phoning himself? Unless, of course, you were bullshitting me and they didn't come from Pope's phone at all, but from someone else's. Which seems a lot more likely, don't you think?'

On the night I'd met her in the Ben Crouch Tavern, I'd observed that something in Emma's girlish demeanour invited people to underestimate her, and I'd made exactly that mistake. I suspected that I wasn't the first.

'All right. I'll tell you what I know and how I know it, but be prepared not to like what you hear.'

She gave a hollow laugh. 'You're a self-confessed mass murderer. Don't worry, I'm fully prepared on that front.'

So I told her. About Blacklip; about Slippery Billy West; about everything. The only things I kept from her were the locations of the killings, and where I'd been these past three years, but even that would have been fairly obvious, given where Blacklip's corpse had been found.

When I'd finished she didn't speak for a while. Instead she just sat there watching me. She gave no indication of how she felt, although it wasn't that hard to guess. I lit a cigarette and wondered if it was worth my while trying to justify what I'd done. In the end, I decided it wasn't. She knew that one of the men I'd killed had been a violent and long-standing child abuser, and that the other had been the hitman who'd slain Malik and Jason Khan. That should have been justification enough.

'Why didn't you tell me all this before?' she asked eventually.

'You didn't need to know. And it wouldn't have made you feel any better about me, would it?'

She started to say something, but I put up a hand to stop her. I could hear movement outside – the shuffling of feet.

We both listened.

The only sound in the room was the faint tinny chattering of the TV in the corner.

A loud knock on the door startled us both. We looked at each other.

The knock came again. 'Emma, are you there?' The voice was naturally loud – deep and authoritative. 'It's DCI Barron. I'm here with DS Boyd. We'd like a quick word, if we could.'

Emma looked alarmed. She glanced over at me for guidance and I motioned for her to let them in. I got up, picked up the ashtray I was using and my drink, and headed for the staircase, trying to keep as quiet as possible.

'Just coming,' I heard Emma call as I reached the third stair.

By the time she'd opened the door I was on the landing, leaning over the edge of the staircase to listen to whatever DCI Barron and his colleague had to say, and hoping that Emma didn't take the opportunity to get her name in lights and a plum job on one of the nationals by telling them about the fugitive currently in her house. I might have trusted her implicitly that morning but I wasn't so sure now, not with the law on the doorstep, and me having just admitted that there were a further two murders to add to my rapidly growing list of crimes.

'What can I do for you both?' I heard Emma ask as they came into the house and she offered them seats.

'You were asking about a gentleman by the name of Jamie Delly last night,' said Barron. 'You called one of my colleagues, John Gallan, asking if he had Delly's address. Would that be right?'

Emma must have said something in the affirmative, because Barron asked why she'd wanted to know.

'I wanted to speak to him about his brother, Jason,' she answered. 'As part of my own investigation.'

The female officer, Boyd, then spoke, but her voice was quieter and I couldn't make out what she was saying. Something about Emma's articles, it sounded like, and her tone was more abrupt.

Barron interjected to inform Emma that the police had been called to Jamie's flat that morning. 'We've been keeping an eye on him as part of our investigation into the Malik/Khan murders, and we received a call this morning from one of his neighbours saying there was a disturbance going on at his place, and the sounds of a struggle. DS Boyd and I were the first to attend. We saw a tall, slim, bearded man of about forty leaving the premises, but he disappeared before we could apprehend him. When we arrived at the flat we found Mr Delly semi-naked in his bathtub having suffered a number of very nasty injuries which suggested he'd been tortured. He's being treated in hospital now.'

Boyd asked Emma whether she knew of anyone fitting that description who might have had links with the case.

Emma said she didn't, and I offered her a silent

thank-you. But I wondered how long it would take them to link the description to the man who'd been involved in the Soho shootings. A while yet, I hoped. There was a lot of CCTV footage to go through and I'd been wearing completely different clothes. But it was a worry.

'What did you think Jamie Delly could tell you about Jason?' asked Boyd, her voice louder and clearer now.

Emma said this was her business, but Boyd replied that given what had happened that morning it was police business as well.

'I'm still interested in finding a motive for the murders,' Emma explained. 'It's a high-profile case but it doesn't seem to be moving very fast. I thought Jamie might be able to shed some light on things. I was going to visit him tomorrow.'

'Well, he's not saying anything to us,' said Barron, 'so if you get any information out of him, please let us know.'

Emma said she would.

The conversation continued with Barron and Boyd trying to find out where Emma was with her own investigations. Barron then suggested that, given the tone of her articles, she should be extra vigilant in case she herself became a target, which was when she told them about the break-in the previous night and the bloodied doll that had been left behind as a warning. After admonishing her for not reporting the incident, and asking to see the doll, he became even more forceful in his warnings. His tone was genuine enough, though, and I was confident that the main reason he was saying all this was because he was worried for her. I wasn't sure I could say the same about Boyd. Her manner was more hostile, which I suppose was understandable. As a woman she wouldn't be so easily impressed by a pretty girl, and, like most coppers, she didn't like journalists nosing into her investigations, particularly when those journalists were being critical.

'We can offer you police protection if you like,' said Barron, promising to take the doll to the station for further examination, but Emma declined.

Boyd then asked if she could use the bathroom. I heard her get to her feet as Emma told her it was first left at the top of the stairs.

As Boyd climbed the stairs, I retreated into Emma's bedroom and went round to the far side of her bed, feeling like a kid again as I sunk to my hands and knees and made myself as inconspicuous as possible in the darkness.

I heard her reach the top of the stairs, but rather than go straight on into the bathroom, she stopped. A second later, the door to the bedroom made a scuffing noise as it was pushed open, and I could sense her in here with me. She moved swiftly across the carpet and I suddenly wondered what on earth I'd do if she discovered me here: the man she'd seen that morning at Delly's place, hunched on the floor in front of her. I began to sweat.

A few more steps and she was almost on me. I gritted my teeth and remained as still as possible, silencing even my breathing and resisting the urge to go for my gun.

It was only when her legs were three feet away from my head that she stopped, and I could see her looking around Emma's desk. She opened the desk drawer and had a quick poke about inside. It looked like she had plastic police-issue gloves on.

I stayed as still as a statue, knowing that she only had to turn her head ever so slightly and drop her gaze downwards and the lives of the four people in this house would be changed for ever. One tiny movement; such huge ramifications.

But she didn't. Instead, she shut the drawer without removing anything, turned on her heels, and left the room. A few seconds later I heard the toilet flushing and Boyd heading back down the stairs. It was at that point that I finally started breathing properly again.

They didn't stay long after that. I couldn't hear what they were saying because I remained in the bedroom, but I heard the front door open and shut, and after what felt like a suitable interval, I got to my feet and emerged from my hiding place.

When I returned to the lounge, Emma was smoking a cigarette and looking stressed. 'I ought to bloody well kick you out,' she told me bitterly.

'What if they talk to my neighbours and one of them saw you coming in?'

'No-one's seen me round here and I'll be very careful that they don't in future,' I promised her, before changing the subject. 'Did you know that when DS Boyd came upstairs she rifled through your desk drawer?'

Emma frowned. 'Did she? What do you think she was looking for?'

'I don't know. Sources, information, anything, I suppose.'

'Isn't that illegal?'

'It is, and anything she found would be inadmissable in court, but it's the sort of thing that happens now and again. The police are like anyone else: they want results, and sometimes they're prepared to cut corners. But I was surprised she felt the need to do that. I mean, most of the sources for your articles on this case have been cops, haven't they?'

She nodded, still frowning.

'Is Barron one of your contacts?' I asked, assuming by the way he'd been talking to her that he was.

'Yes, he's been helpful on this case.'

'I don't recognize the name. Is he based at Islington?'

She shook her head. 'No. He's retired, technically, but they brought him back for this case because the Met's so short of detectives. They're doing that a lot these days.'

'And who was the other guy? The one you

phoned about Delly's address?' Again, it had been a name I hadn't recognized.

'John Gallan. He's a DI at Islington. A nice guy, and helpful too, but he'd still arrest me like a shot if he knew I was harbouring you.'

It was then that I realized quite how much danger I was putting her in by using her as my unofficial assistant, and I knew it was going to have to stop. 'Look, I know I'm causing you problems with my involvement in this, so I'm going to say goodbye now. Thanks for all your help, and if I do end up finding out the motive behind the Malik and Khan killings, I'll let you know. All I'd ask in the meantime is that you don't tell anyone I'm back here.'

'It's not safe for you either, Dennis. My advice would be to return to the place you came from while you're still in a position to.'

Blondie had said pretty much the same thing to me two days ago and, like Emma, he'd had a point. But I was getting close now, I could feel it, and I didn't want to let go. For the last three years life had been easy, but it had also been unfulfilling. The truth was, I liked hunting. For twenty years, prior to my ignominious departure from England, I'd hunted criminals every day, sometimes for insignificant crimes, sometimes for murder, and I'd enjoyed it. I'd enjoyed the chase, the evidence-gathering, the slow but steady peeling away of the layers of fat to reveal the bare bones of the mystery beneath, the one mistake that would ensnare my prey. The fact that the prey usually ended up getting a far lower sentence than his crime deserved was a matter of some disappointment, but never enough to stop me from trying again. And now, free from the constraints of an under-manned and overregulated police force, the prey wouldn't escape so lightly. And I was enjoying the puzzle, too. This was a real mystery – not one of the grimy, pitiful tragedies that make up so much of the world's murder statistics. A series of murders and attempted murders had been committed, yet I still had no initial motive. All I knew was that if I found the motive, all the layers would peel away and I'd be left with my solution. When you're a twenty-year copper, ex or current, you don't turn away from a challenge like that. You revel in it. Even if the stakes were so high.

I walked over to the chair and picked up my coat. 'If you could give me the contact details of the psychotherapist who treated Ann, I'd appreciate it.'

Emma sighed. 'Look, sit down.'

'I thought . . .'

'I know I ought to let you go, but I've invested a lot of effort in this case; it's something that I've watched the police plod through almost as if they don't want to solve it, and because of that, I've been determined to. And now it seems there's even more to it than I thought. Do you honestly think that Ann's father had something to do with it?'

She returned to her original place on the sofa, so I sat down too.

'Well, this is what we've got,' I said. 'Les Pope ordered and arranged the murder of Richard Blacklip a year ago, very shortly after Blacklip had been charged with offences relating to the sexual abuse of his daughter, Ann, which had taken place some years earlier. Ann was the girlfriend of Jason Khan. Jason Khan was shot just over five weeks ago, along with Asif Malik, after Khan telephoned Malik and called him to a meeting in a café. It may well be that Jason had important information he wanted to share with Malik, someone who, according to his brother, he knew from the past. We still don't know what that information concerned. It might have been something to do with Thadeus Holdings, or Nicholas Tyndall and his operations, or Ann herself. Whatever it was, it was something very serious, and Ann was no doubt privy to it as well, because she was killed a few days later. So it's possible it had something to do with the relevations her psychotherapy revealed. But if that's the case, why did Ann live for so long after her father's death without coming to any harm? Why didn't they get rid of her at the time of his arrest if her knowledge was that incendiary?'

'That's why I can't see how it can be anything to do with it.'

'It may not be, but the Blacklip connection's too coincidental to pass up without looking at further. I need to visit the psychotherapist and see what light she can throw on things.'

'Do you think that's a good idea?'

'I don't want you doing it. Barron's right: you are taking a risk if you're seen to still be sniffing around. Leave it with me. I think it'd be wise if you took a bit of a back seat for the moment.'

For once, Emma didn't argue. In fact, she surprised me. She asked me if I was hungry. 'I'm going to cook some spaghetti in tomato sauce. You can stay for some if you want.'

One thing I've learned through life is never to turn down an invitation from an attractive lady. You've always got too much time to regret it.

Which was a pity, really, because had I left there and then, things might have turned out very differently.

# 30

While Emma prepared the dinner, I helped myself to another can of Fosters and turned the volume up on the telly. Channel 4 news was on and I watched a piece about the rise of obesity amongst the country's schoolchildren, complete with grim footage of waddling kids in gym shorts, before Britain's new Lord Chief Justice popped up to be interviewed by the newsreader about comments he'd made suggesting that prison should only be reserved for the most violent offenders. Apparently, he'd claimed that putting burglars, thieves, even first-time muggers behind bars only made them worse.

The new Lord Chief Justice was called Parnham-Jones, and for the interview he was without the old wig and gown; instead he wore a plain black suit with a sky-blue silk tie and matching handkerchief, and was sitting in an armchair next to a roaring fire in his country home. He was in his early sixties, I'd guess, white-haired, with the bearing and aquiline

293

features of a public-school-educated patrician not used to, or much comfortable with, criticism. I would have bet all the money I'd got stashed in my poky little hotel room that he'd never been on the receiving end of a crime in his life. And commentators and politicians wondered why the public had lost faith in Britain's criminal justice system.

Parnham-Jones defended his comments in soothing, thoughtful tones, but with an underlying steel that brooked no dissent, always making a point of addressing the camera directly. Prison, he explained, was the university of crime. Send first- and second-time offenders there and they were not only likely to reoffend but to move on to more serious offences. Far better to ease the terrible overcrowding in the prisons and give them meaningful community-based sentences instead.

To be fair to the guy, he put his point across well, and with the sort of succinctness that TV interviewers love, but you had to wonder how much he really knew about what was going on out there. In my experience, community-based sentences – painting old ladies' houses, cleaning walls of graffiti, drug-treatment programmes – tended to be a bit of a joke. They were badly administered, the criminals often only turned up when they fancied it, and they never felt much like a punishment. I'm not 100 per cent sure that prison's a lot better in terms of turning people away from crime (in the end, criminals commit their crimes knowing full well they're wrong, but not really being too bothered about that fact, so trying to rehabilitate them's a waste of time), but at least when a guy's banged up he's not actually out there thieving, mugging, or whatever. In that sense, whatever the liberals amongst us might say, prison works.

Emma came back in with the spaghetti and a plate of garlic bread and we ate at the table with the TV off.

You get that sense sometimes, or I do anyway, that things are looking up for you, and that the worst is over. In my experience, it's usually followed by a very heavy fall. But as I sat there demolishing Emma's cooking (and it was very good), while quaffing my second can of Fosters, I couldn't help forgetting about my worries.

After we'd finished eating, we cleared away and she put on a CD of Van Morrison's greatest hits. I asked her how she'd got into journalism.

She smiled. 'I've always liked a good story, and I did English at A level, so that was the foundation. Then when I was at sixth-form college, just before our exams, they had a careers fair where representatives from different industries set up stalls in the refectory so that we could go and talk to them. The journalist who came from the local paper was only a couple of years older than me and he was quite nice-looking, so I got chatting to him, we ended up going for a drink, and he got me a job on the paper.

I was meant to go away to uni, but I ended up marrying him. God knows why. I think it was because my dad was so against it. He had all these ideas of what career path I should take. He wanted me to become a lawyer, like him.'

'So where's the husband now?'

'We were young and it didn't last, but by then I'd got a taste for the job. After the split, I moved up to town and I've been working here ever since. The money's not fantastic but it gives me independence.'

I wondered why she wasn't on a national newspaper – she certainly seemed to have enough talent – but chose not to say anything, in case I hit a raw nerve. 'And this place? Is it yours?'

She smiled proudly. 'It is. With a little bit of help from my parents.'

Which was typical. You never saw a poor lawyer. 'You need all the help you can get with the prices these days,' I said, or something equally inane.

She asked me how I ended up being a policeman, and I gave her the honest answer: because at one time I'd thought that it was a useful, socially acceptable job, and I'd genuinely believed I'd make a difference.

'How did you end up as a hitman?'

I cringed a little when she called it that. It wasn't how I saw myself, somehow. 'Is this an interview?'

She shook her head, her expression one of genuine interest. 'No, it isn't, but I would like to know.'

I thought about the answer for a long time, and as I mulled it over I lit a cigarette, as if that would somehow make answering easier. At the same time, I also thought about Malik. I pictured him up there in heaven, or whatever the Islamic equivalent was, looking down at me with a mixture of interest and disapproval as he too waited for my answer. I knew that whatever I said would never have been enough to have earned his forgiveness.

'Because I wasn't strong enough, or sensible enough, to say no,' I said eventually, and hoped that Malik would have at least half approved of that.

Emma was unconvinced. 'But why did you decide to kill people for money?'

I sighed. 'I thought when I did what I did that I was doing the world a favour. I thought I was killing people who deserved it.'

'But Dennis, you can't just be a judge, jury and executioner,' she said, with a hint of educated self-righteousness. 'You haven't got the right to decide who dies and who doesn't. No-one has. And you're still doing it. Only a few weeks ago, you shot the suspect in the Malik and Khan murders.'

'Slippery Billy? He deserved it. If he hadn't been a murderer, I wouldn't have killed him.'

She paused, unsure, I think, what else to say. I'm not the best person to argue with about the ethics of murder, because I can sympathize with other points of view. In the end, I do what I do; and I've done it because at the time my instincts have told me to. It's no justification, but at least it's a reason, and some people don't even have one of those.

Emma sat forward in the seat and watched me intensely. It was a little disconcerting, but somehow I didn't want her to stop. It felt good to be the centre of attention for once.

'Do you really consider yourself one of the good guys, Dennis?' she said softly. 'Don't you ever worry that you might be just as bad as the people you put down?'

She looked beautiful then; the perfectly rounded features of her pale face amidst the flowing auburn hair, and those big, smiling, hypnotic eyes that seemed to drag you further and further in. And I knew that whatever I replied was going to disappoint her.

In the end, I settled for what I thought was honesty.

'No,' I said simply.


We slept together that night.

It just happened. We drank some more, watched the TV, moved off the more difficult subjects (although she tried occasionally to come back to them), and as the evening progressed I'd felt that there was something growing between us. I liked her anyway, and had done since the moment we'd met, but I was also detecting a growing warmth coming back the other way, as if she'd finally accepted me for who I was and was prepared to stop getting too uptight about it. Or maybe it was just the booze.

I'm no Valentino, and like most men I've had less practice than I would have liked over the years, but after the last of the beer had gone and we were halfway through a bottle of red wine, she'd stood up to go into the kitchen for something, and I'd followed her in there. She'd turned round, sensing my presence, and I'd taken her in my arms and kissed her. For a second she hadn't reacted and I'd thought that maybe my confidence in my own charm was misplaced, but then she'd kissed me back – hard and with passion – and a few minutes later, still entwined in each other's arms, we'd danced and stumbled our way up the stairs and into the bedroom, clothes strewn behind us. I'd wondered briefly what the hell I was doing; then, as we fell on the bed and she giggled as I kissed her neck and tugged at her underwear, I'd ceased caring.

Afterwards we lay naked on the bed and smoked, and I experienced a peculiar feeling of detachment, as if somehow I wasn't there and it hadn't really happened. I listened to the sounds of the night – the cars humming faintly past on the main road, the occasional drunken shout from somewhere in the distance – and tried to relax and enjoy the moment. I let my fingers drift down to her belly, pale and flat in the perma-glow of the city's lights, but all the time my instincts were talking to me, trawling back through the many dark experiences of my life and predicting the winding, uncertain path of my short-term future.

And what they told me was as unnerving as it was accurate.

That a fall was definitely coming.

# 31

I was woken by the alarm at seven the next morning after a good night's sleep, which would have benefited from being an hour or two longer. But who was I to complain? Emma's bed was a lot more comfortable than the one in my hotel room, and there was the added bonus of having her in it. I lay where I was, eyes half closed, while she had a shower, but when she came back I could see that she wanted me gone.

'I've got to be in the office for nine,' she said, chucking me my clothes, 'but I'll be on the mobile. I'm not trying to hurry you or anything, but you understand . . .'

I told her I did, and heaved myself out of bed. 'I'll leave you in peace, and I'll check in later when I've got something. OK?'

She smiled but it looked forced. I felt like telling her not to worry; that it wasn't her fault. I don't suppose it was easy for someone like Emma – a nice, well-brought-up girl with a decent job – to come to terms with the fact that she'd slept with a killer. Especially one who was on the run, and currently in her house. She gave me the number of Ann's psychotherapist, Dr Cheney, and I wrote it down, trying not to stare as she pulled on her skirt.

At the front door, there was one of those pauses where neither party's quite sure what to do or what to say. I leant forward and kissed her gently on the cheek, and she turned her face and planted one on mine. It felt good enough.

'See you later,' I said, and hurried out the door without looking back, feeling like a kid who'd stayed out late without telling his parents.

Dr Madeline Cheney was not the easiest woman to get hold of. I called her just after nine o'clock from the Italian café near my hotel and got her secretary. Dr Cheney was busy, I was told in very professional, patient-friendly tones. If I wanted to make an appointment, I could go through her, the secretary.

I decided to come clean (or as clean as I was going to get in this investigation) and told her that I was a private detective, and that my enquiry related to one of Dr Cheney's former patients, Ann Taylor, now deceased. It was urgent, I explained, that I speak with Dr Cheney as soon as possible. The secretary sounded suitably excited and said she'd pass the message on. I thanked her, left my mobile number and rang off.

As I'd hoped, the secretary had taken my request seriously, and her boss returned the call half an hour later, while I was back in the hotel room.

'Good morning, this is Dr Madeline Cheney,' she said guardedly. Her accent was middle class, well-educated, and at a guess belonged to a woman in her early to mid forties. 'You called me earlier. My secretary said it was urgent.'

I introduced myself as Mick Kane and confirmed that it was urgent. 'It concerns Ann Taylor.'

There was a pause before she spoke again. 'Ann? It seems she's far more popular in death than she ever was in life. I've already had the coroner's office on to me this week. What's your connection with the case, Mr Kane?'

I told her the same story I'd originally told Emma: that I was representing Asif Malik's uncle, and that Ann's name had come up during the course of my investigation. She didn't seem surprised by the mention of Malik, so I assumed she already knew about his part in the proceedings.

'I'm very busy today,' she said.

'Is there no way you can fit me in? I wouldn't ask if it wasn't important.'

'Why is it so important? Has something happened?'

'I'm not sure,' I answered, hoping that by being

enigmatic I could secure her interest. 'I can't really talk about it over the phone.'

She thought about it for a moment, then announced that she could see me for half an hour that afternoon at three o'clock. 'But I'd like to be sure that you are who you say you are.'

I'd been half expecting suspicion, so I told her that I'd been working with Emma Neilson, the journalist who'd alerted people to the fact that Ann's death might not have been accidental.

'I tend to agree with her theory,' I added, and gave her Emma's number. 'You could also phone Mohammed Mela, my client, although he can be difficult to get hold of.' I gave her a number off the top of my head, and hoped she'd try Emma rather than him.

Dr Cheney fired off a rapid set of directions to her practice in the village of Aldermaston, a ninety-minute drive away in Berkshire, and told me she'd see me at three. We both hung up.

Now I needed transport. A quick look at the road map in a nearby bookshop showed me that Aldermaston was a fair way off the beaten track. I was going to have to hire a car.

When you live under a false identity, you have to be fully equipped. You don't just need a passport in your new name, you need a driving licence, a birth certificate and even genuine credit cards. It's a hassle, but it pays to be thorough, and I was. Much of my documentation had originated in the UK

304

before I left (I think I always knew that at some point my double life would unravel), but the gaps had been filled using expert forgers in the Philippines. So when I went into the Hertz rental office in Marble Arch later that morning, I knew there'd be no problem.

And there wasn't. Fifteen minutes later, I was crawling through traffic in a silver Ford Orion in the direction of the M25, and hoping that this wasn't going to turn out to be a wild goose chase.

# 32

Aldermaston was one of those quintessential English villages that you see in all the guidebooks. Situated on the edge of the Berkshire downs, and surrounded by green fields and pretty copses of oak and beech trees, it was little more than a collection of houses and converted barns, with the odd thatched roof thrown in, nestling on either side of a road that somehow seemed more suited to a horse and cart than the steady procession of cars that passed up and down it. There was a top-secret establishment that allegedly contained many of the country's nuclear weapons somewhere round here but I didn't see any evidence of it on the way in, and even on a grey, sullen day like this one, the village stood out like a tranquil oasis after the intensity of London.

I drove down what passed for the high street: a narrow road with terraced red-brick buildings on either side, some of which clearly dated back hundreds of years, that contained a handful of antiques shops and estate agents. There was an Elizabethan-style pub on the corner, where the road forked at a near right-angle as it came to a mini-roundabout. A notice board outside advertised high-quality food. I was early so I stopped there for a pint and a steak and kidney pie, which was indeed high-quality but also high-priced. While I was there, I asked the barman – who had a very pink face and a drinker's nose – for directions to the Cheney practice. He obviously knew her business, because he gave me them but conspicuously avoided me after that. I don't think he liked the thought of having the mentally ill dining on his high-quality food.

Dr Cheney's practice was in a large, modern house that I assumed was a combination of home and office, situated a few hundred yards down the right-hand fork in the road. It wasn't quite an eye-sore, but you could argue it came close, with a brand new tarmac driveway out the front that would have amply parked a dozen cars. Today, however, there were only two: a Range Rover and a Fiat Punto. I pulled up alongside the Range Rover and got out. It was ten to three.

There were two doors at the front of the house. A sign on the main one asked all callers to the practice to use the other, so I rang on the buzzer and was let in without preamble. I found myself in a small

307

wood-panelled foyer that bore more than a passing resemblance to the inside of a Scandinavian sauna. An attractive young receptionist sat at a desk in front of me, wearing a white coat and a welcoming smile that showed a lot of teeth.

I introduced myself with a smile of my own, and announced my business.

'Please take a seat, Mr Kane. I'll let Dr Cheney know you're here.' She stood up and disappeared through a door behind the desk, while I admired the certificates from various psychiatric bodies testifying to Dr Cheney's high standards in the field. I know any idiot could buy these sort of things over the Internet and there was no guarantee that they meant anything, but I had a feeling that in Dr Cheney's case, they did.

The secretary emerged a few seconds later to inform me that, if I'd like to go through, the doctor would see me now. The words immediately brought back terrible memories of visiting the medical profession in my youth, and I was glad I had nothing wrong with me. Or nothing Dr Cheney could cure, anyway. The secretary asked if I'd like a coffee, and I thanked her and said that I would. Milk, one sugar. It was all very civilized.

I stepped inside Dr Cheney's huge office, which was decorated in the same style as the reception area but on a significantly bigger scale, complete with a number of chairs and several desks, but no sign of that old classic, the couch. A slim, tanned woman with a well-worn face and wide brown eyes stepped seemingly out of nowhere and shook my hand with a powerful grip. Her eyes appraised me coolly from behind a pair of fashionable black-rimmed glasses, but the smile itself was warm.

We exchanged pleasantries and she invited me to take a seat in front of her desk, which was at the far end of the room. It was immaculately tidy.

'What is it I can do for you, Mr Kane?' she asked, sitting down with her back ramrod straight and folding her hands slowly and carefully across her lap. It was a disconcerting gesture, and if it was meant to put her patients at ease it didn't work, but then I assumed it was being done specially for me.

I briefly explained the facts of the case, as they concerned her. 'Three people are dead: Mr Khan, Mr Malik and Miss Taylor, all of whom are connected with each other. There is, as you're no doubt aware, a major police investigation going on into the murders, but Mr Malik's uncle wants a second opinion.'

'And one private detective's work is better than the combined expertise of the Metropolitan Police?'

'At the moment, the combined expertise of the Metropolitan Police isn't getting very far. The investigation's been going for close to six weeks, and they've yet to make an arrest, let alone bring a charge of murder against anyone. And until Miss Neilson brought up the subject, Ann Taylor's death wasn't even being treated as part of the inquiry. As far as I'm aware, it still isn't. I'm certainly not suggesting that I can do any better than the officers involved in the case, but I'm hoping I can come at it from a different perspective, and get somewhere that way.'

She nodded slowly, as if accepting my answer, while continuing to appraise me. 'You are aware that what is said between a doctor and her patient is entirely confidential. Therefore, I can only repeat to you what Ann wanted brought out into the open, nothing else.'

She paused for a moment while her secretary came in with the coffee, and I told her that I was fine with that.

'How much of the history do you know?' she asked.

'I know the basics. That she was referred to you by another doctor, who felt she had a possible personality disorder that might have been the cause of the violent attack she committed. And that you got her to remember aspects of her past, which led to her father being arrested and charged with offences of child abuse. But I know very little about the details of the abuse, other than that it was very serious.'

Dr Cheney gave me a thin smile. 'Let me explain something to you, Mr Kane. I'm not a great believer in what in most circles these days is called repressed memory syndrome.' I think I must have looked a bit blank, because she continued,

'Repressed memory is when a patient is considered to have undergone a trauma or traumas so intense that the brain's only coping mechanism is to wipe the memories clean. Effectively, the patient forgets what has happened and carries on with life. It's believed by some within the psychiatric field that these memories can be returned to the conscious mind by certain types of treatment, particularly hypnotherapy. Naturally, it's an area of huge controversy, since it allows for accusations to be made where there is no corroborating evidence, and therefore perfectly innocent people can find themselves facing criminal charges for acts they never committed. But this wasn't the situation with Ann. You see, I wouldn't describe her memories as wholly repressed. I think she knew perfectly well what had happened to her, but created a veneer of toughness to try to cope with it. However, when I uncovered what had happened in her past, the accusations she made were not, I felt, taken seriously enough by the police, because of the controversy surrounding this issue of repressed memory. Although the jury at her trial believed her and she was found innocent of the charge against her by reason of diminished responsibility, the police took a more cynical view of her claims, and their investigation into the allegations was wholly inadequate.'

'But they arrested her father, Richard Blacklip.'

'Yes, they did that. They had little choice but to

do that. However, his abuse was what might euphemistically be called the tip of the iceberg.'

'So what were they? The claims she made?'

'That she was introduced to sex at the age of four by her father, shortly after her mother died. That at first the abuse simply involved him touching Ann intimately, then steadily became more serious as she grew older. Intercourse, both vaginal and anal. Oral sex. For years, she slept in his bed every night and believed that what was happening to her was normal, although Blacklip constantly reminded her never to tell a soul, and during the whole time she spent with him, she never did. Her schoolwork was below average, but not significantly so, and she went through the schooling system without any of her teachers becoming unduly concerned, although as time went by, her attendance levels began to drop off.

'Ann described to me how the relationship between her and her father began to change when she was about nine years old. For the first time, he began involving other people – men he described as her uncles, although she'd never seen any of them before. He would take her to different houses, to what he called "parties", where his friends – these men he called her uncles – would sexually assault her, usually in a group setting. She wasn't sure of their exact number – she said somewhere between five and eight, and the majority of them wore masks. Her descriptions of the events that took place, and how things were organized, had the very real ring of authenticity.'

'But, given her background, it's possible she could have made them up?'

Her expression suggested very strongly that it wasn't. 'In my professional opinion, and this is exactly what I told the investigating officers more than a year ago, she was not making these allegations up. She was telling the truth. And this was evidenced by the fact that on further investigation, it transpired that her father had child-abuse convictions dating back many years and under several different names.'

'Christ,' I said. 'Poor girl.' Once again I was reminded of the empty, directionless and ultimately short life of Ann Taylor. Without a father like Blacklip, I wondered how different things could have been. Could she have grown up into a well-adjusted and happy young woman? Of course she could have done. As far as I was concerned, Blacklip had killed her just the same as if it had been his fingers round the syringe that had pumped her full of drugs. If ever I'd needed justification for what I'd done to him back in Manila, then this was it.

'Poor girl, indeed,' repeated Dr Cheney. 'Her life was an absolute tragedy, made worse by the fact that no-one else has ever been charged in connection with any of the crimes against her, and now that her father has also died in mysterious circumstances ... You heard about that, didn't you?'

'Yes, I did. I would have called it good riddance if it wasn't for the fact that there are a lot of questions he could answer if he was still alive. Like who else was involved.'

'It sounds to me as if you think that Ann's death and the deaths of the other people you mentioned – the boyfriend and the police officer – have something to do with these events in her past?'

'I like to take things one step at a time,' I answered carefully. 'At the moment it's only one avenue of inquiry, but it's certainly one that's worth pursuing. Was that the full extent of Ann's allegations, or was there more?'

For a moment Dr Cheney was silent, her eyes boring into mine.

'If there is,' I said, prompting her, 'it's important that I know.'

'Yes,' she said eventually. 'There was more.'

The room suddenly felt very quiet. I wanted a smoke, but I also knew better than to ask in here. There was no way Dr Cheney was a smoker. Sometimes you can just tell.

'I felt, you see, that Ann was holding something back,' she continued. 'But I wasn't sure what it could be. What she'd told me already had been horrifying enough, but somehow it didn't quite fit with the girl I had sitting in front of me. When Ann came to me she had deep-seated emotional

314

problems, and a propensity for extreme violence towards those whom she believed had done her wrong, and during our sessions it became increasingly clear that there was violence in her past, something she'd experienced that wasn't explained by what she'd told me already. That acted as the catalyst for her finally leaving her home and father. After all, she'd been used to the treatment she was receiving; she saw it as normal. I therefore became convinced that something else had happened, something that she desperately wanted to repress because it was simply too traumatic. We had a number of sessions together, and slowly, and as gently as I could, I finally extracted from her what it was.'

Again, silence filled the room. This time I made no prompt. I waited. I knew she'd tell me.

She cleared her throat. 'Because Ann repeated these allegations to the police, and because I believed what she said and would like something done about it, if indeed after all this time it's still possible, I will tell you. But only because of that. According to what Ann told me, the reason she left was because she witnessed a murder.'

I tensed, my mouth feeling dry. 'Whose?'

'A young girl's.'

I exhaled more loudly than I'd expected, remembering Blacklip back in that hotel room. Requesting a little girl to kill.

'What happened?'

315

'The "parties" that Ann was forced to attend by her father became, she said, progressively nastier. The participants started to be much rougher with her than they had been originally. A new participant also became involved, a man who always wore a black leather mask and whom the others tended to defer to. This man was apparently the most violent of them all. Also, for the first time, other young girls were present. She remembered two being there who were slightly older – twelve or thirteen – although she didn't recognize them.'

Dr Cheney stopped for a moment and took a deep breath. 'Later, at another party at which Ann said there were five men including her father present, there was also another girl there, about the same age as Ann. Again, Ann didn't recognize her, but she remembered that the girl was in great distress. She was sobbing and begging her tormentors to stop, but, according to Ann, this simply served to spur them on even more. The violence got more and more out of hand. They started hitting her as they had sex with her, and the abuser with the black mask produced a knife and held it to her throat while she was forced to commit certain acts with him.' Her voice, which up until that point had been dispassionate, cracked a little. 'Ann remembers the girl choking and the man in the black mask cutting her face with the knife, and then someone – she couldn't remember who – ushered her – Ann – out and locked her in an adjoining room. She was made to sit there in darkness for an indeterminate period of time, hearing the muffled and desperate screams of the other girl, until finally they stopped altogether.

'Some time after that, her father came for her. By now he was fully dressed, but Ann said that he looked tired and had several blood spots on his neck. He told her to forget what she'd seen, then led her out of the house, but as they were going past the room where the assault had taken place, the door opened and she saw inside for a few seconds. There were two men on the sofa, both still naked, their masks now removed. They turned away as soon as they saw her and she didn't get much of a look at them because it was what was on the floor that caught her attention. There was a large sack tied at one end, which, by the way it was stretched, looked as if it contained a body. There were several large bloodstains showing through and no sign of the other girl. Whoever had opened the door then shut it very quickly, and Ann said her father became agitated and hurried her out, telling her once again to forget what she'd seen, because if she ever repeated it, the man in the black mask would come back for her. She was eleven years old at the time, Mr Kane. She believed him.'

'And you believed her? I'm not suggesting that she made it up, but if she was truly keen to see her father suffer, is it not possible that she could have told you this just to make sure?'

'I don't think so. She never wanted her father prosecuted; she just wanted to be left alone so that she could forget the whole thing. However, I advised her to tell the police, because I was concerned about what Richard Blacklip might still be doing. Also, I knew that it would help her case if she allowed me to tell the court about what had come out in our sessions, particularly if she was then seen to be co-operating with the police in building a case against him.'

'But the police never followed it up? About the murder, I mean?'

'Not at the time, no. They said they'd looked into it, but without a body, a location for the crime, any other corroborating witnesses or even an exact date, there wasn't a great deal they could do. Obviously they questioned Blacklip, but he denied all knowledge of such a thing. In fact, he denied everything and claimed he was a doting father, but a search of the house uncovered pornographic material involving young children, and further investigation revealed that he'd had these other convictions in the past. And now, of course, he can't be questioned any further.'

'Did Ann give you a description of this girl?'

Dr Cheney gave a little shake of her head. 'Only that she was about her own age, and that she had shortish brown hair.'

I wrote this down in my notebook. 'Have you heard from the police recently?'

She nodded, finishing her coffee. I hadn't touched mine. 'Yes. I had a visit from a policeman a few weeks ago, not long after the shootings you're investigating.'

I was surprised that Dr Cheney hadn't mentioned this earlier. 'Really? About Ann? What did he want to know?'

'He asked similar questions to you. He wanted to know the specifics of Ann's claims. I explained to him that I'd told the police everything at the time, but they'd chosen to do nothing. He apologized and said he was from the murder investigation . . .'

'The one into the deaths of Asif Malik and Jason Khan?'

'That's right. He said he hadn't been a part of the original inquiry into Ann's claims, and asked me to repeat everything. So I did.'

'What was the detective's name?'

'DCI Simon Barron, if I remember rightly.'

'You do.'

'You've met him, then?'

In a manner of speaking. 'Yes,' I said, 'I have.'

'I'm surprised he didn't say anything to you about our meeting.'

I was surprised he hadn't said very much to anyone about their meeting. If he was so interested in what had happened to Ann, why wasn't her death being treated as suspicious? Had he not shared the information he'd received from Dr Cheney with his colleagues? And if not, why not? Maybe Emma could find out.

But I was satisfied with what I'd heard because it meant I was onto something. The scent was getting stronger. I still wasn't 100 per cent sure that Ann Taylor's word could be entirely trusted (after all, she'd been an impressionable eleven-year-old girl), but something had happened, something that someone wanted suppressed very badly. And that someone had a lot of clout.

One thing I've learned down the years is that you don't get answers by asking a few big questions. You have to ask a lot of small ones. It's the only way you'll ever finish the puzzle.

'How long ago, roughly, did the murder of this little girl happen?'

'Ann had just turned seventeen when she came to me last year. At that point she'd been in care for approximately six years, so it would have been about seven years ago. But I can't give you an exact date, because she didn't leave home immediately after witnessing the incident. I think she was too shocked and, frankly, too scared. She thought it might have been a few weeks, even months, later that she finally plucked up the courage to run away. She did say, however, that there had been no more parties. They stopped altogether after that one.'

'But there can't have been many children go missing over that period. Not children that age. Did you ever look into Ann's claims yourself?'

Her expression tightened, the skin stretching with difficulty. I guessed that, like me, she'd had plastic surgery, although I don't think her surgeon was as good as mine.

'No,' she said. 'I assumed the police would do that. I did try to think back seven years to see if I could remember a child-abduction case that made the headlines, but nothing came to mind. DCI Barron said he'd look into it.'

I put my notebook away and drank my coffee down in one. It was tepid. 'Thank you very much for your help and your time, Dr Cheney. It's very much appreciated.'

'But is it helpful? Without real evidence, it's going to be hard to prove anything, isn't it?'

I stood up. 'If what happened to Ann's true, then there'll be evidence somewhere. If I find out anything, I'll make sure I let you know.'

She stood up as well. 'That's what DCI Barron said, but I never heard another word.'

'I expect he never got anywhere,' I told her as we shook hands. 'Or that he didn't have the time to pursue it.'

'But you will, won't you?'

I nodded firmly. 'If the answer to my case is there, I'll find it.'

And I would. I'd come a long way for this. I wasn't going to let it go.

Not now.

## 33

Was this what it was all about? The murder of a child. Was this what so many had died for? Somehow, it still didn't seem right. Paedophiles are furtive creatures; capable of forming into well-organized groups, and certainly responsible for some shocking crimes. But to be able to muster this sort of ruthlessness (and against men too rather than vulnerable children); to hire killers to snuff out their enemies, and then snuff out the killers themselves . . . I just couldn't quite buy it.

But at least I now had something to go on. If a girl between the ages of eight and thirteen had disappeared in southern England in the six months before Ann was taken into custody, I would find out about it. Dr Cheney had said she'd tried to think back and had come up with nothing, but by her own admission she hadn't been putting her life and soul into it. And the police, had they? DCI Barron had come here to see Dr Cheney, but seemed to have left without moving any further forward, since there'd been no follow-up inquiries. Sometimes it's surprising how often investigating officers can overlook facts that don't immediately fit with their theories on a crime, and understandably. On first glance, the murder of Asif Malik and Jason Khan had nothing to do with the out-of-date witness account of an alleged murder of an unidentified child seven years earlier. Only when you had my perspective of events was it possible to see the link.

But Dr Cheney was right. Without any real evidence, it was going to be hard to prove anything against anyone. If I could track each of the individuals down, I could impose my own justice, but I was one man operating alone, and if my true identity was discovered, it would take me out of the equation for ever. What was needed was something tangible to point the police in the right direction. And the only people who could provide this were Andrea Bloom and her boyfriend, Grant, both of whom, I was certain, had been told something by Ann, possibly in the days before her death. Something that they were now too scared to talk about.

Outside, a wet blanket of darkness had enveloped the surrounding fields, and it was raining hard. I hurried back to the car, jumped inside, and drove away.

And a single, worrying thought kept going through my head.

Did Tomboy Darke know more than he was letting on?

I got back into the West End at half past six, having endured a nightmare journey up the M3, and dropped the car back at the rental garage. As soon as I'd left there, I phoned Emma, wanting to catch up and let her know what I'd found out.

But when she answered I knew something was wrong.

'Oh, Dennis, thank God you've called.' She sounded distraught and it was obvious she'd been crying. I was surprised at the intensity of my concern for her.

'Emma, what is it? Tell me.'

'I got a visit today. From two of Tyndall's men.'

My throat went dry, and suddenly I could hear my heartbeat. 'Jesus, what happened?'

'It was when I was leaving work. I was just getting into my car when they came out of nowhere: two big men in leather jackets. They dragged me into a side road and . . .' She stopped for a moment and sounded as if she might cry again, but after a couple of seconds, she composed herself. 'One of them put a knife to my throat.'

'Did he hurt you?'

'No.'

I silently thanked God.

'He pressed it against my neck but he didn't cut me. He was grinning the whole time and he didn't even bother trying to hide his face. The other one was twisting my arms behind my back. Then the one with the knife told me that this was going to be my last warning. Any more articles about the Malik/Khan shooting and they were going to kill me.'

'Did they say they were representing Tyndall?'

'They didn't have to. I knew they were.'

I didn't argue. It was difficult to think who else would have threatened her like that. 'Are you OK? Where are you now?'

'I'm back at home. I'm fine.'

'You can't stay there alone. I'll be over in twenty minutes.'

'No, don't. Please.'

'Why not?'

She sounded edgy. Not right. 'I phoned Simon ... DCI Barron ... after what had happened, and he's arranged police protection for me. There's two officers in a patrol car directly outside the door and they're staying there until I leave tomorrow morning. I'm getting out of the city for a few days, Dennis. Going back to my parents' farm until things die down a little. You understand, don't you?'

I was gutted. Like the worst kind of lovesick fool, I'd had this idea on the drive back that I'd be spending a nice evening with Emma discussing the case over a bottle of wine before having a repeat performance of the previous night's lovemaking.

But I didn't say any of this, because she was right. It was best she laid low for a while. 'Of course I understand. I hope I'm here when you get back.'

'Do you think you will be? What did you find out today?'

I gave her a brief rundown of the meeting with Dr Cheney and what she'd told me. I also told her that DCI Barron had already been to see her. 'He never mentioned anything to you about it?'

'No,' she said, sounding surprised. 'Not a word. I had no idea he was pursuing that line of inquiry.'

'She never heard from him again, anyway.'

'So what's your plan now?' she asked.

I told her that I was going to see if I could back up Ann's story by checking whether any girls had gone missing during the period she'd described. 'I'm also going to go back and talk to Andrea Bloom, Ann's friend. She knows something, Emma. I'm sure of it.'

'But why are you so sure she hasn't told you everything?'

'I was a copper a long time. I can just feel it. She's hiding something. So's her boyfriend. If what they've got is good, I'll try and persuade them to go to the police and make a statement. Then they might start to look more closely at Ann's past. At the moment it's the best I can think of. But don't say anything to DCI Barron about any of this, though. OK?'

She seemed surprised. 'Why not?'

'I'd rather it was kept quiet for now. If I get anywhere, you can tell him then.'

'All right, but be careful, Dennis. You're sailing very close to the wind. And if they do end up treating Ann's death as a murder, what's going to happen with you?'

There were still a few loose ends to tie up, of course. Maybe a visit to Theo Morris of Thadeus Holdings, and even to the enigmatic Nicholas Tyndall. But soon, I hoped, my part in all this would be over. 'I think I'll go home,' I told her.

'I hope we get a chance to see each other again.'

'So do I,' I said, and I meant it.

'But if we don't . . . Well, I don't think I could call it fun, but I'm glad I met you. Take care of yourself, please.'

'And you, Emma. And don't be tempted to hang around. I really wouldn't want anything to happen to you.' I felt like saying something else, something along the lines of how much I cared about her, but I held back.

'I've learned my lesson,' she told me. 'Goodbye, Dennis. And good luck.'

'Goodbye, Emma.'

She rang off and I stood staring at the phone for a while, thinking that fleeting romances were the story of my life. Two years ago, when I'd been in Siquijor Island, I'd met an Australian girl in her thirties who was passing through on her way home. She'd been travelling the world for six years, and was on the last leg of her journey when she shipped up at our place and got a room for a few days. We didn't see a lot of Western women in the Philippines. It wasn't really on the backpackers' trail and it had the sort of moderately dodgy reputation that meant it was usually avoided by women travelling on their own. So Christine had been a breath of fresh air. We'd got talking in the bar on her first night, and I'd taken her out diving the next day. She'd had that relaxed attitude to sex that I've always admired in a woman, and since we'd been the only two on the boat, we'd ended up making love amongst the diving equipment. We'd spent the next week very much together, with me giving her a tour of the island, and her telling me about her travels and the places she'd seen. It had been fun. More than fun, it had been one of those blossoming romances that I'd experienced so little of in my life, and I'd even been thinking about finding some way to follow her to Australia.

But I was kidding myself. In the end, it had just been a fling to her, and seven days after she'd arrived, she kissed me on the lips, told me to take care of myself, and walked out of my life for ever. Just one in a long line of goodbyes.

I knew this would be the last I saw of Emma, but in a way it felt right. She was too young, too pretty, and if I'm honest, too good for me; and since there was no chance of anything ever coming of our relationship, it was best that we parted now, before things got serious.

I walked back to the hotel room and had a shower. The water was lukewarm so I was only in there two minutes and was cold when I got out. I got dressed and lay on the bed, and thought about my next move. I was tempted to go out and have a few drinks, maybe back in Ernie's pub, but I wanted to be fresh the following morning.

I looked at my watch. Seven twenty. I picked up the mobile to call Andrea Bloom, then realized I didn't have a number for her. I asked myself whether it was really worth a trip over to Hackney now to see her, but the alternative was lying in this shitty hotel room staring at the cracks in the ceiling, and in the end that wasn't much of an alternative, so I forced myself up off the bed. I needed food. Then I'd be on my way.

# 34

It had just gone nine o'clock when I turned into Andrea's street, having walked all the way from Angel underground station, and the night was cold. A biting wind rattled round the pavement, scattering pieces of rubbish and keeping the area's citizenry behind closed doors. I was wearing a grey beanie hat I'd bought the previous day to replace my 'I love London' cap, and a scarf pulled up over my face. Only my eyes were visible.

There was a light on in the living room and several lights up on the third floor, although none on the second or in the hallway. According to Andrea, the house was a squat that she shared with her boyfriend, as well as another couple and a single guy. There didn't seem to be much activity for so many people.

I approached the door, hoping that my journey hadn't been wasted, and saw straight away that it was very slightly ajar.

I stopped dead, and listened. The TV was on in the living room. It sounded like a quiz show with plenty of audience participation and the volume was quite loud. I couldn't hear anything else so I pushed the door open slightly, wondering whether or not to knock. Wondering too whether or not to go inside. People don't leave their doors ajar in an area like Hackney. They don't do it anywhere in London, especially not on a freezing cold night like this one.

I pushed it open further and stepped inside, shutting it quietly behind me. I resisted the urge to call out.

From somewhere up the stairs there came a creak, and then the clank of pipes heating up. I wasn't unduly alarmed. This was an old house – 1920s, I'd have guessed. Things creaked in a 1920s place. Again, I listened but there was no other sound.

I had my gun with me but didn't reach for it. It would have been far too difficult to explain away.

Turning left, I pushed open the living room door and the TV suddenly grew louder. The quizmaster was Chris Tarrant, and he was asking the contestant what the capital of Rwanda was. He gave him four alternatives while I scanned the empty living room, noticing that there were a couple of open cans of beer next to one of the seats. They hadn't been there the previous day, and since the room was otherwise tidy, I concluded that they'd been opened this evening. Not that this told me much.

I retreated from the room as the contestant won eight grand for getting the answer right (it was B: Kigali), and started up the staircase as quietly as possible. Two of the stairs creaked loudly as I put pressure on them, but I kept going regardless.

At the top of the stairs a door was open. Although it was dark inside, I could see that it was a toilet, and empty too. There was still no sign of anyone.

Two more stairs to my left led up to the second floor. I went up them into the darkness of the narrow landing. A door immediately to my right was shut.

'Hello?' The voice came from up the next set of stairs at the end of the landing. I recognized it immediately as Andrea's. 'Is that you, Jeff?' she added.

'No, it's Mick Kane, Andrea,' I called back. 'Your front door was wide open. I need to speak to you.'

'What's going on?' she demanded, still out of sight. 'Why's it so quiet down there?'

'I don't know,' I answered truthfully. 'There's no-one in the living room. I think you must be the only person in.'

'I'm not. Maz and Star are in. Or they were a few minutes ago. I heard them.'

'Maybe they've gone out for some cigarettes or something. I just had a couple of quick questions.'

'I don't want to talk to you any more, and I don't like the way you've just walked in our house.

You weren't invited, and it's freaking me out.'

'I'm sorry, but I couldn't phone you because you never gave me a number. I visited the psychiatrist who treated Ann today, Dr Madeline Cheney. She filled me in on a lot of things. I think you can, too. Please? It won't take more than a few minutes and it's extremely important.'

Out of the corner of my eye, I spotted something moving, down near my feet, only just visible in the gloom.

'I'm not talking to you. I'm going back to my room now, and I'm locking myself in. If you don't leave, I'll call the police. I mean it.'

I looked down. A dark line had appeared beneath the door on my right. The line was getting longer, touching the threadbare carpet and forming a small pool where there was a kink.

Blood.

My whole body tensed, and when I spoke next my voice was loud and urgent. 'Andrea, listen to me. You've got to come down, right now!'

I could hear her retreating up the next flight of stairs, back to her room and what she thought was safety. 'I told you,' she shouted. 'I'm going to call the police.'

'There's something wrong, Andrea. You've got to believe me!' My voice was getting louder. There was someone else in this house; someone who shouldn't have been here. I pushed the door and felt it come up against an obstacle. I pushed harder and it slowly opened, forcing the obstruction out of the way.

'Come down here, Andrea, please!'

I reached for the light switch inside and flicked it on.

And saw the corpse.

Registered the sight. Blinked. Registered it again.

It was a young man of about twenty, with spiky, dyed-black hair and dead blue eyes. He was lying in a foetal position, blood still pouring from the huge twin gashes across his face and throat.

Upstairs there was the sound of footfalls on the carpet as Andrea ran back to her room, then the sound of a door shutting.

I pushed further into the room, saw the semi-naked body of a slightly built woman, about the same age, on a low futon bed. She was lying on her back, one arm draped across her breasts and belly, glassy eyes staring at the ceiling. She'd had her throat cut too and the blood was beginning to dye the sheets round her a deep red.

This time I pulled out the .45 and stepped back out of the room, pointing it into the darkness ahead.

Once again the house was silent except for the murmur of the TV downstairs.

'Andrea, if you can hear me, I want you to come down the stairs right now and leave with me. Or else call the police.'

There was no reply. Nothing. Not even a creak.

I could have gone. Turned round and walked. Dialled 999 from a safe distance away.

I could have done, and I wanted to. But I didn't. Instead, I crept down the corridor, turned at the end, and started up the flight of stairs that led to Andrea's room, finger tight on the trigger of the gun.

A stair creaked. Above me was almost pitch darkness. I kept going.

When I reached the top, I stopped. I was on a small, windowless landing. There were two doors to my left, both closed, and one right in front of me, also closed.

'Andrea? Are you there?'

Silence. Not even a breath being drawn. All I could hear was the thudding of my heart in my chest.

I fumbled round for a light switch but couldn't see one, then stepped forward and flung open the door directly in front of me, staring straight into darkness. As my eyes adjusted, I saw a tiled floor with a bath to my right, partly obscured by a shower curtain, and a toilet and washbasin further on. The faint glow of street light eased through the window at the end.

I pulled back the shower curtain. Fast, in one movement.

The bath was empty.

So was the rest of the room.

As I stepped back onto the landing, I heard a faint sob.

335

I stopped. It was coming from one of the other rooms to my left. I knew it could be a trap so I took another step back, then turned until I was facing the two doors, unsure from which one the noise had come.

I stayed where I was. Stock still. Waiting. Listening.

Slowly, ever so slowly, the door nearest to me opened. I held the gun outstretched in front of me, two-handed, waited for what seemed to be a very long time, my arms aching, beginning to shake.

And then Andrea finally appeared, standing upright, staring at me. Frightened, terrified . . .

. . . And dying.

The blood was gushing out of the gaping wound in her neck, each pulse of her heart spurting more. It was everywhere, splattering in a series of arcs on to the carpet in front of me.

For a moment I was too stunned to move, then suddenly she came flying bodily in my direction. I tried to dodge her but she hit me head on, her mouth opening and shutting and making this horrible gasping sound as we both fell back against the top banister in a wet and bloody embrace. I pushed her out of the way, catching sight of the killer as he came towards me, an iron bar raised above his head, dressed in a transparent waterproof jacket and mask, looking like something out of a chemical warfare film. Andrea staggered and fell, still trying to grab hold of me with one hand while the other worked vainly at stemming the tidal flow of blood.

The blow caught me on the side of the head as I raised the gun to fire and I was momentarily stunned. My grip on the gun eased and it dropped from my hand as I grabbed at the banister for balance. He hit me again across the side of the face and this time I went down hard, landing on top of Andrea before rolling off her and trying to get myself into a protective ball. His next blow was a kick that caught me in the guts and made me want to vomit, the one after that connecting with my face. I could hear him grunting with exertion, and the obscene crinkling of his suit as he moved back and forth.

And then he did a strange thing. He stopped and dropped the open cut-throat razor he'd been carrying in his other hand onto the carpet near my head. Blood dripped from it.

As I tried to focus, he stepped back to kick me again. Two feet away, Andrea Bloom lay sprawled and fading on the floor, the blood continuing to flow out of her at a terrifying rate, the carpet now awash with it, but still she watched me with dark, beautiful eyes that pleaded for one last chance to live.

'What the hell's going on up there?'

I recognized the voice. It was Andrea's boyfriend, Grant, and he was coming up the stairs.

The killer paused, then kicked again, but this

time I was ready for it. I got hold of his leg and pushed him away with my last remaining strength. He fell back against the wall, then pulled free and turned and ran past me, lashing out with the bar as he did so and catching me across the arm. I fell back to the floor, my vision becoming fuzzy and my head aching like mad for the second time in a few days. I wanted to lie down, to go to sleep. I could hear the killer running down the stairs, heard him confront the boyfriend, heard Grant cry out as he came off worst, and knew without a doubt that if I stayed where I was and gave in to the temptation to close my eyes, then not only would I go to prison for the murders I was wanted for from three years ago, but I'd also go down for the ones in here. Because I was the one left with the murder weapon and a houseful of corpses.

Using the banister for support, I got to my knees, and then my feet. Andrea had stopped gasping now and her eyes had closed. It was possible she was still alive, but if she was, it was purely academic. Even in the gloom I could see the blood everywhere; could smell the sour, inevitable approach of death. There was no hope. She was gone.

But there was no time to ponder the injustice of her murder. I had to get the hell out of there. I looked round for the .45 but couldn't see it. I squinted, finally spotted it in the corner of the landing, and staggered over to retrieve it. My head did some sort of internal somersault as I bent down and picked it up and I had to steady myself against the wall to stop myself from fainting. I wanted to puke. Badly. But vomit leaves DNA, and I couldn't have that.

I swallowed, made for the stairs, staggered down them, the darkness ebbing and flowing in front of me. Made my way along the hallway towards the second set of stairs, holding the gun unsteadily in preparation for any last-ditch ambush by the killer.

Grant's body was sprawled backwards on the staircase, his right leg bent at an awkward angle, one foot propped against the banister. His face was a mask of blood, his hair thick and matted with it where he'd been bludgeoned with the iron bar. A slither of white was showing where his skull had been exposed and flecks of blood dotted the bare wall behind him.

That could have been me. But no, he'd wanted me alive. Wanted me set up for these murders. Which meant . . .

The Lord alone knew what it meant. I swallowed, resisting once again the urge to vomit, and tried to step over Grant's body, stumbling as I did so and tripping over his leg.

I fell down four stairs, my head pounding like someone was using a pneumatic drill on it, which they may as well have been, forced myself back to my feet, and made for the door.

I banged against it harder than I'd been expecting, and fumbled for the handle, finding it after a couple of seconds and giving it a hard yank.

A welcome blast of icy London air smacked me right in the face, and my vision seemed to clear a little as I made my way down the steps and started off down the street, trying to stay upright, trying to put as much distance between myself and the murder scene as possible. Four people dead, just to keep one mouth shut. I was getting close. I had to be.

When I got to the main road, I fell onto one knee, jarred it, tried to get up, saw the whole world melt in front of me, and vomited ferociously.

I vaguely recall a car pulling up and being lifted to my feet and pushed into the back of it. I vaguely recall there being two men in the front as it pulled away.

Then I lost consciousness.

# 35

I was in a darkened room, lying on my back on a
single bed. The bed smelled clean. My jacket and
shoes had been removed and a light duvet covered
me. I tried to sit up, but the effort made me dizzy
and I lay back down again. I felt my head. It had
been expertly bandaged, but I didn't think I was in
a hospital. There were no monitors beside the bed,
no wires or drips, nothing like that. Just a plastic
chair, which my jacket was neatly folded over, and
a second wooden chair near the door. I looked at
my watch. Ten past three in the morning. The
curtains weren't pulled and outside the night was
dark. I wondered where I was, and whether whoever had picked me up on the street earlier had
seen the gun I was carrying, or informed the police.

I lay there for a long time, staring at the ceiling,
trying to come to terms with my predicament.
Who'd known that I was going to see Andrea
Bloom? Emma had; so had Jamie Delly. I'd asked

Emma not to say anything to Barron, but it was possible she'd let slip something. It was also possible that someone was bugging her phone. Theo Morris of Thadeus Holdings? Nicholas Tyndall? The list of suspects was still too long, but it was narrowing. Unfortunately, so were my options.

There was movement on the other side of the door and it opened. A slightly built black man in his sixties came in. He had a kindly face and I knew straight away that he wasn't going to give me trouble.

He smiled when he saw I was awake. 'I've got something for you,' he said in a quiet voice. The accent was West African. I'd worked with a Nigerian guy back in the late Eighties and he'd sounded very similar.

As he approached the bed, I saw that he was holding a small, horn-shaped flask made of some kind of wood. It had a metal lid on it, and looked old. With surprising strength, he lifted me up by the back of the head and propped me against the pillow. 'Drink this,' he whispered and placed the flask to my mouth, removing the lid.

I was thirsty and my mouth was dry, so I did as he said. The taste was unfamiliar but not unpleasant. Vaguely salty, like weak Bovril, but with an underlying sweetness as well. I glugged the whole lot down, and he removed the flask.

He stood there watching me for a few seconds.

'Do you start to feel better?' he asked at last.

I sat up further in the bed. 'Do you know what? I think I do.' And I did. The thickness in my head was dissipating fast and I suddenly felt far more alert. 'What is that stuff?'

'Medicine,' he said.

'It's a lot more effective than paracetamol. You ought to market it to the drugs companies.'

He continued to smile. 'Are you ready to get up? There is someone who would like to see you. He is in one of the other rooms.'

'Who is it?' I asked, slipping out of the bed and grabbing my shoes, but he ignored the question and opened the door, waiting while I pulled them on.

'Your jacket and gun will be safe in here,' he said, and beckoned me to follow.

Intrigued, and feeling better and better as the medicine or whatever the hell it was kicked in, I stood up and followed him out of the room, the dizziness slipping effortlessly away.

We were in a long corridor with expensive parquet flooring and doors to the left. To my right, a single long window offered a panoramic view of the blue darkness and occasional lights of the sleeping city at night. In the near distance were two tower blocks, surrounded by a carpet of low-rise buildings. I guessed that we were at least six floors above the ground ourselves. I tried to get my bearings, but I didn't recognize the view. I was somewhere in London, but that was about all I could tell you.

I walked along the corridor behind my new friend to another door. He knocked slowly three times, as if it was some sort of signal, and the door was opened by a tall, grim-faced black man who wore sunglasses even though the room behind him was only dimly lit. The man stood to one side, out of view, and my guide turned and beckoned me to follow him inside. I knew then, of course, who I was going to see and I wasn't sure whether I should have been thankful or petrified. Probably the latter, but I followed him into the room anyway, figuring that I didn't have a lot of choice in the matter.

The room was huge, with windows on three sides, although black drapes had been pulled down to shut out the city's light. Candles on ornate holders of varying sizes had been lit all round the room, bathing it in a flickering glow. Shadows ran and jumped across the walls, from which strange, tribal masks and the heads of exotic animals stared out menacingly at all those who entered. Low futon-style sofas and large patterned cushions were scattered about the room, and at the far end, sitting on a low wicker chair with a high back like a throne, was a well-built and handsome black man somewhere in his early thirties, drinking what looked like a coffee and smoking a cigarette. Sitting like grim guardians on either side of the chair were two dolls, much larger than but very similar to the one that had been left on Emma's bed, which told me something I already knew.

The man in the chair smiled and motioned to one of the sofas next to him. At the same time, my guide left the room, shutting the door behind him, while the man in the sunglasses melted effortlessly into the shadows somewhere to my right.

I walked over to the sofa and slowly sat down on it. The man in the chair waited until I'd got myself comfortable before speaking.

'I'm going to assume you know who I am,' he announced in a pleasantly resonant North London accent.

'I think I can take a guess,' I answered, reaching into my shirt pocket for my cigarettes. They weren't there.

'Please, have one of these,' said Nicholas Tyndall, removing a pack of Marlboro Lights from the pocket of his own shirt – a black silk number – and lighting one for me. 'You might want to know why I had you brought here,' he suggested.

I said it wouldn't be a bad idea.

'You were in a bad way when my men picked you up. If we'd left you there, you would have been picked up by God knows who, and that may not have been such a good thing.' He paused for a moment while he took a drag on his cigarette, watching me with a playful expression. This was a man who oozed natural charisma. And menace, too. There was real menace emanating from where

345

he was sitting. You knew that if you crossed this man, you were in a lot of trouble. Although maybe I was stating the obvious since any man who sits in a cavernous candlelit room surrounded by voodoo-like ornaments is going to be someone you'll want to stay on the right side of.

'As I heard it,' he continued, 'you'd just left a house containing a lot of dead bodies. People – innocent, I understand – who'd been murdered very recently. Their throats slit. Their heads bashed in.'

Not for the first time that day, I could hear my heart thumping. I cursed the fact that I'd left my gun in the other room.

'If the police had seen you lying on the pavement, they would have taken you in. Perhaps connected you to that house. Perhaps even connected you to other things. Who knows?'

Our eyes met and I held his gaze. There was something very unnerving in it. I felt that if you kept looking, you'd unearth grim secrets that you'd far rather not see. Behind him, the flickering shadows partly illuminated a tapestry of a man with a scythe in one hand and what looked like a sack of bones in the other.

'What do you want with me?' I asked at last, not at all sure I wanted to hear the answer.

'You've been observed asking questions,' he said, emphasizing the word 'observed'. 'Questions about the shooting of Asif Malik and Jason Khan. In fact, yesterday you threatened two of my men with a gun when you went round to visit Khan's brother, Jamie.'

'I didn't threaten them. I asked them to leave the premises.'

He smiled. 'No matter. They weren't being careful enough, and they were caught out. They'll learn their lesson. The fact is, Mr Kane . . . That is your name, isn't it?' There was a hint of laughter in his eyes when he said this, as if he knew damn well it wasn't. But I didn't rise to the bait.

'Well, the fact is, Mr Kane, the shooting of Messrs Malik and Khan has caused me a great deal of trouble. A lot of people – your friend Miss Neilson of the *North London Echo* included – seem to think that I had something to do with it. Since you've been asking questions in an unofficial capacity, and working, so far as I can see, a lot harder than the police, you must have your own ideas about who's responsible. Do you think it's something to do with me?'

'No,' I said, 'I don't.'

He took a deep breath that seemed to make him grow larger in the room, and his expression suddenly became very serious. 'Good, and by saying that you've answered your own question. The reason I had you brought here is because this whole thing is nothing – I repeat, nothing – to do with me. Jason Khan did some work for some people who know some other people who do some work for me, but I never met him when he was alive and consequently had no interest in seeing him dead. As for Malik, he was no danger to me. He had been involved in investigating my business affairs in the past, but as far as I'm aware that all ceased when he joined the National Crime Squad some months ago. And why would I want to kill a police officer, especially one who was such a high-profile target as Malik was? It would just put undue pressure on my business affairs, which is something I obviously don't want. I'm not interested in making enemies of the law, Mr Kane, but it seems that I have done, and that's why the focus of this police investigation is aimed at my associates and me, which is a state of affairs that I do not want to continue. The trouble is, everyone thinks I did it, which suits the true perpetrators of the crime just fine. However, if they could be uncovered, then the pressure on me would ease, would it not?'

'I guess it would,' I said, finishing my cigarette and stubbing it out in a cast-iron ashtray shaped like a hand, which was resting on the side of the sofa.

'And this is why I want to hire your services.'

For a moment, I was taken aback, but then it struck me that it seemed a logical request.

'How close are you to identifying the perpetrators?' he asked.

'I'm getting there.' I thought about the missing-girl lead I'd got from Dr Cheney. 'I've got something I want to follow up tomorrow, which may well get me a lot closer.'

'I see you carry a gun. A high-calibre one, too. But it only contains two bullets. Have you got any more?'

I told him I didn't.

'There are some dangerous adversaries out there. I can supply you with another gun, and some ammunition, plus a flak jacket. They may go some way to helping you survive.'

'I could do with some transport as well,' I said, thinking that a car might come in useful in the days ahead.

Tyndall nodded. 'That can be arranged. I'll also pay you five thousand cash. Another five if you unmask the people involved in killing Malik and Khan and gather the evidence needed to get the law off my back. Does that sound fair to you?'

I could have told him that I didn't work for anyone, that I was my own man, but in this game you've got to be a realist. Like I said, he was the sort of bloke it was best to stay on the right side of, and it wasn't going to make a great deal of difference to my investigation whether he was paying me or not. At least with him as my employer, I had someone backing me up.

'Yeah, it sounds fair. I'll take the job, but I want you to call the dogs off Emma Neilson. No more voodoo dolls through her letterbox or threats in the street.'

'I don't like upsetting women,' said Tyndall, sounding like he meant it, 'but that girl has caused me no end of problems. If you can get her to stop writing libellous articles, I'll leave her be.'

'You've got my word,' I told him. 'She's heading out of town tomorrow and she won't be back for a while. By the time she returns, this'll all be over.'

'You think so?'

'I'm sure of it.'

Tyndall leaned back in his seat, making himself comfortable. 'I hear you've also had a lot of trouble from people who want you out of the way.'

'You could say that.'

'I think I might have alleviated it somewhat.'

I raised my eyebrows. 'What do you mean?'

He smiled, and this time it was the smile of a predator. Then he leaned down and picked something up from behind the chair. It was the transparent mask worn by the killer of Andrea Bloom and her housemates, complete with black, protruding mouthpiece for breathing. It took me a couple of seconds to realize that it was still attached to the killer's head – the exposed white neckbone jutting out from underneath the plastic.

Tyndall held the head by the neckbone and with his other hand removed the mask. Blondie – my nemesis since I'd arrived here four days ago (Jesus, was it only four days?) – stared dully across the room at me, his mouth slightly open, his face splattered with blood where they'd severed the head. Tyndall relinquished his grip on the bone and held the head up by its hair.

'When people fuck around with me,' he said, 'I fuck them around one hell of a lot worse. Do you understand what I'm saying?'

I looked at him, then at the head, then back at him. 'I think I'm beginning to get the picture.'

'Good.' He returned the head to the floor, out of sight. 'Before he died, this dog told us that he'd received his orders to go to the house tonight from a man called Theo Morris, who was apparently his employer. Does this man's name mean anything to you?'

'It does. He works for a company called Thadeus Holdings.' I motioned in the direction of where he'd put the head. 'Did he say why he didn't try to kill me tonight?'

Tyndall seemed surprised by that. 'I thought he did try to kill you.'

I shook my head. 'He tried to beat me up a bit and knock me out, then he deliberately dropped the murder weapon next to me. I'm assuming he wanted me and it found by the police at the scene so I could be set up for the killings.'

Tyndall shrugged. 'I don't know anything about that.'

'I'll find out,' I said. 'I'm going to be questioning Theo Morris in the next couple of days. I'd appreciate a clear run at him.' There was a heartbeat's pause while we looked at each other. 'In other words, I don't need any help.'

'All right. However, I expect to hear from you every day with progress on how you're doing. What's your phone number?'

I told him. He nodded but made no effort to write it down.

'When you leave here tonight you'll be supplied with an encrypted email address. Send your progress reports to that address. If we need to get hold of you, we will. Now, how are you feeling?'

'Good,' I said, touching my head. 'Surprisingly good. What kind of medicine did your friend give me downstairs?'

Tyndall's smile was amused this time. 'Have you ever heard of Muti, Mr Kane? It's a form of African medicine, and those who follow it believe that if you remove the body parts of a person as they die, those parts can be used to make some very potent medicine. When taken, they can give the recipient untold strength. Particularly when the body parts belong to a fallen enemy.' The smile grew wider and I looked away, hoping he was joking. 'Claude, can you show Mr Kane out? And make sure we get a car brought round. One that can't be traced.'

Tyndall stood up. So did I, but with a little less conviction than I'd displayed when I'd got out of bed a few minutes earlier. 'You'll have to excuse me,' he said. 'I'm a little tired tonight. It was good to meet you.'

He put out a hand – the one that had been holding Blondie's head by the neckbone – and because I was still wearing my gloves, I reluctantly shook it.

'I wish I could say the same,' I answered, turning round and following the guy with the sunglasses out of there.

I was led back along the corridor, past the room I'd been in and round the corner to a lift. There, the man who'd given me the medicine appeared, and with his customary smile placed a silk blindfold over my eyes. I was taken down to the ground floor, where I was kept standing in silence for a few minutes. Finally I was ushered through a door and out onto the street. A car pulled up and I was helped into the front passenger seat and informed not to remove the blindfold until I was told. Then the car pulled away.

Ten minutes later, permission was given. I took the blindfold off and opened my eyes. I was being driven by a young white man I didn't recognize along the Euston Road past St Pancras Station.

'Where do you want dropping off?' he asked.

I told him Paddington, and he continued driving in silence through the bare night streets before pulling up outside the station fifteen minutes later.

'It's all yours,' he said, getting out of the car and leaving the engine running. 'There's a holdall in the boot with all the stuff you've been promised.' He shut the door and walked round the back, jumping into another vehicle that had stopped behind us.

I clambered across into the driver's seat and watched as they pulled away, turned left and disappeared from sight, leaving me wondering whether the whole night had been some strange and terrible dream.

# Part Three
## THE HUNTERS

# 36

I thought I would have woken up late the next morning after all the activity of the night before, but at just after nine I opened my eyes and realized that the last thing that had passed my lips had almost certainly been a cupful of someone else's blood. I was sure I could still taste it in my mouth. What was worse was that it appeared to have done me a lot more good than harm. My head was clear, and when I removed the bandage round it in front of the bathroom mirror, the injuries looked to have partly healed. For some reason, my next thought was of Blondie. I wondered how much they'd tortured him before he died. I also wondered whether they'd removed any of his organs, and whether they would have been used for a specific ritual. Then I stopped wondering, because I was beginning to feel sorry for the man who the previous night had slaughtered four people and who'd done his utmost to kill me.

The world is a hard, dark place. It's inhabited by some brutal people. I'd met a disproportionate number of them in the past few days, although I had a feeling that none was more brutal than the man I was now effectively working for. But then I was pretty sure he hadn't killed my friend. Someone else had, and I knew I was getting steadily closer to finding out who.

But I was also riding my luck. When I'd come in the previous night, the guy on the desk had seen the bandage I was wearing and had given me a strange look. Someone might have seen me at Andrea Bloom's house. The footage from the CCTV in Soho would be released soon and might give a better picture of me than I'd bargained for. Whichever way I looked at it, pretty soon my second chances were going to run out. If I wanted to find out who was behind the murder of my friend, then I was going to have to hurry.

I went for breakfast at the Italian place. They knew me there now and the woman behind the counter greeted me with a smile and hello, which I thought was a nice touch. I plumped for more traditional fare that day and ate a full English breakfast of bacon, eggs, sausages, tomatoes and chips while I read the paper. There was no mention of the events of the previous night. By the time I'd finished, I felt heartily refreshed and the imaginary taste of blood in my mouth was gone. I paid my bill, told the woman to have a nice day, and went outside to phone Emma.

She answered on the third ring.

'How are you feeling?' I asked.

'Better than I did last night. I'm leaving as soon as I've finished packing. How did it go with the girl?'

'Not good. They beat me to it.'

'Is she . . . ?'

I sighed. 'Yeah, she is.' I didn't add that her housemates were dead too. 'Did you say anything to Barron about her?'

'No, of course not. You asked me not to.'

'Because I'm wondering how the hell they knew about her.'

'Hold on. You're not accusing me of anything here, are you? You don't think I'm anything to do with this?'

'Of course not, but I'm beginning to get worried about the quality of information the people we're up against are getting hold of, that's all. I'm thinking they may be bugging your phone. They may even be listening now.'

'Shit, Dennis. This is getting far too heavy. I'm going to hang up and leave right away. And I think you'd better get out, too.'

'Don't worry about me – worry about yourself. How are you getting to your parents' place?'

'Driving. It's a lot easier than the train, and once I'm out of London it'll be a lot quicker, too. I'll be honest, I'm really glad to be going now. If I never hear another word about this case I'll be happy. I wish I'd never written a word about it. And if you're listening, whoever you are, I'm not going to write another word about it, either.'

'Just lie low for a while and it'll blow over,' I told her. I thought about adding that I'd probably got rid of her harassers, but decided against it. It was better for her if she didn't know. Maybe better for me, too, since I'd resigned myself now to the fact that this was it between us, a feeling that was confirmed when there was a pause down the other end of the phone, which seemed to suggest that she wasn't sure what else to say to me. I remembered Christine, the Australian girl, being similarly lost for words when we'd parted at the port of Larena in Siquijor. What do you say?

I said, 'Take care.'

She said, 'You too.'

Even now, months later, I wish that those were the last words to each other we ever spoke.

# 37

Seven years ago, a young girl had allegedly lost her life during a sadomasochistic orgy, during which she was brutally murdered at the hands of a number of men. Five participants had been there that night, according to Dr Cheney. One had been Richard Blacklip. And perhaps one had been Pope, but I didn't even know that for sure. What I did know, however, was that if it had happened as Ann had said (and I believed it had), then the girl in question would almost certainly have been reported missing by someone. It was just a matter of finding out who.

Not for the first time in the last twenty-four hours, I cast my mind back seven years. I have a good memory for heinous crimes. For instance, I can remember the time when three children were murdered by strangers over the course of a weekend, in two separate incidents. The summer of 1994, it had been. I woke up to the news on Capital Radio on a sunny Monday morning. Three kids dead. It made me think that the world really was going mad, and all my efforts as a copper were for nothing if there were still people out there capable of that sort of outrage.

But it's also rare, and seven years ago I could think of no specific case, certainly nothing that was unsolved. It was possible, of course, that one of the paedophiles had sacrificed his own daughter. For most people that's a thought too shocking to contemplate, but, believe it or not, there are people out there who've actually done such things. The thing is, though, they've usually been caught. Kill a young family member and, even if you don't report them missing, someone somewhere's usually going to notice that they're no longer around. Which left me with the conclusion that there was going to be a record of this girl's disappearance somewhere. If I looked hard enough, I'd find it.

My first port of call was a cyber café on the Edgware Road. I bought a coffee, went online and looked up the National Missing Persons Helpline.

The National Missing Persons Helpline is a registered charity that deals with the thousands of people who go missing every year in the UK. They include a hundred thousand children under the age of eighteen. That's a lot of kids out on the streets. Thankfully, the vast majority just disappear for a day or two and then come back home, but I remember a representative of the charity telling me a few years back, when she'd come to the station to give a talk, that even if 99.9 per cent of the cases were solved and the kids found, that still left one hundred children completely unaccounted for. It wasn't a thought I wanted to dwell on.

I found the number for general enquiries, logged off and phoned it.

The woman who answered was busy (with a hundred thousand people disappearing every year, it'd be difficult not to be), but helpful, too. I explained that I was a private detective working for the legal team representing a young man who was on remand for murder. Part of his defence was that he'd been abused as a boy by a paedophile ring, and that he claimed to have seen a female child murdered during one incident. The woman at the other end, who sounded in her sixties and was probably a volunteer, gasped when I said this, and I immediately felt guilty.

'To be honest with you, madam,' I said by way of explanation, 'it's not likely that the story's true, but I wouldn't be doing my job properly if I didn't follow it up.'

'No, of course not,' she replied uncertainly.

'Is there any way I can check on this man's claims?' I asked, giving her the dates in question. 'I know you keep records of missing children.'

'We do,' she said carefully. 'We have a

comprehensive database and we never remove names from it, even if the person concerned is found, but it's not accessible to the public. And I can't give out any information. However, we are capable of carrying out comprehensive searches of our database, if we receive a request from the police. Can't you go through them? I'm sure they'd be interested.'

But that was the problem. I couldn't.

I knew better than to try to strong-arm the information out of her, so I thanked her for her time and rang off, disappointed but not entirely surprised. If detective work was that easy, there'd never be such a thing as an unsolved case.

I finished my coffee, left the café and went to retrieve the car that Tyndall had provided me with. It was a black Kia four-wheel drive that I'd left over near Hyde Park the previous night, and when I got there and eventually located it, it had already received a ticket. No-one can accuse London's parking authorities of inefficiency. Still, it didn't bother me. I wouldn't be paying it. I peeled it off, chucked it on the passenger seat, and drove out onto Park Lane, heading for my next port of call.

The British Library's newspaper arm – the place where they keep microfiche archives containing two hundred years' worth of back issues of selected newspapers – is situated in a drab suburb of post-war residential housing in Colindale, North

London. The building itself was uglier and smaller than I expected and looked more like a factory or a functional modern schoolbuilding than a library. It faced onto a main road almost directly opposite Colindale underground station.

I showed my false passport at the door as ID and was given a one-day reading pass by the man at the desk. A notice said that all coats and bags had to be left in the cloakroom for security reasons, but luckily he didn't ask me to remove my jacket. If he had done, he'd have probably seen the .45 revolver sticking out of my jeans, and if he'd missed it, plenty of other people wouldn't have. But he let me through with a smile, informing me that archived copies of *The Times* were kept on the next floor up.

I was going to have to do this the hard way. According to the records, Ann had been taken into Coleman House children's home in Camden on 6 June 1998, and she had claimed to Dr Cheney that the murder she'd witnessed had taken place some weeks before that. I decided to concentrate my search on issues of *The Times*, from 1 January, to see if there were any reports of children who'd disappeared or had died in unusual circumstances. I felt sure that something like this would be reasonably big news, so I narrowed my search to the first five pages of each issue. It was hardly a scientific methodology, but then I was a one-man band with severely limited resources, and I didn't see any other way.

The microfiche machines were bulky contraptions situated in a darkened back room. I found a spare one and spent the next ten minutes trying to load the film spools containing the editions of *The Times* from 1 to 10 January, without any success whatsoever, until finally a pretty Spanish student took pity and showed me how to do it.

The year had begun with the usual batch of bad news: Loyalist gunmen on the rampage in Northern Ireland; bloody massacres in Algeria; gangland killings; a string of domestic tragedies. Things didn't improve much either, but then again, when do they?

There was the trial of the teenage thug who'd buried a carving knife up to the hilt in the head of a twenty-eight-year-old charity worker as she sat alone on a suburban train with her back to him, purely because, according to him, she was 'the only target visible'. There was the trial of Victor Farrant, the rapist released early from his sentence who went on to murder his new girlfriend and batter another woman half to death. His girlfriend was a divorced mother of two, and as Farrant was returned to prison (this time, presumably, to complete his sentence), her anguished kids were quoted as asking why on earth he'd been let out in the first place. One, I thought, that Britain's new Lord Chief Justice, Parnham-Jones, might like to answer in one of his fireside chats.

What struck me as I read was the sheer number

of brutal crimes committed in the UK by people whose only motive seemed to be the sadistic gratification their violence gave them. In the Philippines, people killed. They killed a lot more than they did in England, as even the most cursory glance at Manila's murder statistics would demonstrate, but in general those killings were the direct result of poverty or ideology. Few people there murdered for pleasure. Here, where people had money and freedom, they did. It was a depressing thought, because it suggested that where the violence of humankind was concerned, things would never get better.

But for the moment, such lofty issues didn't concern me.

I kept reading. Trawling. Searching.

It was time-consuming work. I estimated I was taking about three minutes per issue, so each month was taking me more than an hour and a half. By the time I got to March, it was almost half past three and my eyes were hurting. I thought about stopping for a while, taking a break and ringing Emma to see if she'd arrived home, but I didn't want to lose my place at the machine. One more hour, then I'd call it a day.

1 March – nothing. 2 March – nothing. 3 March, something caught my eye. The bottom of the front page. I read it through; then read it again.

## MAN ARRESTED AFTER DAUGHTER
## GOES MISSING

A thirty-six-year-old man has been arrested by
police after his daughter was reported missing by
neighbours. John Martin Robes of Stanmore, North
London, was taken into custody by police investigating the disappearance of his twelve-year-old
daughter, Heidi, who had not been seen for several
days previously. Heidi's mother is not believed to
live with the family and police were yesterday trying
to trace her. Neighbours claim that Robes and his
daughter could often be heard arguing loudly, and
that Heidi had some behavioural problems. A
spokesman for her school said that everyone there
hoped and prayed that she would be found safe
and well, but added that she had run away before.

There was no photograph.

I took out my notebook and wrote down the
details. Then checked 4 March, this time the whole
paper, but there was no further mention of the
arrest or the fate of the missing girl. Sometimes
when a kid from the wrong side of the tracks goes
missing – and this is especially true when they've
got a bit of a history – there's very little publicity
surrounding the disappearance. It can be a lottery.
A pretty, middle-class girl under the age of ten from
the Home Counties is going to get a ton and a half
of newsprint dedicated to her. A tough young
thing of twelve, born and bred on a council estate

and a teenager in all but name, just hasn't got the same selling power, and in the end, that's what it always comes down to.

But was she the girl I was looking for? I brought up the issue of 5 March, found nothing, then checked the 6th. There, on the right-hand column of page two was a short report sandwiched between news of a strike by Heathrow baggage-handlers and more Anglo-American bombing of Iraqi military installations. It stated that John Martin Robes had been charged with the murder of his daughter, Heidi, even though no body had been found, and was due to appear before magistrates that morning. Again there were no pictures of either accused or victim, but my interest was aroused, the main reason being the lack of a corpse. A corpse provides the police and the CPS with a lot of the evidence they need in order to secure a conviction. Take that away and nailing the killer becomes an uphill task. It made me wonder what it was the police had on Robes. The problem was it wasn't going to be that easy to find out. There was usually a minimum of six months between an arrest and a trial – it can sometimes take as long as a year – so it meant going through a lot more back issues of *The Times*, or finding a quicker means to locate the date. I decided to use the Web.

There were a number of PCs with Internet access tucked away on the opposite side of the room from the microfiche machines and I found one that was free. On the screen was a large icon representing something called *The Times* software. I clicked on it and a box appeared, prompting me to type in a keyword. I typed in the name 'John Robes' and looked at my watch. Five to four.

Five seconds later, a list of hits appeared in chronological order. At the top were the articles I'd already picked up in the March editions. After that there was nothing until 26 October, when a few brief lines outlined the first day of the trial of John Robes for the murder of his daughter. There was another piece on 28 October, detailing Robes's testimony on the witness stand, in which he'd tearfully denied all knowledge of his daughter's death, but had been unable to explain how a knife with her blood on it had been found in his house, as well as a bloodstained piece of her clothing. But the trial obviously hadn't caught the imagination of the media or the public, because again the article was short and there wasn't a further mention of the case until 3 November, when a headline announced that John Robes had been found guilty of murder and sentenced to life imprisonment.

I began reading the article. There were photographs this time – one of father, one of daughter. I only took the briefest look at him. He was a youngish-looking thirty-six, with an angular face and dark blond hair in a side parting, and in the photo he was smiling broadly. As is so often the case, he didn't look like a killer. And Heidi wasn't what I was expecting, either. She looked younger than twelve, with straight, light brown hair cut level with her chin and a much rounder face than her dad's. She was smiling too, in the same broad manner as the man who'd allegedly killed her, and her cheeks showed cute dimples. She didn't look like the sort of girl who had behavioural problems.

I stared at her image for a long time, knowing Dr Cheney's description, though very basic, matched with that of the girl smiling out at me. The years have been kind to me where tragedy is concerned, and I've learned to detach myself from the suffering of others, both those whose deaths I used to investigate and those I've caused. But the past few days had stretched that detachment to the limit. The murders of Ann Taylor and Andrea Bloom, two kids fighting against all the odds to make a life for themselves, coming after the death of my old friend Asif Malik, had hit me harder than I'd been prepared for. And now, as I sat there in the forced silence of that darkened windowless room on a cold December afternoon staring at the picture of a girl who'd died, helpless and alone, seven years earlier, for the first time in a long while I felt like crying.

Turning away from the pictures, I scrolled down and continued reading. John Robes, the article stated, had been found guilty of murder after a trial lasting just over a week. Once again, the fact that no body had been found was mentioned, but the forensic evidence of the knife and the clothing, coupled with the further discovery of a blood-stained gardening glove which two witnesses claimed to have seen in Robes's possession in the weeks prior to Heidi's disappearance, proved damning.

Robes had also admitted to having had a violent argument with his daughter on the night he claimed she'd run away, during which he'd struck her, but he continued to deny any part in her death. The jury hadn't believed him, and after a fourteen-hour deliberation had pronounced him guilty. Robes had broken down in tears at this point, and had taken several minutes to compose himself. The judge had then sentenced him to life imprisonment, calling his act 'as incomprehensible as it was barbaric', and had bemoaned the fact that Robes had provided no explanation as to why he'd done it, nor given any indication as to where the body was.

Something caught my eye and I froze. Down at the bottom of the article.

'Jesus Christ,' I whispered audibly, ignoring the looks of the other people on the PCs.

For a full ten seconds I didn't move, the shock rooting me to the spot. I've faced guns before; been shot at; been certain I was about to die. But nothing has ever incapacitated me as much as what I was looking at right now.

Because now I knew what had happened.

Jumping to my feet, I turned and walked away as fast as I could, knowing without a doubt that Ann Taylor's story was true and was the reason she'd died, and that the twelve-year-old Heidi Robes was the victim who had been murdered in the paedophile orgy. And that it was essential that Emma had reached her parents' home safely, because otherwise she was putting herself in extreme danger.

You see, she knew one of the men who I was now sure had been involved on that dark, terrifying night seven years ago; the man who seemed to keep popping up wherever I turned, and who'd been quoted at the bottom of the article as he talked to the assembled press outside the post-verdict court-room. It had been a harrowing case for all those involved, he'd said, but at least now justice had been seen to be done. Ironic words indeed, but understandable from the man who'd led the police murder investigation.

Detective Chief Inspector Simon Barron.

# 38

It all made sense. They'd had an inside link on the police investigation from the beginning, and it had to have been someone senior. Barron was a DCI, an officer privy to the most confidential information on the inquiry, including the name of the prime suspect: Billy West. He could have leaked the name without drawing suspicion to himself. And it had been Barron who'd been to see Dr Cheney asking questions about Ann; who'd not said anything to anyone else about what he was doing. And doubtless, it had been him too who'd been feeding Emma with the stories linking Nicholas Tyndall to the Khan/Malik murders, as he'd worked to deflect attention away from the true culprits.

Outside it was dark and the traffic on the main road had built up. I fumbled in my coat pocket for my phone and switched it on hurriedly. My hands were shaking and I silently cursed the fact that Emma had ever become involved in this case, and that I hadn't done more to stop her.

The phone rang to indicate that there was a message. I pressed the callback button and waited while the number rang twice.

It was Emma. She sounded breathless and excited. Static screeched in the background. 'Sorry about this, Dennis, but the job's got the better of me. I'm on the hard shoulder of the M4, somewhere near Swindon. I've just had a call from Simon Barron. He thinks he's onto something, but he's worried. He's saying that the people we're looking for have definitely got an insider on the murder squad. He wants to meet me at some offices over in Wembley. He says there's someone there he wants to introduce me to.' She gave me an address, adding that it was on an industrial estate near the new stadium. 'He must have found out about your involvement as well. Not that he knows who you really are, of course, but he knows that you're an investigator working the case, and that you've been speaking to Jamie Delly and Dr Cheney. And also that you've been helping me. He said I should call and get you over there, too. So I'm driving up there now. It's . . .' there was a pause while she checked her watch, 'five to one, and I'm about an hour and a half away. Hopefully, see you there. Call me. I really think we could be onto something here. Talk soon. Bye.'

The world seemed to melt around me, and the cars passing by became lost, watery silhouettes as I realized that I was too late, and that I'd surely helped Emma Neilson into her grave. An hour and a half away at five to one. It was now five past four. Even if she'd hit heavy traffic and got lost, and her journey had taken double the time, she'd still be there by now. And possibly dead.

The message ended, and I scrabbled at the phone with shaking hands, pressing 5 for redial.

Her mobile rang. And rang. Then went to voice-mail. I left a message as I hurried down the road towards the car. 'Do not go to that meeting with Simon Barron,' I shouted into the mouthpiece, making no effort to hide the panic in my voice. 'He's the insider on the murder squad, the one we want. If you go to that meeting, he'll kill you. I'm serious. If you get this message, call me back straight away.'

I rang off, then listened to her message again, writing down the address of the meeting place in my notebook. The car was two minutes' walk away – one minute if I ran – and I was on the right side of town for Wembley, so, traffic permitting, I had a chance of making it there in the next half-hour.

A cold wind whipped across the Colindale Road and I pulled up the collar of my jacket and tried to do the distance in a minute, running as fast as I could and dodging between faceless passers-by, not knowing what I was going to find when I finally stopped.

# 39

It had started to rain again as I turned off the roundabout and into the huge Wembley Park industrial estate. The road that ran through it in a shallow incline towards the immense building site that was the new football stadium was already busy with the first wave of commuter traffic. Huge, featureless business units and warehouses, swathed in the dim half-light of neon signs and glowing street lights, reared up on both sides, while every fifty yards or so another road branched out, clustered with further monotonous examples of the same bland architecture.

I was sweating, my hands sticky on the steering wheel, peering through the rain for the turning I wanted. I couldn't seem to see it. The site of the new stadium with its giant looping arch loomed closer and closer. It meant the end of the estate. It meant I'd missed the turning and wasted another precious few minutes. I could hear my heart hammering in my chest. Imagined Emma at Barron's mercy, and knew that my actions, my stupidity and my selfishness had helped to get her there. One victim in a long fucking line. I counted to ten in my head, urging myself to stay calm, to detach myself from the situation. To push her image out of my mind.

Another turning appeared on the right. I slowed down, looking for the road sign. The car behind me honked impatiently. I ignored him and slowed further. Then I spotted it, squinting through the windscreen wipers, my nose inches from the glass.

It was the one.

I pulled into the middle of the road without indicating and waited for a gap in the oncoming traffic. The car behind me couldn't get through and beeped again. I still ignored him. He beeped a third time. I felt like jumping out of the car, pulling the .45 and blowing out one of his headlights. Instead I closed my mind to everything except the task ahead, my fingers drumming loudly on the steering wheel, waiting.

There were ten yards between two of the cars coming towards me. Hardly a gap at all, but it was going to have to be enough. I took my chance and accelerated across, looking ahead for the offices of a company called Tembra Software.

The road was about a hundred yards long and dotted with storage units and warehouses. It came to a dead end in front of a large 1960s-style concrete building four storeys high, that was swathed in darkness apart from two illuminated windows on the third floor. A concrete wall topped with long ornamental black railings like spears bordered the plot, separating it from the businesses on either side. There was a rectangular concrete sign about two metres high at the entrance to the building's main car park. The sign was unlit, but as I drove towards it I was able to make out the darkened lettering: TEMBRA SOFTWARE. I was in the right place. The gates to the car park were open, but there were no cars inside and I could see from the tired state of the building's exterior that Tembra must have gone out of business some time ago.

I slowed down and pulled up at the side of the road twenty yards short of the entrance. I needed to make my decisions carefully. Barron was expecting me. He knew I'd come here in search of Emma because the bastard had been one step ahead of me the whole time, using Blondie to pick off all those potential witnesses whose information could help to solve the Malik/Khan murders. I was no longer in any doubt that Barron had been a participant on that night seven years ago, that he'd been one of the five people in the room when Heidi Robes had been murdered, because I couldn't believe that he'd be protecting these people unless he was one of them. And now he was finally tying up the loose ends. He'd finish off Emma, then finish off me. I wondered if he already knew my true identity, and, if so, whether that was why he'd told Blondie not to kill me if I turned up at Andrea's place the previous night, but to leave me there with the murder weapon and the corpses. Dennis Milne, the killer, returns.

I got out of the car and closed the door quietly. Behind me, the traffic rumbled endlessly past on the main road through the estate, but it was quiet at this end. The warehouses on both sides of the Tembra building had their shutters down, and appeared deserted. There was no sign of Emma's car anywhere.

I looked up at the two lights on the third floor. There was no-one in either of the windows, no flickering shadows, but I felt sure that Barron was in there, and that if he was, so was Emma. This was definitely the place where he'd want to finish this thing; in the darkness, away from any witnesses. I figured he wouldn't have anyone with him. He was trying to cut all links between himself and the crimes of his past. It would be far better to operate alone on this one and be safe in the knowledge that he wouldn't have anyone else to deal with later. That meant he'd either be by the front door waiting for me to come in that way or, alternatively, up on the third floor (in my opinion the more likely location). He'd know that when I turned up I'd come inside to investigate, because I'd want to know whether or not Emma was still here. He'd be able to watch for my arrival far more easily from the higher vantage point. So that meant that the front door was probably free.

But caution told me to avoid it, even though it was the most direct route and time wasn't on my side. Instead, I headed through the empty car park of the warehouse next door and made my way along the narrow alleyway that separated it from Tembra's boundary wall. When I was out of sight of the two illuminated windows and level with the rear of the Tembra building, I reached up, grabbed hold of the railings and scrabbled up the wall until I managed to get a toehold in the tiny space between two of them. Using the top of the railings to pull myself upright, I very carefully lifted one leg over them. The metal spikes scraped against my jeans, and I was conscious that one slip and I could end up castrated. I repeated the process with the other leg, then half jumped, half slid down the wall.

Somehow I landed on my feet, painfully but unscathed, to find myself in Tembra's empty rear car park.

Which was the moment my mobile started ringing.

I was wearing the black leather jacket I'd bought and the phone seemed to take for ever to find, but eventually I located it and pressed the answer button, putting it to my ear.

'Hello?'

'Dennis? Please . . .' The words were a terrified, forced whisper.

'Emma! Where the hell are you? Are you all right?'

'I'm at that place I was meant to meet Simon,' she hissed, her voice shaking. 'I'm in trouble . . .'

I could hear background noise. Footsteps. Emma cried out in fear.

'I'm coming to get you,' I told her frantically. 'Don't worry.'

But I was already talking to a dead phone. I held it to my ear for a few more seconds, waiting until I was sure she wasn't going to make another call, then switched it off.

So she was alive. And Barron was impatient. I had no doubt that it was he who'd controlled that phone call, just to make sure that I took the bait. But at least now I had a chance of success. They wouldn't expect me to be here already. If he'd seen me, he wouldn't have bothered getting Emma to call.

The rear of the building was shabbier than the front, and someone had spray-painted rune-like patterns that may have been gang signs on the brickwork between the ground-floor windows, several of which had been smashed behind the metal security bars. The smoked-glass double doors that led out into the car park had probably been quite plush once, but were now worn and scratched. They were also locked.

I walked round to the other side of the building, looking for another way in, my footsteps sounding artificially loud on the chipped tarmac. The first-floor windows weren't protected by bars, and one was broken, with a single piece of jagged glass jutting up from its base. A drainpipe ran beside it and I contemplated shinning up it and getting in that way, but it felt loose to the touch.

I was going to have to go in the way he wanted me to. I looked at my watch. Five to five. Rush hour. The rain continued to pound down and I knew that this could be Emma's and my final resting place – a bland and derelict building on a lonely industrial estate in the midst of this cold, teeming city. The thought frightened me.

But fear's good. Fear keeps you alive and hones the senses. Fear is what can get you out of these situations.

I started walking again. Slowly and quietly, circumnavigating the building. Time now suddenly back on my side.

When I reached the corner of the wall that faced the building's main entrance, I slowly poked my head round. The double doors were closed, but unlike the back ones, they didn't appear to be locked. Beyond them was darkness, with no sign of anyone. I moved back out of sight, leant down and picked up a loose chunk of cement and chucked it round the corner at the lower part of the doors. It struck with a light tap, and I waited to see if this aroused anyone's curiosity.

Five seconds passed. Nothing happened.

It could have been a trap, but in the end I had no choice. I stepped out of the shadows and, drawing the .45, tried the handle. The door opened with a squeak that probably seemed a lot louder than it actually was, and I stepped inside, half expecting to hear the sound of a weapon being cocked, then the final, deadly explosion of gunfire. But the corridor ahead of me was empty. Half a dozen linoleum steps led up to the next floor. I crept over to the bottom and listened.

Again, nothing. Not a sound.

The steps climbed at rigid right angles between the floors all the way to the top of the building. A dim half-glow from the street lamps outside provided the only light. In the distance, a long way off, I heard the sound of a siren. Nothing moved. I started up the steps, my finger tensing on the trigger of the .45.

The siren faded into the night and the silence grew louder.

I reached the first floor. Above me, shadows from the city ran across the grainy, bare walls.

I kept going, straining to hear any sound from above, and fighting to stop myself from breaking into a run and announcing my presence prematurely.

All my life I've had a ruthless streak, an ability to shut myself away from the suffering of others and not let it get to me. You need that when you're policing the crime-worn streets of London, or when you're living and running a business in the Philippines. Or when you kill people for money. I relied on that ruthless streak now to shut out Emma's suffering, while I concentrated on preparing myself for Barron.

The siren began again in the distance, a long slow whine, joined shortly afterwards by a second. Charging off towards the scene of another bloody crime. It was a noise that reminded me of home. Of life here in the big, violent city. Always some emergency going on. A never-ending conflict between the haves and the would-haves-if-they-could-get-their-hands-on-it, and the people meant to keep them apart – the coppers. Men like Asif Malik, who'd paid the ultimate price for his work in such a thankless job. And once upon a time, men like me, who'd instead been corrupted by it.

I reached the third floor and stepped onto a landing with a large window at the end that looked out onto the industrial estate. A solitary picture – a cheap-looking abstract that was barely visible in the gloom – hung crookedly from the wall. There were corridors to my left and right. The one to my right was where I'd seen the lights earlier. It stretched for about fifty feet, with doors facing each other on either side, all of them wide open, before ending at a windowless wall with part of its brickwork exposed. The second and third doors on the left led into the rooms with the lights on.

Instinctively, I looked over my shoulder and found myself staring back at a perfectly symmetrical corridor going down the other way. Except on this one, all the doors were closed. Barron was not making this very easy for me, but then I'd expected that.

I waited where I was for several seconds, aware that the sirens were getting closer, then slowly walked towards the lights, holding the .45 two-handed in front of me.

I passed the first couple of open doors and peered into empty offices, long since stripped of fittings and furniture. I kept going, conscious of the sound of my footfalls on the linoleum. He had to know I was coming. Even tiptoeing as quietly as possible, my approach must have been audible amidst the dead silence of the corridor.

I came to the second set of doors. To my right, darkness. To my left, light. I took a step forward and looked in.

Something immediately caught my attention. A leg, partly concealed by the angle of the open door.

The sirens had been joined by a third, the whining getting louder as they entered the estate.

A trap. It could be a trap.

With a sudden lunge, I kicked the door wide open and burst into the brightly lit office, gun swinging in a wide arc.

And groaned.

Because I was too late. Had always been too late. And had walked once again into a trap that had been expertly set for me.

# 40

For a moment, I simply stared at the corpse, unable to move. Full of regret that yet another innocent life had been taken.

Then I shook myself out of my torpor and walked over to him.

DCI Simon Barron was slumped against the wall at a slightly crooked angle, his eyes closed, his white shirt and pale blue tie drenched in blood. I could see that he'd been stabbed a number of times in the chest and abdomen in what must have been a frenzied attack. The entry wounds were clearly visible, and the blood that had flowed freely from them had now coagulated. A pool had formed round the top of his legs and had dyed the edges of his khaki raincoat crimson. His face was white and I guessed he'd been dead a while. An hour or two, at least.

The noise of the sirens was now continuous and coming closer and closer. Through the window I could see the blue and white flashes of light dancing across the night sky above the estate's buildings. The vehicles were on the main road but no more than a couple of hundred yards away, and as I watched the first police car turned into the cul-de-sac and approached the Tembra Software building at speed.

At that moment, I knew they were coming for me.

I turned and ran like I've never run before, charging along the corridor and across the landing, taking the steps three and even four at a time. The third floor became the second floor, the second the first, and outside I could hear the cars pulling up and the shouts of the arriving police officers as they began to secure the area. I knew they would go round the back and surround the building to make sure their fugitive didn't get out. I had to beat them to it.

I turned left on the first floor and raced down the corridor, trying to remember where I'd seen the broken window. When I got to the last door on the right, I opened it, ran inside, and saw that I'd guessed correctly. Running forward, I kicked the glass jutting up from the base of the window and knocked it flying. It shattered loudly as it hit the ground. I clambered out, cutting my leg in the process, and slid down the nearby guttering. There was a tearing sound as it came away from the wall. I was still five or six feet from the ground and had to jump the rest of the way. I hit the concrete hard, a piece of the guttering landing on my head, then turned to run round the back of the building.

I heard someone shouting 'Stop! Armed police!' from behind me, but I kept running, across the empty car park and up to the wall at the back, taking it in one go. Rather than trying to manoeuvre myself over, I simply went head first and hoped for the best, the best being in this case a painful landing on my hands, followed by an involuntary two-second handstand and then a forward roll into a puddle, during which the .45 fell out of my waistband, though thankfully didn't discharge.

I jumped up again, retrieving and replacing the gun in the process.

I was in a large builders' yard filled with various pieces of plant, a handful of combi vans and a number of metal sea containers. Plenty of places to hide, and no sign of anyone. I was tired, but adrenalin, coupled with the knowledge that the police were right behind me, kept me moving. I could hear one of the coppers shouting that I'd gone over the wall, and he sounded close, so I started running again.

I cleared the builders' yard in the space of thirty seconds and found a hole in the fence at the other end which led onto one of the estate's roads. I went straight through it, ran a further hundred yards, turned into another road and ran down that. When I got to the end, I turned right and slowed to a walk.

There weren't many pedestrians about, but there was enough slow-moving traffic to delay any vehicle-bound pursuit.

I knew then that I should have called it a day. I could have walked away and got on the plane back to the Philippines, confident at least that the reason Malik had died was connected somehow with what had happened seven years previously, and that Pope, Blacklip, Slippery Billy and now Blondie had been punished for it. There were unanswered questions, of course, such as exactly what it was that Jason Khan had found out months after the end of Ann's sessions with Dr Cheney that had prompted him to meet Malik and for the killing spree to start, but no-one could say that I hadn't done my bit for my old colleague and friend, and that I had given him some measure of justice, even if his family would never know the true story.

I should have called it a day, but of course I didn't. Somewhere out there was a man who had worn a black leather mask and tortured a young girl to death one night, and who, quite possibly, still walked free. I wanted to find him, and those still helping him.

And this time I knew where to look.

# 41

I waited for him in the dim, reddish light of the underground car park. I knew he'd come. His car, a Jaguar S-Type Sedan, perfect for a man of his seniority, remained parked in his spot. He was working late that night. It was half past seven and I'd been there close to half an hour, standing in the corner shadows not far from the pedestrian entrance. Men and women in business suits came through every so often, the high-pitched ding of the lift or the tattoo of footfalls in the stairwell announcing their arrival. Their numbers were getting fewer now as the evening wore on, and only a couple of dozen vehicles remained, dotted about the cavernous room.

My leg hurt where I'd cut it on the glass. Before I'd come here, I'd found a pharmacy and bought a basic first-aid kit. I'd then returned to my room in Paddington, strapped it up crudely with the bandage, and finally cleared the place of all the essentials, before checking out. I was now beginning to get used to the dull throbbing of the wound. To be fair, I was now beginning to get used to injuries in general, having received more in the past five days than I'd had in the previous ten years. It was the price I had to pay for operating alone.

I was doing some stretching exercises to encourage the circulation and warm up a bit when the lift dinged again. A couple of seconds later, a shortish man with thick black curly hair and a moustache emerged, his footsteps echoing as he strode purposefully towards the Jaguar, a briefcase in one hand. As I watched from my vantage point ten yards away, he flicked off the car alarm remotely, then opened the car boot and chucked the briefcase in, before heading round to the driver's door.

As he got in, I drew the short-barrelled Browning pistol Tyndall had supplied me with and came out of the shadows, screwing on the silencer as I walked towards his car. The engine started with a low rumble that hinted at a lot of power.

He didn't see me until I'd pulled open the front passenger door and deposited myself in the seat next to him. A shocked expression shot across his face and he started to protest, but I wasn't having any of that. I smiled and shoved the silencer against his cheek, using enough force to push his head back against the window. He ended up in a position that looked very uncomfortable.

'My wallet's in my jacket pocket,' he spluttered. 'Take it, please.'

'No thanks, Theo,' I said. 'I've got a better idea. I'm going to ask you a question and you're going to answer it truthfully. Otherwise I'm going to shoot you in the face right now, then drop you in the back seat and let you bleed to death while I drive your nice flash car out of here.'

I waited for Theo Morris to protest, to tell me he didn't know what the hell I was talking about, but he said nothing, just whimpered slightly. His expression slackened, or maybe it was just the way the silencer was pushed against him, but I knew that he was aware that I was the man he'd either been trying to have killed or framed these past few days, and I could tell that he wasn't going to bother playing the innocent. I also had a feeling that he wanted to unburden himself. It was something in his eyes. Defeat? Guilt? Probably both. This guy was no ruthless pro. He might have been good at handing out orders from the comfort of his air-conditioned office, but he wasn't the sort to get his hands dirty. Somehow that made him worse.

'What's the question?' he asked after a long pause.

'I think you know, but I'll ask it anyway. When you sent those men to kill Les Pope on Sunday, and to kill Andrea Bloom at her home in Hackney yesterday, on whose authority were you acting?'

'Oh, God . . .'

'He can't help you now, Theo. Only *you* can help you.'

'I swear I didn't know it would end like this. I didn't ask for the bloodbath last night. I just wanted Crown to shut the girl up. How was I to know he was such a bloody psychopath?'

'Crown? Was he the blond guy? The one who was sent to meet me on Saturday with the ticket back to the Philippines?' Theo tried to nod, but it was difficult in the position he was in. 'Well, Crown's dead now. And so will you be unless you answer my question.'

He paused again and I leaned forward and pushed harder on the gun. His cheek began to go red and he grunted in pain.

'My boss,' he said. 'The company's CEO, Eric Thadeus. He got me to organize it. I wouldn't have done it, but—'

'But he paid you well, no doubt.'

'I told you, I honestly didn't know that it would end up like it did. I didn't want it to get messy.'

Theo Morris was only a little guy, and slightly built, too, apart from round the belly area. But I guessed that when he was in the boardroom he was full of confidence and swagger. This was definitely a man who lived his life knowing he was one of the top guys in his closeted little world, a big fish in the corporate pond. Only now, as he sat here helpless with me, was he discovering that true power came not from the influence you held amongst your kind, but from the barrel of the gun, and unfortunately for Theo, he was facing down the wrong end of it.

'Where's Eric Thadeus tonight?'

'I don't know.'

'Yes, you do. Don't lie. There's no point. Whatever he's promised you that you haven't already got, you're not going to get now, so don't waste your time protecting him. He's finished, and you're staying with me until I find out where he is.'

'He's at his place in Bedfordshire. He's staying there until tomorrow. After that he's flying out to another of his homes in the Bahamas for a couple of weeks.'

I kept the gun where it was for a couple of seconds, then decided he was telling the truth, and removed it from his face, positioning it instead across my lap with the silencer still pointing in his direction.

'All right, turn off the car phone.' He did as he was told. 'Now start driving. We're going to Bedfordshire.'

Theo looked at me like I was mad. 'He's got security there.'

'I'm sure he has. Start driving.'

I think he knew there was no point in arguing or begging for his life, so he put the car in reverse, pulled out of his space and settled once again for telling me he'd never wanted it to end like this.

I told him to shut up. I really wasn't interested.

The drive was long, silent and uneventful. Theo tried only once to make conversation but barely managed a few words before I cut him off and put the radio on, turning the volume up. I didn't want to hear anything from him – not small talk, not excuses. Nothing. As far as I was concerned, he was as guilty as all of them.

I tried not to think, working hard to empty my mind of all its fears and doubts. I'd been betrayed, and betrayed badly; I was trapped in a country in which I'd been a fugitive from the law for three years. If I was captured, I'd be lucky to see the outside of a prison cell again. If I escaped, I wasn't at all sure I could go back to where I'd come from and carry on as before in business with a man I'd once trusted, but who now had questions of his own to answer. Tomboy Darke had relationships with people who'd been involved in some horrific acts, and things between us could never be the same again. But now wasn't the time to dwell on that.

The radio station we listened to as Theo drove was Magic FM, which specializes in easy listening tunes. They played 'The Boys Of Summer' by Don Henley, followed by a couple of old Elvis Presley numbers. Neither of us sang along, although Theo appeared to relax a little and his driving became less erratic. I noticed that he was still sweating, which was understandable.

At eight o'clock, the news came on. As Magic was a London-based station, the top story was the massacre at Andrea Bloom's place the previous evening. Theo sighed loudly and tutted as the newsreader reported that two men and two women had been stabbed and bludgeoned to death at a house in Hackney, in what she called 'another terrifying tale from the violent city'. The identities of the victims had not yet been released and the police were keeping an open mind regarding the motive, which usually meant they didn't have a clue. There was no mention of Barron's death in Wembley, but no doubt this would follow soon enough.

I lit a cigarette, sat back and watched Theo as he drove us up the M1 in the direction of Bedfordshire.

A little over an hour later, some ten minutes after we'd pulled off the motorway, we passed through a pretty village which was little more than a collection of houses and a church, and took a left-hand turn. The road started to climb up a tree-lined hill, and large detached houses appeared on both sides, all set back from the road, the majority behind imposing gates. It was a fitting spot for the wealthy to live in, allowing them to look down on the rest of the village from their superior position.

'How far?' I asked Theo.

'We're almost there.'

'Point it out to me as we pass, but keep driving.'

'There it is,' he said half a minute later as the road began to flatten out. He was pointing to a white-washed stone wall about ten feet high coming up on our left. As we passed the wrought-iron gates, I caught a glimpse of the house itself, which stood at the end of a long drive. It was a huge, Elizabethan-style double-fronted mansion, with latticed bay windows and tar-blackened wooden beams running from roof to ground.

Several more houses followed on the left, before giving way to woodland. About a hundred yards further on, I spotted a single-lane track veering off into the trees. 'Pull down there,' I ordered Theo.

He did as he was told and his face took on a panicked look. This was the end of the line for him, the point at which he'd find out whether he was to live or die.

Twenty yards down the track I told him to pull over onto the verge.

'I'm not going to say a word about this, you know,' he told me as he brought the Jaguar to a halt. 'I don't want the police involved any more than you do.'

'What sort of security does Thadeus have at this place?'

'I've only been up here a couple of times. On those occasions, he had a night watchman, but that's it. He's also got cameras in the grounds.'

I thought that he might well have more security tonight, just to be on the safe side. Until he had confirmation that I was out of his hair.

'All right, cut the engine.'

'I thought I might be able to go. I've told you—'

I pushed the gun into his ribcage and he turned off the ignition. 'Out.' We both stepped out of the car. 'Open the boot.'

He went round and reluctantly flicked it open.

'Now get in.'

He started shaking. 'Don't kill me. Please.'

'You deserve it, Theo. You're the lowest form of scum, getting other people to do your dirty work, but I'm not going to kill you. Unless, that is, you're still standing there in five seconds.'

He stared at me imploringly, then must have decided that he had nothing to lose by begging for his life. He told me that he had a wife and kids, and could I spare him just for their sakes, because he knew he didn't honestly deserve to live, and if he could turn back the clock, then by God he'd do it like a shot. I got the feeling he'd never begged for anything before, but it was worth the effort. His wife and kids were probably as rotten as he was, but I didn't like the idea of adding yet another small tragedy to the many that had been played out during this whole bloody saga, so when he finally raised his leg up to clamber in the boot, I smacked him hard across the back of the head with the butt of the gun and bundled him, unconscious, inside.

I shut the boot, took the keys from the ignition and locked the car. Theo Morris was going to have an uncomfortable night, but, as he himself had pointed out, it was no more than he deserved.

## 42

I started walking back in the direction of the village.
Above me the sky was an angry morass of clouds
skitting west to east, obscuring the light of the
three-quarter moon at regular intervals. A hard
wind whipped about my shoulders, colder than the
one I'd left behind in London, and I pulled up my
collar in a futile effort to curb the draught that
threatened to whistle right through me.

The house next door to Thadeus's place was a
wide single-storey ranch-style building, complete
with a huge wagon wheel attached to an artificial
rock in the driveway. There were four cars parked
up and plenty of lights on inside, but the owners
were obviously less security-conscious than Mr
Thadeus, because the main gate was open.

I stepped onto the drive and made my way over
to a path at the side of the house, keeping close to
the wall that linked the two properties. I could
hear the clink of glasses and the high-pitched

laughter of middle-aged women who'd had too much to drink. It sounded as though there was a party going on in there, and I felt vaguely jealous that they probably had nothing more to worry about than hangovers the next day.

Halfway down the path, a newish-looking garden shed backed onto the boundary wall. I climbed on top of it as quietly as possible, and peered straight into the thick foliage on Thadeus's side of the wall. Not hearing any movement on the other side, I heaved myself up and over the wall, sliding down until I hit the ground with little more than a rustle of leaves and a grunt. Recovering, I pushed my way through the bushes and slowly poked my head out the other side.

I was about twenty yards from the corner of Thadeus's house. Between me and it was a neatly trimmed lawn that looked beautifully green, even in this light. There was a small single-storey gate-house behind one of the gateposts, which was not visible from the road outside. A light was on in the gatehouse and I could see the balding profile of a man sitting in there. There were several screens in front of him, which were obviously the views from security cameras, but he didn't appear to be watching them very closely. From the angle of his head, I guessed he was reading a book and trying to look as subtle about it as possible, just in case the boss was watching. There was only one way of checking whether or not Theo was right about him being the only security, and that was to wait.

So that's what I did.

Five minutes passed. Then ten. I was on the verge of concluding that Thadeus was confident there was no way I was coming for him, so had not bothered beefing up his protection, when a guard in full uniform and a peaked cap ambled round from the back of the house, smoking a cigarette. He had an Alsatian dog with him. I'd half expected this. The guards had to have something to scare away intruders, since I suspected that neither of them had any weapons of their own. It's one of the quirks of British law that you can employ security guards to protect your life and property, but their powers of arrest and use of force are so limited that they're largely ineffective. Even if their dog bites you, they could be found liable in a civil court – but observing this hound, I didn't think he was going to present too much of a problem. He was obviously well-fed and looked fairly close to retirement. The guard with him, who looked pretty close to retirement himself, was having to pull on the lead just to get him to keep to the ambling pace. The dog stopped and I thought he might have caught a whiff of my scent, but he cocked his leg and took a quick leak, while the guard puffed loudly on his smoke, pausing between drags to clear his throat.

I slipped back into the cover of the bushes, pushed my scarf up so it was covering my face from the bridge of my nose down, and waited as the dog finished his business and they continued their walk. The keys on the guard's belt jangled loudly as he got nearer. The art of surprise had clearly never been a major part of his repertoire.

I watched as they drew level with me, about ten feet away. The dog still didn't seem to smell anything, but as he came within sight of the gatehouse twenty yards away, he began to speed up. Maybe it was dinner time.

I came out as silently as possible, took four quick strides and placed a gloved hand over the guard's mouth, pulling him back into a tight embrace. At the same time, I pushed the silencer into his cheek. The dog turned and growled angrily. It looked like he was going to attempt to earn his keep for once. I had to act fast.

'Call the dog off or it dies,' I told him in muffled tones, 'and keep very quiet. Now.' I removed my hand, but kept the gun in exactly the same position.

'It's all right, Prince,' the guard whispered nervously, leaning down to pet the dog, who relaxed his posture slightly. 'Calm, boy,' he said, then looked at me. 'I don't want any trouble, mister. I'm not going to resist, all right?'

'You do what I say, no-one'll get hurt. I've got no interest in you.' I let go of him. 'Now keep walking and make for the gatehouse. When you get there, go inside as you would do normally, and I'll take over from there. And please don't try anything, because I will kill you. I guarantee it.'

My voice was calm, which in my experience is usually the best means of convincing someone that you're serious, particularly when you're threatening to shoot them. Come over all panicky and nervous and they'll think that maybe they haven't lost all control of the situation, and try and do something about it. Particularly old-timers like this guy. He might have been pretty crap at his work, but I'd bet he still took pride in it, and wouldn't want to be made to look a fool.

I gave him a push and he started walking. The dog continued to growl, but followed when he gave it a pull on the lead. I wasn't sure what I was going to do about old Prince. I couldn't very well kill him (not after seeing what the death of Tex had done to its owner), but I couldn't exactly leave him loose, either.

'How many in the house?' I asked him. 'And answer quietly.'

'I don't know. This is my first night here. We only got called up on short notice.'

'But you were met by someone?'

'Yeah, the guy who owns the place. He's the only one I've seen.'

'OK, keep quiet now.'

As we reached the gatehouse, he opened the door and stepped inside, just like I'd told him to. Prince squeezed past him.

'All right, Bill?' said the one sitting down with the book, still obscured from my vision. 'Anything happening?'

I took that as my cue to come in and point my gun at him.

He turned round, saw me with my face hidden by the scarf, and adopted an expression of alarm that was so dramatic, it looked comical. He raised his arms quickly, then froze like a kid in a game of Mr Wolf. The book dropped loudly to the floor. It was a hardback with a title I didn't recognize. He started to speak, but I cut him off with a snapped 'Be quiet!' I turned the gun on Bill and told him to secure the dog.

Bill was sensible. He didn't argue. Neither did he ask me what I thought I was doing, or tell me I was making a big mistake. He just connected Prince's lead to a hook on the wall. There was still enough slack for the dog to move around, but not to get at me.

'Now muzzle him.'

Bill found a muzzle on the worktop, beside a kettle and a couple of mugs, and leant down to do the honours.

I turned back to Bill's colleague. 'Move away from the desk and face the wall.'

He paused, staring at me like he knew it was the end, and I had to tell him again, adding that if he co-operated nothing would happen to him. I motioned with the gun towards the wall. Finally, he did what he was told, but he still didn't look too sure about it, even with my words of reassurance.

Then, out of the corner of my eye, I saw Bill move

his hand towards the hook. He was going to try something. I couldn't believe it. I swung round and his hand stopped six inches from its target. He tried to put on an innocent expression, but it didn't really work. I started to tell him that it wasn't worth dying a hero, but before I could finish, his friend lunged forward and rugby-tackled me round the waist with surprising speed, one hand grabbing wildly for my gun arm, before clamping over my wrist with a strength driven by adrenalin.

'Help me, Bill,' he shouted, panic in his breath.

Bill went for the hook again, and I fell back hard against the door frame under the weight of the assault, my gun arm forced skywards.

Reflexively, I pulled the trigger. It might even have been completely accidental, I'm not sure. Either way, the result was the same. The silencer spat and the bullet caught Bill in the head. At least, I thought it did. He cried out and fell backwards, tripping over Prince before landing on his arse, both hands clutching at the side of his head.

'I'm hit!' he wailed, as blood seeped through his fingers. Prince jumped on him, whining balefully. 'I'm down, help me.'

As Bill's colleague turned round to see what was going on, he relaxed his grip on my wrist and I took the opportunity to pull my arm free and shove the silencer against his cheek.

'Oh God,' he said, at which point I kneed him very hard in the bollocks and pushed him away. As he doubled over in pain, I grabbed hold of him and pushed him back into the seat he'd been occupying until a few seconds earlier.

I turned to Bill. He was wailing, and Prince was now licking the blood running down his fingers with worrying enthusiasm. 'You've shot me,' he said, sounding like he was going to be with us for a few seconds yet.

'In the ear,' I replied. 'I shot you in the ear, and it was an accident. If you want to blame anyone, blame your friend,' I said. 'Now get up and muzzle that dog, like you were meant to do in the first place.'

At first he didn't move, but when I threatened to shoot him in the other ear he finally managed to take his hands away from the wound and do as he was told. It was still bleeding but, unlike Jamie Delly's, the ear remained largely intact.

I got Bill's colleague to open the drawers of the desk in front of him, and located a pair of plastic handcuffs in the second one down. I sat them both in the corner, next to Prince, and got Bill's partner to cuff them both together at the wrist and throw me the key. They assured me that they wouldn't do a thing if I left them as they were, but they were hardly immobile, or likely to be true to their word, so I hunted round until I found a ball of thick green string and a pair of scissors in another drawer, and bound them together back to back, before tying a double reef knot at the end. You wouldn't have to be Houdini to get out of it, but it would take a while, and a while was all I wanted.

'I need an ambulance,' said Bill when I'd finished. 'I'm losing a lot of blood. I feel faint.'

He wasn't losing a lot of blood. The bullet had somehow only managed to cause a minor flesh wound, but I was beginning to feel sorry for them both, so I found a clean rag, wet it in the sink and wrapped it round his ear.

I removed a small bunch of keys from Bill's belt and asked him which one opened the house.

'I don't know,' he answered. 'He never told us. This cloth's really cold. It's dripping water everywhere.'

I got back to my feet. 'Remind me never to hire your security outfit,' I said, and left them there, explaining that I'd call an ambulance shortly so long as they were quiet. 'Make a noise and you can stay like that all night.'

When I was outside, I found the key for the gatehouse door and locked it. Then I turned and, as quietly as possible, began making my way towards the house, keeping close to the foliage.

# 43

The rear of the property looked out onto a second lawn as large as the first, with a swimming pool at the far end. There were lights on inside the house, but the curtains were drawn so I couldn't see anything. I moved quietly forward and listened at one of the windows, picking up the sound of muffled voices. So they were here. I looked at my watch. Nine twenty-five p.m.

A substantial conservatory jutted out from the house and I walked across and tried the French windows that led into it. They were locked. I fumbled in my pocket for the keys, and tried them one by one. The fourth one opened the door and I crept inside, gently closing it behind me and removing the Browning and silencer from my pocket. The interior of the conservatory was bathed in the dim quarter-light provided by the lamps in the other rooms. Two long sofas ran down each side of it and a mahogany coffee table in the middle contained a selection of magazines. I noticed a *Country Life* and a *Good Housekeeping*, as well as the latest statement of accounts for Thadeus Holdings. Nothing controversial, then. But that was only to be expected. Like so many paedophiles, Eric Thadeus was bound to be a good actor.

The door connecting the conservatory to the rest of the house was open, and I went through into a panelled hallway with impressive watercolours of country scenes on the walls. The door to my left was ajar and I could hear voices drifting through from further inside the house. I stepped across the polished floorboards carefully, not wanting to make any noise as I made my way over to the door.

It led into a large pine kitchen with black granite worktops. On the far side of the room, another door was open, through which I could hear the clink of glasses as well as the voices of the people I'd come to kill, far clearer now.

'I'll open some more wine,' I heard the man say, and a second later his chair legs scraped across the floor as he got up from the table.

I made no move to hide as Eric Thadeus, a bigger man than I'd been expecting, dressed casually in chinos and a cotton shirt, came striding into the room carrying an empty wine bottle. I noticed he had worn leather slippers on. Then, as he saw me and opened his mouth to speak, I shot him in the left leg about six inches above the knee. He gasped, dropping the wine bottle as his leg went from under him. The bottle shattered on the floor's terracotta tiles and he fell awkwardly amongst the glass, banging his head on the door frame as he did so. I stepped over him and into the house's lavish dining room, leaving Thadeus moaning in agony and clutching at his shattered leg.

'Hello, Emma,' I said, raising the gun so it was pointed at her head.

She was at the far end of the table, the remains of a glass of white wine still in her hand. Her red-gold hair was tied back in a ponytail, and the elfin face beneath it a mask of shock. 'Dennis, please, I can explain.' She put the glass down on the table and burst into tears. 'He made me come here,' she sobbed.

'Sure he did. You look like you're under a lot of duress.' I walked over to the table, keeping the gun pointed at her head. 'Do you have any idea what this man's done, or the suffering he's caused?'

'You don't understand,' she replied, looking at me pleadingly through the tears. She was a damned talented actress, I had to give her that, and her expression was so genuine it made me doubt her role in all this myself. Even though I knew she was as guilty as sin. 'Thank God you're here,' she continued. 'He's got my parents hostage. He's had them for days. Either I do what he says or he's going to kill them.' She got to her feet and I

413

saw that she was wearing a sleeveless white dress that made her look years younger.

'Stay where you are.'

She was sobbing uncontrollably now. Almost like a child. 'But they're downstairs in the cellar, that's where he's been keeping them. I've got to see them and check they're all right. Please, Dennis, you've got to believe me. I can prove it.' She came towards me, and I told her again to stay where she was. But she kept coming, because she knew as well as I did that I couldn't shoot her. The doubt must have been evident on my face. In the kitchen, Thadeus continued to wail loudly and dramatically in an effort to summon help.

'Emma, stop. I'm serious.'

She stopped. Five feet away, standing there with a vulnerability that made my legs go weak. She was truly beautiful in her misery, her big hazel eyes begging me to believe her. And I wanted to. Christ, I wanted to. I was faltering, and we both knew it.

There was a sudden sound behind me, and the next second I was pitched forward as someone grabbed me round the middle and knocked the gun out of my hand. It clattered to the floor, landing at Emma's feet. I hit the dining-room wall head on, knocking a painting off it.

Dazed, I didn't have time to think about resistance as I was pushed down to my knees and my arm pulled up painfully behind my back. I managed to look round and saw that I was being

414

manhandled by a powerfully built young man in the same security guard's outfit as Bill and his friend. Unfortunately, this was where the resemblance between him and them ended. This guy, with his dark buzzcut and rugged outdoor features, was definitely ex-military, and by the speed and effectiveness of his assault, I'd have said marines or paras. Now I was in real trouble.

'You don't understand,' I told him through gritted teeth. 'These people are guilty of some horrendous crimes.'

'Shut the fuck up!' he demanded, then turned to Emma. 'Pardon my French, miss. I don't like criminals. I think you'd better call an ambulance for your father.'

Emma's face broke into a relieved smile. 'Oh, thank God you've come,' she told him. 'This man was going to kill me.'

'Don't listen to her,' I hissed, but his response was to put more pressure on my arm and I had to stop speaking as I gritted my teeth in pain. It felt like the damn thing was breaking.

'You were saying something about people in the cellar, miss?' he asked. 'Is there anyone down there?'

She started to cry again, then picked up the gun by her feet. 'Yes, it's my parents,' she sobbed. 'They're being held hostage . . .'

Her sobbing stopped abruptly as she turned the gun round so it was pointed at him. She gave him a sweet smile through the tears. 'But don't you worry your handsome little head about that.'

I tried to say something, but she never gave me the chance. With the coy little smile still very much in place, she pulled the trigger.

The gun hissed and the grip on my arm relaxed as the security guard tottered and fell to one side, a big red mark appearing where his right eye had been. His body shivered violently, then lay still. She was as good a shot as she'd claimed when she'd first pulled a gun on me.

'My, my, Dennis, you are proving resilient,' she said, her smile taking on a malevolence that until that moment I'd never seen. 'We keep putting these obstacles in your path, and you keep overcoming them. You were meant to be in custody facing murder charges by now. That's the whole reason you've been kept alive this long. Mind you, I think we should have suspected that you'd make it here.'

'Who are you?' I whispered, unsure what else to say.

'I'm Emma Neilson, of course; the woman you slept with. And this . . .' she motioned with the gun towards the door, beyond which Thadeus continued to moan loudly, 'this is my father.'

She took a sip of wine, enjoying my reaction, oblivious to the security guard lying dead on the floor a few feet away. It made me wonder how I could have been so blind to the blackness within her, how my instincts could have failed me so utterly.

'I suppose you thought he only went for kids, didn't you?' she continued. 'Well, they've always been his favourite, I have to admit, but he was married once. To my mother. Only she died in a car crash. They called it an accident, but I don't think so. I think he had a hand in it.' She walked past the body, still keeping the gun trained on me, until she was a yard from the door and looking through it. 'Isn't that right, Daddy? You had Mummy killed so you could have me? Because you're a dirty fucking pervert.' There was an undertone of bitterness in her voice, but also a measure of triumphalism, as if she was only now finally asserting her power.

'Help me, love,' I heard him say. 'Get an ambulance, please.'

She ignored him, turning her gaze back to me. Her face no longer looked pretty. It looked vicious. 'Do you know something?' she demanded. 'He started fucking me when I was eight years old. Eight. That's how old I was. And every time he did it, he'd give me an expensive present. A piece of jewellery; an antique doll. Once, when I'd been a particularly good little girl, he even bought me a miniature Aston Martin to drive round the garden in. Can you believe that?'

I didn't say anything. I didn't honestly know what I could say.

'And then when I was sixteen, and I had more

417

presents than any girl could know what to do with, he stopped. Just like that. I'd got too old for him. He continued to give me the gifts, of course, and made very sure that his beloved daughter received everything she could ever want, but the sex finished. I was damaged goods. And he never gave me one fucking word of explanation, either. He simply carried on like nothing had happened. Bastard.' She spat the last word into the air, and I had the feeling it could have been aimed at any man.

'Emma, please,' moaned Thadeus. 'Finish him and get me some help.'

She ignored him. 'But what my father doesn't realize is that these days he's the one who's damaged goods. He means nothing to me.' Her words faltered slightly at this point, and I got the feeling that perhaps in some terrible way he meant far more to her than she was letting on. 'The only reason I even talk to him is because he's got what I want. The company. And now you've come along and things look like they might work out just right. Dennis Milne – fugitive from the law, brutal murderer – breaks in here, murders Eric Thadeus and his security guard before Thadeus's daughter overpowers him and shoots him with his own gun.'

'They'd never believe you,' I said, only too aware how plausible her story sounded.

'Oh yes they will. Your DNA's going to be discovered at the murder scene of Simon Barron, on his clothes, along with some of your hairs that I managed to remove the other night when you were asleep. It's also going to be found at the house where four people died last night, if it hasn't been already. I'll tell the police that both DCI Barron and I were some way to outing you as the man behind the murders of Khan and Malik. You killed Barron, and now you've come here to kill me.'

I felt my throat constrict. She'd played me perfectly. 'Motive?' I asked, aware that the word came out like a croak.

'Who knows what goes on in the diseased mind of the killer?' she replied, without much in the way of irony.

I watched her carefully, and had no doubt at all that she'd done what she claimed with my DNA. I'd always known she was switched on, and I think somewhere in the back of my mind I'd also known that certain things about her didn't add up – the amount of money she had; the sketchy family background; the fact that, in the end, she'd done everything to point my search for the truth in the direction of Nicholas Tyndall – but I simply hadn't wanted to suspect someone so pretty and vivacious. Someone I'd slept with. For an instant my thoughts flashed back to Coleman House and Carla Graham. I'd made that mistake before.

'So, it was you who killed Barron?'

'He was getting too close,' she said simply, giving a bored shrug. I could see she was about to end this conversation.

'But what I can't understand,' I said, playing for time, 'is if you're some big-shot heiress, how come you were working as a reporter for some provincial paper?'

'We needed someone on the inside, particularly given the size of the investigation into the café shootings, and I've always been good at writing. It was just a matter of greasing a few of the right palms to get me a job on the *Echo*. Nothing's very difficult when you've got money.'

I thought back to my initial call to the newspaper. 'No wonder the guy who answered the phone at the *Echo* didn't like you.'

She snorted derisively. 'Do you think I care? I'm the one with all the cards, Dennis. And I've played you all for fools. Even Tyndall, with his pathetic threats and silly little dolls, didn't scare me. In fact I found it quite exciting. And all I had to do was flutter my eyelashes at these hardened coppers and every one of them fell for my charms. Including you. The brutal hitman.'

I managed a half-smile, which I think annoyed her. 'Brutal? I don't begin to compete with you.'

'No,' she said, stretching out her gun arm, ready to fire. 'You don't.'

I willed myself to remain calm as I continued to look for my moment. 'How did the whole thing begin? I know it was with the therapy, but what did Jason Khan know? And why did he and Ann die so long after she'd exposed Blacklip for who he was?'

She shook her head dismissively. 'Sorry, Dennis, but I can read you like a book. You're just trying to delay things and I haven't got a lot of time. Comfort yourself with this: for an old man, you were very good in bed, and it was fun to sleep with another killer.'

And then she fired: three carefully aimed rounds that slammed into my chest like lead punches.

I gasped as my body jackknifed, and I felt myself rolling sidewards.

'Now it's your turn, Daddy,' I heard her say, her voice soft and gentle, and through the thin slits of my eyes I saw her turn and face her father in the doorway, raising the gun to finish him off too.

'Emma, no,' he pleaded. 'What are you doing? I love you.'

His voice had taken on a desperate urgency, and suddenly something in her expression changed. A ripple of doubt crossed her face, weakening the killing glare. There was something else there, too. It might have been love; it might have been hate. It was impossible to tell which, but when I think about it now, I'm convinced that it was both.

The gun in her hand shook ever so slightly, and for a long tense moment, she hesitated.

And consequently never noticed as I sat up, still reeling from the force of the bullets, the worst of which had been absorbed by the flak jacket Tyndall had given me, and pulled the .45 from where it had been concealed in the front of my waistband underneath my jacket, lifting it two-handed in her direction.

'Just one more obstacle, Emma,' I said as she turned my way, her face stretched tight with alarm.

She mouthed the word *NO*, the syllable seeming to go on for ever, and started to raise her gun.

Which was the moment I pulled the trigger, realizing that in the end she deserved it as much as any of them.

The bullet struck her right in the middle of the chest, her white dress erupting in red as the shot lifted her off her feet and slammed her against the wall. Her own gun went off, the bullet ricocheting off the floor and flying up into the ceiling, and then I fired a second time, this time hitting her in the face and blowing the back of her skull away. A huge chum-like mixture of blood, brains and bone shot three feet up the wall as Emma slid down it, her face disappearing under a falling red curtain.

I heard Thadeus cry out in pain, grief, maybe even relief, but the cry was weak and there were still questions he had to answer.

Staggering to my feet, I took two deep breaths and walked over to the door. He was leaning back on the door frame where I'd left him, still clutching his leg. Blood stained the tiles and ran in a steady stream across the kitchen floor. His face was pale.

'You've killed her,' he whispered. 'My baby.'

'She was no-one's baby, Thadeus. You made sure

of that. She was a monster, and one you created. I almost wish I'd let her kill you.'

'She wouldn't have killed me,' he snarled through gritted teeth. 'Couldn't you see that? She loved me. She was my little girl. And you've murdered her. You may as well do the same to me. It's all over now.'

'Not quite, it isn't. I've got some questions for you. If you answer them, I'll make it quick. If you don't, it'll be slow and it'll be painful.'

'Fuck you, Milne,' he spat, sending flecks of thick white saliva onto my jeans. 'I'm not going to make your life any easier. Our secrets will die with us and there's nothing you or any other bastard can do about it. Because you've got nothing left to threaten me with. The only thing you can do is end my life, and I'm ready for that now. Today's as good a day to die as any.' He spread his arms out, welcoming my final shot. 'So go on, do your worst.'

So I did.

I did things to him that I'm ashamed of, because those things debased me and dragged me far too close to his dank, black level. I ignored his cries for mercy, I ignored the blood that splattered my clothes, I ignored the stomach-churning disgust that grew as I applied the pressure. I ignored every-thing except the task of making him talk, knowing full well that both the ghosts of my past and the ghosts of his would never forgive me if he didn't.

And talk he did. In the end, he told me

everything, and when he'd finished, I bent down and used the pistol that Nicholas Tyndall had provided me with to shoot him once in the head, an act which put us both out of our misery. I think at that moment he was pleased to go. Not because he really was in pain, although doubtless there was an element of that, but for other less obvious reasons. I genuinely believe that somewhere in his dark heart there was a part that was weighed down heavily with guilt, particularly where Emma was concerned. I believe that he loved her, and I believe too that she loved him. It was a corrupt, twisted love but it was there nevertheless, and by his actions when she was a child, he'd betrayed that love, and knew it.

It didn't make me feel any more sorry for him. Eric Thadeus had ended the life of Heidi Robes, and in doing so had sentenced her father to a life behind bars for a crime of which he was not only innocent, but also a victim. Only the cruellest of minds would have countenanced that. Thadeus was scum. He deserved everything he got. But Emma? I tried not to think about her.

Instead, I turned away and left them there together.

# 44

Eric Thadeus told me that Jason Khan died – and Asif Malik died with him – because of a television programme.

This, effectively, was what started everything off. Jason had known for some time about the abuse his girlfriend, Ann Taylor, had suffered at the hands of her father and his so-called friends in the days when she still lived with him. Her trial for GBH had taken place before Jason met her, and having come to terms with the details of her past herself, she'd told him everything when they'd become lovers, including the fact that she'd witnessed a murder seven years before.

Thadeus confirmed that the murder victim had been Heidi Robes, and that she'd been killed during a violent sex game that had got out of control. Usually the parties they held never went that far, or so he'd claimed. I wasn't so sure.

Thadeus called his group of paedophiles the

Hunters, and there was a perverse hint of pride in his voice when he mentioned their name. One of the Hunters, and a participant on that night, was Les Pope. Pope had been charged with getting rid of Heidi's body and framing her father, John, in order to keep suspicion as far away as possible from the group. According to Thadeus, Pope had used one of his lowlife clients to do the dirty work, something that the client had obviously done very efficiently, given how things had turned out.

Even when Ann's account of the murder became public some years later, and the second participant from that night, Richard Blacklip, was subsequently arrested, things still hadn't got out of hand. Blacklip got bail, was supplied with a false passport and a ticket to Manila, and then it was simply a matter of Pope telephoning Tomboy to organize his murder, thereby avoiding the possibility of a problematic trial, where the truth of the Robes murder might have come out.

And up until two months earlier, the truth looked like it might have remained buried for ever. I'm sure it would have done, too, if it hadn't been for the television programme.

I don't suppose either Jason Khan or Ann Taylor made a habit of watching *Newsnight*, BBC2's late-evening current affairs programme, but for some reason – call it fate, if you like – they were both sat in front of it on the evening when the producers chose to interview the newly installed

Lord Chief Justice, Tristram Parnham-Jones.

I still wonder what Ann's reaction must have been. She'd never seen the face of the man in the black leather mask – the most violent of all her father's 'friends' – but she remembered his voice clearly enough. Would always remember the smooth, controlling tones of the person who'd molested her and then taken a knife to a screaming and pleading Heidi Robes. And now this man – who, years later, must have continued to haunt her dreams – was the one on the television talking. There was, she was adamant, no mistake.

But what could she say? The police hadn't found any evidence to back up the claims made at her trial regarding the murder she'd witnessed, and no-one had been charged in connection with it. Who was going to believe her now, if she started accusing the most senior judge in the land of being a child murderer on account of his voice? I could see her point. They'd think she was mad. She'd already been threatened with a spell in a psychiatric institution once, and would be fully aware that claims like that, from someone with her background, would probably get her carted straight off to one.

But Jason was different. Jason was a street thug and a hustler, whatever his rushed conversion to Islam might have suggested, and he would have sensed an opportunity to make some serious money. His problem, of course, was how to use the potentially explosive information he was holding to best effect, so he turned to his solicitor – a man he knew to be corrupt – for help organizing some form of lucrative blackmail.

What Jason didn't know was that Pope was only representing him in legal matters in order to remain close to Ann and keep tabs on what she was or wasn't saying. The Hunters, it seemed, were very careful and very thorough, and initially that thoroughness paid off. Pope strung Jason along, while simultaneously planning his murder. But Jason must have got wind of what was going on, because he'd phoned Asif Malik, a senior detective and fellow Muslim, requesting that they meet up urgently. Presumably (although no-one knows for sure), Jason was going to spill the beans.

His phone, however, was being tapped on Thadeus's orders, and the call was picked up by the Hunters, who were now keen to get him in the ground as soon as possible. Billy West watched Jason leave his home to go to the meeting, and instead of killing him there and then and saving Malik's life, he'd got greedy and shot them both.

There had been five men present on the night of the Heidi Robes murder. Five Hunters: Eric Thadeus; Les Pope; Richard Blacklip; a man called Wise who, Thadeus told me, had died of cancer three years previously; and Tristram Parnham-Jones.

Only Parnham-Jones still survived.

# 45

I left the house the way I'd come in and headed back to the Jaguar, dialling 999 as promised, to call an ambulance for Bill.

I couldn't hear anything from Theo in the boot when I reached the car, so I got inside, turned on the engine and started driving. I had no idea where I was going.

As I drove, I thought through the case, and in particular Simon Barron's part in it. How had he got so close to Emma and Thadeus, when everyone else on the investigation was convinced that the man behind the slayings was Nicholas Tyndall? I'd never know, of course, but as a former detective myself I could surmise. My guess was that Barron had realized some years ago that by convicting John Robes of the murder of his daughter, he'd made a terrible mistake. I felt sure that somewhere further down the line he'd come across the name Richard Blacklip and discovered that he was part of a wide and well-connected paedophile ring. Obviously there couldn't have been a great deal of evidence against any of them for anything, but something about them must have led him to believe that it was they, not her father, who had murdered Heidi. This would have put him in a terrible position, made worse by the fact that, according to what Thadeus had told me, John Robes had committed suicide in prison several years earlier. Unable to tell anyone else of their possible involvement for fear of what it would do to his own reputation, it may well have been this knowledge, coupled with his unending sense of guilt, that had pushed Barron into premature retirement.

However, like all coppers, he could never entirely let go. So when the Met issued a rallying call for retired detectives to come back and help in London's burgeoning murder investigations, he'd volunteered. I don't suppose he'd known at the time how much the Malik/Khan case impinged on the one that had caused him so much pain, but it wouldn't have been that difficult for him to make the connection once he'd found out Ann Taylor's real identity. The problem, from Barron's perspective, was that no-one on the investigation seemed that interested in Ann's death or the light her testimony of child abuse years earlier might throw on the case, so he'd used the *North London Echo*'s investigative journalist, Emma Neilson, to publicize his suspicions. He'd fed her information, ignorant of her own duplicitous role, hoping that her articles would prompt a rethink of strategy within the investigation. I don't suppose Emma had been too keen to draw attention to the fact that Ann's death might not have been suicide, but she would have had little choice but to adhere to Barron's wishes and write the articles if she wanted him to remain onside.

And then Barron had found out something that suddenly made him a dangerous liability. It could well have been the name of someone else involved. He'd probably even confided to Emma who it was, and, in doing so, sealed his own fate. She'd lured him to an isolated meeting place, doubtless with the promise of information of her own, and had then silenced him for ever, nearly succeeding in getting me arrested in the process. Very neat. And very ruthless. She really had been a cunning operator.

But something nagged at me, something that I just couldn't get out of my head. You see, it was the timing. Heidi Robes had been abducted and murdered seven years ago. According to Thadeus, one of Pope's lowlifes had got rid of her body and planted the false evidence of her father's guilt. Tomboy Darke had left London for the Philippines seven years earlier, having made enough money (by his account, as an informant) to set up a business there. One of Tomboy's criminal trades when he'd been back in England had been burglary. Coincidence? Let me tell you something, speaking as a copper: there's no such thing.

It was eleven o'clock when I pulled off the M1 just short of Leeds and drove until I found a deserted lay-by. I got out and switched on the mobile, ignoring the banging coming from the boot. As I walked across a piece of scrubland towards some trees, I dialled our dive lodge in Mindoro. It would be a little after seven in the morning there.

Lisa, our part-time receptionist, answered. It was nice to hear her voice and it was a good line.

'Mr Mick,' she said. 'How are you?'

I told her I was good and she asked when I was coming back. 'Never,' was the answer, but I didn't tell her that. Instead I said it would be soon, and she said she'd look forward to it. I asked her if Tomboy was there.

'Yes, he is around here somewhere. I get him for you. See you soon, Mr Mick.'

A minute later, he was on the line. 'How are things?' he asked.

'Take a walk,' I told him. 'So you're out of anyone's earshot.'

He asked me once again how things were. He sounded nervous, but not unduly so.

'Cold,' I said. 'What's it like there?'

'Warm,' he answered. The conversation was awkward, but then I'd expected that. 'I'm in the dive shop now,' he said eventually, 'and there's no-one about. You can talk.'

'Good.' I sighed, wishing that it hadn't come to this. We'd been good mates once. Even a week ago. Now, though, the whole world had changed. 'I know everything, Tomboy.'

'What do you mean?' There was no mistaking the nerves in his voice now.

'You know what I mean. I know about the girl Pope and his friends killed at their little get-together all those years back, and I know that they used you to get rid of her body.'

'What are you talking about?'

'Her name was Heidi, by the way. Heidi Robes. And she was twelve years old. And her old man, the one whose house you broke into to plant the evidence, he's dead now. He was found guilty of her murder, even though they never had a body, and he finally topped himself two years back. He'd lost his wife first, then his only child. I'm amazed he lasted as long as he did.'

The silence at the other end of the phone spoke volumes. Tomboy didn't have to say anything; we both knew that what I said was right.

'You'll never be able to bring either of them back, and you'll never be completely able to shake off the guilt of what you've done all in the name of greed, but you can do one thing to make things a little better. There's one man amongst those paedophiles who's so far escaped the fate that's coming to him, and he's now the Lord Chief Justice in the UK, if you can believe that. He raped that girl, and one way or another, even after all this time, I'll bet he left some DNA evidence on her. They weren't so clued up about it seven years ago. So what I want you to do is tell me where you buried the body.'

Tomboy cleared his throat. 'I don't know what to say,' he croaked, sounding like he'd just lost his life savings on a horse that had fallen a yard short of the finishing line.

'You do. I've just told you what to say. I want to know the location. It'll never get back to you, I promise.'

'Mick . . . Dennis . . . Look, I . . .' His voice trailed off. 'Pope was blackmailing me, you know? I had to do it. I wouldn't have done normally, you know that. He found out I'd grassed up Billy West for a job he'd done, and he was threatening to tell him. You've got to believe me.'

'The location, Tomboy.'

He told me that he'd taken her to woodland down in Dorset, not far from the coastal town of Swanage. 'There's a lake in the middle. She's in there, weighted down with chains. Or she was, anyway. In a wooden box.'

I made him give me directions and he tried to remember as much as possible while I wrote it all down in my notebook, the phone pressed to my ear. By the time he'd finished he was crying. 'I wish I hadn't done it, Dennis, but he made me. He had stuff on me. He could have had me killed. I did it because it was my only chance of escape.'

Part of me wanted to tell Tomboy that I understood, but in the end, how could I? 'You're very lucky that you're six thousand miles away,' was all I could manage.

'Is that it, then?'

'For us, yes. Just hope I never decide to come looking for you.'

I rang off, and stood for a while staring at the spindly bare trees in front of me as they rose up like gnarled, many-fingered hands in the winter night; wondering if I'd done the right thing by coming here and tearing up the past. It would have been so much easier if I'd never heard about Malik's death; had never shot Slippery Billy West, or found out about his part in the whole bloody chain of events. If I'd simply carried on life in paradise with my old mate Tomboy, ignorant of what he too had done in his past. Diving, drinking, letting one day drift into the next.

But the world never works like that. Life's hard, and it's unfair. And if ignorance is bliss, then knowledge is essential. There are some terrible people walking the earth, and even now they might be coming for you or me. If you're not watching, not acting, not neutralizing them, then one day they're going to have their hands around your neck, and it'll be too late.

People say that one man can't justify being judge,

jury and executioner. Some have even said it to me. I suspected Parnham-Jones himself would say it. And in many ways I can agree. But there are times when you need to take a short cut to justice. Because the alternative – letting the guilty get away with crimes too sickening to contemplate – simply doesn't bear thinking about.

As I turned to walk back to the car, the phone rang again. I didn't recognize the number so I picked up and said nothing.

'I called to see how you're doing,' said Nicholas Tyndall. Bizarrely enough, after all that had happened that day, his voice came across like a breath of fresh air.

'It's over,' I told him wearily.

'And the people who've been trying to fuck up my business?'

'All dead. Including the reporter.'

'Miss Neilson? You know, I always had a feeling about her.'

'Well, she was a part of it. A lot more cunning and a lot more vicious than either of us gave her credit for.'

'You're not upset she's gone?'

'I'm upset she was what she was.'

'We're all what we are, my friend.'

He was right, but I still couldn't help wondering what Emma would have been like if she hadn't had Eric Thadeus as a father. And that was the sad thing: we'd never know.

'Do I owe you any money?' he asked.

'No, we're quits. You might get a bit of heat for a while, but it'll be over soon, I promise you.'

'That's what I like to hear. Thanks for your good work. Maybe we'll do business together again some time. I could always use men like you.'

'No thanks. This is the end of it. We won't be talking again.'

'Suit yourself,' he said.

I said I would and hung up. Then switched off the mobile and chucked it towards the gnarled old trees. It was someone else's problem now.


I drove north until eventually I came to the North Yorkshire Moors. It was there, amidst cold bleak hills, with not a tree or dwelling in sight, that I opened up the boot and told Theo Morris that he could go.

'Where?' he asked.

'Wherever you like,' I said. 'But go now while I'm still feeling charitable.'

That did the trick. He jumped out and without so much as a backward glance took off in the direction of an undulating valley below. He might have been cold, tired and lost, but I guessed that he was also extremely relieved.

I got back in the car and continued to drive.

# Epilogue
## THREE WEEKS LATER

It was late afternoon on Christmas Eve and raining steadily as the car pulled up at the end of the track and came to a halt. The driver was only partly visible through the fogged-up windscreen as he scanned the surrounding undergrowth for signs of activity.

I waited thirty seconds, then stepped out from behind a nearby beech tree and made my way over to his window. I was wearing a long grey raincoat, a grey beanie hat, and a black scarf that obscured most of my face but left my eyes and mouth uncovered. In my hand was a sealed waterproof bag containing the document I'd been working on for the past three weeks, as well as the co-ordinates for the final resting place of Heidi Robes.

The window came down as I approached and DI John Gallan eyed me warily. He was an honest-looking guy a couple of years younger than me, with a decent head of curly black hair that I would have thought was beyond regulation length, and a face that bore enough laughter lines to suggest he was good company.

'What I've got here is of the utmost importance,' I told him when I reached the window, sounding like a character in *Mission Impossible*.

'So you said on the phone,' he replied, staring at the bag, then back at me. 'What is it?'

'It's information that relates to an old murder investigation. Someone was tried for the crime and convicted, but didn't do it.'

'Why come to me about it?' Gallan asked, making no move to take the bag. 'Why not just drop it at a police station?'

'Because I've read about you and some of the cases you've worked on, and I think you can be trusted. I also think you'll give the contents your full attention. Especially when you see the name of the person involved. It's important that it's in the hands of an honest man.'

'How did you get hold of this information?'

I couldn't help but smile a little at that. It was a typical copper's response – trying to find out as much as possible. I'd have asked the same thing in his position.

'Let's just say circumstances led me to it.' I handed the bag to him through the window, and he placed it on the seat beside him.

'And that's the best I'm going to get, is it?'

I nodded. 'That's it. And it's also the end of my

involvement.' I stepped away from the car. 'Anyway, thanks for coming. And Merry Christmas.'

'I'd wish the same to you,' he said, watching me with a thoughtful expression on his face, 'but I don't know who you are. You might not deserve a Merry Christmas. Do you?'

I thought about it for a second. 'I don't know,' I said at last. 'I think that depends on your opinion.'

'Well, my opinion is that if you're a good man you deserve one, and if you're a bad one you don't.'

'That reminds me of something an old friend of mine would have said. Well, from what I've heard, you're a good one, so enjoy it.' With that, I turned away and started walking.

'You still haven't answered my question,' he called out after me, but I kept going, and soon afterwards I heard him reverse down the track the way he'd come.

The problem was, I couldn't answer his question, because I genuinely didn't know.

Twenty years ago, it had all been so different. All so black and white. I'd been a young probationer then and on the way up, dreaming of a future I could shape through my own efforts. I'm not sure if I was ever an idealist, but I honestly did think I was doing the right thing, and even though it's a long time since the police have been looked at by their peers in a positive light, I was proud of what I did. I thought it was a better job than being a business-man or a computer programmer. Less money, but much more to it. I think I dreamed that one day I'd get married and have a couple of kids; that I'd rise through the ranks until I was a DCI or even a DCS; that I'd stand up for my fellow coppers against government interference; that I'd tell the Home Secretary that he had to cut back on the paperwork and give us the freedom we needed to bring the bad guys down. That people would sleep safely in their beds, knowing that men like me were looking after them.

Never once did I dream that I'd be a murderer.

But then you don't, do you?

When I got back to my car, it was beginning to get dark. I started the engine and drove away without looking back.

THE END

# Acknowledgements

A lot of people helped in the writing of this book. So, in no particular order, thanks to Pete, Sam, Doc and all at El Galleon, Mindoro Island, Philippines, for answering my many questions and providing me with an introduction to expat life there. I particularly enjoyed the walks between Sabang and Puerta Galera, Pete. To Matt for helping me find the best place to dump the bodies. To Waggy in Manila who was the best (and, dare I say it, the cheapest) guide I could have hoped for. Sorry so much of what you showed me was cut from the final document! To Selina Walker, my editor at Transworld; Amanda Preston, my agent; and my wife, Sally; all of whom provided constructive criticism of the various drafts, and whose comments made it a far better book than it would otherwise have been. And to my invaluable sources amongst law enforcement and its related arms, none of whom (as usual) wish to be named.

I owe you all a drink. See how this sells and you might get one!

SIMON KERNICK'S NEW THRILLER

# RELENTLESS

IS NOW AVAILABLE FROM BANTAM PRESS


HERE'S A TASTER . . .

# 1

I only heard the phone because the back door was open. I was outside breaking up a fight between my two kids over which one of them should have the bubble-blowing machine, and it was threatening to turn ugly. To my dying day, I will always wonder what would have happened if the door had been shut, or the noise of the kids had been so loud that I hadn't heard it.

It had just turned three o'clock on a cloudy Saturday afternoon in late May, and my whole world was about to collapse.

I ran back inside the house, into the living room, where the football was just kicking off on the TV, and picked up on about the fourth ring, wondering whether it was that permatanned bastard of a boss of mine, Wesley 'Call me Wes' O'Shea, phoning to discuss a minor detail on a client proposal. He liked to do that at weekends, usually when there was a football match on. It gave him a perverse sense of power.

I looked at my watch. One minute past three.

'Hello?'

'Tom, it's me, Jack.' The voice was breathless.

I was momentarily confused. 'Jack who?'

'Jack . . . Jack Calley.'

This was a voice from the past. My best friend when we were at school. The best man at my wedding nine years earlier. But also someone I hadn't spoken to in close to four years. There was something wrong, too. He sounded in pain, struggling to get the words out.

'Long time no speak, Jack. How are you?'

'You've got to help me.'

It sounded like he was running, or walking very quickly. There was background noise, but I couldn't tell what it was. He was definitely outside.

'What do you mean?'

'Help me. You've got to . . .' He gasped suddenly. 'Oh Jesus, no. They're coming.'

'Who's coming?'

'Oh Christ!'

He shouted these last words, and I had to hold the phone away from my ear momentarily. On the TV, the crowd roared as one of the players bore down on the goal.

'Jack. What the hell's happening? Where are you?'

He was panting rapidly now, his breaths coming in tortured, wailing gasps. I could hear the sound of him running.

'What's going on? Tell me!'

Jack cried out in abject terror, and I thought I heard the sound of some sort of scuffle. 'Please! No!' he yelled, his voice cracking. The scuffle continued for several seconds, and seemed to move away from the phone. Then he was speaking again, but no longer to me. To someone else. His voice was faint but I could make it out easily enough.

He said six words. Six simple words that made my heart lurch and my whole world totter.

They were the first two lines of my address.

Then Jack let out a short, desperate scream, and it sounded like he was being pulled away from the phone. There followed a succession of gasping coughs, and instinctively even I, who'd lived my life a long way from the indignities of death, could tell that my old friend was dying.

And then everything fell eerily silent.

The silence might have lasted ten seconds, but was probably nearer two, and as I stood frozen to the spot in my front room, mouth open, too shocked to know what to say or do, I heard the line suddenly go dead at the other end.

The first two lines of my address. The place where I lived an ordinary suburban life with my two kids and my wife of nine years. The place where I felt safe.

For a moment, just one moment, I thought it must have been some sort of practical joke, a cruel ruse to get a reaction. But the thing was, I hadn't spoken to Jack Calley in four long years, and the last time had been a chance meeting in the street, a snatched five-minute conversation while the kids – much younger then, Max just a baby – shouted and fidgeted in their twin pushchair. I hadn't had a proper chat with him – you know, the kind friends have – in, what, five, six, maybe even seven years. We'd gone our separate ways a long time ago.

No, this was serious. You don't put fear like that into your voice deliberately. It's a natural thing, something that's got to come from within. And this most definitely had. Jack had been terrified, and with good reason. If I wasn't mistaken, and I would swear to God that I wasn't,

I'd just heard him breathe his dying breaths. And his last words were the first two lines of my address.

Who wanted to know where I lived? And why?

Let me tell you this: I am an ordinary man with an ordinary desk job in a big open-plan office, leading a team of four IT software salesmen. It's not a huge amount of fun and, as I've already suggested, my boss, Wesley, is something of an arsehole, but it pays the bills and allows me to own a half-reasonable detached four-bed house in the suburbs, and at thirty-five I've never once been in trouble with the boys in blue. My wife and I have had our ups and downs, and the kids can play up now and again, but in general, we're happy. Kathy works as a lecturer in environmental politics over at the university, a job she's held for close to ten years. She's well liked, good at what she does and, although she probably wouldn't like me saying so, very pretty. We're the same age, we've been together eleven years, and we have no secrets. We've done nothing wrong; we pay our taxes and we keep out of trouble. In short, we're just like everyone else.

Just like you.

So why did some stranger want to know our address? Some stranger who wanted it so badly he was prepared to kill for it?

Fear kicked in, that intense terror that starts somewhere in the groin and tears through you like an express train until it's infected every part and is ready to develop into outright panic. The instinctive flight mechanism. The sick feeling you get when you're walking empty streets alone at night and you hear footsteps coming from behind. Or when a man smashes a beer glass on the corner of a bar and demands to know what the fuck you think you're looking at. Real fear. I had it then.

I replaced the phone in its cradle and stood where I was for a long moment, trying to think of a rational explanation for what I'd just heard. Nothing presented itself, and yet at the same time even the most paranoid explanation didn't make sense either. If someone wanted to speak to me, then they presumably knew who I was. In which case they could easily have found out where I lived without asking a man who barely knew me any more. They could have looked in the phonebook for a start. But they hadn't.

'Daddy, Max just hit me for no reason.' It was Chloe coming back into the house, grass stains on the knees of her jeans, her dark-blonde hair a tousled mess. At five, she was little more than a year older than her brother Max, yet vastly more sensible. The problem was, he'd already overtaken her in bulk, and in the anarchic world of young kids bulk tends to win through in arguments. 'Can you go and tell him off?' she added, looking put out, as innocent of danger as all children are.

Someone was coming here. Someone who'd just killed my oldest friend.

The last I remembered, Jack Calley had been living five or six miles away, just outside Ruislip, where London finally gives way to the Green Belt. If he'd called me from near his home then the person he'd given my address to would be about a fifteen-minute drive away at this time of day. Maybe less if the traffic was quiet and they were in a hurry.

'Daddy, what are you doing?'

'Hold on a sec, darling,' I said with a smile so false it would have embarrassed a politician. 'I'm just thinking.'

It was two minutes since I'd put down the phone and I could hear my heart beating a rapid tattoo in my chest. Bang bang, bang bang, bang bang. If I stayed here, I was putting my family at risk. If I left, then how was I ever going to find out who was after me, and why?

'Hey, sweetie,' I said, keenly aware of the strain in my voice, 'we've got to go out now, round to Grandma's.'

'Why?'

I squatted down and picked her up. 'Because she wants to see you.'

'Why?'

Sometimes it's best not to get into a dialogue with a five-year-old. 'Come on, darling, we've got to go,' I said, and strode outside, carrying her in my arms.

I saw that Max had abandoned the bubble-making machine in the middle of the lawn and was now at the bottom of the garden, his head poking out of a makeshift, canvas-sided camp at the top of the climbing frame. I shouted at him to come out because we had to go. His head immediately retreated into the camp. Like a lot of four-year-old boys, he didn't like to do what he was told. Usually this wasn't much of a problem. I tended to ignore it and let him do his own thing. Today it was a disaster.

Jack's words played over and over in my mind. 'Oh Jesus, no. They're coming.' The urgency in them. The fear. They're coming.

They're coming here.

I looked at my watch. 3.05. Four minutes since I'd picked up the phone. Time seemed to be moving faster than it usually does.

'Come on, Max, we've got to get moving. Now.'

I ran over to the climbing frame, still holding onto Chloe, ignoring her complaints. She tried to struggle out of my arms, but I didn't let go.

'But I'm playing,' he called out from within the camp.

'I don't care. We've got to go now.'

I heard a car pulling into the road out front. This was unusual. The housing estate we live on leads nowhere and is simply a horseshoe-shaped road with culs-de-sac sprouting off it. Drive along it and eventually you end up right back close to where you started. Our house was on the corner of one of the culs-de-sac, and a car came down it once every twenty minutes at most.

The car slowed down. Stopped.

I heard a car door shut, further down in the cul-de-sac. I was being unduly paranoid. But my heart continued to thud.

'Come on, Max. I'm serious.'

He giggled, blissfully unaware of my fear. 'Come and get me.'

I put Chloe down and reached inside the camp. Max retreated as far as he could go, still giggling, but his expression changed when he saw the look on my face.

'What is it, Dad? What's wrong?'

'It's all right, nothing's wrong, but we've got to go round to Grandma's quickly.'

He nodded, looking worried, and scrambled out.

I took them both by the hand and, trying to stay as calm as possible, led them through the house and out to the car. They were both asking questions, but I wasn't really listening. I was willing them to go faster. In the distance, I could hear the cars out on the main road. Above me came the steady roar of a passenger plane circling beyond the unbroken ceiling of white cloud. The neighbour's new dog was barking and someone was mowing their lawn. The comforting sounds of normality, but today they weren't comforting at all. It was as if I was in some sort of terrifying parallel universe where danger loomed on all sides, yet no-one else could see or understand it.

I strapped the kids into their car seats, then realized, as I was about to get into the driver's seat, that I'd better take some overnight gear for them, just in case they were out of the house for any length of time. I tried to think what I was going to say when I turned up at my mother-in-law's with them. The best man at my wedding just phoned me for the first time in years; then, as we were speaking, he got murdered, and now his killer's after me. It sounded so outlandish that even I would have questioned my own sanity, if

I hadn't been so damn sure of its authenticity. And Irene had never liked me much either. Had always thought her daughter, with her strong academic background and her Cambridge degree, was too damn good for a glorified computer salesman.

3.08. Seven minutes since I'd picked up the phone.

I was going to have to tell Irene that something had come up at work. That maybe it was best if the kids spent the night with her. And then what? What happened tomorrow?

I told myself to stop trying to analyse everything and to just get moving.

'Stay in the car, OK? I'm just going to get some overnight stuff.'

They both started to protest, but I shut the door and ran inside and up to each of their bedrooms, hastily chucking together pyjamas, toys, toothbrushes, everything else they were going to need, and shoving them in a holdall, knowing with every step that I was racing against time.

3.11. As I came running out of the house, I recalled the gurgling, coughing noise Jack had made as he was being attacked. The sound of death – it had to be. But who wanted to kill a middle-of-the-road solicitor like Jack Calley, a man who was doing well but hardly setting the world on fire? And, more importantly – far more importantly – who wanted to find out from him where I, lowly salesman Tom Meron, and my family lived?

As I reached the car, I cursed. Both kids had unclipped their seatbelts and were fooling around. Chloe had clambered through the gap in the front seats and was now playing with the steering wheel, while all I could see of Max were his legs sticking up in the air as he hunted for something in the back. They were both laughing, as if there was nothing whatsoever wrong with their world – which there wasn't. It was just mine that was going mad.

I opened the door and flung the overnight bag past Chloe onto the passenger seat. 'Come on, kids, we've got to go,' I said, picking her up and pushing her back through the gap in the seats. 'It's very important.'

'Ow! That hurt.'

'Get back in your seat, Chloe. Now.'

I was sweating as I ran round to the back passenger door, pulled it open, yanked Max up and shoved him bodily into his seat. With shaking hands, I strapped him back in, then reached over and did the same to his sister.

'What's happening, Daddy?' asked Chloe. She

looked frightened, not used to seeing her father acting so strangely.

I'm not a panicker by nature. There's not much in my life that would instigate panic, if I'm honest, which was why I was now finding it hard to stay calm. This all felt like a bad dream, something that should have been happening to someone else. An elaborate hoax that would end in laughter all round.

But it wasn't. I knew it wasn't.

I scrabbled around in my jeans pocket for the car keys, found them and started the ignition. The dashboard clock read 3.16, but I remembered that it was four minutes fast. Eleven minutes since the call. Christ, was it that long? I reversed the car out of the drive and drove up to the junction, indicating left in the direction of the main road. The relief I experienced as I pulled away and accelerated was tangible. I felt like I'd escaped from something terrible.

I was being stupid. There had to be some sort of rational explanation for what I'd just heard. There just had to be. 'Calm down,' I muttered to myself. 'Calm down.'

I took a deep breath, feeling better already. I'd take the kids to Irene's, drop them off, phone Kathy, then just drive back home. And there'd be no-one there. I'd look up Jack Calley's number, call and see if everything was all right. From the safe cocoon of my moving car, I began to convince myself that Jack hadn't actually been hurt. That the ghastly choking hadn't been him dying a lonely death. That everything was fine.

A one-hundred-yard-long, relatively straight stretch of road led from the entrance of our cul-de-sac to the T-junction that met up with the main road into London. As we reached it, I slowed up and indicated right. A black Toyota Land Cruiser built like a tank was moving towards us down the main road at some speed. I could see two figures in caps and sunglasses in the front seats. When it was ten yards away, the driver slowed dramatically and swung the car into the estate, without indicating. I was about to curse him for his lack of courtesy, when I noticed that the side windows of the vehicle were tinted, and I felt a sense of dread. An unfamiliar car driving onto the estate only eleven minutes after Jack had called me. At a push, Jack lived eleven minutes away. The timing was too coincidental.

I watched its progress in the rearview mirror, a dry, sour taste in my mouth, fear causing my heart to rise in my chest. Our cul-de-sac was the third one down on the right, just before the road bent round sharply. The Land Cruiser passed the first cul-de-sac, then the second.

Fifteen yards short of ours, the brake lights came on.

Oh no, no. Please, no.

'Daddy, why aren't we moving?'

'Come on, Daddy. Come on, Daddy.'

The Land Cruiser turned into our cul-de-sac, then disappeared from view. I knew then as much as I knew anything that its occupants were coming for me.

I pulled onto the main road and accelerated away, the voices of my two children and Jack Calley – desperate, dying Jack Calley – reverberating around my head like distant, blurred echoes.